To Chris, Beth, Claire and Jonathan,
without whose love and support
this book would never have been written.

Echo Hall

Virginia Moffatt

W F HOWES LTD

This large print edition published in 2019 by
W F Howes Ltd
Unit 5, St George's House, Rearsby Business Park,
Gaddesby Lane, Rearsby, Leicester LE7 4YH

1 3 5 7 9 10 8 6 4 2

First published in the United Kingdom in 2017
by Unbound

A CIP catalogue record for this book is available
from the British Library

ISBN 978 1 52885 452 8

Typeset by Palimpsest Book Production Limited,
Falkirk, Stirlingshire

Printed and bound by
T J I

Yet looking through these pages after months of writing, I find they are filled with accounts of pain and injustice and horror, the sins of the fathers visited upon their children . . . I was in Sarajevo and once, as Serb shells whiffled over my head, I stood upon the very paving stone upon which Gavrilo Princip stood as he fired the fatal shot that sent my father to the trenches in the First World War. And of course the shots were still being fired . . . It was as if history was a gigantic echo chamber. That was the year in which my father died. This is therefore the story of his generation. And mine.

Robert Fisk

Woman much missed, how you call to me, call to me,

Saying that now you are not as you were

When you had changed from the one who was all to me,

But as at first, when our day was fair.

Thomas Hardy

REMEMBRANCE

2014

I should not remember this place, and yet every step towards the house unnerves me with its familiarity. The war memorial on the road from the village, the aromatic scent of the fir trees guarding the estate, the cawing of the rooks circling overhead, remind me that I have been here before. I was only a year old when I left. It should not be possible for me to remember this, and yet I do.

Perhaps it is because the stories our mothers tell us embed themselves so firmly in our DNA it is as if we lived the experience too. Or the location of our birth imprints itself upon our psyche, so that when we return it is as if we never left. Or perhaps it is just that Echo Hall has been on the edge of my memory for so long that being here feels like a homecoming.

Nonetheless, I hesitate before I pass through the large oak doorway, unsure whether I am prepared to become a tourist in my own life. Maybe it is enough to have reached its hard, grey walls, gazed up at the unforgiving windows, seen the skies louring overhead. And then I think how coincidental it is that I am visiting Sandstown on the weekend the National Trust has chosen to open the house. I realise the chance to visit my first home is too good an opportunity to miss; if I cross the threshold I might understand the past more fully.

So I enter, pay the fee and pick up a brochure describing the history of the Flints – a dry tale of dust and stone, slate and finance that misses the point entirely. Standing here, in the dark lobby, the grandfather clock in its rightful place, I am overwhelmed with a familiar sense of sadness. The ghosts may be long gone, but Mum was right – unhappiness seeps through the walls, even now.

I decide to begin at my beginning. I know exactly where to go: through the green baize door passing the old servants' kitchens and turning right into the main kitchen. It has been reconstructed as it would have been 100 years ago, in my great-great-grandmother's time, just before the war to end all wars. On the night Mum's waters broke in here, there was an old gas cooker, an oak table and Formica cupboards on the walls. Now, the cooker has been replaced by a Victorian range; wooden shelves line the walls, piled with the cooking implements of the period; the table is laid as if the cook is about to prepare a meal, the walls adorned with recipes and household instructions relating to the Edwardian era. It is as if time has looped back on itself, returning the house to its starting point.

I wander back to the hall and enter the living

room on the west side of the house – the site of my birth. An elderly couple are already there, examining the display of furniture separated from the rest of the room by a rope. The man is reading out a description of life for the lady of the house in a loud voice. The narrative grates; it bears no relation to reality – my great-great-grandmother was a dour woman, with no time for worldly distractions. It was her sister who enjoyed the finer things in life, although she lost them all in the end. The man finishes; his wife nods with interest, and they depart, leaving me alone.

I close my eyes, remembering Mum's description of my delivery: how she crouched on all fours, gripping the sofa legs, grunting and screaming as I pushed my way from the silence of her womb into a dizzying new world. For a moment, I imagine I am there: the feelings are so strong my body shakes as if once more I am making that dark dangerous journey into life. I open my eyes, and steady myself on the wall. There is definitely something about this house; no wonder it had such a powerful effect on Mum.

My phone buzzes. It's Dad:

How's the revolution going, Comrade Phoebe?

He does love to tease. I'm about to text him an Emma Goldman quote when I remember it should be off. I shove it in my pocket. I will call him later for our weekly bout of political sparring, and tell him about this trip; but for now, I want to explore further. To my disappointment, most of the East Wing and the upstairs are still closed to the public. I glance at my watch. It is two o'clock; I have to be back at the conference by six. There is time for a walk, at least. I traipse back down the corridor by the kitchens, and out through the back garden. I climb the hill. I know instinctively where I will find the gap in the hedge, the gate through to the woods that will take me to Arthur's Stone.

And, as I follow my mother's footsteps, her stories lead me on.

IN THE HOUSE OF THE NEWLY-WEDS

1990

CHAPTER 1

Looking back on it, I never really believed that Adam and I would last. Our loose connection was just too fragile to survive, based as it was on a chance meeting, a veneer of attraction, my need for someone to cling to. Mum's death had left me stumbling in the fog and, for a little while, he seemed to provide a solution, a way out, a very light to guide me home. After the slow painful drama of the cancer ward, I needed something lighter and Adam was able to provide it – a summer of love full of frenetic energy as we chased raves, dabbled with ecstasy and indulged in sex on the beach. It was fun at the time and so far removed from my usual way of life that it helped numb the grief I was feeling, but deep down I knew we couldn't go on like this forever. As the summer drew to a close – the nights turned cooler and the leaves began to falter on the trees – he seemed to sense it, too. He called me less often, and was unavailable so many times that I began to prepare myself for the inevitable.

I suppose that's why I wasn't surprised when he left without explanation. His persistent refusal to introduce me to his grandfather had begun to suggest that we had no future together. So his sudden departure seemed a fitting end to our brief romance, the inevitable comedown from the summer's high. I threw myself back into my work as a therapist, drowning myself in the troubles of others rather than dwelling on my own. I was so sure he was gone that I didn't even think of him when I picked his postcard up off the mat a week later. The picture of a fox striding across a cathedral buttress could have been chosen by anyone; the name of the place – Sandstown – was unfamiliar. It was a jolt to see Adam's handwriting when I turned the card over.

> Echo Hall
> 3rd September 1989
>
> Dear Ruth,
> Sorry to leave like that. There wasn't time to call. Granddad's had a stroke. He's very ill. I'm afraid I'll be here for a while. Will ring when I can.
> Love Adam x

Though I knew Adam was wealthier than me, I hadn't realised his family owned a hall. Mum would have enjoyed that: she loved country houses. The thought made me smile for a moment, and then I sighed. Mum wasn't coming back, and I'd be a fool to think that this wasn't his way of letting me down gently. I put the postcard on the fridge and continued with my daily business, determined to put him behind me.

It never crossed my mind, then, that this was just the beginning. That Adam would return in November, as suddenly as he had left, with Champagne and an unexpected proposal. That, despite being unsure about marriage, I might, by then, have my own reasons for accepting. I couldn't have imagined any of that the day I received his postcard. Nor could I have anticipated how quickly my life would change so that, in February, I would find myself sitting next to my new husband, stroking my swollen belly as we drove north.

The day had started clear and bright, but by mid-afternoon the clouds were forming and the air was growing colder. Adam's hands were fixed to the wheel; he was concentrating hard on the road, as wisps of white mist wreathed themselves around the car. We had been quiet for miles. It was still weird driving through Birmingham without calling in on Mum; and, now the excitement of the wedding was out of the way, it was just beginning to dawn on me that I had no idea what lay ahead. Perhaps Adam felt it too. He had barely said a word since turning off the M6, and so I slept, until the car suddenly shuddered to a halt.

I sat up to see a mass of sulphurous clouds rolling across the road.

'Where are we?' I asked.

'About five miles from Shrewsbury.' The car in front jerked forward. Adam raised his foot off the clutch, following suit. 'Sorry to wake you; the fog took me by surprise.'

'Shrewsbury? Nisha lives round here somewhere.' My best friend had recently moved to a pacifist community; I hadn't realised she would be so close.

'Oh joy.'

I tried not to wince. Adam's opinions of Nisha were matched only by hers of him. He thought her a hypocrite – claiming benefits in order to protest against the state; while she considered an ex-soldier who adored Margaret Thatcher to be beneath contempt. They both had a point. It had hardly mattered last year when I didn't think we had a future. But now we were married, I'd have to find a way to broker a peace between them. It wasn't going to be easy.

I gazed out of the window. Through the fog I could make out the shapes of trees at the side of the road. In the dying light of the late-afternoon sun, the vapours glowed muddy-yellow. Perhaps, because Nisha was on my mind, it made me think of mustard gas; the hunched hawthorn bushes emerging from the mist, a row of weary soldiers. I glanced across at Adam; he was bent over the wheel, a look of fierce concentration on his face. For a moment he seemed like a stranger; to re-assure myself I reverted to a familiar game.

'You've a one-way ticket to the moon. Who would you take?'

'Hmm . . .' he said, lifting his hand off the

steering wheel for a moment, running his fingers through his wavy hair, a habit that had endeared me to him from the start. 'It would have to be . . . Kylie Minogue.'

'Kylie Minogue?!'

'She's so small, I'd have more room in the space-ship. Wouldn't it be great to see her bouncing around in moon-boots?'

'The hair though.'

'I think it's cute . . .' Noticing me shiver, Adam turned the heater up. 'What about you?'

'Mel Gibson.'

'That Neanderthal?'

'I love his accent. He'd be wild and wacky, and he'd kick bad guys into outer space.'

Adam's laugh was comforting. The last few weeks before the wedding and the move had been so full of plans and preparations, I'd begun to feel we'd lost our capacity for fun.

'This is nice.' I stroked his thigh.

'Hmm.'

Somewhere behind the clouds, the sun was sinking, discolouring the sky from yellow to a grubby orange-brown.

'Do you want me to drive?'

'It's all right, I know these roads.'

I sat back, secretly relieved; I didn't fancy driving in these conditions, particularly once the sun had set. By now the fog was so dense, the outside world seemed muffled and remote. We made such slow progress that sometimes it felt we were hardly moving at all. Occasionally, when it thinned a little, we latched on to the lamp of a car ahead till it turned off and disappeared down a side road. But after Shrewsbury, we hardly saw another vehicle. It took another hour to reach Sandstown; a journey that Adam said normally took half that time. Here we turned off the main road, inching our way along a winding country lane, that criss-crossed between England and Wales. In the thick vapours, villages surprised us – stone walls of houses leaping up from the pavements, their yellow lights pale beacons in the darkness. Sometimes, the fog parted, and I could just see the tops of skeletal trees arching over our path. The air filled with moisture, so that even the inside of the car began to feel damp. I shifted in my seat, and patted my bump, a reassurance to myself that all was well.

'Nearly there,' said Adam, as we came upon a sign for Whetstone, a small village whose main street was illuminated by a row of street lights. A gap in the fog revealed a collection of slate-roofed houses, a church, a graveyard of tombstones tumbling in different directions, a tiny village school. At the edge of the village the war memorial loomed. As we began to climb the wooded hill, the fog thickened again. The road bent back on itself sharply through conifers and bare decid-uous trees. The car's beams picked out small details: roots grasping the side of the hill; mosses and the remnants of bracken, fighting for space

8

on the black rock. Rivulets of water ran onto the wet road. Adam slowed almost to a halt as the head-lamps lit up an entrance, marked by two pillars, covered in lichen. We drove up a steep path that zigzagged through the closely packed fir trees. Water dripped off the branches. We emerged from the wood onto a gravel driveway beside a wide lawn, stopping in front of a large square house.

'Wow,' I said.

Nothing Adam had told me had prepared me for this. The high front door was framed by two rows of tall windows, with bays at either end of the house, their panes black and vacant against the grey stone walls. Above them a smaller row of gabled windows ran under the roof. They must have been the servants' quarters once, though Adam had said there were only two left now: Mrs Davies, the live-in housekeeper, and her son, Tommy, the groundsman who lived in the coach house at the back.

'Here we are then,' said Adam, helping me out of the car.

Here we were indeed. I had hardly time to take stock before a small woman with curly white hair came out to greet us.

'Mr Adam,' she beamed.

'Hello, Mrs Davies.'

'You must be the new Mrs Flint.'

'Ruth.'

'I like the sound of Mrs Flint better, my lovey. It's been too long since we've had a Mrs Flint in the house . . . And so lovely to have a baby on the way, too. Come in out of the damp air.'

She bustled us in. Adam strode after her, completely at ease. I followed behind, overawed by the dark oak panels on the walls, the large staircase on the right side of the lobby, the grandfather clock in the corner.

'You're gawping,' said Adam.

'It's a bit . . .'

'It's not as scary as it seems.' He squeezed my hand.

Mrs Davies ushered us through a door on the left into a room that was panelled like the hall. Red velvet curtains were drawn over the window. The long dark table was laid for two. Even though there was a roaring fire, the place had a desolate air.

The housekeeper shepherded us to our seats.

'Your granddad is asleep, Mr Adam,' she said, pouring red wine for him and water for me. 'He's not so good today. The doctor's been. He said with a bit of rest, Mr Flint should be right as rain in the morning.'

'Thank you,' said Adam.

'You must be starving. I'll get your dinner.'

Adam sat back in his seat and raised his glass with a broad grin. 'Welcome home, Mrs Flint.'

I raised my glass and smiled back. I knew how much Adam loved this place, how keen he was that we should move here. And I respected his desire to take care of his grandfather. For weeks I'd been letting his conviction persuade me it would be alright; but now we were here, I'd never felt so far from home in my life.

After dinner, Adam insisted on letting me rest as he unloaded the car. I sat in the sitting room on the west side of the house, watching the news of Mandela's release with delight. But I switched over when Adam entered; even a dull *Poirot* episode was preferable to an argument about politics on our first night. Though the plot was ludicrous and the solution obvious, it passed the time until the fire began to die down and we were ready for bed. Adam killed the remaining flames, spreading the white ash across the hearth to make sure no spark remained. Immediately the room temperature plummeted. The hallway outside was even colder, our breath steaming the air as we made our way up to bed. After years of living in small well-heated houses and flats, this was going to take some getting used to. I was glad to fall into bed, thankful for the familiar warmth of Adam's body. I was asleep in minutes.

It was pitch black when I woke again. I waited for my eyes to adjust, but the room remained absolutely dark. So dark it felt physical, as if the night itself was pressing down on my chest, crushing the life out of me. I could barely breathe. I didn't want to disturb Adam, but I couldn't sleep like this. I had to let some light in.

I climbed out of bed. The air was icy. I felt my way along the side of the mattress and the furniture till I reached the window. Grey light entered the room as I drew the curtains and I began to breathe more easily. The fog had lifted and, though the night was largely cloudy, occasional shafts of moonlight lit up the driveway. In the distance I could make out the shapes of the fir trees we'd driven through earlier, standing 80 feet tall, like guards on the edge of a prison. I shivered and turned back to bed, but the light from the window didn't reach very far. The room was still dark. I needed to open the door, too.

As I was doing so, I heard a sound. At first I thought it was just the wind. Then I heard it again: a voice speaking in the hall. There was a pause, and another voice replied. I wondered whether Adam's grandfather had got up and was talking to Mrs Davies. It was none of my business, I knew, but something drew me to them. I crept to the top of the stairs. The first voice was a man's – clear and cold.

'She is dead, then?'

A mumbled assent.

'And the child?'

'Yes.'

The voice sighed. 'So be it – it is God's will.'

Hesitantly, I moved down a stair or two. The hall below was black, except for a single beam of moonlight that danced on the face of the grandfather clock. I moved forward to see who was

12

talking. No one. I went further down. Still no one. I reached the bottom of the staircase. The hallway was empty.

I stood there for a moment, not sure what to do. Then, in a panic, I went back to Adam as fast as I could. I switched the lamp on and shook him.

'Adam.' My heart was beating fast.

He groaned and rolled over. It took me several shakes before I was able to wake him.

'What's the matter?' he asked, peering at me with alarm. 'Is it the baby?'

'No, no, nothing like that.'

'What then?'

As I explained, I realised how ridiculous it sounded.

'You dreamt it,' said Adam.

'It was real,' I said. 'I mean, I don't believe in ghosts, but it was real.'

'You're pregnant, you're in an unfamiliar place – it was a bad dream, that's all.'

'It was real.'

'I'm sure it felt real, but it wasn't.' He yawned. 'Things are always weird in the middle of the night. Come here.'

He turned off the lamp and pulled me towards him, but gradually, as my shivers reduced, he relaxed, his body slackening into sleep. Soon he was snoring, leaving me alone with my thoughts. It was just a dream, I kept telling myself. It was natural enough to be anxious about birth at this stage of my pregnancy. It was just a dream. But the disturbing voice stayed in my head, repeating the words over and over again.

I lay awake for a very long time.

CHAPTER 2

I must have fallen asleep eventually, because it was mid-morning when I woke again. I stretched out an arm expecting to find Adam, but he was gone. The first day in our new home, and I'd been left alone. Disappointed, I hauled myself out of bed to open the window. The air was cold and, after London, shockingly clean; an aromatic scent of fir trees lingered. The fog of the previous night had completely cleared. The sun was hanging in a pale-blue sky, dodging clouds that drifted in the breeze. At the bottom of the hill, fir trees towered over the edge of the estate before making way for the broadleaf woods beyond. Through their branches I could just make out the spire of the church, and beyond that, a sliver of water shimmering in the sun. A car braked at the corner, the screech of the wheels disturbing the rooks in the rookery in the middle of the woods. They flew around in circles, cawing loudly before settling back on their straggly nests. The scene was so peaceful it banished the terror of the night; suddenly I was keen to explore.

I dressed quickly and stepped out of the bedroom,

pausing to take in my surroundings properly. A large landing bridged the gap between the east and west sides of the house, its walls covered in dark oak panels and decorated with a series of photographs. It was marked by a wooden banister, which turned at the top of the stairs just in front of me. Mrs Davies's rooms were across the landing. To my right, a long corridor extended to the back of the house. Though it felt a little like snooping, after the events of the night I felt compelled to investigate. I walked down the gloomy hallway, opening doors onto a bathroom and bedrooms till I reached the final one at the back of the house. It was furnished in a similar fashion to ours: tallboy, wardrobe, double bed. Even though it was clean and tidy, it smelt of damp. Black mould spread in tiny dots across the ceiling, collecting in a mass at the bottom of the far wall. A large spider scuttled across the floor. I am not a fanciful person, yet when I entered I was overpowered by a sense of malice, as if some previous inhabitant had left behind a residue of ill-will. Trying to shrug the feeling off, I walked over to the bay window. A large garden sloped up the hill, bounded by a row of fir trees at the top. It was pretty enough, but my eyes were drawn to the West Wing, where another room, that looked like a sister to this one, jutted out. Black curtains were drawn over the windows, reminding me somehow of a funeral parlour. The feeling of malevolence was even stronger here; for a moment I was full of an irrational

16

rage that didn't belong to me, but was somehow connected with the other bedroom. Then it occurred to me that perhaps I had no business here, and besides, I was hungry; it was time for breakfast.

Mrs Davies was crossing the landing as I emerged from the corridor. Although she didn't ask what I'd been doing, I felt as if I'd been caught doing something wrong. I blushed. Luckily, she didn't seem to notice. She told me that Adam was at the quarry; she was going to the shops and I could help myself to breakfast. I wandered down to the kitchen where I grabbed bacon and eggs from the fridge and lit the ancient gas cooker that was propped against the far wall. The food was soon sizzling away so loudly that I didn't notice the door open until I heard the clatter of metal on the stone floor. Startled, I turned round to see an old man with white hair that flopped over his eyes, just like Adam's. But these eyes were full of shock, not affection. He stood in silence, staring at me.

'I'm Ruth,' I said. 'Adam's wife . . .'

He still stared.

'You must be Mr Flint. Mrs Davies said it was OK to cook.'

He drew a breath. 'Of course. I'm sorry, just for a moment . . . standing by the cooker . . . you reminded me of someone.'

Though he declined my offer of food he agreed to join me for a cup of tea. Once seated, he straightened his back, sitting upright, his hands placed stiffly on the table. I made the drinks, bringing them over before fetching my food and sitting down myself. He nodded thanks, without smiling. He didn't say a word. I began to eat, looking at him from time to time in the hope he might speak. He remained silent, staring above my shoulder at the wall opposite. It was hard not to avoid his disconcerting gaze. Though his eyes were the same shape as Adam's they were grey-blue, reminding me of the sea in winter – cold, dark, unfathomable. Adam had warned me his grandfather could be difficult; clearly, he hadn't been exaggerating. I paused between mouthfuls, casting around for a conversation opener, unable to produce anything more original than, 'I hope you are feeling better?' which seemed to break the ice. When he smiled, his face softened, the crinkles round his mouth increasing his resemblance to Adam.

'Yes. Thank you.'

This was an improvement, but not much. How I wished I'd been able to meet him earlier; it would have made this so much easier. But in December, I was vomiting for England and had been advised total bed-rest; by the time I recovered, the wedding was upon us.

'I'm sorry we've not met before,' I said. 'I was so ill at Christmas, it wasn't possible.'

'I'd have liked to be at your wedding, but I had the same problem.'

'What a pair of old crocks,' I laughed.

He didn't laugh with me, but his smile was a shade warmer. 'You are here now. And very welcome too,' he said. 'I hope Mrs Davies made you comfortable last night?'

'She did. She's marvellous.'

'I don't know what I'd do without her.'

'It must be a big job, taking care of this place.'

'We don't use all of it, but still . . . We're lucky to have the old communication system – I can reach her whenever I need to.' He nodded towards a board on the wall, marked *butler, housekeeper, cook, chambermaid*. Each name had a bell above it. 'There's a pull in every room, and bells in the old servants' quarters and corridors. If I ring, Mrs Davies can hear when she's upstairs. And since it is two-way, she can call for help too.'

'How romantic.'

'Hardly. It simply ensured the servants knew their place, remaining invisible to the inhabitants of the house.'

I supposed it did, but still, I was intrigued. 'I expect in a house like this, there are lots of interesting family stories . . .'

His body stiffened and his smile vanished. In a chilly tone, reminiscent of the voice I'd heard in the night, he said, 'Not really.'

He pulled his walker towards him, stood up and left me staring at my empty plate, wondering what I'd done wrong.

★　★　★

19

Adam rang after I'd finished the washing up, full of apologies for abandoning me. He claimed he'd meant only to check on things while I was sleeping, but once he'd arrived he'd found too many things needing urgent action. Perhaps because of my encounter with his grandfather, I was frostier than I intended to be; despite his promise to be home at four I ended the call abruptly. By now, I was feeling out of sorts, so having nothing better to do I stomped down to Whetstone, hoping it would improve my mood. There wasn't much there: a school, a tiny shop, a pub that was closed till five, and the church. I'd never been one for religion, but when Mum was dying I'd found myself drawn to such places. The stillness, quiet and flickering candles had helped calm my anxious fears. The door was open, so I wandered in. It was cool and quiet; sunlight streamed through the stained-glass windows, casting multi-coloured patterns on the floor. I felt more peaceful immediately. At the tomb of a medieval couple I stopped and stared at the inscription describing a long and loving marriage. I wondered how they had managed it, and whether Adam and I stood any chance of being as happy.

'Kindness.' Suddenly I could hear Mum's voice. 'That's what kept us together, kindness . . . forgiveness . . . and your Dad's rubbish jokes.'

She'd told me that while she could still talk, about a fortnight before she died. A couple of days later Adam found me sobbing in the hospital chapel, on a day when watching Mum in pain had been too hard to bear. I was a blank stranger, but he'd been kind to me then and I liked him for it. He was visiting his old colonel in the next ward, which was another thing I liked him for. After that, we used to meet for cups of tea and offer mutual support. I liked the fact that he listened without judgement and, being an orphan himself, understood what I was going through. My friends were all sympathetic to a point, but none of them had a clue what this felt like. It was good to find someone who'd been through it before, who could guide me through this strange, sad landscape. So, on the night my mum and his colonel died, it made absolute sense to go to the pub and get wrecked. It made sense to prop each other up at the funerals that followed. And afterwards, when they were over, when we both said we were done with crying, it made even more sense to throw ourselves into a frenzy of parties and raves. Life was for living, after all.

Reflecting on this in the church, I was ashamed of my snippiness with Adam earlier. He was only being a dutiful grandson. And wasn't it his sense of duty that had drawn me to him in the first place? I resolved that when he came home, I would take Mum's advice. If kindness and forgiveness worked for my parents, I was sure it would work for us.

Luckily, my tetchiness had passed Adam by, and he simply snorted with laughter when I told him that I'd lit a candle for us in church.

'When did you get so soppy?' he said.

We were standing on the landing, looking at family photographs just before dinner.

'I'm not. It's just . . .' I wanted to explain, but I couldn't find the words, so instead I turned to a picture of his mother as a little girl, standing next to a slightly older boy.

'Who's this? He looks terribly like your granddad.'

'Uncle Will.'

'You've not mentioned him before.'

'He left for Australia years ago. No one knows what happened to him.'

'A family secret. Fascinating.'

'Not particularly. He and Granddad argued, and he left.'

His vehemence was puzzling, but I was more curious about the photos. The family resemblances were striking. In several, had it not been for the clothes, Adam's grandfather might have been his twin. In one picture, he stood in RAF uniform holding a chair, his floppy curls cropped. He was not smiling, but his face seemed kinder than I'd have expected, given my encounter earlier. It was his wife, Veronica – her WREN jacket buttoned tightly over a large bust – who had the face of a tyrant. Further back, Mr Flint was in pre-war pose: reading in the garden, unaware the camera had caught him; emerging from the sea, his body glistening with water; in a more formal photo with his brother and parents. They were a stern pair: a tall man with steely eyes and ramrod back, standing

22

beside a small squat woman with a jowled face. She was dressed in black and had the look of a bulldog that was about to attack.

'My great-grandparents – Jacob and Leah.' Adam broke into my thoughts. 'And that's Granddad and his brother Henry. Henry died in the war. Jacob had a brother – Reuben, I think. Like Uncle Will, he emigrated. They didn't stay in touch.'

'What about these two?' I asked, pointing to a small round frame enclosing a portrait of young women with oval faces. They looked like china dolls; their skin was pale as porcelain.

'Leah and her sister Rachel.'

'Honestly?' I couldn't believe the difference between the soft young face and the flabby cheeks of middle age.

'Life was harder then, wasn't it? Even if you were the lady of the house.'

'I'd love to know your family stories.'

'They were born, lived here, inherited the quarry and died.'

Adam's tone was as abrupt as his grandfather's had been earlier, but I was distracted for the moment, for as we reached the west side of the landing, I noticed a door like the one in the hall. Realising it must lead to the room I'd seen earlier, I turned the handle.

'What are you doing?'

'I want to have a look.'

'There's nothing down there.'

'What about the room at the end?'

23

'It's just a room.' At that moment, the bell rang for dinner. He took my hand. 'Come on, Granddad hates people to be late.'

I was puzzled by his reluctance, but I let him drag me away; I had no desire to upset his grandfather twice in one day.

Mr Flint was already seated at the head of the table when we entered the dining room. To my relief, he smiled when I greeted him – my earlier transgression forgiven. I was bursting with questions, but as Mrs Davies bustled in with the plates, I decided now was not the time to ask them. Instead, I confined my curiosity to the history of Whetstone and its environs while tucking into a delicious dinner: succulent steak that melted on the tongue, crispy roast potatoes and mint-soaked peas.

My new life was perhaps a little unsettling, but at least the food was good.

CHAPTER 3

After the sunshine of my first day, a fog descended on the hills and never quite left. Mist permeated the house with a permanent grey gloom. Our bedroom reeked of damp. I woke each morning to find moisture on the covers. I was rarely warm.

Life fell into a routine of sorts. Adam left early for work; I rose late. I brunched, browsed the well-stocked bookshelves and curled up on the sofa with stories I hadn't read in years. From time to time I would wander down the hill to Whetstone to post a letter. The post office was located in the village shop, a dusty dark cave, its shelves filled with cereal packets and tins that looked as if they'd been there for a decade at least. It appeared to be as unloved as its proprietress, Ivy, the people in Whetstone preferring to shop at the supermarket in Sandstown. I never saw anyone else going in there but me, and even I was only ever there to buy a stamp or some envelopes.

On the way back, I often stopped for a rest by the war memorial. Such landmarks aren't obvious in the city – offices and high-rise flats tend to crowd them out – but here in the countryside, the Celtic cross dominated the single road out of the village. I stared at the names marked in stone. I'd grown up in peace-time, untouched by war; yet in this village no family appeared to have survived unscathed. Not even the Flints, Henry's name being among the dead of the Second World War. And I was struck by how often names were repeated across the generations: Jones, Clark, Thomas, Edwards. What must it have been like to lose a father, brother or son in battle – not once, but twice? The name Tommy Davies featured in both wars. I wondered if they were related to our Mrs Davies, but I didn't ask her at the time. In those early days I was still a stranger, and it seemed too intrusive a question.

In the afternoon I'd rest, then have a bath and wait for Adam to arrive home for dinner. Sometimes I was downstairs in time to open the door to whatever health professional was visiting that day – usually the physiotherapist, sometimes the doctor, and on one occasion a district nurse. As I showed her to Mr Flint's room, she seemed keen to chat, telling me that she'd recently moved into the area from Liverpool. Perhaps, like me, she felt in need of someone to talk to. I wasn't intending to see her out, but I happened to come out of the living room as she had finished. She was walking across the hall when she stopped, staring at the wooden panels, the staircase and the front door, as if trying to remember something.

'Can I help you?' I asked.

'I'm sorry . . . I just thought, for a moment . . . the place seemed familiar. Déjà vu, I expect.'

I thought nothing of it as I showed her to the door. Mr Flint was recovering so well, there would be no need for her to return. I said goodbye, expecting never to see her again.

Though Mrs Davies was often about, she was busy cleaning, cooking, preparing bed linen. It made me feel guilty to see her working so hard, but she always refused my help. I rarely saw Mr Flint, and when I did, his conversation was limited to monosyllables. He generally waited till Adam was home before putting in an appearance at dinner, and then I often wished he'd stayed in his room. The meals fell into a pattern. Adam would tell us of some minor achievement, such as the completion of an order, only for his grandfather to criticise the percentage he'd negotiated. Each dinner ended the same, with the pair of them glaring at each other, and my small talk petering out with the dessert. I was always glad when Mrs Davies cleared the plates and Mr Flint departed for the evening.

It was a life of sorts, a limbo in which I was no longer busy treating patients, but not yet busy being a mother. The evenings I spent with Adam were pleasant enough, but a far cry from the heady excitement of the previous summer, when every night we spent together seemed rich with possibility. And, after the initial holiday feeling had passed, I

27

began to miss the friends I'd left behind. The sound of the post van on the drive began to make the difference between a good day, and a bad.

One morning, about a month after our arrival, I heard the noise of wheels on the gravel. I was hoping for a letter, but I was disappointed. There was just a parcel for Mr Flint. It was loosely covered in brown paper, ripped to shreds in places; it fell apart as I took it from the postman, revealing a notebook bound in leather. The fly leaf fell open on the inscription, *Daniel Clarkson*. There was an envelope inside addressed to the old man. I carried it in to him.

'There's a parcel for you; I'm afraid it's been bashed about in the post.'

'Thank you,' he said. But when he glanced at the inscription, his hand shook, and the tone of his voice altered. 'Put it on the desk, please,' he said, dismissing me with a curt wave.

As I walked out, I sensed him half-shifting in his chair. I thought for a moment he might be going to open the parcel but I was wrong. When I looked back he was sitting upright, staring at his book, though he didn't appear to be reading it.

Baffled, I asked Adam about Daniel Clarkson when he returned home.

'The name sounds familiar,' he said. 'Why do you ask?'

I explained about the parcel. 'Of course . . . he was . . .' He hesitated. 'A friend in the RAF.'

For a moment, I was sure he had been about to say something else.

'He didn't seem happy to receive it,' I said.

'Granddad doesn't like to talk about the war. He was shot down. He nearly died.'

I wanted to believe him, but there was something about his answer that didn't ring true. The longer I stayed at Echo Hall, the more I felt Adam was holding out on me and I didn't understand why. It wasn't just the fact that he and his grandfather refused to talk about the family; they also seemed to be hiding something about the door upstairs. Every time I approached the subject they refused to discuss it. Still I persisted, until eventually Adam snapped that the key was lost and would I please, please drop it. I dropped it to keep the peace, but all the while I was left wondering: what was it that they were keeping from me?

Since there was no one to talk to about these mysteries, I found myself brooding far more than was good for me. So I was grateful when Nisha rang one day to say she was in Sandstown and was hitching a lift up to see me. I hadn't seen her since the wedding, and her arrival proved a welcome distraction. I'd wanted to go out for a proper walk since my arrival, but had been nervous about going alone. So after a bowl of lentil soup supplied by Mrs Davies, we set out to explore the hills behind the house. The sky was full of scowling grey clouds, a marked contrast to the virulent green grass of the back garden. As we reached the

29

fir trees at the border of the estate, Nisha turned to look back.

'Wow,' she said. 'How on earth have you ended up living with the landed gentry?'

'They're not really landed gentry.'

'It's a far cry from Hackney . . . No dysfunctional families round here.'

I looked back at the curtained window that continued to pique my curiosity. 'I'm not so sure of that.'

'What do you mean?'

I told her about my suspicions as we exited the garden onto a public bridleway that led to the woods.

'How exciting,' said Nisha.

'Adam might be right . . .' I said, treading the soft earth littered with last year's decaying leaf-fall. 'That I'm imagining things.'

'But you don't think that?'

'No.'

Something rustled in the bushes; a blackbird hopped in front of us, then, sensing our presence, flew off. Knowing how much Nisha disliked Adam, I didn't want to admit to having doubts about him, to explain how hurt I felt that I was being kept out of family secrets. *What on earth are you doing with him?* she'd said when she first met him. *Tory boy if ever I saw one.* I had tried to explain that, after a winter locked in the cancer ward, I needed to be free. That he had been kind to me when I most needed it. And that he was light and lovely, offering me glamour and sparkle. He banished smells of disinfectant, memories of morphine, the vision of a mother withering to the bone. She hadn't understood then. She wouldn't understand that, now we were married, I had to believe he wasn't shutting me out again, as he had done when his grandfather was first ill.

'Are you alright?' asked Nisha, as I paused to catch my breath.

'Fine, just walking for two . . .'

She laughed and we moved onwards, branching so many times we had to check the map. Recent rain had left the trails sticky with mud. In some places the soil was black and oozing with silted water. We clambered round these patches as best we could, until the woods began to retreat into bushes. Our route snaked through a grassy slope covered in droppings, the mud giving way to rock and pale-grey stone. Sheep scattered on our approach. The wind chilled our faces, but our bodies warmed with the exertion. At last, we reached our destination: a series of grey boulders standing nearly six feet high, roofed by flat stones, halfway up the hill.

'Why is it called Arthur's Stone?' asked Nisha.

I consulted the guidebook. 'Apparently Arthur met Guinevere here. And then Guinevere met Lancelot, until Arthur discovered them. Should be called Guinevere's Stone really. It was probably some kind of burial ground . . . Oh, and the valley is also a natural echo chamber.'

31

'What fun.' Nisha walked to the edge of the plateau, calling out, 'Hellooooo!'

Her words returned faintly across the valley. I joined in with her shouting till the novelty faded and we turned back to explore the stones. It seemed a popular spot for lovers; their messages were engraved everywhere: *Amy loves Darren, Jim for Jules, EF & JF, Pete and Sue forever, J loves R.*

'People are so naff,' said Nisha.

'You've just never been in love.'

'And you have?'

'I got married, didn't I?'

'Hmm.'

'How about you, anyone on the horizon?'

'Simon. He's very sweet.'

It was my turn to hmm. Very sweet was Nisha's usual kind of bloke. They all followed a pattern – absolute adoration on both sides, based on a total willingness of the boyfriend to be a doormat, till Nisha tired and moved on. I didn't need her description – *ponytail, scrawny, writes poetry* – to smile to myself that she'd done it again.

The afternoon was turning cold, the sky darkening. It was time to go back. We took care on the downward path, but it was dusk by the time we reached the woods. The fog was returning from the valley, reducing visibility even further. We chose forks that seemed right but soon we were surrounded by dark trees and bushes, spectral in the dimming light.

'Which way now?' asked Nisha.

'I'm not sure.' I looked around, trying to remember what the paths had looked like earlier. The clouds ahead broke a little, and to my relief I could see a figure a few hundred yards ahead of us. A woman, I thought. She was standing by a track that branched left. I hadn't seen anyone ahead of us before, but I supposed she'd come on a different path and had lost her way. She was carrying a baby in her arms.

'Can you help us?' I called. 'We're a little lost!'

'Who are you talking to?' asked Nisha.

'That woman.'

'I don't see anyone.'

I pointed, but she was gone. The only visible shapes were tree trunks and bent shrubs.

'She was there a second ago,' I said, puzzled by her speed. 'She must have taken that fork.'

We plunged left in pursuit. To my relief, the path soon widened, and we began to recognise the route we had taken earlier. Soon we were back at the gate onto the estate. We saw no sign of the woman and her baby. I assumed she had walked back to the village by another track, and thought no more about her.

CHAPTER 4

A few days later, I found myself struggling up the hill against a strong easterly wind that seemed determined to force me back. It was so exhausting I had to take frequent rests; and, though I was wearing several layers of clothes, every inch of me tingled with cold. At the top of the drive, I could see Mr Flint wrapped in a thick winter coat, pushing his walker towards the house. He seemed to be in as much difficulty as I was. I caught up with him a few yards from the front door.

'What are you doing out here?' I gasped.

'Needed some air.' He spoke in sharp bursts of breath. The wind had whipped his cheeks bright red. 'I didn't think it would be quite so blowy.'

'I had to stop three times on the way back.'

'The last couple of months are the worst,' he said. 'Everything is such an effort.'

His interest took me by surprise. 'I am getting a bit fed up,' I admitted. 'I'll be glad when the baby arrives.'

'I'm looking forward to it.'

This was amazing, the longest conversation we'd

had since my arrival. We entered the building, heading for the kitchen. Mrs Davies had left some fairy cakes on the table. They were light and airy, melting on the tongue.

'These are delicious,' said Mr Flint, tucking into his second. 'Everything tastes wonderful now I don't have to stick to the diet the doctor prescribed.'

'I must find out her recipe.'

'You must forgive me – a combination of dull food and poor health has made me rather anti-social.' He smiled. 'From now on I intend to make more of an effort.'

Since he was being so amenable, I decided to risk an awkward question. 'Adam said the key for the door upstairs was missing. Can you think where it might be?'

He pushed his cup back. 'No.' His eyes hardened and his mouth fixed into a rigid flat line.

'Couldn't we get another one cut?'

'There's no need.'

'Why not?' The fresh air seemed to have made me reckless.

'There's nothing up there.' His voice shook with anger.

'I'm sorry,' I said, 'I didn't mean to upset you.'

But the pleasant mood had evaporated, and he disappeared back into his room. He didn't re-emerge till dinner, during which he hardly spoke. Fortunately Adam was caught up with quarry business, and didn't notice. When he suggested I come and help out the next day I was quick to accept, keen to avoid another tricky encounter with the old man.

I drove to Bryngraean the next morning, the grey clouds hanging low in the sky, threatening rain. I crossed the Welsh border about a mile from Whetstone, taking a road that twisted and turned on increasingly improbable gradients. I tried not to think about the sharp drops to my left and focused on the way ahead. I grasped the wheel tightly, my back hunched, my foot permanently on the clutch. As I climbed higher, the air became cooler and damper; white mist swirled around the car. The entrance to the quarry was on a bend, so sharp I almost missed it. I braked and turned the car under the rusty metal barrier, then drove up the steep slope. Piles of wet black slag marked the side of the track; the road ahead was marked with potholes, filled with muddy brown water. Straggles of mist hovered above the puddles, making me think of gases rising above no-man's land. What an earth drew Adam to this desolate place?

I followed the bend in the road. To my left, rusting tramways sloped down the hillside to the town of Tref y Bryn below. On my right, the remains of a small village clung to the hillside: dilapidated cottages with caved-in roofs and crumbling walls; a well with a broken winch; a grey-stone chapel with shattered windows. My journey ended at a plateau where huge mounds of black shale towered over a huddle of slate-grey buildings. A couple of large trucks were parked in the corner piled high with newly cut slabs of slate. As I locked the car I could hear the sound of an explosion from further up the valley; it was so loud the baby jumped. Clouds of dust billowed out from the source of the blast, clogging my mouth and nostrils. I coughed violently.

Adam emerged from one of the buildings. 'Come in. This will stop in a minute,' he called above the noise.

He led me into the main office: a long room with tiny windows at either end, the double glazing the only attempt at modernisation. In the far corner, a leather-bound ledger lay open on a sloped oak writing desk. The shelves above it stretched around the room, packed with the accounts of the past, the dates on their spines going back to the previous century. In the centre of the room a rickety table was piled with papers, old catalogues, files, engineering reports, all placed in haphazard fashion. The only semblance of organisation was on the smaller table, where someone had attempted to keep the files in some kind of order. No wonder Adam had been working so late. Seeing the chaos, I was more than happy to help out, and was soon absorbed in the work, matching each invoice with the ledger note. Despite the double glazing, the windows rattled every time the trucks drove past; I tried not to let them distract me. I began to make progress, piling the paid invoices in one tray, the unpaid in another, struck by how ill Mr Flint must have been before his stroke. His handwriting, bold and flowing at the beginning of the previous year, gradually became shakier and shakier; the entries became less frequent, the details less clear, leaving me with a pile of unsures at the end of the morning.

'What's the damage?' asked Adam, as we sat eating ham sandwiches.

'There's about a quarter to pay, some of them red. About five thousand pounds, I think.'

'Ouch.'

'Is it that bad?'

'It's tight . . . And we don't have much room for manoeuvre. I used to think this quarry would go on forever. But the latest engineering reports suggest the main seam may be drying up.' So this was why he'd been so distracted since we'd arrived. He'd always wanted to run the quarry; it would be terrible if he had to give up on the idea before he'd even got going.

'What'll you do?'

'I've got an idea.'

He took me by the hand and out into the yard, quieter now the explosions had stopped. We walked to the back of the site, up a broad path to the top of the terraced hill. The tram-tracks followed us on the left, past the remains of a small ruined building, defunct machinery rusting in its centre. At the top of the slope the tracks turned towards us, joining a larger tramway that led to the entrance of a tunnel. A small yellow train – a driver's carriage and five trucks – stood waiting for us. Adam helped me on board, climbed into the driver's seat and started the engine.

I've never been keen on caves or underground spaces, but Adam was so excited I didn't like to object. I gripped the rail as we descended into gloom, turning back to catch the last glimmer of daylight at the entrance. It reminded me of a myth I'd loved as a child – Persephone being kidnapped by Hades. Her final desperate look before the descent into hell. I shivered; suddenly the myth felt all too real. We turned a corner, plunging downwards. The slate walls were close enough to touch, the ceiling crowding down on our heads. A chain of wall lamps flickered orange-black against the damp rock, fighting off the darkness. The air grew colder.

To take my mind off the encroaching shadows, I asked, 'How is slate created?' My words steamed the air.

'Metamorphic rock begins as mud, deep in the earth – malleable, flexible, the crystals arranged in different directions.'

I wanted to grab Adam's hand, but he needed both to drive the train. I forced myself to concentrate on what he was saying.

'Pressure and stress force the crystals together, squashing them into straight lines. They harden to form rigid layers of slate.' Adam seemed unaffected by the clammy atmosphere. 'The process is reversible. Over time the stone is weathered by rain, wind and sleet. Rocks fall. The slate breaks up, becoming malleable, till it crumbles to the free-flowing mud from which it came.'

'You sound like a tour guide.'

'Funny you should say that.' The train rattled to a halt in a man-made gallery. A ring of lamps lit up the bottom of the cavern. A ladder with tiny slats stretched up the side of the cave, 60 feet above us.

'Did men really climb up there?' I asked.

'They carved rock from the walls, creating these fantastic arches,' said Adam, his voice full of energy. 'Imagine this lit up.'

'It would be impressive.'

'I'm thinking of developing it as a tourist attraction. That way we could keep the quarry going even when the main seam is finished. Mark's interested.'

Mark was our best man, Adam's oldest friend from school. He ran a company specialising in historical reconstructions of Victorian industries. This site would be perfect.

'What about your grandfather?'

'There's the rub.'

The lights blinked, flickered and then went out. I gasped. My heart started to pound. The darkness closed in, as black as it had been on my first night at Echo Hall. Water dripped from the ceiling. Adam was a few feet away, but I couldn't see him. The blackness pressed in on me; I could barely breathe.

'Get me out of here,' I began to sob, calling out for him.

He was quickly there, grabbing my hand, taking me back to the truck. We reversed back up the track. It was a long, slow climb, but as the lights flickered back on, I felt myself breathing more freely. We came to the bend and turned towards a tiny circle of light. The air grew warmer; the tunnel began to brighten. The circle became larger, until at last we reached the surface. I staggered out of the carriage, gulping the air, the horror receding with Adam's apologetic hug. I was grateful for his comfort, and glad he had something he was so passionate about, but it wasn't an enthusiasm I could share. I left him in the office, driving home in a steady drizzle.

When I arrived at the house, the lights were off downstairs. I could hear hoovering upstairs, but otherwise the house was still. The hallway was dark, damp and uninviting. Twenty rooms to choose from and none of them felt like home. I wanted to cry. And then, just as I had decided I might as well go for a nap, I was overwhelmed by a wave of spite that seemed to be emanating from Mr Flint's room. Once more I was gripped by a strong presence whose sole intent seemed to be to inflict sorrow and pain. I froze, unable to move, until Mr Flint's yell broke the spell. Alarmed, I rushed to open the door and for a moment, in the grey gloom, I could have sworn I saw two figures by his chair. But when I turned on the light, there was no one there; I was jumping at shadows again. The sense of malice dissipated, leaving Mr Flint bent double, hands held over his ears, whimpering.

'No, no, I won't . . .' he mumbled, over and over again.

I reached over, shaking him as gently as I could. Gradually his arms relaxed, his body stilled. He opened his eyes, staring at me in alarm till he recovered his wits.

'Are you OK?'

'I was dreaming.'

'It seemed like a bad one.'

'My parents . . .' He paused. 'They were not the kindest of people.'

I waited, and then he said, more to himself than to me, 'Why did they tell me? Why didn't they leave me alone?'

'Tell you what?'

He looked up at me, startled, as if he'd forgotten I was there. 'It doesn't matter . . . It was all a long time ago.'

He wouldn't be drawn further, but in the red hearth light, he seemed more human; his face was softer, more malleable. It was easy then to stay and chat, offering comfort for a while.

Just as I was leaving, he said, 'It really is a pleasure to have you here, Ruth. Bringing new life into the house.'

The warmth of his words was encouraging. Perhaps, I reflected on my way upstairs to change,

I was finding a place in this family after all. But as I reached the top of the stairs, I caught sight of Mrs Davies. She was carrying the vacuum cleaner, and seemed to be coming away from the green baize door. Was that where she'd been vacuuming? I thought of confronting her then and there, but I was worried about causing more upset. If I wanted to find out what was going on here, I would have to do it by stealth.

CHAPTER 5

After my trip to the quarry, I made little progress in my investigations. Having been rebuffed so often, I didn't dare ask Adam and his grandfather about the locked door again. Mrs Davies did not appear to go near it, and though I searched everywhere I could think of, I could not find a key. Eventually I tired of looking, but the thought of the door preyed on my mind. It entered my dreams, a portal to a world of shadowy figures, choking darkness and hidden malice. Dreams I was glad to wake from, reassured by Adam by my side.

Though my nights were troubled, the days at least began to grow bright. As March drifted into April, tiny green buds appeared on the trees. Tractors began to plough the fields. Lambs appeared on the hillsides, dancing up and down the slopes with an agility I envied. The air grew warmer, and the skies were blue more often than grey. By the time Easter arrived, the buds had burst, sprinkling the trees with leaves; the hedgerows were scattered with white blossom and yellow daffodils sprouted on the lawn. With the arrival of sunshine, Echo Hall took on a more cheerful air, the garden filled with the honey scents of hyacinth and wisteria. Sometimes, I almost felt as if I liked the place.

'Do you know, that myth really makes sense now,' I said, as we set off for lunch with Mark and his wife Helen.

'What myth?'

'Persephone and Ceres . . . Winter is the mother mourning her daughter; spring the celebration of the girl returning.'

'You've experienced spring before.'

'It's different in the country . . .'

'You're more aware of the seasons,' said Mr Flint, from the back. 'I've always liked that story.' He caught me by surprise; I'd not taken him for the literary sort.

'Exactly. You notice every bud opening, every new blade of grass,' I said.

They both laughed. For the first time since I'd arrived at Echo Hall, they seemed relaxed, happy almost; as if being away from the house freed them from its stern grip.

We arrived an hour later, walking up the garden path to the sounds of a baby crying and a shout of 'It's mine!' from the front room. Mark answered the door; a scent of roast lamb wafted from the kitchen where Madonna was exhorting us not to choose second best from a tinny radio.

'Come in,' he said, leaving us to make our way as he rushed in to prevent his sons from pummelling each other.

'Sorry about that,' he added, diverting them with a pile of Lego. 'Helen's tied up with the baby, so I'm left to referee.'

I smiled. I'd liked Mark from the moment I met him. He had calmed my nerves on our wedding day with a slew of terrible jokes. And, despite being every bit as right-wing as Adam, he'd somehow managed to win Nisha over when he dropped her home afterwards. Now, watching him sort out the children, I appreciated he was a good father too.

Helen hadn't made it to the wedding – it had been too close to her due date – so I was interested to know what she was like. While Mark fixed us drinks, I examined the room, trying to get a sense of her personality. It was painted ochre, decorated with blue and white tiles. The floor was of polished wood, covered with large rugs. Two small palms framed the fireplace.

'Helen's Middle Eastern theme,' Mark explained as he handed me a glass of lemonade. 'She's good, isn't she? I keep telling her she should go into business.'

It was lovely, if intimidatingly perfect: more like a museum than a living room, and rather impractical. As the boys began to fight again, they nearly knocked the palm trees flying.

'*Mark*.' Helen entered the room with the baby on her shoulder. 'Can't you sort them out?'

'I was just getting drinks.'

'You're useless,' she said in an exasperated tone, scolding the boys before turning to me. 'It's lovely to meet you, Ruth.' She shook my hand. 'I've got one last thing to do in the kitchen and we'll eat when Mum gets here. Can I trust you to hold Alice for five minutes, Mark, while I finish off?' She handed him the baby, heading back to the kitchen.

'Meet my little princess,' he said.

'When do they start getting interesting?' asked Adam.

'She's interesting right now.'

'That's a matter of opinion.'

'You wait till yours comes along, mate. You'll soon change your tune.'

'Humph.'

'He will, won't he?' said Mark, sitting down next to Mr Flint.

'Indeed he will.' I hadn't taken the old man for the baby sort either, but he was totally absorbed by the child. 'She's a real beauty.'

'Isn't she?'

'About eight weeks, I'd say.'

I couldn't have guessed that if I hadn't known Alice's birth date. How did he know?

'Spot on.'

'You must be pleased to have a girl.'

'Especially after these two little thugs. They're gorgeous, but . . . boys will be boys. You can't stop them fighting.'

'I'm not so sure of that,' I said.

'Watch it, Mark, you'll get her on her soapbox.' Adam grinned.

'I have studied the subject.'

'The famous dissertation . . .' This was a matter on which Adam and I often sparred. My final-year project had concluded that parental influence dominated male and female behaviour. Adam thought it nonsense. 'She thinks it's down to the sins of the father and all that.'

'It's a viewpoint, I suppose.' said Mark. 'And when delivered by a beautiful woman, how can we disagree?'

'Now you're just being patronising.'

'Not at all. Beauty and intellect. A perfect combination. No wonder Adam married you.' He grinned at me, and for some reason I felt myself blush. It was idiotic. He was my husband's best friend, but suddenly he seemed extremely attractive. I was grateful for the arrival of Helen's mother, Fiona, who provided us all with a distraction, allowing me to gather my composure before lunch.

The meal was delicious and the company proved pleasant, until I made the mistake of praising Helen's interior-design skills.

'I was just saying to Ruth that you should go into business,' said Mark, gazing at her fondly.

'Like that's likely to happen.' I was taken aback by the sharpness of her retort. 'When you're always away with your building projects.'

'That's my job,' he protested. 'It's not as if I'm in the reserves, like Adam, and have to give up all those weekends . . .'

48

'Work or not, someone in this family has to be around for the children, don't they?'

She had a point. I'd not minded Adam's occasional weekends away last year – they'd provided a welcome break from the intensity of our relationship. After his grandfather became ill, he'd been given leave of absence and I'd half-forgotten it was coming to an end. Now the baby was coming, I realised I wasn't too keen on him continuing even if he would be leaving in 18 months.

'Will you be sorry when it's over?' asked Mark.

'Yes and no. It takes up a lot of time, and I'm married now.' Adam looked at me and smiled. 'But part of me wishes I could see some proper action before I finish.'

'You don't know what you're talking about,' said Mr Flint.

Adam flushed. 'I was just saying. Your generation had a chance to prove themselves. My army experience was mainly kicking around NATO bases in Germany and Cyprus. I just wish I'd had the opportunity to do something real.'

'Only a fool would think that.'

Adam reddened.

Time to change the subject. I turned to Fiona. 'Do you live close by?'

'Along the street. We moved here when Jim retired.'

'It must be nice to have Helen and Mark so close.'

'Yes. I love being near the grandchildren.'

Unexpectedly, my eyes filled with tears. It was

nearly a year since Mum died; I missed her all the time, of course, but I hadn't stopped to think I'd miss her even more when the baby was born. I glanced down at the tablecloth, trying to pull myself together.

Fiona chattered on, oblivious, talking so rapidly I lost the thread. 'They were childhood sweethearts of course.'

'Who?'

'Mark and Helen. We used to live next door to Mark's family.' She gazed at them across the table with a fond smile. 'And still just as much in love as ever.'

I hadn't seen much sign of Helen's affection for Mark, but I could see why she'd chosen him. He was kind, caring, the type of man who'd have caught my eye if we were both single. Which of course we were not. I turned back to Adam and squeezed his hand as if I needed to remind myself how lucky I was. If he hadn't been there for me last year, I'd never have got through it.

We stayed till tea time. It was a pleasant enough afternoon, and once the meal was over, Helen did seem more relaxed as she snuggled up to Mark on the sofa. Perhaps her mother was right; perhaps they were still very much in love. Nonetheless, as the afternoon wore on, I began to get bored. The children were sweet, but the constant discussion of every detail of their lives dragged after a while. I was glad when it was time to leave. We drove back over the hills as the sun was beginning to set. By the time we arrived home its red-gold rays cast a warm glow from the windows; for once the place looked vibrant, welcoming, alive. But the minute we stepped inside, I was assailed by the same familiar chill; and was it my imagination, or did both Adam and Mr Flint immediately seem less relaxed?

Later, at bedtime, Adam asked how I'd got on with Helen. I could see he wanted us to be friends, so I tried my best.

'She was alright.'

'Only alright?'

'She was horrible to Mark. Never stopped nagging him.'

'She's always like that after a new baby. Lack of sleep, I expect. Give her a chance – honestly, she's lovely. By the way,' he added, as we pulled the covers over us, 'were you OK at lunch? You seemed a bit upset by something Fiona said.'

'It was just that Mum won't . . .' I cuddled up close to him, glad to be held.

'. . . be here for the baby. Of course. It's her anniversary soon. Shall we go to Birmingham?'

'That would be great.'

I closed my eyes. This was why I loved being with Adam: he understood without me having to spell it out. I drifted off to sleep, comforted by the thought.

★   ★   ★

51

But over the next few days, whenever I considered the trip to Birmingham, I couldn't face it. So Adam suggested an alternative. Why didn't we visit *his* parents' grave and we could think of all our parents at the same time? I approved: our mutual losses had drawn us together in the first place, and now they were part of the ties that bound us. So on the day of the anniversary we walked down to Whetstone and entered the tiny cemetery at the back of the church. Tall yew trees surrounded the graveyard, their dark-green leaves obscuring the light. Green mosses ran across the grass; grey and brown lichens covered the stones. The graves were piled higgledy-piggledy, as if some toddler had knocked them over like bricks. Presumably because they were such an important local family, the Flints were buried in the centre, their graves marked by large decorated crosses – the Jacobs, Aarons and Reubens going back generations. Adam's great-grandparents, Jacob and Leah, were there, alongside a plain cross in memory of their son Henry, killed in 1942. Adam's parents, Eve and Paul Harrington, were close by, next to his grandmother Veronica. Holding hands in front of their graves, conscious of the baby moving inside me, Mum suddenly felt close, our future connected with our past. We stood for what felt like hours, united in our griefs, until at last Adam said, 'I need to be getting back.'

'Of course . . . and thanks,' I said. 'This has

been just right.' I looked down at the stone one last time, struck by something. 'Your name . . .'

'What of it?'

'Your mum . . . she married a Harrington. So why are you called Flint?'

'Erm . . .' The question seemed to flummox him. 'Just a quirk of Granddad's. When I came to live here, he made me change it by deed poll. Keeping the family name and all that.'

'I see.' It seemed as rational an expectation as any, but as we left the graveyard, I couldn't help but wonder whether, as with the locked door, there was more to it than that. Living at Echo Hall was like catching something out of the corner of your eye and not quite being able to see what it was. I had the sense that I was missing something vital about the Flint family, but I couldn't quite work out what.

CHAPTER 6

One day, near the end of April, I found myself unexpectedly alone in the house. Adam had taken the day off to drive his grandfather to visit friends. I'd planned to go along too, but in the morning I was overwhelmed with exhaustion and at the last minute stayed at home. Just after they left, Mrs Davies was disturbed from her hoovering by the news that one of her grandchildren had had to go to the hospital. She was needed round at the coach house to look after the others, so Tommy could go and help his wife. She hurried out of the house in such a state of consternation that she forgot to put the vacuum cleaner away. As I went to move it, I discovered she'd also dropped her keys. I picked them up, fully intending to leave them in her bedroom, when it occurred to me that one of them might open the door. It was two o'clock. She wouldn't be back for a while, and I wasn't expecting Adam to be home till six. Plenty of time to explore, and no one would be any the wiser. I climbed the stairs, and tried the keys in the door.

After several attempts, one turned with a satisfying

click, exposing a long corridor similar to the one on our side of the house. I wandered down, looking in the bedrooms, but they were all empty. Adam and Mr Flint had been telling the truth. There was nothing to see here. I'd let my rapid change of circumstance, unfamiliar home and pregnancy throw me off balance. Trying not to feel too disappointed, I reached for the handle of the last room. I might as well satisfy my curiosity. The latch was stiff; it took several attempts to open it. When it finally gave way, I was propelled over the threshold into a thick, choking darkness. Emotions lingered here, as they had in the bedroom on the other side of the house, though in this room the walls seemed soaked with sadness, horror, despair. Hardly able to breathe, I forced my way across the room, drew the curtains and opened the windows. Light and air flooded in; the feelings receded. It was just a bedroom, nothing more. It smelt musty and was furnished with a bed, a dressing table, a cupboard, a pile of boxes and a trunk. Why had Adam and his grandfather been so reluctant for me to come in here?

I walked over to the wardrobe, opening it to find a couple of fur coats, a scarf made with real fox heads and several cotton dresses with padded shoulders and short sleeves. An odour of mothballs emanated from them. At the end of the rail, I noticed a blue silk dress. It looked as if it had been restyled from an old ball gown. Whose were these? A servant's hand-me-downs from her mistress? I turned to the boxes, searching for answers.

The first one was full of books, a Bible resting on the top. I picked it up. A name was written inside: *Elsie Forbes, 1935.* Whoever she was, Elsie Forbes was clearly educated. The box was crammed full of classics, with the occasional nod at what would then have been the height of modernity: *Burmese Days, The Power and the Glory.* She had good taste. I picked up a slim volume of Thomas Hardy, which fell open on a well-thumbed page. I shivered. The poem had been one of my favourites at school:

Woman much missed how you call to me, call to me, Saying that now you are not as you were, When you had changed from the one who was all to me, But as at first, when our day was fair. Can it be you that I hear? Let me view you, then, Standing as when I drew near to the town, Where you would wait for me; yes, as I knew you then, Even to the original air-blue gown! Or is it only the breeze in its listlessness Travelling across the wet mead to me here, You being ever dissolved to wan listlessness Heard no more again far or near? Thus I: faltering forward, Leaves around me falling, Wind oozing thin through the thorn from norward And the woman calling.

Elsie Forbes, whoever she was, had written in the margins: *ghostly lover disappears, Heathcliff and Cathy?* That made me shiver, too. I'd had the exact same thought when I'd read Hardy's poems for his long-dead wife.

It was a bit unnerving to be sharing opinions with a woman who'd lived here several decades ago, but I was intrigued. Who was she? I undid the catch on the trunk. It was filled with personal memorabilia – theatre stubs, bus tickets, a flier for dances at the Adelphi Ballroom. There were several packs of letters bound together with a red ribbon. I picked one up at random, undid the ribbon and opened the first letter. It was from Elsie Forbes's sister, Het, telling of her move to London, her forthcoming pregnancy and her husband's new job in the Docklands. Perhaps Elsie was a chambermaid, then?

I picked up another bundle of letters. The hand-writing looked familiar. I extracted one from the collection, opened it, and then put it down again. I couldn't believe it. I read it again just to make sure I hadn't made a mistake. The letter was short and to the point:

Echo Hall
September 1935

My Dearest,
You are Something Else,
I want Nothing Else,
In this whole wide world but you.

57

I would for-go All Else,
And be with Naught Else,
If I could only be with you
So never say What, Else?
And never say Why, Else?
Or .... Else
Without you I'll be blue.
Your ever-loving
Jack xxxx
PS Sorry for the dreadful poetry, more
Daniel's line than mine.

My head was reeling. Jack was Mr Flint's name.
And this certainly looked like his handwriting.
Why had he written love letters to a woman I'd
never heard of? Another letter provoked even more
questions.

Echo Hall
1st January 1936

My Darling Else,

I hope that you are well and have had a
better Christmas than mine. Echo Hall is
as grim as ever. My father was at his most
severe in his Christmas Day sermon. I sometimes think he forgets the message of the
season, he is so eager to remind his congregation of their failing ways. I wish I had you
here with me, you would liven things up a
bit. Instead I have to endure Father's treatises

58

and Henry ogling his new girl, Veronica. She's frightful, all piety and butter wouldn't melt but she runs rings round him. Father of course adores her; she has the right note of reverence for his every saying. But behind the sweet exterior I can sense nerves of steel. Poor Henry is totally mad about her, but I think he'll live to regret being involved with her, she's a Tartar underneath. Mother is stern and sad as always. Once upon a time I could make her smile, but not any more. Like Father she prefers to spend her time praying to her God who seems a very miserable deity to me. All fire and brimstone and condemnation of the sinner. I suppose I'll have to let you run the gauntlet and meet them all one day – Mother, Father, Henry and now Veronica. But I don't think I am yet equal to the task. I'll need all your strength and all your help and all your love when that time comes. Luckily for me you have enough courage for both of us.

I'll be back in Liverpool on the 18th, I'll get the late train so don't wait up for me. I think Daniel will be there a couple of days earlier, so he can keep you company till I'm back.

Forever yours, Jack x

I sat back on my heels, puzzled. Veronica was Mr Flint's wife. Why had no one mentioned she'd been going to marry Henry first? How had Mr Flint's feelings turned from such loathing to love? And who was Elsie Forbes? Why were her possessions here? There was something else nagging me about the letters, but I couldn't quite think what.

I turned my attention to a collection of photographs. One was of Mr Flint before the war, his name scrawled on the back. In another, a young man with dark curly hair stood against a gate: *Daniel at home.* Daniel, that was it. The name on the diary Jack had received. Was this the same Daniel? A third picture showed the two of them on either side of a young woman. They were by the seaside, and all three were laughing. She had linked arms with both of them, but was leaning towards Jack, in a way that implied intimacy. I turned it over. *Me and my boys, summer, 1935.* This must be Elsie Forbes. She seemed happy, good-humoured, the kind of person you'd want for a friend.

The wall beside me was turning pink; shadows were falling over the boxes. Outside, the sky was turning red-gold. It was time to go. I sorted the letters back into their piles and replaced the books and photographs. On a whim, I kept the last one, stuffing it into my cardigan pocket. I locked up, returned the keys to Mrs Davies's room and sat in the front room waiting for Adam to return. Sitting down, I realised how tired I was. I closed my eyes and put my feet up on a stool. Within minutes I had fallen asleep.

*　　*　　*

'Mrs Flint!' A voice called in my ear. And then again. 'Mrs Flint.'

For a moment, I thought I was back in my flat in Hackney. 'Huh? What?'

'It's dinner time.' Mrs Davies shook me again.

I woke properly and followed her into the dining room. Adam and his grandfather were already there.

'How was your afternoon?' Adam asked, as Mrs Davies put a steaming bowl of soup in front of him.

'Not bad. I rested mainly.'

I wanted to tell them both what I'd done, to ask about Elsie Forbes, but their previous reactions hadn't inspired me with confidence. I needed some time to work out how to tackle this. I began to eat my soup and listened politely as they talked about their day. The room was getting warmer and I'd almost forgotten about the photograph when I took my cardigan off. The picture fell to the floor just as Mrs Davies placed a plate of beef stew in front of me.

She leant over to pick it up. 'You've dropped something, my lovey,' she said. She put it on the table and left the room.

'What's that?' Adam asked.

I didn't move fast enough. Mr Flint had seen the photo.

'Where did you get this?' he asked, his voice rising.

There was no point hiding the truth. 'The back bedroom.'

'I told you not to go there.'

'I don't understand why.'

'It's family business.'

'I'm not family?'

He did not answer. Instead he pushed his plate away, his face ash-white. 'Adam, could you help me to my room, please?'

'I can explain,' I said.

'Don't bother,' said Adam, as he helped the old man up. I toyed with the stew, waiting for him to return, but he didn't come back. Eventually, I left the table, taking the plates through to the kitchen where Mrs Davies tutted at the waste.

As I came out of the kitchen, I heard the front door bang. I rushed to it, too late to stop Adam from driving down the hill. I thought of knocking on Mr Flint's door, but remembering the look on his face, I thought better of it. I went into the lounge and turned the television on. I flicked between the channels, but I wasn't really paying attention. I waited till eleven, but Adam still wasn't back, so I climbed the stairs to bed. At midnight, I was aware of lights up the drive, the sound of an engine coming to a halt. I sat up for a long time waiting for Adam's foot on the stairs. He never came.

CHAPTER 7

It had taken weeks to get used to sharing a bed with Adam; now I couldn't sleep for his absence. I tossed and turned, trying to get comfortable, but my bump was too big, the pillows too lumpy; and my mind was filled with argument.

I must have slept, I suppose, because the screeching of rooks startled me at about half-past five. Dawn was beginning to break: grey light was sneaking through the blue-black clouds. I closed my eyes, willing myself to go back to sleep. It was no good. I was wide awake. I'd hardly eaten anything the previous night; now I was hungry. I wasn't sure if I could face Adam yet; if I went downstairs now, I might be able to avoid that awkward conversation for a while. I crept into the kitchen, placed bread in the toaster and put the kettle on. Outside the sky was lightening. It was going to be another clear day. The toast popped. Though I felt sick, I forced myself to eat it. It was dry and stuck in my throat.

I was just finishing when Adam came in. His clothes were crumpled, his hair tousled.

'Hello,' I said.

'Hello.'

We gazed at each other. I was first to turn my eyes away.

'I'm sorry . . . I shouldn't have . . .'

'Too right you shouldn't have.' He pushed his hand through his hair, a gesture I normally found endearing. Today it felt like a threat. 'What on earth possessed you?'

'I was curious. You said there was nothing to see. I thought you were hiding something. Turns out I was right.'

'It's family stuff.'

'Marrying doesn't make me family?'

'It's not like that.'

'Well, what is it like? We're about to be parents, Adam. How can we do that if we don't trust each other?'

Adam was saved from answering by Mr Flint entering with a clatter of his frame.

'I'm sorry,' I began.

'I'm sure you are, Ruth, but you went against my express wishes.'

'If you'd just told me what was up there, I wouldn't have gone looking.'

Mr Flint considered this for a moment. When he spoke, his voice was colder than his words. 'I suppose there's some truth in that. Very well. I will tell you. And then I never want to discuss it again.' He pulled the chair out and sat down at the table. Adam sat down next to him, still refusing to return my gaze. 'Elsie Forbes was my wife.'

'I thought your wife was called Veronica?'

'Veronica was my second wife. I married Elsie first.'

'What happened?'

'She died. During the war. In this house. In that room.'

'I'm sorry . . . I didn't know.'

'I don't like to be reminded of it, of her. I couldn't bear to throw her things away, so we locked the room up. Later on, I married again. And that's the end of it.'

It was a reasonable enough explanation, yet I couldn't help but feel he was holding something back. But his tone was so final I said nothing more, and began to prepare breakfast. Adam had thawed enough by the time it was over to give me a peck on the cheek, but I was glad when Mr Flint went back to his room.

After he left, I turned to Adam. 'Why didn't you tell me?'

'I wanted to,' he sighed, 'but it isn't easy, growing up in the Flint family. We're just not the kind of people who talk about difficult subjects. When tragedy strikes, like Granddad's first wife, like my parents, we just deal with it and move on.'

I opened my mouth to protest.

'Ruth, you asked if you were family? Of course you are. Of course *we* are. But this is what my granddad wants. Maybe I should have explained this before, but I'm telling you now. This is what it means to be a Flint.'

I thought he was wrong, but I could see now wasn't the time to say it. At least he'd come back to me. At least he'd tried to explain. He kissed me before heading off to work, leaving me to tell Mrs Davies that we'd had an early breakfast. Now I was tired and wanted to go back to bed. I fell asleep immediately.

Mrs Davies woke me at lunch with a cup of tea and the message that Nisha had called, inviting me to a talk in Sandstown that night. I was still tired, but it seemed the perfect excuse to avoid a potentially difficult evening at home. With any luck, a bit of space between Adam and I would ensure that by tomorrow things would be back to normal. I ran a bath, thinking about the events of the previous day as I watched the bubbles building in the water. Despite Adam's warning, I couldn't help but wonder about Elsie Forbes and who she was to Mr Flint. What had happened to her that made him behave like this? Why didn't he want to discuss it? I stepped into the bath, sinking into its warm waters, relaxing with the scent of lavender. If Mr Flint had been a client, I'd have said something painful had happened, so painful that he couldn't bear to talk or even think about it. In which case, there was no point in me pursuing it further. The more I pushed the more he'd retreat, and the chances were I'd alienate both him and Adam. No, I realised as I ducked my hair under the water, I'd have to be patient. I would have to put aside my curiosity and stop asking questions. Instead, I should try and build a better relationship with the old man. Perhaps then he would able to trust me and be willing to share his secrets. Decision made, I climbed out of the bath, got dressed and headed off towards Sandstown.

It was a bright evening; the sky was a pale blue, the sun's rays lighting sparks of fire over the barley fields. Summer was coming: the verges had burst into life, with grasses, buttercups and campion jostling for space under a canopy of cow parsley. I reached the edge of town within half an hour, passing a series of dull housing estates full of tiny box-like houses that looked the same. It seemed an ugly place until I entered the main road, where the Edwardian houses and tree-lined avenues were much more attractive. I parked near the station by a large hotel called the King George. It was probably quite splendid in its heyday, but now the previously white walls were smudged grey and covered in lichen, while the paint was peeling off the black gables. On the terraced house opposite, a faded advert for milk was just visible on the brickwork. Nisha had given me instructions, but I managed to take a wrong turn and found myself walking by the cathedral that dominated the skyline. It was a Gothic masterpiece complete with arches, columns and flying buttresses; its roof was covered in animal gargoyles. I gazed up at the fox, cat and spaniel that had featured on Adam's postcard. Last summer I had never heard of this place; now it was part of my neighbourhood. Sometimes, it was hard to keep up with how much my life had changed.

Someone pointed me in the direction of the Meeting House and I arrived with 10 minutes to spare. I entered the meeting room where 20 wooden chairs were arranged in a semi-circle. An urn steamed on the long trestle table at the back of the room. The walls were painted white and decorated with pictures of famous Quakers: George Fox, William Penn, Elizabeth Fry. One faded poster proclaimed the message *Pacifism is not peace at any price . . . but Love at all costs*. Another was emblazoned with the CND symbol surrounded by a circle of people; by the door there was a large photo of Greenham Common surrounded by thousands of women. I wandered over to it, gazing at the cheerful crowd. I was somewhere in that throng, joining hands with my sisters in a cause I'd once fervently believed in. But that was a long time ago, when I used to believe in causes, before one of the sisterhood betrayed me and I'd given up on passion for good.

Four or five people were already seated. Nisha was standing at the front talking to a tall woman whom I guessed was Liz, the speaker. I walked over to them.

'You look ready to drop!' Nisha cried, giving me a hug. 'Good job we've got boiling water to hand.'

'It's ages yet,' I reassured her as she made the introductions. Liz barely acknowledged me. It was pretty rude, but I gave her the benefit of the doubt; perhaps she was concentrating on her talk.

I found myself a seat. Nisha sat down next to me. 'So are you getting excited?'

'Nervous, more like. You should have seen the film we watched in antenatal class. I had no idea.' The seats were beginning to fill up around us.

'You'll be fine.'

'You don't have to go through it.'

The room hushed as Liz began to talk. I thought the title 'The End of Empire' was pretentious, and was about to say so when I caught the captivated look on Nisha's face. I'd seen that look before – my friend in hero-worship mode. Though I knew better than to criticise one of her idols, I knew from experience that such relationships rarely ended well for her. I made a mental note to prepare myself for the fallout, and concentrated on the speech. Though I hadn't warmed to Liz, she began well, describing the fall of the Berlin Wall, the triumph of nonviolent revolution, the collapse of the USSR and end of their empire. Outside the sky was beginning to darken, grey-blue clouds building towards nightfall as she described the dangers of Russia's crumbling warheads, and a world with only one super power.

'What will America do?' she asked. 'How will it manage the problems of the Middle East? Of post-war Iran and Iraq? Of Palestine and Israel? The dwindling oil markets? What kind of world policeman will it be?'

She continued in similar vein for another half-hour. My mind began to wander. When I was a student, I used to come to meetings like this all the time. Back in my marching days, such speakers had me out on the streets at the drop of a hat for every left-wing cause going: pro-choice, CND, anti-apartheid, gay rights. I'd thought I'd live like that forever, till I'd returned home early one day to find my lover Jeremy in bed with my best friend Gail. At the time our relationships were so defined by our politics, their betrayal was enough to turn me off activism for good. I glanced across at Nisha. As the years had passed, everyone else in our circle had moved on, except her. She never stopped marching, all the way through the '80s, for every hopeless cause and passionate dream. She was always so sure of herself, never afraid to make a bold choice, regardless of the consequences. Now, listening to Liz's concluding remarks – that we needed vigilance against world leaders, to support our local arms-trade group, to campaign for human rights in Iraq and Iran – I could see she'd be marching for a long time to come. Suddenly I envied her. It was years since I'd been that clear-sighted, a situation only worsened by the fog that had enveloped me after Mum's death.

After the talk, we went for a meal. I could have done without Liz's presence, but I couldn't think of an excuse to exclude her. Unsure where else to go, I suggested the King George Hotel. Despite the peeling paintwork, it looked charming from the outside, so I was disappointed to find the dining room so tatty. I'd been hoping for faded elegance, not Formica tables covered in red plastic tablecloths, several of them torn. In the corner of the room a large TV screen rolled out a loop of continuous pop videos. The mid-week menu was unadventurous: burgers, scampi, pizza. I was too hungry to care too much, settling for haddock and chips. There was no vegetarian option, so Nisha and Liz made do with chip butties. Nisha didn't seem to mind, but I could see Liz was fuming.

'That was an interesting speech,' I said, trying to break the ice. 'Do you really think we need to be vigilant? Isn't the world safer now?'

'We should all be worried about the collapse of an empire, however bad. The winners are at their most powerful; they need to flex muscle. Believe me, the US will find an enemy somewhere – the generals at the Pentagon can't let their toys gather dust.' She stabbed at a chip viciously. 'They'll find an enemy, they'll find an excuse, and then . . .'

'And then?'

'For us? A war on the far side of the world, so remote we will watch on TV before switching off at tea time and forgetting all about it. But for the other side . . .'

'What?'

'It will be hell.'

CHAPTER 8

If I was honest, I wasn't too keen on Adam leaving me for reserve training three weeks before my due date, particularly when I'd had pains on and off for several days. But when I suggested that he might stay, he said it was only for a couple of days, besides the midwife had said they were just false contractions called Braxton Hicks; it was unlikely that anything would happen just yet. Besides, he added, I wouldn't be alone – his grandfather and Mrs Davies were close by. He was probably right; and after our recent quarrel, I was keen to make amends. I made an effort to be cheerful as he left, fully intending to lie down and rest after he had gone. But after an hour of trying and failing to settle in a comfortable position, I felt a sudden urge to get out of the house. When I stepped out of the door, it was a delight not to need a jumper. Although it was only eleven, the morning was already hot, the sky azure blue, the trees fully leaved – vigorously green.

I strode down to the village rapidly, determined to make the most of this unexpected energy. As I reached the High Street, I spotted a small procession of children ahead – the girls wearing their prettiest frocks and headdresses of flowers, carrying posies, the boys in smart suits. Of course, it was the May Day procession. Mrs Davies had taken a day off because her eldest grandchild was going to be a May princess. She must have been one of the four girls following the carton on which the May king and queen were perched. They were being pulled by four boys whose coordination left a little bit to be desired; the vehicle wobbled and veered down the road. I fell in behind, enjoying the ritual meander through the village as the group sang songs to elderly residents who handed out sweets in return. There was a pleasant, friendly atmosphere, and for the first time since my arrival I felt connected to this tiny community. People round these parts had been performing the ceremony for centuries; the past was coming to life in front of me, and I was part of it. The procession ended at the village green, where to my delight the children performed country dances culminating at the maypole. Each child took a colour: red, green, yellow, blue, purple, orange, dancing in between each other with a dexterity I couldn't quite believe possible. It was mesmerising, watching as they wound the ribbon tighter and tighter round the maypole, weaving the colours into a neat pattern. Across the green I saw Mrs Davies applauding loudly as her granddaughter completed the last circuit. My stomach tightened with a dull pain. I ignored what I took to be another false contraction as it struck me that, in a few years' time, my own child might be doing the same. The thought was an attractive one; I returned home with a warm glow, and a feeling that I almost belonged.

The morning's activities had done me good. I had a big lunch and afterwards, for want of something better to do, drove over to see Helen. Adam was right, she was easier to get along with on her own. Even so, I was pleased when Mark turned up early from work. I much preferred his company, and on his insistence stayed for supper with the family.

It was half-seven when I left, and I drove home slowly, partly because the light was fading, and partly because I kept having to stop due to Braxton Hicks. They had eased off by the time I got home, and I settled down to watch a Bond movie. It was ridiculously over the top, but it proved a useful distraction from the gnawing anxiety that was beginning to build the closer it came to bedtime. My body didn't feel quite right, and without Adam to reassure me I became fretful. At midnight, I climbed the stairs to bed. The heat of the day still lingered in our usually cold bedroom; it was too warm to sleep. I tried cooling myself with a flannel, but it did no good. I tossed and turned, unable to get comfortable. I must have dozed for a while, but at three I woke to feel a tightness round my waist, as if I were being pulled into a corset. It took my breath away for a few moments, and then subsided. I thought it must be another of the

Braxton Hicks, but it was followed soon after by a sharper pain. I tried to reassure myself it was nothing, but I couldn't sleep like this. I decided to get up and make myself some warm milk.

The kitchen was full of shadows. I turned on the light, wincing with a small electric shock. As I switched the kettle on, I heard Mr Flint's walker in the hall – damn it, I'd woken him up. But when he pushed the door open, he seemed cheerful enough.

'Couldn't sleep?'

'Feeling a bit uncomfortable. Probably just a Braxton Hicks. You?'

'I'm often awake at this time.'

'Would you like some hot milk?'

'Please.'

I put the milk pan on. As I watched it heat up, my body began to strain against me. This time the sensation was less like a corset and more like an iron band. A bubble or two appeared on the surface of the milk as the band pulled harder. I gasped.

'Are you alright?'

I could hear the note of concern in his voice as I lost sight of the frothing milk and clutched on to the side of the cooker.

'That doesn't look like a Braxton Hicks,' he added.

'I think you're right,' I said, as the pain receded.

Before I could say anything else, I heard the sound of the milk rising and felt something wet on the side of my thigh. I looked at the pan as the milk bubbled over. I must do something about that, yet here was liquid running down my leg, gushing all over the stone floor.

The old man pulled himself up by the metal frame. The sound of scraping the floor brought me to my senses. I turned the hob off; the contents of the pan sizzled for a moment and then died down, leaving a lingering smell of burnt milk.

'I think we'd better get you to a hospital.'

'I think you're right. I'll just . . . I must . . . I think . . .' It was impossible to go on. Another wave of pain had me in its vice-like grip and I could hardly breathe.

Mr Flint's voice reassured through the mist. 'I'll go upstairs for Mrs Davies.'

'Are you sure you can make it?'

'I'll take it easy and hold the rail.'

I nodded, clasping the side of the table, trying to remember what they'd said in antenatal class. He clattered to the door, pushed it open and struggled through. Then I heard a loud curse, the sound of clanging metal and a thump.

'Mr Flint?'

'I need a hand.'

I pulled myself off the chair; the band felt looser. I made it to the door, breathing more freely. My damp pyjama trousers clung to me. Mr Flint was lying on the floor, his frame beside him, so I moved as quickly as I could to pick it up. As I reached him, the pain redoubled, forcing me to my knees.

Mr Flint's giggle seemed to come from another planet. 'Talk about the cripple leading the incapacitated. I think we need to call for help.'

I nodded, trying to frame the words as he called out in a thin voice. There was no answer; the door was too thick. Another contraction prevented me from helping him stand up and we clung to each other. Through the pain, something kept coming back to me: *in the kitchen, in the kitchen.* Mr Flint called again, but his voice had no strength.

'This isn't working,' he said weakly.

'You're right,' I agreed, and then, as the pain drifted away, it dawned on me: the servants' bells.

'Stay here,' I said.

I probably had enough time to get there before the next contraction. I staggered up and, moving at tortoise speed, forced myself across the carpet, still leaking water. *Oh dear God, the mess.* I reached the door; I had another minute before the pain kicked in again. I made it to the table, Mr Flint called out encouragingly. I pushed myself forward and reached the pulley system, ringing the bell for the landing. I rang and rang as another contraction reached its peak, until I heard Mrs Davies's voice exclaiming at the sight of the old man on the floor.

She was quick and efficient. She soon had him back on his feet and organised a change of clothes for me. While she fetched my bag I paced the living room, trying to breathe through the contractions that were coming so fast there was hardly any respite. But as she came back in, I suddenly stopped, a shudder of pain forcing its way through me, nearly knocking me to my knees. I let out a guttural roar from deep within my body.

'Ruth? Are you OK?' Mr Flint sounded more concerned than he had done all evening.

'Not . . . sure . . .' I gasped, grabbing the side of the sofa.

'I think we need to stay put,' said Mr Flint.

Mrs Davies nodded.

'What about the hospital?' I asked.

'Ruth. Your baby is coming now. You need to stay here and we'll deliver it for you.'

Mr Flint's voice was suddenly strong and authoritative. I couldn't quite take it in, yet something made me obey. Mrs Davies covered the floor with towels and I found myself kneeling down, pantless, gripping the sofa. Behind me, Mrs Davies helped Mr Flint to his knees. Normally I'd have been embarrassed, but the need to push overwhelmed everything else. I just wanted the pain to stop. Mrs Davies sat on the sofa, massaging my shoulders.

'When I say push, you need to push as hard as you can . . . get ready . . . PUSH . . . and breathe.'

Push and breathe . . . Push and breathe . . . Push and breathe . . . We seemed to be there for hours, Mrs Davies at my head, Mr Flint behind me, moonlight streaming through the open curtains. I thought the pain would never end. At last, at the point when I thought I had no energy left, he said, 'This is it . . . one last push and you've done it.'

I pushed and pushed and suddenly felt something catapult out of me. For a moment, everything was quiet, then there was a yell – a beautiful, ear-splitting yell. I turned round. The old man was kneeling, covered in blood, holding a tiny screaming baby.

'Congratulations, it's a girl,' he said, smiling.

The ambulance arrived 10 minutes later, after I'd delivered the placenta. They checked us over and pronounced us safe to stay at home. Mrs Davies cleaned up, and by six, I was sitting on the sofa, feeding the baby and drinking tea. I was flushed with excitement, adrenaline pumping through my veins.

'How on earth did you know how to do that, Mr Flint?' I asked.

'I trained as doctor . . . I delivered lots of babies. It's like riding a bicycle; it never leaves you.' I was astonished, but before I could enquire further he added, 'By the way, I think, after this evening, we can dispense with formalities . . . Call me Jack.'

I squeezed his hand and nodded.

Adam arrived shortly after, still in uniform, which made him seem different somehow – sterner, less carefree. He was full of apologies that he'd not been there, so I bit back *I told you so* and handed the baby to him. Immediately he softened as he beamed at the sight of her.

'Have you got a name?' asked Jack.

'We said Phoebe for a girl, Jack for a boy,' said Adam. Phoebe was my mum's second name; I'd always liked it.

'Phoebe's lovely,' said Jack.

'And since she was born by moonlight . . .' I laughed.

'Phoebe it is,' said Adam.

I smiled at them both. For the first time since my arrival, I felt part of a proper family. Then, all of a sudden, the events of the night hit me and I was overcome by a wave of exhaustion. Adam helped me to bed, where I slept till lunchtime. Phoebe woke at the same instant, demanding a feed, setting the pattern that would follow for weeks.

A hush fell over the house as we all adapted to the presence of our new arrival. The days blurred into nights – an endless round of squalling, feeding, nappy-changing, burping. My breasts dripped milk and stank of cheese. The bathroom reeked of Napisan. I barely slept. I hardly noticed when food was placed in front of me. I thought and spoke only of Phoebe. Time came to a halt.

In an attempt to get some sleep, Adam moved out of the bedroom at the end of the first week. Drained and barely conscious, I hardly noticed that he had left.

CHAPTER 9

Ash-white arms were round my neck, dragging me down into a clammy cave. Darkness was all around, pressing my chest so I couldn't breathe. I tried to pull away; the arms tightened their grip. Somewhere in the distance I could hear someone screaming, a cold voice saying over and over again, 'She is dead, then?' I tried to escape but my arms and legs were heavy. I could not move.

Phoebe's crying broke through the dream, pulling me back into a bewildered wakefulness. I forced myself out of bed, turned on the lamp, fetched her from the cradle and settled her into her feed, still shaking from the nightmare. In the early weeks of my pregnancy, when I thought Adam had abandoned me, I'd had a similar dream every night. Each morning I'd woken to an empty bed, an overwhelming sense of loneliness and a feeling I couldn't do this on my own. So I'd taken myself off to the abortion clinic, only to run away at the last minute, not being able to face that alone either. When Adam turned up out of the blue, his proposal seemed to provide the perfect way out.

Although I had never really imagined getting married to him, I pushed back any doubts I had and said yes. It seemed like the easiest option, the safest bet, the right thing to do at the time.

Now Phoebe was here, I knew I'd made the right choice, but I hadn't realised how lonely she would make me feel. Adam was around for the first week after she was born, but then he disappeared to the quarry, worried, he said, by the finances. I hadn't made any friends since my arrival, so unless Nisha or Helen visited, I saw no one apart from Jack or Mrs Davies. When Adam came home from work, Phoebe was at her most fractious – suckling but not feeding, unable to sleep yet too tired to be awake – and I was at my most exhausted. Some nights it wasn't till eleven that she finally went off, by which time Adam and I were too tired to speak. I didn't begrudge him sleeping next door – there was no point us both being this tired, particularly when he had a business to run; it just didn't feel like we were in this together. I'd accepted his proposal because I didn't want to be on my own, yet it seemed as if I was anyway. What was the point in that?

Phoebe finished her feed. I picked her up, burped her and settled her back in the cradle. At least, I thought as I lay back down, things were better with Jack. Since Phoebe's birth he'd seemed softer, kinder, and much easier to be around. The impromptu delivery seemed to have brought him on physically, too. He was walking better, ditching the frame in favour of a stick. He was going out more and even talking about spending some time at the quarry. Perhaps that's what we need, I thought as I drifted off; if Jack were able to help out a bit, Adam might be home more, and we could be a couple again.

When I woke again, sun was streaming through the windows. It was a warm day, so after breakfast I took a blanket and spent the morning sitting with Phoebe under the oak tree on the lawn. Only a few weeks before it had been covered in a shimmer of green; now it was in full leaf. The hills opposite were dressed in bright-green bracken interlaced with heather. I felt optimistic and energetic; after lunch, it was easy to begin planning Phoebe's christening.

I wasn't originally that keen on the idea, and was surprised that Adam had proposed it. It was only when he pointed out that his mother had been baptised, married and buried in the village church, and that he himself had been christened there, that I acquiesced. When the day came, I was glad he'd persuaded me; being part of a family ritual helped me feel I belonged.

'Will you care for Phoebe and help her to take her place within the life and worship of Christ's church?' the vicar asked.

'With the help of God we will,' Adam and I replied.

Mark and Helen, the godparents, joined us. I glanced across at Jack; his lips were repeating the words too.

'Do you reject the devil and all rebellion against God?'

'I reject them.' Again, I noticed Jack's lips moving.

'Do you renounce the deceit and corruption of evil?'

'I renounce them.' Adam bent his head as he said the words with emphasis.

'Do you repent of the sins that separate us from God and neighbour?'

'I repent of them.'

Adam hadn't seen, but Jack appeared to be crying. Feeling he would be embarrassed by my gaze, I turned my attention to Phoebe. She gave a surprised yelp when the water was poured over her head. I patted her down and she smiled and gurgled at me, eliciting a laugh from the small congregation. The service concluded with prayers and we emerged into the sunlight. As we were standing around introducing our guests to each other, I noticed Jack walking towards the gate by the graveyard. For a minute, he seemed about to go in, but then he stopped and turned round, rejoining us as we walked towards the car.

Back at the house, he surprised me by offering to look after Phoebe, and walked around the lawn with her as we sorted out drinks for the guests. When I had served everyone, I wandered towards him.

'You seemed very thoughtful in church.'

'All that talk of the devil – it reminded me of my father.'

'Oh?'

'He was a great believer in the work of the devil.' He gazed down the hillside, his voice low and sad. 'You know, his father planted those fir trees. They were half the height when I was a boy, yet I always felt trapped by them and by his sense of the man I was supposed to be. I spent my whole childhood trying to escape my father and grandfather, to become a different kind of person . . . for nothing. Somehow I turned into them anyway. What was it Adam said about your dissertation? The sins of the fathers? I hated my father, and yet I behaved exactly like him. I failed my children, particularly Will. And that's my inheritance. To have lost my son for good.'

'I'm sure that's not true,' I said.

'It's too late for me to change.'

'It's never too late.'

He said nothing. He handed Phoebe back to me and walked towards the house, leaving me to rejoin our guests. He did not reappear for the rest of the day.

Adam threw open the French windows and, while Mark and Helen's boys ran around the grass, the men began a heated discussion about the World Cup. Nisha, who'd grown up with football-mad brothers, was in her element, but I was quickly bored by the endless analysis of each critical moment: Gazza's tears, the missed goal opportunities, Pearce's failed penalty. I began a conversation with Helen about their recent trip to Turkey. Adam was right: I should make an effort; and, given how busy Nisha was, I could do with another friend. I was nodding politely at her descriptions of amphitheatres and catacombs when she suddenly changed the subject.

'This Kuwait business must be worrying for you.'

'What about it?' I'd been so caught up with Phoebe I'd not been paying much attention to the news.

'It's looking like war,' said Helen.

'Really?' It seemed impossible, sitting here in the sunshine with the children playing. 'What's it got to do with us?'

'We're allies,' said Adam, overhearing. 'We can't sit this one out.'

'Funnily enough, we were Saddam's allies before the invasion.' Nisha's intervention was sudden and uncharacteristically angry. 'We've been selling him weapons right up until this summer. What on earth gives us the right to condemn him now?'

'That was business. This is expansionism. He has to be stopped.'

'Whatever the consequence?'

'Sometimes, there's no choice. Imagine if we'd left Hitler alone.'

'We might have saved millions of lives.'

Adam glared at her, 'We'd probably all be speaking German.'

I thought they were about to come to blows but luckily Mark asked Adam to check a match statistic, and Nisha let it drop.

It was only as the party was breaking up that she returned to the topic.

'Sorry about earlier,' she said, as she hugged me goodbye. 'It just makes me so mad. Two years ago no one wanted to know Saddam gassed his own people in Halabja. Now, though . . .'

I had no answer but a returning hug.

By nine, everyone had left except Helen and Mark, who were staying the night. We sat in garden chairs by the front lounge. Phoebe was comfortable only with me, so I wrapped her in a blanket and held her close. The night was still warm. The sun glowed white behind the hill, spreading up into the sky until it met pale blue. A single star came out. An owl hooted in the distance.

'So are you going to be dusting off the old rifle soon?' asked Mark, pouring his friend a glass of wine. 'How exciting.'

'I'm not sure it's that exciting for Ruth,' Helen said. 'Why don't you tell us about your plans for the quarry?'

For the first time since I'd known her, I was grateful for her direct approach with her husband. I didn't want to think about mine going to war just now.

We talked into the night as the air cooled and the sky darkened, leaving a sliver of light shining on the horizon. At twelve, Helen said she was tired and went to bed.

'I'll be up soon,' said Mark.

'Don't be long,' she said.

I should have gone with her, but Phoebe was fighting sleep. She fed, stopped, and fed again. I wouldn't be able to rest upstairs; I might as well be down here in company, particularly when that company included Mark. Adam poured another glass for himself and Mark as I wandered up and down rocking the baby to sleep. By the time I'd placed her in the Moses basket, the two men were half-asleep themselves.

'Nice . . . night,' said Mark. The words hung there.

Adam replied. 'Yes . . . Getting cold . . . isn't it?'

'A bit.'

For a while, no one spoke at all.

Then Mark sat up, suddenly alert. 'Shooting star.'

'Where?'

'Over there, to the right of the woods.'

'I can't see it. Can you?' I turned to Adam, but he'd drifted off.

'Look, there's another.'

I strained and strained but I still couldn't see anything.

Mark got up from his chair. 'Come over here, it's easier to see if you're lying down.'

Feeling slightly self-conscious, I lay down on the dry grass beside him.

'Now,' he said, 'look to the east. It's a meteor shower – the Perseids – always happens this time of year. Out of the corner of your eye, look for some movement.'

We lay there, expectant. Nothing happened. Then all of a sudden, I saw it – a silver globe of light streaking across the sky. I shrieked with delight. Then another and another. The sky was full of explosions, criss-crossing the sky, as if someone had lit a box of fireworks. We stayed for what seemed like hours, the excitement of each passing meteor keeping us together in anticipation of the next. Every now and then we caught each other's eye and grinned. Once, it seemed to me that Mark's gaze held more than just a mutual enjoyment of the moment. I turned away, shocked by the intimacy. I lay still, my heart beating fast. We were close enough to hear each other breathe, close enough to touch, close enough to . . . Before I could allow the thought to form in my brain, I heard a little mew, and then a louder whimper.

'Phoebe.' I jumped up quickly, not looking at Mark. 'It's getting late.'

'So it is. I'd better go up.' He staggered off.

I prodded Adam. 'Time for bed.'

I picked Phoebe up and sat down to feed her. Adam followed Mark inside, giving me a peck on the head as he passed. Outside the sky had turned deep black. The stars sparkled silver. The air was cold. I wrapped the blanket round us. As Phoebe tugged on my breasts, I remembered the promise I had made earlier in church – that I would renounce deceit and evil. I repeated it to myself, again and again, trying to convince myself it was true.

I am not the type of person who cheats on her husband.

I am not.

CHAPTER 10

In the weeks after the christening even I couldn't ignore the news about Iraq, which seemed to dominate every radio and TV bulletin. Now, as I turned off the motorway towards Nisha's house, I switched off a report about hostages, partly to concentrate on my route, but also to stop myself thinking about the possibility of Adam being called up. He was pretty relaxed about it, but I could see he was itching to go and do his bit, as he put it. I wasn't sure what troubled me more: the fact that the generals, as Liz had predicted, had found themselves an enemy, the thought of my husband going to war, or the realisation that in my heart of hearts I couldn't support his actions.

The last of the harvest had been collected, and the stubble from the fields billowed grey smoke against a bright-blue sky. Although the sun shone, there was a chill in the air; soon it would be time for warm jumpers and raincoats. I'd decided to visit Nisha on the off-chance, but I hadn't banked on the confusing country roads and it was another half an hour before I arrived at the brightly painted sign: *Emma Goldman Farm*. I turned up a dirt track, passing a field of cows on one side, a large garden on the other. The track ended in front of the house; there was no lawn, just a yard of dirty brown earth that must be grim in wet weather. The air reeked of cow dung. I put Phoebe in a sling and walked up to the gabled porch.

The house stretched away from the front door forming an L-shape at the end. It would have been quite impressive had the walls not been such a grimy grey, the paint peeling, the window frames rotting. A wooden carving hung from the porch roof: *If I can't dance, it's not my revolution*. I smiled: a typical Nisha house, right down to the paint flaking off on my knuckles when I knocked. Nobody answered. I peered in through the window to see an office, the tables covered with papers, the walls decorated with photocopied newspaper articles and a sign saying *No Nukes*. I knocked again; no answer. The door opened at the first push, so I wandered in. In the distance I could hear raised voices. I followed the sound to a long room at the base of the L, where I found the household gathered on sofas. Nisha broke off from talking when she saw me, and suggested to the others that they take a break.

'Thanks,' she said, as she took me through to the kitchen. 'You interrupted at just the right moment.'

I took Phoebe out of her carrier and began to feed. The kitchen was filthy: washing-up piled in the sink, three-day-old pans soaking on the side, the red and black tiles on the floor looking like they hadn't been washed in months. Nisha seemed oblivious to the mess, taking the last two clean cups from the cupboard as she put the kettle on.

'What was all that about?' I asked.

'There's talk of a peace camp in Iraq . . .'

'Isn't it dangerous?' I said, thinking about the news report.

'It's not just that. I think there's too much work to do here for us all to go.'

A young man with a ponytail wandered in from the garden. He walked up to her and began to massage her shoulders. This must be Simon.

'You OK? That was a bit tense in there,' he said.

'Fine,' she said, shaking him off. 'This is my friend Ruth.'

'You're right, of course,' he said. 'Somebody needs to take care of the garden.'

Nisha didn't seem inclined to discuss it any further; she changed the subject to my trip to London. We chatted about the lives of various friends and acquaintances till the meeting was reconvened. As I left, I could hear the argument building up again. I was glad to leave them behind.

Adam was still at the quarry when I arrived home. Jack had dinner with me but seemed subdued, and retired early. I put Phoebe to bed in her new room, and then awaited my husband's return. We'd agreed before I left that it was time we shared a bed again, but somehow I felt nervous. Luckily, he arrived home full of excitement that he and Mark had worked out a business plan and he was convinced the visitor centre was viable. I was grateful he'd brought a bottle of Champagne with him, as it relaxed me enough to go upstairs, where we were soon pulling each other's clothes off.

'Nice to be back,' he said, kissing me.

I kissed him, but even with the Champagne, it was an effort. It had been months since we'd done this; I wasn't sure I remembered how. I forced myself to think of a time and a place when sex was simple, enjoyable, when I'd wanted him as much as he wanted me, remembering an afternoon on a hidden beach last summer. We'd made love to the sound of screeching seagulls, under the bluest of skies, our bodies fluid and in harmony, resulting in a moment of exquisite pain and pleasure that I'd never had before or since. Now he tasted dry, the motion of his hands mechanical, the pressure of his body on mine hard and heavy. To my horror, just as Adam came, all I could think of was Mark. He tried to continue for my sake, but I pushed him off.

'I'm sorry, it's been a while.'

'It's OK.' I replied. 'I'm just a bit rusty.'

That seemed to satisfy him; he turned over with a grunt, falling asleep straight away. I lay watching the rise and fall of his back for a long time, hoping I was right, till, conscious that Phoebe would be waking me in a couple of hours, I too drifted off.

It was strange having him in bed again. I wasn't quite sure I liked it until the morning, when I saw the grin on his face. This . . . I'd missed this, waking up together, starting the day with him by my side. How often had that got me through the dark days after Mum's death? And now we had Phoebe, we had so much more to look forward to. I returned his kiss with more warmth then the night before, finding I had the energy to jump out of bed.

I was feeling in such a good mood, I decided it was time that Phoebe and I braved the Whetstone mother and baby group. I rarely saw anyone apart from Nisha, Helen and, occasionally, Mark, who I thought about far more often than was good for me. I ought to try, I decided, to make some new friends. The minute I arrived, I realised it was a mistake. There were only a handful of women, and they all seemed to know each other. One or two of them made a feeble attempt to bring me into the conversation, but their efforts petered out, and I remained in the corner, the outsider. Afterwards I pushed the buggy back through the village, my previous elation completely drained away, sunk in the depressing thought that Whetstone could never provide the companionship and warmth I'd left behind in London. I was just reaching the school when I saw Jack entering the graveyard with a bunch of red roses. Curious to know what he was doing, I followed.

I walked up the slope to the church and along the path to the gate. I found Jack kneeling at a headstone in the far corner, some distance from the Flint graves. The roses were on the ground by his side. He appeared to be crying.

Feeling like an intruder, I was about to turn away, but at that moment a sparrow hopped in front of us and Phoebe giggled in delight. Jack looked up and saw us.

'I'm sorry,' I said. 'I didn't mean to impose.'

'You're not.'

I came over to the graveside and inspected her inscription. *Elsie Flint. Born 11th September 1915. Died 22nd December 1943.*

'It's her birthday today.'

'Yes.'

'She was so young.'

'She was . . . She would have been 75 today. I can't imagine her that old.' He pulled himself up, holding on to the gravestone for balance. 'Perhaps she was lucky to live without these aches and pains.'

'Perhaps.'

We turned out of the graveyard and began to walk up the hill.

'Jack,' I asked tentatively, 'what happened to Elsie?'

'I don't know. Not really.' He sighed. 'We were so in love at the beginning. Like all young couples should be. We had Will, I'd begun to practise medicine, I wanted to be a GP but then . . .' We had reached the war memorial; he nodded at it as we passed. 'The war came. She and Will couldn't stay in Liverpool, so I brought them here. I knew she'd find it difficult with my parents – that they wouldn't like her, nor she them, but it seemed like the best way to keep my family safe.'

We were approaching the edge of the estate. I looked up towards the grey house, looming above the fir trees. 'And it wasn't?'

'It was alright in the beginning. Elsie was a very tolerant person. She made an enormous effort to make things work.' As we climbed the hill Jack began to walk faster, as if he was keen to get the conversation over. 'And in the early days I could get home sometimes. When Evie was born, my colonel let me home to see her. A wonderful weekend. But after that, we didn't see each other for over two years.'

'That must have been tough.'

'Separation does things to couples. We were both under strain in different ways, I suppose. It wasn't the same next time we met. We'd both changed.' We had reached the lawn. 'And then . . .'

'And then?'

'I was shot down. I nearly died, and it was weeks before I was well enough to come home. When I finally came round, all I could think of was her . . .' His voice shook. 'Which was when they told me she had died. Scarlet fever, they said.'

'You don't think it was?'

He didn't look at me as we arrived on the door

step. 'It didn't make sense. She was young, fit and healthy. Scarlet fever was all but eradicated by 1943. But that's what my parents said at the time, and I believed them.'

'And now?'

We stepped over the threshold. He stopped and looked at me sadly. 'Now I am an old man. I have lost too much. Two wives and a daughter, dead. My son has emigrated. Now I think I need the truth, but I don't know where to start.'

'Let me help,' I said. 'Maybe there are some clues in Elsie's room.'

'Maybe.' He hesitated, then said, 'Wait a minute.'

He went to his room, and came back with a key. 'For upstairs,' he said. 'See what you can do.'

It was only after he had gone that I realised I hadn't asked him about Daniel Clarkson. I thought I might try later, but at dinner he was quiet and taciturn and I decided to leave it for another time.

Over the next few days, the weather took a turn for the worse as grey skies and fog returned to the valley. The news from Iraq continued to be gloomy. One night Adam announced that he had been called up. He would be leaving just before Christmas. Inside, I became fretful about Phoebe's alarming cough, and anxious about Adam's departure. Outside, the world edged towards war.

CHAPTER 11

The bracken had died back in brown swathes on the hills; the sky was squally grey, and russet leaves scattered the ground beneath the oak tree. I turned from the window, took Phoebe back to her room and placed her in her cot. I was relieved that, after a fortnight of severe infection, she was finally breathing more easily. For the first time in days, I felt able to leave her. Ever since Jack had given me the key, I had been itching to get into the back bedroom. Now was my chance.

I wasn't sure what I was looking for. More letters perhaps; notes about her life; maybe even a diary. I pulled the trunk out, rifling through the contents, and was delighted to find four leather-bound diaries at the bottom, inscribed *Elsie Flint* in a neat elegant hand. I picked them up and was about to leave when the wardrobe door swung open. For some reason, I felt drawn to the dresses, running my fingers through the silk and cottons. On a whim, I took out the cut-down blue dress and tried it on. It was a little tight in places, but the silk felt smooth on my skin, and the empire waist helped disguise my baby stomach,. But as I clicked the final hook in place, I was filled with a dizzying sensation: a mixture of bliss and horror, as if the dress had been both source of pleasure and pain.

There was a brush on the shelf, along with a few ancient-looking hair pins. I picked them up and played with styles – curling my hair on top, then letting it flow in waves like Vivien Leigh. I gazed in the mirror. Wasn't there an old legend that if you brushed your hair in front of a mirror on Halloween, you saw the face of the man you would marry? I had no need of such nonsense, and yet I found myself brushing and gazing in expectation. Something moved in the corner of the room. I turned around, but there was nothing there. When I turned back to the mirror, I dropped the brush. There was a woman standing beside the door. I looked behind me again. Nobody. But she was there in the mirror, wearing the same dress, her auburn hair loose in long waves to her shoulder, her lips painted bright red. She smiled at me, as if greeting a friend.

I touched the glass, looking at her smiling face, as two words formed in my head: 'Find Will.'

I said them aloud, 'Find Will?'

She nodded. Then she was gone.

Will. That was Jack's son. Adam's uncle. The one who had gone to Australia. The son Jack wouldn't talk about. I was thinking that perhaps he might be prepared to talk about him now when I heard a yell. I ran downstairs. Jack was in his chair; his eyes were open, even though he was clearly asleep.

'Elsie, Elsie!' he shouted, before slumping back in his chair, eyes closed.

Hesitantly, I went over and touched him on the arm. 'Jack?'

He woke up. 'Elsie? 'The hope in his voice was heartbreaking.

'No, it's Ruth.'

He stared at me for a moment, taking in the blue dress, the way I'd done my hair. It took a moment or two before he recognised me.

'Of course,' he said. He sat back in his seat, recovering his breath. 'For years they told me to forget . . .'

'Who?'

'My parents. Veronica. I still hear their voices are still in my head, telling me to forget.'

'Why listen?'

'At first I didn't, but then they told me that before her death, she had an affair. With my cousin Daniel.'

'Did she?'

'I thought so at the time. They seemed to have absolute proof.'

'And now?'

'Since Veronica died, I've found myself troubled by dreams. In some, my parents are at my shoulder, telling me Elsie was never trustworthy. That I was right to forget her. To remarry, give up medicine and do my duty by the family and stay here so I

101

could inherit the quarry. But in others . . .' he half-sobbed, 'in others, I hear her calling my name. Sometimes she appears, telling me that she only ever loved me. I reach out for her, thinking this time, this time, she will be there . . .' He paused and gazed up at me sadly. 'But when I stretch out my arms to embrace her I wake up alone. Which is when I remember that my parents had always hated her. That Daniel always denied the affair. That he begged to meet me to explain, but I always refused. And that my son Will accused my parents of killing her.'

'What?'

'At the time, I thought Will was just trying to make me angry.

He said it in the middle of an argument about him taking over the quarry. I thought he'd calm down the next day, but he walked out of the house that night, writing from London repeating the accusations and telling me he was emigrating. I was furious with him. So I let Veronica persuade me that he was unbalanced. She discouraged communication with him. It was easier to do that than to think he might be right. I let him go.'

'And now?'

'Now I find myself asking, suppose Will was telling the truth? Suppose my parents killed her? All these years of hating her, and believing in them. All wasted . . .'

I squeezed his hand. 'It's not too late. We have Elsie's diaries and Daniel's. They might help.'

He nodded slowly. 'His widow, June, said if I read them I might see things differently . . . But I haven't been able to face it.'

'Then let me.'

'Do you think it is possible to be reconciled with the dead?'

'I'm sure it is. And the living. We should find Will too.'

He was happy then to agree to my suggestion that I contact the Australian Embassy to try to track Will down. Adam was less pleased. He'd spent so many years supporting Jack's desire to forget, he found it hard to believe the old man had changed his mind like that. And he was worried that raking up the past would only cause him hurt. But since Jack and I were so determined, there was nothing he could do about it. I wrote to the embassy that night.

The next day, on the way back from the post box, I saw a small group of people by the war memorial gathered for Remembrance Day. I stopped, watching as a woman with grey hair laid the wreath underneath the names: Jones, Clark, Thomas, Edwards, Davies, Flint. So much loss in such a small place. Mrs Davies was there, head down as she listened to the prayers. The vicar drew the service to a close, talking of sacrifice, courage, the willingness to work for a greater cause. *Lest we forget*, he concluded: they died for us, so that we might live. *Lest we forget*. A simple statement and one I could subscribe to surrounded by people for whom this was still personal. As the crowd began to disperse, Mrs Davies spotted me, we walked back home together.

'Nice of you to come, my lovey.'

'I happened to be passing.'

'I always like to remember my husband at this time. And his father before him, though of course Tommy and I never knew him.'

'I saw their names on the cross. I wondered if you were related.'

'It was all a very long time ago. I'm just glad the boys today don't have to join up like they did. Particularly with this nasty business in Kuwait.'

'Yes.' Phoebe stirred a little in her buggy as we reached the bottom of the drive, and then went back to sleep.

'Mind you, I don't like the thought of Mr Adam going off there.'

'No,' I didn't want to think about that too much. And besides, something had occurred to me. 'Mrs Davies, did you know the first Mrs Flint?'

'Of course I did. Lovely woman she was, too.'

'Were you here when she died?'

'In 1943? No, my lovey. I was keeping my mother company, down near Cardiff. Old Mr Flint wrote to tell me. Very sad it was. That poor man. Imagine surviving his injuries, only for that to happen.'

We reached the front of the house.

'I was very sorry about it,' Mrs Davies continued. 'She was always kind to me, particularly when my

Tommy died. I wished I could have been here to help. But I only came back here a few years after the war.'

She bustled off to the kitchen to make lunch, refusing my assistance. I sighed. Another blind alley. I just had to hope that the embassy would respond.

As usual, it took a visit from Nisha to lift my mood. She was in fine spirits when I picked her up from the station.

'Maggie, Maggie, Maggie, Out, Out, OUT,' she called as she passed through the ticket barrier.

'Don't say that in Adam's hearing,' I said. 'He's devastated.'

'Sorry, I can't help it; I've been waiting for this moment for years.'

We walked into town and found a pretty cafe with chintz tablecloths and porcelain ornaments. We sat down and ordered baked potatoes.

'And did you see that new TV series? *House of Cards?* Opening with the old bat going . . . Talk about life imitating art.' We laughed.

The waitress brought the food over. 'We don't see many of your sort round here,' she said, placing the food on the table.

'Brummies, you mean?' said Nisha.

The waitress flushed, and left us.

'How do you stand it?' I asked.

'I don't, really . . .' she said. She changed the subject. 'By the way, I have some news. I'm not going to Iraq.'

105

'Good.'

'I'm too much of a coward.'

'No, you're not.'

'Yes I am. I'm terrified. What if we were taken hostage? Or bombed? I just can't do it.'

'How's Liz taken it?'

'I didn't tell her.' Nisha reddened. 'Nor Simon. We had a community meeting, debated whether some should stay or not. We couldn't reach consensus so we had a vote. Luckily for me, Simon is loyal. We won four to three. Annie, Erin and I are staying behind, the others are going. Liz isn't too happy with me, but she had to accept it.'

'Well I, for one, am glad. I couldn't cope with two of you going to war.'

I was relieved that she would be staying behind, but on my way home I couldn't stop anxious thoughts crowding in. In a few weeks' time, Adam would be leaving for Iraq. I thought of Mrs Davies and all the others by the war memorial. They'd sent their family and friends to war, hoping they'd be safe, imagining they'd survive, only for them not to return. Suppose that happened to him? To us? The thought was too horrible to contemplate.

CHAPTER 12

As November drew to a close, Adam and I found ourselves in constant conflict. Jack's decision to let me look at the diaries and search for Will clearly rankled with him. I, in return, was still resentful that he had kept so much from me. I couldn't quite believe his reassurances that he had no more secrets. And underneath it all lay the knowledge that he would soon be leaving for Iraq. Initially I had just accepted the inevitability of his departure; but, as the date drew nearer, I began to fight him on that, too. He was so adamant he was doing the right thing I couldn't bring myself to disagree. Instead I appealed to his sense of responsibility for me, Phoebe and Jack. I begged him to ask for a deferral, but he refused, saying it was his duty; and that was that. Night after night we repeated the same tired argument, getting nowhere, until late one evening he gave up. Instead of shouting back at me, he sat down on the bed, put his head in his hands and said, 'Can't you be supportive, just this once?' He looked so lost and vulnerable that all of a sudden my anger dissipated. I sat down beside him and took his hand; soon he was sharing his anxieties about what lay ahead, and how much he needed me to back him. He so rarely admitted weakness; it was easy, then, to provide encouragement, and I resolved to try harder.

In an attempt to demonstrate my wifely support, I decided I should organise a leaving party for him. Since Mrs Davies and Jack would be away for the night, the Saturday before Christmas provided the perfect opportunity. Then Helen offered to leave the kids with her mum so she and Mark could help, which gave me another idea. For weeks Adam had been talking about his plans for the quarry, but he was convinced Jack wouldn't agree to them. I thought he was wrong. Jack had softened so much over the autumn I felt he would be more receptive than Adam imagined. So I suggested he and Mark could broach the subject before Jack left, while Helen and I were getting things ready. Though Adam took some persuading, he too was trying to make an effort; he let me talk him into it.

But it all went horribly wrong from the start. Helen and I were moving furniture in the dining room when we heard shouting from the front room. We hurried to see Jack standing by the doorway, yelling at Adam.

'It's all beginning to make sense to me now,' Jack was shouting. 'Your eagerness to leave the job you loved. Your shotgun wedding.'

I was puzzled. What did our wedding have to do with anything?

'It's not . . .' Adam rose from his chair to plead with him.

'You pretend to help me. All the while you're making deals behind my back.'

'That's not it.'

'Oh no? Do you think I've forgotten the last time you two did this? You always were a greedy little tyke.'

'Granddad . . .'

'Your trouble is, you take too much for granted. I have a son, remember. And thanks to your wife, he'll be home before you know it.'

He walked across the hall and into his room, banging the door behind him. Adam sat back down, crestfallen.

'He'll come round,' I said.

'I told you, Ruth. I told you not to interfere.'

There was nothing I could do but go back to the party preparations. Presently Mark popped his head round the door, saying he'd take Adam to the pub to calm him down. Soon after Jack's friends arrived to take him to Chester, and Helen and I were left alone. I enjoyed her company more than I expected too, though I still preferred Mark, and was grateful when he and Adam returned to help us.

It was nearly seven before we were done. Adam and the others were soon dressed and ready, but I wanted to make sure Phoebe was properly asleep. I sent them downstairs while I tried to settle her.

I paced up and down with her on my shoulder, thinking about the row. I'd been so sure that Jack would be amenable; his response had shocked me to the core. It was only when I was placing Phoebe in her cot that it occurred to me. Today was 22 December: the day Elsie died. No wonder Jack had reacted badly. The quarry was all he had left. I'd chosen the worst day possible to suggest he give it up. I sighed as I pulled my new blue satin dress over my head. I'd have to try my best to put things right tomorrow.

Just before going downstairs I glanced at myself in the mirror. I'd lost some baby weight and for the first time in months, I felt attractive: a woman, not a mother. I smiled, determined to enjoy myself tonight. As I descended the staircase, Mark emerged from the living room and wolf-whistled appreciatively. 'Hello, gorgeous!' I blushed as we passed in the hall.

At first, the party went well. I danced with Adam, then Mark, and later joined Helen for a rousing chorus of 'Sisters are Doin' It for Themselves'. But as the evening wore on, the men began a drinking game. Adam invited me to join in, but I refused. When we first got together, such games seemed fun, and made me feel one of the boys. Now they seemed puerile. I wandered into the dining room, where I found Helen and most of the other wives standing by the punchbowl, moaning about their husbands. Helen was furious with Mark for participating and was particularly scathing about his failings. I couldn't understand it. The game was stupid, but it wasn't that terrible. Besides, unlike Adam, Mark had the sense to stop after a while. Why didn't she appreciate him more?

The night dragged. Conversation after conversation with people I had little in common with. I drank more than I intended, drifting between rooms, feeling light-headed and out of place. Eventually, at midnight, when most people had left, or, like Helen, gone to bed, I had had enough. I grabbed some bin bags and began to tidy up the front room. Looking at the mess, I tried not resent the fact that Adam had already passed out in a chair. The party was for him, after all; he shouldn't have to clear up.

'Need a hand?' Mark appeared just as I was propping open the door to the kitchen.

'You're an answer to prayer,' I said.

It didn't take too long after that, and by the time we were done we both had a second wind. We sat in the kitchen drinking whisky, talking about Adam's departure.

'Don't tell him this . . .' I said. 'But I don't think he should be going. I don't believe in war. Particularly not this one.'

'He's doing the right thing. The Iraqis killed babies in incubators. They've got to be stopped.'

'Wouldn't diplomacy be better?'

'You pacifists are so naïve. Don't you get it? If we don't stop it, people are going to die, and all

111

the talking and peace marches in the world won't save them.'

There was a noise in the corridor. A door banged. I thought nothing of it; I was too wrapped up in Mark.

'I don't see it quite like that.' I smiled at him, daring him to continue the argument.

He moved closer, changing the subject. 'You know, if you need anything while he's away, all you have to do is ask.'

He was lovely. His deep-blue eyes were warm, affectionate.

'Thanks.' It was wrong, but I couldn't help myself; something was happening and I didn't want it to stop.

'What are friends for?' He put his arm around my shoulder and squeezed.

There were just the two of us. I turned my face to his, and, thinking he was doing the same, leant in to kiss him.

He jerked away immediately. 'What are you doing?'

'I'm sorry . . . I thought . . .'

'No, *I'm* sorry.' Mark reddened. 'I seem to have given you the wrong idea.'

Oh God. I didn't know where to look. How could I have been so stupid?

'It's my fault,' I said. I made my excuses and rushed upstairs to bed.

Adam hadn't yet come up, so I pulled the covers over me, trying to forget what I had done. Why had I behaved like such an idiot? Last year, I couldn't get enough of Adam. Now I was throwing myself at his best friend. What was wrong with me?

When I woke at six, I was alone. I looked into Phoebe's room. She was still asleep. The bed next to her was empty, but it looked as if it had been occupied. I went downstairs and found Adam in the kitchen nursing a cup of tea. He had huge bags under his eyes and looked as if he had barely slept.

'What happened to you last night?' I asked.

'You promised me you'd be supportive.'

'What?'

'You promised, Ruth. To back me. But I heard what you said to Mark.' I blushed. 'Telling him you didn't think the war was right, that you didn't believe in me.'

'That's not what I meant.'

'It's what it sounded like.'

'You should have come in.'

'I was too upset. I went to bed.' That must have been the door banging. Thank goodness, he hadn't seen what followed. 'You're always talking about honesty but you don't practise what you preach.'

'I'm sorry.'

'You know what was worse? You told my best friend instead of me.'

Feeling guiltier than ever, I apologised profusely. Eventually, he began to calm down, and when I brought Phoebe down everything was almost normal until we began to discuss the events of the previous day.

'What did Jack mean yesterday?' I asked. 'When he said you'd done this before?'

Adam blushed. 'It was just before I left school. Mark was setting up in business, and he thought the quarry was the perfect place to start. I'd had a row with Granddad, so we made some plans behind his back.'

'What happened?'

'When he found out about it, he cut off my allowance. I wasn't entitled to a grant, so I joined the army to fund university and make a life for myself.'

'Yet you came when he needed you.'

Adam shrugged. 'Family's important.'

'What about the inheritance?'

He shifted in his seat. 'My namesake – my great-great-great-grandfather – founded the family business, imagining his eldest son would take it over. But Reuben Flint was a musician who wanted to write symphonies. He abandoned the business. Adam Flint was furious, and came up with a clever solution to stop anyone else doing the same. He wrote a codicil into the deeds of the house. Sons can only inherit the quarry if they are married and live here with their children. If no sons are to be had, grandsons will do, as long as they keep the Flint name.'

'So, in order to inherit this place, you have to live here, with your wife and child?'

'That's right.' Adam stared at me as if trying to

work out what I was thinking. 'But it's irrelevant. Honestly.'

'I thought you were in the process of leaving me last autumn. I'd come to terms with it, and then you came back. There was me thinking it was romantic, that you must really love me to offer me everything. All the time it was to get your hands on that sodding quarry.'

'It wasn't . . . I didn't . . .'

'Ever since I've been here you've been hiding things from me. Making me feel I'm not quite up to the job of being a Flint. Turns out our whole marriage is based on a lie.'

He was about to protest when Helen and Mark came down, forcing us to put our quarrel aside. I could hardly look at Mark, but luckily the kitchen soon filled with guests, so it was easy to avoid each other. It was nearly one before everyone had gone and we'd tidied up; Adam had promised to pick Jack up and he hurried off once the last guest had departed.

I sat in the front room while Phoebe played in her travel cot, thinking about the last few weeks: the lies, the arguments, my disastrous attempt at seducing Mark. I had to admit it – I'd been kidding myself, thinking this marriage could work. Adam and I had been wrong from the start. We'd both got into this under false pretences; it was clear to me now that we were totally incompatible.

★   ★   ★

It was cowardly to go without saying goodbye, cowardly to let my husband go to war unblessed, but I couldn't stay a moment longer. I packed some bags, threw in the diaries, left a note on the phone table and carried Phoebe out to the car. Fog blew in shapeless clouds across the front lawn. The air was cold. Water trickled from the gate posts at the bottom of the drive. The rooks sat in their nests, hunched like mourners watching a funeral procession. I drove down the black wet road into Whetstone. Through the mirror I watched the fog swirl round Echo Hall until it was completely engulfed. I put my foot down, and sped through the village.

We were on our own now.

A PLACE OF SAFETY

1942

JACK

You don't think too much before a mission. It doesn't do. If you think, your head explodes with statistics: how many flights, what your chances are. If you think, you remember the men who went down in flames in front of you. It doesn't do to think.

It doesn't do to think. To worry where your bombs might be falling. And on whom. Instead you lie on your narrow bed trying to read the poetry book Daniel sent you, not understanding a blessed word. You read and reread the letters Elsie sends. Behind her careful choice of words, you detect your father's presence: censoring the expression of her thoughts. Perhaps you were wrong to send the warmth of her into the cold arms of your parents. Though how else could you protect your family from the German pilot doing the same as you tonight?

As you wait for the daylight to fade, you try to reassure yourself. She is safe. With the kids. Daniel is there to watch over her. Allowing you to do the job that must be done.

Soon it will be time for supper. The talk will be

loud, the jokes blue, but you will not join in. Crudity was never your style, even when you were a medical student. Afterwards, you will go with your crew to the hangar to get kitted up. The trucks will come to take you to the Lancasters. As you climb in the cockpit, you will take out the picture you carry everywhere, the three of you in happier times. You will place it in your sight line, as you do on every trip: a Very light to guide you in the dark.

But you do not think of that now. You close your eyes and you think of her: lavender perfume, a red ball dress, the softness of her hair. You whisper, Elsie, Elsie, Elsie. Her name: the talisman that will save you.

ELSIE 1

The night Jack proposed, he bought Elsie a red lamé dress and took her dancing at the Adelphi Hotel.

'When I'm qualified,' he said, 'I'll set up practice in Sefton Park. We'll buy a big house and come here every Saturday.'

She laughed, taking him onto the dance floor, enjoying the firmness of his arm on her waist. Round and round they glided, the ballroom lights sparking the gold threads on her dress. Red-gold, red-gold, round and round, like the carousel she used to ride on as a child.

The child on her lap stirs; Elsie opens her eyes. The land girls are working the black horse, ploughing furrows as they lay a late spring crop. A girl with light-brown hair stands on the edge of the field, her head bent forward to light a cigarette. For a moment, Elsie thinks it is Daniel's girl, June, but then the woman looks up. It isn't June at all, it is someone else; the bus sweeps past before she has time to work out who. Susie, perhaps? They turn a corner sharply; the gas canister clatters, waking Will. Disorientated after his nap, he begins to whimper. As she soothes him, Elsie feels like weeping too. They are both a long way from home.

The bus stops by the grey church and cemetery, set back in the shadow of the hill. The gravestones have shifted over the years. Once they were upright, but now they point in all directions, their surfaces black with lichen, the inscriptions faded. Elsie isn't superstitious but for some reason it always makes her shiver to walk past. She is glad to cross the road to the teacher's cottage by the village school.

Today is a half-term holiday. Daniel is in the back garden turning over the black soil with a large spade. From behind, he could almost be Jack, though the mop of curly black hair gives him away the minute he stands up. It's funny, she's always thought of Jack as the physical one. Daniel, with his sleeves rolled up, is a revelation. He has muscles after all. A girl might admire them if she wasn't already spoken for.

'Digging for Victory?' Elsie asks, as Will runs to the birdhouse.

'A few carrots would be nice.' Daniel stretches his back and rubs his ankle, as if to remind her of the reason for his absence from the frontline.

'I've got your shopping.'

'Thank you.' He receives the offered bag. 'Any treats?' Last week she'd managed to get her hands on a miraculous steak.

''Fraid not. They'd run out of beef, although they kept a bit aside for the in-laws.'

'The luck of the wealthy.'

'I'm sorry teachers don't get such dibs.'

It would be natural to invite Daniel to join them for Sunday lunch, but she knows he won't come. Even if he did, Jack's parents would not make him welcome, though she can't understand why. He is Leah's only nephew, after all.

'Come in. I'll make you a sandwich.' He limps up the path.

They follow him through the tiny house into the front parlour. Elsie fiddles in her bag for bricks, setting Will to work building towers, while Daniel prepares the food.

'Have you heard from Jack lately?' he calls from the kitchen.

'Last week. Full of black lines. It didn't really tell me anything.' She tries to hide the disappointment in her voice. After all, this is what war does – blacks out the lights and the conversations between lovers.

'It must be hard,' he says, as he brings in the sandwiches.

'Yes.' Elsie doesn't want to dwell on it. 'I thought I saw June today.'

'She's gone away.'

'Where to?'

'Her mother's not well.'

'Will she be back soon?'

'Hard to say.'

'You must miss her.'

'Hmm.'

'Let me know when she's back. I've been saving clothing coupons for a proper shopping trip.'

'Will do.'

'Not that there's much to buy, mind you. I just fancy some real stockings . . .'

Daniel laughs. 'They always look real to me.'

'Cheeky boy, looking at my legs. 'She sighs. 'I know it's terribly frivolous, but I do miss having decent clothes to wear. Since Leah offered, I've been working my way through her old clothes, making do with the dresses I find. Even so . . .'

'. . . it would be nice to have a new dress for once? That's not frivolous at all,' says Daniel. 'We all have things we miss from before.'

Will has finished his sandwich. Bored by the grown-up talk, he rises from the table, wandering over to the mantelpiece, where a framed photograph catches his eye. 'Mummy, Mummy, that's you.'

Elsie glances up to see her favourite picture. Bank Holiday weekend, five years ago: she is with her boys at Southport, before the beach was occupied by barbed wire and watch-towers.

'You've had it framed.'

'I thought it deserved pride of place.'

'And Daniel,' says Will, pointing to Daniel's skinny body leaning against his mother.

'That's right,' says Elsie, smiling.

'Who's that?'

'That's Daddy.' Elsie's eyes fill with tears.

'Daddy's flying. Neeah, neeah, neeah.'

'Careful!' Elsie calls, but it is too late. Will cannons into the fireplace. Trying to catch his balance, he knocks the picture off onto a pile of coal. He falls to the floor with a crack and a thump.

'Will!' Elsie's cry is too sharp; the little boy bursts into tears.

'It's alright, honestly,' says Daniel, as Elsie lifts Will up to comfort him.

Daniel picks up the photograph. The frame is shattered; fragments of glass spray over its surface and coal dust seeps through the cracks, obliterating the images underneath.

'That was your only copy – now it's ruined.'

'I'll fix it,' says Daniel, shaking the broken glass into the bin. 'Besides, I don't need the photo. I remember everything.'

Later, she wonders exactly what he means by that statement, but just now she is glad for an excuse to leave. Suddenly, Daniel reminds her too much of the man who is missing, and it is more than she can bear. She gathers her bags, takes Will's hand and makes her goodbyes. The road ahead bends round the corner and up the hill, where it is swallowed by the dark pines lining the Flint estate. Beyond the trees, Leah and Jacob lie waiting for them, like a pair of venomous spiders. It isn't the home she wants; it isn't the home Jack promised; but at this moment, it is the only home she has.

On the long trudge home, Will still smarts from his telling-off. He drags his feet, refusing to speak to her. The sun has long disappeared behind grey clouds that begin to drip into a drizzle. By the time they reach the war memorial, their clothes are damp. They follow the twisting road into the woods edging the estate. Water trickles around the roots grasping the hillside, over the grass-green mosses and dead bracken, onto the grey wet road.

As they reach the gate, Will finally speaks. 'I'm cold.'

'Nearly there.' Elsie brightens her voice. 'Let's be explorers. You be the leader.'

'We're climbing through the jungle,' he says. 'There are elephants up here. And tigers!' Rooks circle above them, cawing a welcome home. Will rushes ahead, searching for imaginary animals.

'Mind out for cheeky monkeys!' calls Elsie, chasing him through the lichen-scarred pillars into the driveway.

He is surprisingly fast; she doesn't catch him till they are nearly at the front door. When they reach it they are both red-faced with exertion, and giggling. The giggles evaporate as they enter the house to find Leah standing in wait for them – a gargoyle in black gazing down from the gallery above.

'You're late.'

'I'm sorry.'

'We have been waiting to go out.'

We? Who else is here? As if in answer, a door closes on the landing, followed by heavy footsteps and the soft voice that always grates. 'Evie has settled down for her nap.'

Veronica. Like Leah, she is in black, marking the recent mutual loss that seems to have bound them even closer together than before.

'Veronica is taking me to see Mrs Stephens,' says Leah.

Bereaved families together, thinks Elsie sourly, then scolds herself for her unkindness. It is true that Leah is rarely pleasant; even so, no one should have to suffer like that. The two women descend the stairs.

'I hope you don't mind, Elsie, only she was so tired.'

'Not at all. It was very kind of you.'

'She's like a little doll, isn't she?' As usual, Veronica is all smiles. 'You do so awfully well with the children. I don't know how you manage . . .' She reaches the final step. 'What a lot of shopping you have! Here, let me help you.' She picks up a bag. 'Why were you late? We've been waiting such an age.'

'We dropped Daniel's shopping off. He gave us lunch.'

'He should do his own,' said Leah, following them through the green baize door to the kitchen.

'He works during the week; he doesn't have much time to shop.'

'He should ask his young lady go do it.'

'She only has Saturday afternoons off. Besides, Geraint Thomas sorts out all the land girls' rations.' Elsie begins unpacking the food, handing packages to Will to put in the pantry. Leah picks up a box of tea and a bag of flour, placing them in the cupboard beside the range.

'People will talk.'

Elsie is tempted to say, *Let them.* Instead she asks, 'Why would they?'

'Your husband is away fighting a war; his cousin is not. And yet you spend your time with the man who stays behind.'

'He can't fight, Mother. He's got a gammy ankle.'

'It gives the wrong impression.'

'You've got to admit, Elsie,' says Veronica, 'it does look a little queer.'

'Will was with me. Daniel's like a brother . . . he's family.'

Leah mutters something inaudible. Elsie recognises the signs: when Leah is in this mood, nothing she does will be right. She carries on putting away the provisions, trying to stop the useless tears from forming.

'We'd best be off,' says Veronica, when the shopping is put away.

It is a relief when they have gone, and Elsie can be alone. Normally, she would take Will outside to play while Evie sleeps, but today, all she wants to do is lie down herself. She heads up the stairwell, Will rushing ahead, two steps at a time. Outside the rain begins to beat down on the windows. The house is bathed in grey gloom, the corridors reek of damp, the dark oak panels seem to press the walls inwards. Elsie's wet clothes are sticking to her, and now the exhilaration of the run home has evaporated, she is feeling cold and miserable.

At the top of the gallery, she pauses to catch a glimpse of Jack among the sombre family portraits. There he is in happier times, wearing his favourite tweed jacket – the one that makes him look so striking – particularly when standing behind Henry and Jacob, dour in their black workday suits. Here again, emerging from the sea at Bangor, his fair hair darkened into wet curls, his broad shoulders glistening like Johnny Weissmuller's. And her favourite, sitting on the front lawn, totally absorbed in the book he is reading, unaware the camera is focused on him. There are none of their wedding, of course. Nor has she yet merited an addition to the family tree. Marrying in secret has marked them with a permanent lack of respectability, which not even grandchildren can erase.

She enters the nursery to check on Evie. The little girl is sound asleep, her chest rising and falling with deep even breaths. Elsie would give anything to experience such peace.

'Can I play with my Meccano?' asks Will.

'As long as you don't wake Evie.'

Will runs over to the toy box, taking pieces of metal out. He starts fixing them together. With any luck he will stay like that for hours. She stands at the doorway for a moment, envying his absorption in the task, the simple pleasure he takes from linking pieces of metal, creating strange machinery that only a child could imagine. He looks up and smiles, a signal she can slip away. She leaves him there, going to her bedroom where she throws herself on the bed. This is the one place in the house where her thoughts and feelings are truly her own. The one place where, for a brief hour, she can be free.

DANIEL 1

She has gone, leaving Daniel alone with a ruined photograph, broken glass, the regret of an afternoon spoilt. He grits his teeth as he dismantles the frame, trying not to curse the little boy for his carelessness. He shouldn't blame Will; after all, he is only a child. But the picture is no good like this: the glass shattered, the figures obscured. He clears off as much of the soot as he can, shaking the debris into the bin. He is debating whether a wet cloth will make things worse when there is a knock at the door. He rushes to open it; there's always a chance Elsie might have forgotten something, that he might be able to entice her back inside.

'June . . .' The disappointment must have shown on his face, for her smile droops as he greets her.

'That's not quite the welcome I was hoping for.'

'Sorry.' He leans forward to kiss her. 'I wasn't expecting you. I'm just feeling a bit out of sorts. How marvellous to see you.' He laces his voice with extra enthusiasm, trying not to feel too much like a heel. It's not that he doesn't like June; it's just that she's not Elsie. 'How was Easter? And more importantly, how's your mother?'

'That woman is remarkable. A week ago, she could barely eat a bowl of soup. Yesterday she was cooking hot pot and I knew it was time to go.'

'Oh?'

'Once she's in charge of the kitchen, I'm just a hindrance.' June laughs as she steps into the house. 'Have you been lonely without me?'

'Of course.'

'Not that lonely,' she says, spotting the plates in the parlour.

'Elsie and Will came by with the shopping.'

'Ah, that explains the mess by the fire then.'

'Yes.'

Daniel begins to tidy up, slipping the photograph into the drawer; for some reason he doesn't want to share that particular story with her. It might draw her into an intimacy he isn't sure he's ready for. Seeing the rain has stopped, he proposes instead that they take an afternoon stroll, followed by supper at the Whetstone Arms; she accepts with alacrity.

'Must make the most of my last night of freedom. Now the nights are getting longer, I'll be tied to my hoe; there'll not be much time for courting, I'm afraid.'

'We should make hay then,' Daniel says lightly.

'Ha, ha . . . very funny.'

As they leave, the sky is still full of grey clouds that occasionally break to reveal patches of blue sky. Every now and then a ray of sunshine pierces through, casting a yellow glow over the village, warming the grey-stone cottages. They take the Sandstown road, walking alongside hedgerows, so recently bare, now bursting with life. Grasses jostle for space with buttercups and thistles, overtopped by a canopy of cow parsley. The vividness of the green against the increasingly blue sky raises Daniel's spirits as they make their way to their favourite spot, the water meadow by the stream. All of a sudden he feels happier, more relaxed. The clouds are beginning to disperse; the late-afternoon sun is warm enough for them to sit for a while. He spreads out the rug he carries in his rucksack, lighting a cigarette as he sits down. June takes one from him, lying down with her head in his lap as they listen to the trill of the curlews. He almost feels peaceful. If he is not certain of his commitment to her, at least he can create the appearance of a relationship while he makes up his mind about it. Here, as far away from Echo Hall as he can possibly be in Whetstone, it doesn't seem faithless or unkind to stroke her hair as the breeze ruffles through the grass and the ducks splash in the water. The kiss of the woman in front of him almost dispels the myth of the one who lives up the hill.

The sun begins to set; the returning clouds are cast pink and purple as it dips under the horizon, and the evening turns cooler. Daniel has nearly forgotten Elsie, which has always been the point of spending time with June. It is natural to take her hand, walk back to the pub with her, order one of Ellen Morgan's dry pasties and a pint of bitter, and almost feel he is in love. In such a mood, it is possible to make plans: a cinema trip at the weekend, a concert in a fortnight, talks at the Meeting House. For June is superior to Elsie in one respect: as a Quaker, she understands and shares his opposition to this war. It is the one topic of conversation that flows freely between them, the one that he cannot easily discuss with Elsie. How can he, when her husband is out there in the thick of it? The evening has proved a useful reminder that he didn't just take up with June as a distraction; she has qualities of her own he can admire and respect. When he drops her off at her billet, he is calmer and more contented then he has been for some time. Marching back to his cottage, he resolves, as he often does after such a night, that he will focus on the woman he has, rather than the one who is permanently out of reach. A resolve that lasts as long as it takes him to hang his coat, and notice Elsie has left her scarf behind. In a rush, the aftermath of lunch comes back to him: the excited child, the broken frame, the spoilt photograph. What was it he said to Elsie? It doesn't matter. He doesn't need it; he remembers everything. That day on the beach is one he can never forget, no matter how much he wants to, no matter how hard he tries . . .

★　　★　　★

133

Daniel had always envied the ease with which Jack approached women. That day, sitting in the Queen's Head, a simple proffer of a cigarette across the table and Elsie was touching his cousin's finger-tips, ever so slightly. In exchange, Daniel was left, like a chump, to face Millie, with her toad eyes and broad smirk.

'I don't like cigarettes, myself,' she said. 'You not having one, Daniel?'

'I don't smoke.'

'We have something in common then.'

'Perhaps,' he said, looking anywhere but at her hopeful gaze.

In the corner of the pub, a courting couple sat talking in a cosy alcove. Above them, a beam of sunlight shone through the red window rose. Dust motes danced in its track, like sparks from a fire. Daniel turned back to the table.

'Light me up, Jack,' said Elsie, leaning towards him.

'With pleasure,' he said.

'Thanks.'

She sat back in the red leather seat, her auburn hair framed by the green wall tiles behind her. The air was stuffy; they were all feeling sleepy after lunch. At first, the conversation was light-hearted, till Jack noticed the headline on a paper left by a previous customer.

'Oh Lord, further expansions of the RAF.'

'That doesn't sound good' said Daniel.

'Looks like they're expecting a war'

134

'Do you really think it will happen?' said Elsie. 'It doesn't seem possible today.'

'War can't break out in sunshine?' said Jack.

'You know what I mean. What would you do, if it came to it?'

'Air Force, I suppose. I hate to follow my father in anything, but he does have the connections . . . and I don't think I've got it in me to shoot someone face-to-face.'

'What about you, Daniel?' said Elsie.

He was saved from answering by Millie, who stood up, pulling Elsie with her. 'All this talk of war,' she said, 'on a day at the seaside. We should be having fun. Let's freshen up before we promenade.'

The men laughed, but after the women had gone, Jack asked, 'What about you, Daniel? Will you follow in your father's footsteps?'

'I'm not like him.'

'I thought you Quakers were against fighting.'

'We are. I am. As Dymond said, our Saviour has "unequivocally forbidden war". I can't fight. Not ever.'

'That means jail, then.'

'I can't do that, either. I lack my father's stoicism.'

'You have to do something.'

'I'm hoping it won't come to it.'

'Daniel, Daniel, look about you.' Jack shook his head. 'It's coming. Maybe not this year, or next, but it's coming. You've got to have a plan.'

'I have had half a thought,' said Daniel, hesitating. He lowered his voice. 'I might need your help.'

'With what?'

'Declaring myself medically unfit. I could do something useful, like teaching.'

'There are always people who do that sort of thing . . . but I couldn't get directly involved.'

'You'd help, though?'

'If it came to it.'

'You don't think me a coward?'

'Daniel.' Jack's grey-blue eyes were full of warmth. 'I've known you all my life. The way you've stood up to my father over the years – you're no coward.'

The women returned before Daniel had a chance to respond.

'Sunshine and ice cream,' said Millie. 'Come on.'

It was irritating that Jack automatically took Elsie's arm, leaving Daniel to follow behind with Millie. He kept his hands in his pockets to deter her; somehow she still managed to hook her arm through his, dragging him along the crowded promenade. A group of girls passed by, glowing in the Bank Holiday sunshine. They were pretty enough, but they couldn't hold a candle to Elsie. It wasn't fair, Daniel thought, looking at his cousin. Jack had always had the best of everything, always got exactly what he wanted – why should he have Elsie too? Then he remembered Jack's offer of help, and felt ashamed of himself.

They stopped at the pier, where Jack took photographs. Behind them the sea glinted, Air Force blue. The beach was packed with holidaymakers. Small children splashed in the water while their parents stood around, skirts raised, trousers rolled up, trying not to get wet.

'I want one with my boys,' said Elsie. 'Take it, will you, Millie?'

As Jack showed her friend the mechanics of the camera, Elsie pulled Daniel towards her. He took her arm, wishing he had an excuse to hold her more tightly. Her skin was soft; she smelt of lavender. Millie waved Jack towards them. He took Elsie's other arm with a casualness, expressing, not exactly ownership, but a certain kind of closeness. Although she held on to both men, she leant her head towards Jack; Daniel felt like an interloper.

'That's great – the Three Musketeers.' Millie looked down into the box. 'Smile. And . . . one for luck.' She grinned at them. 'Perfect.'

The group moved apart. For a moment, Jack and Elsie's arms remained entwined, leaving Daniel with a sensation he remembered from childhood: the boy locked out from the big house.

At dusk, they went to the fairground, where they hooked ducks, shot at targets and rode the roller-coaster. When they saw a carousel, Elsie yelped with delight. 'I love these,' she said, climbing on a red and gold horse. Jack jumped on the one alongside her.

'Thrown together again,' said Millie, as she and Daniel mounted the horses behind.

Daniel didn't answer. He was gazing at Elsie: the curl of her hair on her shoulders, the trimness of her waist, the shape of her legs beneath her blue dress.

'Are they courting?' Millie asked.

'No, I don't think so.'

'Only they look quite close.'

'We're all good friends,' said Daniel as lightly as he could, but as the carousel started, his stomach tightened into a knot. Round and round they went, faster and faster, red-gold, red-gold. He urged his horse onwards, onwards, until he realised that no matter how fast he went, he could never, ever catch them up.

ELSIE 2

Elsie lies on the bed, clutching the covers, her fingers tracing the place where Jack should be. When he first left, she used to lie here while Will napped, holding the bedclothes, drinking in Jack's smell. But the scent faded years ago; and since Old Mrs Davies left for the armament factory in Birmingham, Elsie has been too busy for such indulgences. He is long gone, leaving only an imprint, an echo of himself lingering in her memories: seaside trips, dancing, the night they watched the Perseids . . .

They had been at Echo Hall three weeks, and already it felt like years. Jack was out most of the day, helping at the doctor's surgery while he and Henry waited for their commissions. Elsie spent her time seeing to Will's needs, trying to adjust to her bewildering new life in the vast lonely hall. Each new day brought another sign that war was imminent. Bill Marshall, the recently appointed air warden, visited with advice on blackouts that sent Leah and Old Mrs Davies scurrying into Sandstown for enough material to cover the vast windows at Echo Hall. The two Mrs Davies, old and young, spent a week at the sewing machines making curtains. Down in Whetstone, the council sent men to remove the white lines in the middle of the road; a notice came to every house announcing that gas masks could be collected from the village hall; another requested that households make themselves available for the evacuees who would soon be coming from London.

The household was not immune either. The servants, whose numbers were already depleted, were leaving every day – to join up or work in the factories. Seeing the vacant rooms they left behind, Elsie asked if Het could bring her family, to avoid being evacuated among strangers. Jacob was quick to announce there would be no space; he had already offered to store artworks for the Ministry of Culture. To her annoyance, Jack refused to argue with his father, and she was forced to tell her sister she couldn't help. Het responded to say she understood; but between the brief lines, Elsie detected coolness, disappointment, anger even. It was hard not to be resentful as the paintings began to arrive, filling up the spare bedrooms and the corridors of the servants' quarters. Helping the war effort was all very well, but surely people came before pictures?

Though she knew war was inevitable, Elsie prayed each day for some miracle that would bring all this activity to an end. The declaration, when it came, would bring twin evils. Jack's departure was bad enough, but already she sensed that living with her parents-in-law was likely to be a trial. Behind their claims to welcome their new daughter, she detected a sense of family obligation, coupled with a deep disappointment at their son's choice of wife.

On the night of the Perseids, the family gathered for dinner in the dark oak dining room, oppressive in the heat of the August night. Veronica joined them, as she often did in those days, making the most of her last days with Henry. The meal, as usual, was conducted mainly in silence. Jacob and Leah rarely spoke to each other, unless to discuss matters relating to the family or household. Their conversations were politely formal, yet underneath, Elsie thought she detected something else – a mix of rage and bitter envy that mystified her. But when she mentioned it to Jack he just shrugged, saying weren't everyone's parents a bit peculiar? Whatever the truth of the matter, she was always glad when someone finally opened their mouths.

On this occasion, it was Jacob who turned to Henry. 'Did you remember to place the order for Jones and Sons?'

'Yes, Father.'

'Good. I think this will be a beneficial relationship for all of us.'

'He mentioned his uncle in Shrewsbury might be looking for a supplier.'

'Excellent. Are you going to meet him?'

'I'm going over there next Thursday. After Veronica and I have chosen a ring.'

Leah's flabby pale cheeks glowed at the news. 'Are you closer to setting a date?'

'Father is still very ill, Mrs Flint,' said Veronica. 'We can't get married till he's better. But we felt it would be a good omen to buy the ring now.'

'We will pray for his speedy recovery,' said Jacob.

'Congratulations,' said Elsie.

'Yes, well done,' said Jack. But afterwards, when they went upstairs to bed, he said, 'I don't know what he sees in that girl. She's got him right where she wants him. Mother, too. But behind that smile . . .'

'What?'

'A tyrant lurks.'

'You're exaggerating.'

'Maybe . . . a little . . . She's not my cup of tea. It's his funeral, I suppose.'

They entered the bedroom where, to her surprise, he pulled a knapsack from under the bed.

'What are you doing?'

'Shh. Come with me.'

'What about Will?'

'It's all taken care of. Old Mrs Davies is looking after him. This way.'

He took her through the green baize doors in the old servants' quarters and past the cloth-wrapped paintings. The corridor ended with a bedroom on the left, the twin of Leah's room on the west side of the house. To the right, a staircase ran up to the attic rooms, and down to the back of the house.

'The servants' staircase. We can escape unseen.' Jack grinned.

'Why the secrecy?'

'My parents wouldn't approve of us leaving Will in the middle of the night, even with Mrs D in charge. There's something I want to show you.'

They crept out of the back door and up the sloping lawn. The moonlight carved out tree shadows. After weeks without rain, the grass was dry, crunching under their feet. Jack took her hand. 'Come on.' They ran up to the fir trees at the top of the garden, arriving at the gate breathless.

'We're not going walking at this time of night? It's pitch-black.'

'I came prepared.' Jack flourished a torch.

'My Boy Scout.'

'I've been running around these woods all my life. I won't lose you.'

Even with the torch, the going was difficult. They scrambled over tree roots that were flung across the path, trying to avoid rocks and stones that leapt out at them in the darkness. An owl hooted. Above them, creatures fluttered between the branches.

'Bats,' said Jack. 'Pipistrelles, I think.'

'Ugh.'

'It's all right, they're very small.'

'Won't they fly in my hair?'

'They'll swoop right over you.'

'How can they miss in the dark?'

'They use sonar. Sound waves that bounce off objects like us and warn them to get out of the way.'

'Clever.'

'Very. I read somewhere the boffins in the navy are trying to work out if sonar can be used to help the war effort. Once it gets going, of course.'

'Really?'

'Very hush hush. Still,' Jack strode ahead as they emerged from the black trees onto the hillside again, 'we don't want to talk about war tonight.'

'No, we don't.'

Elsie followed him up the moon-illuminated path, picking her way over the stones and gravel. A sheep baaed across the field, its call answered by another close by. The night was still quite warm. Above them, the sky was inky blue, speckled with thousands of silver stars. Ahead of them, Elsie could make out a series of boulders, erect like gravestones on the hillside.

'Here we are,' said Jack. 'Arthur's Stone.'

He opened his rucksack, pulling out a rug, a bottle of wine and a corkscrew.

'You really are prepared.'

'Always.'

They sat down. Jack poured the wine and they clinked glasses. He lit a cigarette. Elsie peered down at the valley below. Trees huddled to the side of the hill, sheep-shapes shifted across the grass; in the distance, a light bobbed across the field.

'What's that?'

'Geraint Thomas harvesting the hay.'

'At this time?'

'When the days are as good as this, you have to make the most of them. You never know when the rain will come.'

'This is lovely . . . but wouldn't we see more by daylight?'

'We didn't come for the view. At least not that view. Lie down.'

She lay next to him. He put his arm around her, nuzzled his chin in her hair. His breath smelt of wine and Woodbines. 'Now look up.'

Elsie looked up at the sky, thousands and thousands of tiny lights shrinking her into insignificance. 'They can make you feel small, can't they?'

'You outshine them all.' He kissed her, then took a drag of his cigarette. 'Try looking to the east, out of the corner of your eye.'

'What am I looking for?'

'A flash of light, streaking the sky. There. Did you see?'

'No.' Elsie gazed at the sky. Then, 'Yes . . . I saw that one! And that one. There's another, and another.' The sky was ablaze with explosions, silver streaks of light criss-crossing each other in the blackness. 'It's like someone's lit a box of fireworks. What are they?'

'The Perseids – a meteor shower. Happens every year at this time.'

'They're marvellous.'

'I wanted to share this with you, before . . .'

'Sshh.'

She stroked his hair, snuggling closer, her arm moving with the rise and fall of his chest. Presently, he stubbed the cigarette out and kissed her. The grass rustled with the movement of some tiny creature making its way to bed. Above, the display of meteors continued to light up the sky. The night encircled them.

Afterwards, they lay drinking wine and smoking cigarettes, watching as the meteors slowly ceased their dance, the stars returning to their static state. The air began to cool reminding them how late it was. They dressed in fits of giggles, fumbling with stockings and zips in the darkness. Just before they left, Jack said, 'Hold up,' and returned to the back of the stones. Elsie followed. He picked up a piece of slate, scraped it against the rock, and discarded it for another. After several attempts he found one that satisfied him. For a moment, she wondered what he was doing, then saw in his flashlight the names of the people who'd been here before: *J loves R, H for S, T and K forever.* He smiled as he carved *EF & JF* on a blank spot in the middle.

'There. According to local legend, our love can never die.'

'As if it ever would.'

'Always worth being sure.'

'You daft thing,' she laughed, kissing him. 'Time for bed.'

Though they were cold and tired, they lingered on the path, soaking in the moonlight, the sheep calls, the owl hoots, making the night last. When they finally arrived at Echo Hall they picked their way across the lawn as quietly as possible so as not to disturb the household. Elsie thought they had managed it, but as they reached the back door, she glanced up at Leah's room. Her mother-in-law was standing by the window. She returned Elsie's gaze with a malevolent stare. Elsie caught her breath.

'What's the matter?' asked Jack.

'Nothing. Someone walked over my grave, that's all.'

They slipped back up the backstairs and into the nursery, where Mrs Davies had fallen asleep in the rocking chair, so sleep-muddled she barely registered the lateness of the hour. As Elsie stumbled out of the room, Will stirred in his bed, beginning to whimper.

'You go in, I'll be there in a minute,' Elsie said, but by the time she'd settled Will, Jack was fast asleep, his face peaceful, his breaths regular. She climbed into bed beside him, tracing her fingers across his body, imprinting him in her memory. This night would have to last for a long time.

The clock chimes three o'clock. Elsie turns over, reaching for the prayer book on the bedside cabinet. Before he left, Jack suggested they swap his Book of Common Prayer for her Missal. That way, he'd said, however far apart they were, they'd always be united in prayer. It always helps when she feels this blue; today is no exception. The book falls open on a psalm:

Consider, and hear me, O Lord my God: lighten mine eyes, that I sleep not in death. Lest mine enemy say, I have prevailed against him: for if I be cast down, they that trouble me will rejoice at it.

But my trust is in thy mercy: and my heart is joyful in thy salvation.

I will sing of the Lord, because he hath dealt so lovingly with me: yea, I will praise the Name of the Lord most Highest.

In the next room she can hear Will singing to himself as he plays with his Meccano; Evie is stirring in her cot. Soothed by the prayer, she rises, with strength enough to see to their needs.

DANIEL 2

'Danny and June sitting in a tree,

K- I- S- S- I-N-G,

First comes love, then comes marriage,

Then comes baby in a baby carriage.'

The group of 10-year-old girls hush their giggles at Daniel's approach. He affects not to hear.
'Bang! Bang! You're dead!'
Across the playground a group of boys shoot each other with sticks. Such games are inevitable, particularly in wartime; still, it pains him to see the relish with which they play at killing. He hates the thought that this is what they aspire to, what heroism means to them. He rings the bell, calling two of the gigglers to him.

'Jenny, Sarah, please will you lead the lines back into class?'

'Yes, Mr Clarkson.'

Still smirking, they shoo the younger children

into their lines, the boys continuing to fire their pretend weapons, clutching their fake wounds, till Daniel has had enough.

'Stop that now. Break time is over.'

The boys drop the twigs, shuffling back into the school room. The younger children retreat to the far end, where Miss Mason is setting sums. Daniel marshals the older ones into their seats, under the large arched window.

'I hope you've all written your weekend reports?'

'Yes, Mr Clarkson.'

'Who'd like to start?'

'Mesirmesirmesir . . .'

Every hand is up, every voice pitched in a high squeal. Daniel always tries to be fair, never picking the same person two weeks running: one week a boy, the next a girl. It is the boys' turn this week. Peter Hill hasn't been chosen for a while. He is red-faced, bursting with his news, leaping to the front the minute he is selected.

'ThisweekendmyDadcamehomeonleave.'

'A bit slower, we're not in a hurry.'

Peter takes a deep breath, trying to slow down with limited success. 'My Dad isintheNavy. He is fighting Hitler andalltheotherJerries. He has just come back from doing convoys to Russia. The Jerriesaretrying to bomb the shipswhichcarry food. MyDad is verybrave and shootstheJerriestostop them doing it. It willhelpus win the war. WhenI'mgrownupI'mgoingtojoin the Navy andfightJerriestoo. The End.'

'I can't wait till I'm grown up and can fight,' says Alan Edwards.

'I'd kill hundreds of Jerries,' says Bert Williams.

'I'd kill thousands,' says Jenny Jones.

'Don't be silly, girls can't fight,' says Peter.

'That's not fair.'

'Girls would just cry all the time. They're not brave like boys,' says Alan. 'Isn't that right, sir?'

'I know some very brave girls,' says Daniel. He hesitates. He has a feeling his father would have debated with them: what makes a man courageous – wielding a gun, or acting on his conscience? He was always one for arguing that children should think beyond the obvious. Daniel has never had this knack, or perhaps it's just that he's too timid. Someone is bound to report him to the school board if he steps too far out of line. And what will getting sacked achieve? He promised Jack he'd stay here to look after Elsie. Who would do that if he were forced to leave? Besides, what right does he have to preach of conscience?

As usual, he ducks his own question, praising Peter before moving to the next child, and the next. Yet the thought pursues him throughout the day as he wades through reports and fractions, spelling tests and reading *Just William*. It is still there when he and June catch the bus into Sandstown for the talk at the Meeting House.

'Do you think I should have said something?'

The bus rattles out of Whetstone. It is the beginning of harvest season. The land girls are out in the

151

fields, scything the wheat and barley, placing the sheaves on the trailers.

'Perhaps it wouldn't have done any good.'

He should appreciate the concern on June's round face; for some reason it irritates him. Ever since she's returned from her mother's he finds himself comparing her more and more unfavourably with Elsie. It isn't very fair of him, he knows, but he can't help wishing that it is Elsie sitting beside him, Elsie offering him sympathy, or challenge, it doesn't matter which. The bus sweeps down the road through the purple-heathered hills. Behind them the sun is sinking, casting red-gold rays through the window, giving the momentary impression that the bushes and fields are subject to a series of fire storms, the after-effect of a beautiful but deadly air raid. They turn a corner, cutting off the light, and the hills are cast into shadow. Aware he has been silent for too long, he says, 'Good of Geraint to let you come out this evening.'

'I'll pay for playing hooky. I'll be last off the fields for the rest of the week, believe you me.'

'Did he ask what the talk was about?'

'No, and I didn't tell him either. He's good-hearted, old Thomas, but I suspect he'd think me unpatriotic if he knew.'

They are reaching the edges of Sandstown, passing the large black-and-white houses of the wealthier inhabitants, past the road that leads to his grandfather's old home. He thinks, not for the first time, how different his life could have been.

152

If his parents hadn't met, if his father had been another sort of man, he might have spent his early years in one of these houses, instead of shabby lodgings on the other side of town. He might have grown up to attend the local grammar school, believing that war was necessary for the defence of the nation, for the maintenance of the empire. He might now be out on the frontlines somewhere, fighting for a cause he believed in. Instead, he skulks here, plagued by his wretched conscience and his inability to live up to his father's legacy.

The streets narrow as they reach the huddled red-brick houses near the centre of town. Every now and then a gaping hole appears where a house should be – the work of a stray bomber returning from Liverpool, shedding the rest of its load. There aren't too many; Sandstown is a long way from the besieged cities and, in the main, is surviving the war fairly unscathed. The bus deposits them near the cathedral, where they alight. Their path takes them underneath its magnificent edifice and they stop, as is their ritual, to observe the animal gargoyles on the buttresses.

'I love that cat – the expression on its face is so solemn,' says June.

'I rather like the look of that fox,' says Daniel.

'I thought the spaniel was your favourite.'

'The fox caught my eye today – it looks so bold and adventurous, don't you think?'

And sly and deceitful. The thought is in his mind before he can suppress it. He doesn't mean to, but every step he takes with her continues the lie that she will in time mean everything to him. They turn the corner into Parker Street. Soon they will pass the Shire Hall, where his parents met. June will expect him to comment, as normal. He always hates that conversation; it raises too many expectations. He turns left into Jelf Road to avoid it.

'Hey, where are you going?'

'Short-cut.'

'Is it?'

'You'll see.'

Ten minutes later, they still haven't reached their destination.

'I thought you said it would be a short-cut,' says June. 'We'll be late.'

'I could have sworn it was quicker,' Daniel puffs as they reach Walton Street. 'Never mind, we're here now. And we can't be that late – George and Frances have only just arrived.'

But as they enter the Meeting House, the lights are already down, the black-out blinds drawn in preparation for Edward Norton's slideshow. He stands by the projector, ready to speak. The two couples slide into the back row as he begins. The slideshow offers grim viewing: picture after picture of bombed-out streets, survivors standing beside the remains of their homes, bodies on stretchers being dragged from the scene.

'We are beginning to visit the London Blitz on Germany, a hundredfold,' Norton concludes. 'God knows where it will end.'

George asks, 'What's the purpose of such raids? Payback for last year?'

'To destroy the German war economy, lower morale. The theory goes that if we break down the spirit of the people, they will beg their leaders to stop, bringing the war to a close.'

'Wasn't that a German trick?' asks Daniel.

'When you resist tyranny with violence, you often end up mimicking the very actions you once condemned,' says George.

'True, but unfortunately it does have an effect,' says Edward. 'If you have no railways, no warehouses, no shops, you cannot function as a nation. Whether it makes the country pull together with a Blitz spirit or unite to get rid of their war-mongering leaders, who knows?'

'What can we do?' asks June. 'It seems so hopeless.'

'The country is divided on the bombings. The Battle of Britain is still fresh in people's minds. We can write letters – to the papers, to the Ministry of War, to our MPs, calling for an end to the raids. We are organising a vigil outside Parliament in September to mark the fourth anniversary of the start of the war. If any of you are able to attend, come and talk to me about it afterwards.'

The meeting breaks for refreshments: tea and coffee, served out of large urns in the corner of the hall.

'Perhaps we should,' says June to Daniel as they stand with their drinks, waiting for the lumps of milk powder to settle.

'Should what?'

'Go to the vigil.'

'Maybe.'

'We could always say we're off to London visiting relatives. That way Geraint Thomas and the school board need never know.'

It was such passion that drew him to June in the first place; he'd be foolish to throw her over for some idiotic hope that one day Elsie might be free to choose him. A hope that could come to fruition only in the worst of circumstances.

'It's a thought.' He knows he won't act on it; and, not for the first time, he wishes he was as brave as his father, or as Jack. What is wrong with him? Why can't he have their courage?

Later, as he is dropping June off, she exclaims, 'Oh, I almost forgot. The weather's supposed to turn at the weekend. Geraint said we should ask our friends to help on Friday, so we can get as much done as possible.'

'I might drop by after school.'

'Elsie's coming, I think – she said Will might enjoy it.'

Daniel hates himself for knowing that this news increases his chances of attending; even more so on Friday, when he forces himself to ignore his headache to join the party in the fields. He wouldn't make such an effort for June alone. The sky is cloudless; the sun beats down with no sense of an imminent storm. The job is mostly done; the good-natured crowd is taking a break, sitting in the shade or resting on hay bales. He casts around for June; with so many eyes watching, it is important that he seeks her out first, placing his arm around her shoulders before searching for Elsie. She is standing under the oak tree with Will. They are both red-faced and drinking lemonade. When they spot Daniel they wander over, Will full of excitement at the day's adventures.

'I jumped in the hay!' he announces proudly.

'I hope you did some work too,' says Daniel, squinting in the glare of the sun.

'He was very helpful, actually,' says Elsie. 'He's been piling sheaves. He'll sleep well tonight.' She hugs June. 'Thanks for suggesting it, June – we've had a splendid day. Almost makes me want to be a land girl.'

'It's alright on a day like today. You should try it in the middle of winter when you're trying to break the frozen ground with a pick-axe.'

'Think I'll stick to sunshine,' Elsie grins, then glances at her watch. 'Oh Lord, is that the time? I promised Leah we'd be back by five.' She gives Daniel a hug. 'Sorry I can't catch up, Daniel. You know what Leah's like.'

Daniel hugs her back, pretending not to mind, nodding *Yes I know* . . . Disappointment has always laced their friendship, yet no matter how many times it happens, the pain pulses through him, like the headache throbbing in his temples. A constant ache that can never be relieved.

ELSIE 3

The news of Jack's unexpected leave fills the house with excitement. Will, who has vague memories of his father's last visit when Evie was a baby, has to be sent into the garden to run off his constant desire to impersonate an aeroplane. Evie, at two and a bit, is too small to understand what a father means. She responds to the activity by rushing around giggling. Leah, who has not received guests since Henry's memorial service, rings round the neighbourhood inviting everyone available to tea. Once roused she is unstoppable, refusing to pay attention to Elsie's suggestion that Jack might prefer a quieter homecoming. She is determined her remaining son will be welcomed home as a war hero. The only concession Elsie is able to manage is ensuring Daniel and June are on the guest list. After that she and young Mrs Davies are tasked with cleaning the whole house till it is spotless. Even Jacob is not immune to the news, going so far as to give the quarry workers a half-day holiday.

Elsie hasn't cleaned this much since the old days at her father's boarding house. Even though Jack is worth the effort, at nightfall she is exhausted. In the bathroom, she catches sight of herself in the mirror. A couple of bobby pins have fallen out; strands of hair stray across her face. She has a smudge on her nose and her face is puce. She looks a fright. Not a face to greet her husband after two years. She has a couple of days till his arrival; there's time to rifle through Leah's old dress collection to see if there's a frock that can be spruced up for the occasion. She peers through every cupboard in Leah's suite of rooms, but she cannot find anything suitable. Her mother-in-law's preference for black and grey is all very well for everyday clothes, but not when she needs something knockout.

She is about to give up when it crosses her mind that perhaps there might be something in the East Wing, left by some former inhabitant. Evie and Will trail after her as they fight their way through the government paintings piled on the beds and against the walls, but there is nothing to find. The previous residents have long gone, taking their wardrobes with them. It is not until Elsie reaches the final room at the end of the corridor that she finds what she has been looking for; though when she first enters, it doesn't seem that likely. The curtains are drawn and the room is pitch-black. Evie whimpers. Even Will loses his cheerful chatter. The room is soaked in sorrow, as if some earlier occupant had lived with a deep and enduring grief. Elsie strides across it, drawing the curtains and opening the window. Light and air flood in. The feeling recedes; it is just a bedroom, after all. The children climb on the double bed and start bouncing on it. Other than that, there is a dressing table and two wardrobes. The first cupboard is empty, but in the second she finds three ball gowns that can easily be cut down. They smell of damp and mothballs, but they should be alright with a bit of airing. She stands at the mirror, trying each in turn. A picture comes into her head of a young girl getting ready for a party, delighting in her beauty and the excitement of an evening ahead. Eventually she selects a deep-blue silk, trimmed with Nottingham lace. It should be simple enough to turn it into a perfect three-quarter-length after-noon dress – just the thing to raise Jack's spirits. She'll give him a homecoming to remember.

But it all goes wrong, right from the start. Jacob leaves to collect Jack before she is even up. The morning is damp and cold: a thick autumn mist blankets the garden. Elsie paces up and down the hallway, waiting for the sounds of the car on the drive. At seven, she hears the honk of the horn; she runs to the front door, flinging it open. Two light beams penetrate the cloud, pale beacons illuminating the hill. A submarine-like vehicle heads towards her, finally taking on the familiar shape of the Bentley as it reaches the front of the house. Jack struggles out of the car with his kitbag. His hair is cropped short; he has grown a small moustache.

His eyes are lined with purple shadows; it looks like it's been a long time since he's had a good night's sleep. She had fully intended to throw her arms round him the minute she saw him, but now, faced with this uniformed stranger, all she can manage is a peck on the cheek. Still, he is here at last, and they have 24 hours, 24 . . .

'You weren't at the station.' Jack is uncharacteristically sharp.

'Your father left early.'

'I decided to leave at six,' says Jacob. 'Jack and I have had business to discuss.'

Elsie's heart sinks. No wonder Jacob went alone. She knows what business this is – Jack giving up medicine and coming home to take over that sodding quarry. He'd better not agree, she thinks, as they walk back into the house; he'd better not.

Before they've had a chance to recover, the children emerge from the nursery to see what all the fuss is about. Will has been up since six. Perhaps it is lack of sleep, or that the actual fact of a real father can never live up to an imaginary one; whatever the reason, at the sight of Jack the little boy turns away.

'That's not my Daddy. My Daddy doesn't have a moustache.'

'He's grown one since he's been away.'

'That's not my Daddy.'

When Evie hears her brother, she screams.

It takes several moments to convince Will of his parentage, grudgingly admitted on production of his father's identity card. Evie is not so easily pacified. She yells so much that Elsie is forced to take her upstairs to calm her down. When they return to the kitchen, Jacob has already taken Jack to his study while Leah makes it clear that Elsie's job is to rustle up as many cakes as she can from their meagre supplies of dried egg and flour. The precious Jack hours tick away: 23, 22, 21 . . .

Lunchtime is no better. Evie doesn't shout at Jack, but nor will she speak to him. She spends the whole meal sitting on Elsie's lap, gazing at her father with eyes deep with suspicion. Will behaves so badly that he is banished to the nursery. Elsie tries to catch Jack's eye to show how sorry she is, but he seems intent on ignoring her, listening instead to Jacob's account of the doings at the quarry. Elsie wills Jack to stand up to his father for once, to put an end to this talk of slate so he can spend some time with her and the children before the guests arrive. But he doesn't, seeming content to go along with his parents' plans to keep them apart. After the meal, Leah sweeps her into the kitchen to wash up. When they return, Jacob has taken Jack over to the quarry, leaving Elsie to her usual routines on the one day they could have been disrupted. By the time the party is approaching, there are only 16 precious hours left. At least she has managed to finish the dress, she thinks, though as she wrestles with the hooks she wishes she'd taken it out a little. At last she is done. She pins up her hair, dabs a little lavender perfume on her neck, scrapes the remains of her lipstick over her mouth. She allows herself a rare moment of vanity in front of the mirror, acknowledging she is a sight for sore eyes before turning her attention to the children. They hear the car scrunching over the gravel as Elsie finishes tying the ribbon on Evie's dress.

'Now,' she says, 'shall we start again and show Daddy how pleased we are to see him?'

The children nod, united in contrition. She lets them go downstairs ahead and join Leah at the door to provide Jack with the greeting he should have received earlier. She remains on the landing, watching in relief as, this time, Will shows Jack the Meccano aeroplane he has been making all week, and Evie at last permits him to hug her. It is going to be alright after all. She descends the staircase, keen to make an impression. To her gratification, he gazes up at her open-mouthed in admiration. She can see his eyes appreciating her calves; he smiles as if imagining what lies underneath the silk of her skirt. It is going to be alright after all. Then Jacob steps into the house, and the illusion dissolves.

'Where did you get that dress?' His voice is harsh, his face pale as if he has seen a ghost.

'Upstairs, in the back room.' Elsie is puzzled. 'Mother said I could use her old clothes.'

Leah, who has been focusing her attention on Jack, turns round. Her face reddens as she sees what Elsie is wearing. 'My clothes. I said you could wear my clothes. Not hers.'

163

'Elsie, I think you'd better get changed,' says Jack, his voice taut as he looks from one parent to the other.

'What's wrong with this one?'

'I think it was Aunt Rachel's.'

'Oh Lord.'

Jack and Daniel have often said that there was no love lost between Leah and her dead sister. Though what her old dresses are doing in the house, and why Jacob should be so affected, is a mystery to her. But there is no time for questions; guests can be heard on the drive. She runs upstairs and changes into the first thing she can find – a faded pink cotton frock. It makes her feel dowdy the minute she puts it on.

By the time she returns downstairs, the room is full of Leah's cackling cronies, women who rarely have a good word for Elsie. Veronica is holding court in the centre, her face set with determined courage. It has been several months, but she is still wearing the black armband on her WAAF uniform, a reminder of her tragedy. Elsie can see that this stoic grief is admirable, but it is still infuriating – even in bereavement, Veronica is proving she would have been the better daughter-in-law. Thank goodness Leah let her invite Daniel and June. It is good to see their friendly faces, though there is barely time to speak to them as she rushes from guest to guest, making sure she doesn't offend Jack's parents any further. At half-past four she looks up to see Daniel and Jack sneak out for a quick walk round the grounds. Though she's glad they are getting a chance to chat, she can't help but feel resentful that they haven't taken her.

'Penny for them,' says June, coming over to table where Elsie is putting more cakes on plates.

'I wish Jack and I could have some proper time together . . .'

'Maybe later.'

'It's been hideous so far. Jacob didn't let me go to the station, the children have been little monsters and then I put my foot in it by wearing an old dress of Daniel's mother's.'

'What was wrong with that?'

'Heaven knows. It seems to have shocked Jacob. Leah's not speaking to me, and Jack is furious.'

'You should ask Daniel.'

'You know what he's like . . . never wants to speak about the past.'

'He says he was too unhappy.'

'Look, I'd better go,' says Elsie. 'I can see Mrs Caswell calling for more tea . . . but thanks, June. You're a brick.'

The party drags on and on . . . Tea, cake, dreary conversation. Daniel and Jack returning flushed from their exercise. The children pulling at her, bored by the formality; Jack forced into conversation with everyone but her; Jacob and Leah watching her every move as if willing her into another mistake. At last, the guests depart . . . 12 hours left. Now it is the children's bedtime. With all the excitement, it takes much longer than usual to settle them. It's nearly nine o'clock before she is able to come downstairs, by which time Jacob is turning on the radio for the evening news. When it's over, he ends with the ritual of evening prayer. It is eleven before Elsie can finally take Jack upstairs and have him all to herself. Eleven o'clock! Only eight hours of the precious leave left. Elsie sits on the bed, determined to salvage what she can.

'I'm sorry about today.'

'What on earth got into the kids?'

'They haven't seen you in over two years.'

'That excuses the abominable scene at lunch? Your inability to get them to sleep tonight?'

'They're over-tired.'

'My parents think they're spoilt.'

'You'd rather I favoured their style of parenting then?' Elsie is so angry she stamps the floor with her feet.

'No . . . but . . . Evie . . . She screamed at the sight of me . . . Will was uncontrollable.'

'They needed time to adjust.'

'So why didn't you bring them to meet me?'

'Your father . . .'

'You could have stopped him.'

'As you did? When I wanted Het to live with us?'

'That was different.'

'That was worse. My sister asked for our help. She begged for our help . . . and you were too much of a coward to stand up to your father.'

Jack turns away. 'It wasn't like that . . . You don't understand . . .'

'I understand perfectly well. Everything you ever told me about your father is guff. You may dislike his rules, but when it comes to it, you'll never disobey them.'

'This is my father's house. What was I supposed to do?'

'Stand up for your wife. Or, failing that, you could have claimed family obligation, the Christian duty he's always so proud to proclaim.'

'It's not that simple . . .'

'But it would have been simple for me to get to the station this morning? You really are a prize hypocrite, Jack, the worst.'

The argument continues till they wear themselves out. At midnight they creep into bed, turning their backs on each other. As Jack drifts off to sleep, Elsie lies in the darkness. She has wanted him by her side for so long, but now he is here, she might as well be alone. She finally drifts off into an uneasy sleep, but at four, Jack's thrashing wakes her up. He is moaning, disturbed by nightmares. When he finally wakes, he is trembling and suddenly it is easy to turn to him, to provide comfort, consolation, the bad words forgotten in an instant. Three hours to go, and the leave has just begun.

DANIEL 3

Daniel is surprised when Leah's invitation drops on his doormat. It has been a while since his aunt has spoken to him; even longer since he's been invited to the house. He guesses Elsie must have had a hand in it, bless her, though it's only the prospect of seeing her and Jack that makes him accept. After all these years, the thought of entering Echo Hall still fills him with dread. He is glad, when it comes to it, that he has June by his side. Despite his reservations about their relationship, it is better than arriving alone. To calm his nerves he points out landmarks as they climb the hill.

'Jack and I used to get up to all sorts of mischief in those woods. We built ourselves a shelter, made dams, sneaked feasts down by the stream.' He pauses as they reach the front lawn. 'And there's the oak tree we used to dare each other to climb.'

'Really?' June looks up. 'It must be 40 feet at least.'

'It used to be only half that height. I wouldn't fancy trying it today.' It is surprising how the constraints of childhood still affect him. He is as reluctant to leave the base of the tree and face his uncle and aunt as he was 20 years ago, when Jack was calling him down.

'Are we going in?' June interrupts his reverie.

He shakes his fears away, nods and they turn towards the house. Jacob greets them at the door with the thinnest of smiles, his sea-grey eyes lacking any sign of welcome.

Leah shakes his hand with cold politeness. 'We're in the east sitting room. This way.'

The room is crowded with people Daniel hasn't seen in years: Aunt Leah's gaggle of friends, standing in their usual spot by the fireplace, passing judgement on all who enter. He watches them take note of his arrival, whispering their vile comments to each other. In the past, such behaviour was enough to make him blush and dive out of the room; today he is pleased to discover how easy it is to ignore them – that, finally, they have lost their power to hurt him. Jacob joins his coterie of factory owners and businessmen. They are gathered by the table, discussing the price of goods, the balance of the markets; their erect backs and dark-grey suits remind Daniel of a row of gravestones. Veronica is in the centre of Leah's crones, fitting right in. She smiles at Daniel in a manner that suggests she endorses all their views about him. He smiles back politely, turning away. Of course he feels sorry for her; who wouldn't? But he's always thought her a cold fish, not his type at all. He casts around the room for Elsie, unable to spot her straight away. At least Jack is here, talking to one of his father's friends with the carefully constructed appearance of interest that he developed as a child. He looks older; his face is lined, he's sporting a moustache. He stands differently too, as if the horrors and griefs of the last two years weigh on him. Which they probably do. Jack catches sight of them and excuses himself to fight across the room so he can shake Daniel by the hand.

'This must be June.'

'Hello,' June smiles. 'It's lovely to meet you at last. I've heard a lot about you.'

'Likewise.'

The door opens; Elsie enters. She's as beautiful as ever, though the pink dress she's wearing doesn't suit her. It makes her look tired, faded. Daniel is about to call her over, but Leah intercepts, giving her a plate of cakes to pass around the guests.

'I'd love to catch up, properly, but this isn't the place,' says Jack.

'Why don't you boys slip out for a walk?' says June. 'I'll entertain the troops.'

Daniel flashes her a smile, grateful that tact is one of her strengths. He and Jack need no other invitation; they are out of the house before Leah and Jacob have time to notice. Out of old habit, they march down the front path, past the oak tree on the lawn, through the row of pines, under the rookeries where the rooks caw in hoarse tones above them, into the woods at the bottom of the estate. The mist has dispersed but the air is damp, the ground moist underfoot. Their feet slip a little on the wet leaves.

'Do you think it's still there?' says Jack.

'Wouldn't it be marvellous?'

They enter a familiar copse of oak and beech. The leaves are beginning to turn, their orange, yellow and brown shades lighting up the dull day. They take the right fork and there – by the stream, towards the old hollow where they once played – to their delight the house they'd constructed out of fallen branches is still standing, complete with the logs they used to sit on.

Jack laughs, his face looking 10 years younger. 'To think we built something so sturdy.'

He stoops down to enter. Daniel follows. They hunch over the log seats, like two old men sitting by the fireside.

'It's good to see you, Jack.'

'And you.' Jack grins. 'June seems a nice girl. Will there be wedding bells soon?'

'Maybe. I don't know. Look here . . .' Daniel stares at the ground for a moment. 'Are you alright?'

'Why wouldn't I be?'

'You seem . . . older, grimmer.'

'We don't sleep much.'

'I expect not.'

'It's not just flying missions. It's in between. That's when the mind starts to work overtime. Counting who's missing. Calculating the odds of it being your turn next. Worrying about what damage last night's bomb did.'

'June and I saw some pictures recently. Of the after-effects of bombing raids.'

'Don't tell me.'

'They were terrible, Jack, terrible.'

'Do you think I don't know that?' Jack pokes at a piece of bark with a twig. 'That the Jerries won't strike back in return? Look Daniel, I don't like this ruddy war any more than you do. But we're in it now. The sooner we finish, the sooner we can all come home.'

'Sorry,' says Daniel. 'You don't need a lecture from me, of all people.'

'No, I don't. You know I'd rather be defending the skies from bombers than doing the bombing . . . But it's not that simple. Besides, you should see the state London's in.' The bark crumbles, revealing a colony of centipedes and woodlice that scurry for cover. Jack throws the stick down. 'Tell me, how is Elsie, do you think?'

'Bearing up, I'd say. She misses you like hell.'

'Really?'

'Really.'

'Only she didn't come to the station, and she's been so cool. I was wondering whether she'd gone off me.'

Daniel fights down a shameful sense of glee at the idea that Elsie might be falling out of love with Jack. 'You're a prize chump if you think that.'

'I don't suppose I do, really. It's just . . . not seeing her for an age. And having so little time.'

'I'm sure she's done something to show you how she feels.'

'Well, she was wearing a knockout dress earlier.' Jack scuffs the ground with his feet, watching a cloud of dust appear.

'What happened to it?'

'I didn't realise at first . . . till Father pointed it out.'

'Realise what?'

'She'd adjusted one of your mother's.'

'Ah.'

'Needless to say, it didn't go down too well.'

'I bet not.'

'Have you ever told her about your parents?'

'No. It feels too complicated. I'd have to tell her everything else, too. You won't, will you?'

'Of course not. I promised . . .' Jack's eyes sparkle. 'How is the ankle, by the way?'

'Beginning to weigh on me, if you must know,' says Daniel. He stands up, stooping his head as he walks out of their construction, and wanders over to the stream.

'What do you mean?' asks Jack, joining him. He picks up a stone, puts it between forefinger and thumb before skimming it across the water. Daniel picks up a handful, flicking them one by one across the stream. They jump across the surface like tiny bouncing bombs.

'You're over there, doing what you're doing. I

don't agree with it, but I understand it. While here I sit, too scared to tell people what I think in case I lose my job; only willing to go to a vigil if I don't tell anyone where I'm going; not being prepared ever to admit I won't fight, in case they jail me. I'm not as brave as you. I'm certainly not as brave as my father. I'm beginning to ask myself, what kind of man am I?' Daniel throws the last stone with an intense fury; it bounces four, five, six times before sinking with a plop by a pile of rocks.

'The best of 'em,' says Jack. 'Don't be so hard on yourself. Who's going to look after Elsie if neither of us is here?'

Daniel grins. Jack has always had this habit of making things alright. He glances at his watch. 'We'd best be getting back. They'll be missing the star turn.'

When they return to the house, the room is half empty. June looks as if she's had enough; and, though Daniel is sorry to say goodbye to Jack so quickly, he is glad to get away.

'Poor old Elsie,' says June, as they reach the schoolhouse. 'Living up in that gloomy place with that terrible pair. However does she stand it?'

'I don't know.'

'I think we should take her out, cheer her up a bit.'

'That's a marvellous idea.'

'*Gone with the Wind*'s on at the flicks next week. If my aunt is home, she could look after Elsie's kids for her. We could go to the Saturday matinee.'

'That's wonderful of you, June. I don't deserve you.'

'Of course you don't,' June smiles. 'I'll ring them in the morning.'

To Daniel's delight, Elsie is enthusiastic about the idea when she pops in to see him the next day.

'It's so kind of you and June to take me out. I just had to let you know how grateful I am. I don't know what I'd do without you two.'

'It's our pleasure.'

'I've told the old bats we're going to a double bill, *In Which We Serve* and *Mrs Miniver*. I don't think they'd approve of Scarlett O'Hara.' Elsie grins. 'Pulling one over them. And nicking the radio to listen to *ITMA*. The only pleasures I have left.'

Still, the afternoon, when it comes, proves disappointing. The film is longer than Daniel had anticipated, far too melodramatic for his tastes. He'd hoped to sit between the women, but June arranges herself in the centre; he is forced to put an obligatory arm round her shoulders, trying to catch a hint of Elsie's lavender scent. That the women enjoy the film doesn't help, either. It's as if their sisterly appreciation has united them against him.

When it ends, Elsie breathes a contented sigh. 'That was wonderful. Thank you so much.'

'Don't mench,' says June.

Daniel had hoped that the three of them would grab a bite to eat afterwards, but to his dismay Elsie has to rush to collect the children. He watches her hips swaying up the aisle, wondering what it might be like to pull them close to him . . . Then, conscious of the woman beside him, he censors his imagination. June likes to sit till the music has ended and the last credit has rolled on the screen. When the lights come on and the usherette begins to turn the seats up, they realise they are the only people left.

'Dinner?' says Daniel, in an attempt to make amends for his mental infidelity.

'Don't mind if I do.'

'It was pay day yesterday. Let's blow it on a meal at the King George.'

The hotel is dressed in war-time colours, the once-white walls painted sober blue so as not to be picked out by searchlight. Every inch of the bay windows is blacked out, so that no chink of light can penetrate. They take their usual table in the corner, not far from the grand piano, then order a steak and kidney pie apiece. When the pies arrive, the pastry is leather, and the tiny amount of meat inside has congealed with the watery gravy that tastes predominantly of flour.

Two soldiers wander in, each with a girl on their arm. They sit at the table opposite, puffing smoke and telling jokes in loud voices. By the bar, a group of older men are arguing about the progress of the Desert Rats. As Daniel pushes back his plate to light a cigarette, a brunette in a black dress sits down at the piano and begins to play. She has a strong contralto voice, with enough tunefulness to make up for the missed notes and erratic tempo of her rendition of 'We'll Meet Again'. 'She's no Vera,' says Daniel, sourly.

'Don't be unkind. Her voice isn't bad.'

'Her playing is.'

'What's got into you all of a sudden? Didn't you like the film?'

'Just a bit out of sorts, that's all.'

'Join in the chorus,' says the singer. June needs little encouragement.

As he listens to her, Daniel feels wretched. June is perfectly lovely. She is good, kind and she loves him. It isn't her fault that Elsie got there first. Here she is, her eyes shining in adoration, thinking he feels the same, and all he's doing is stringing her along. She sways and smiles as she sings.

'Come on, everyone,' cries the piano player. 'Final chorus.'

The soldiers and their girls are singing their hearts out. Even the men by the bar sheepishly join in. Only Daniel is silent as the performance ends with cheers and applause.

'You really have got the glums, chum,' says June. 'What's up?'

This isn't fair. He isn't being fair. Daniel swallows, 'The thing is, June . . .'

'The thing is what?'

'Us.'

'What about us?'

'I'm no good to you.'

'I think I'll be the judge of that.'

Daniel gazes at the eyes that are trying not to fill with tears. He has nothing to offer her but cold words that have to be said. 'It's not your fault. It just isn't working anymore.'

'Daniel, that's not true.' June can't hide the tremor in her voice now.

Daniel stares at his beer. 'I am sorry. I am so sorry. You deserve better than this. Better than me. I'm just no good to you anymore.'

She stands up. 'You're a fool, Daniel Clarkson. Throwing this away.' She picks up her jacket and marches out of the dining room without a backward glance. It is done. He sits back, closing his eyes, as the woman at the piano sings a love song as if to mock him. If only he and June were meant for each other. But there's no point pretending anymore. It's all over between them. He is on is own now.

ELSIE 4

Elsie has read and reread Jack's letter so often that it is covered in creases. After the disappointing leave, it is the only proof she has that things are really alright between them. Though she and the children are supposed to be getting ready for chapel, she can't resist reading it again.

15th October 1942

My Darling Elsie,

I had to write the minute I got the chance. I've slipped Jimmy Green at the censor's office five bob to get this in the green channel to avoid those filthy black blobs everywhere. For once, I want you to be the only one able to read what I have to say.

I cannot bear that my leave was so disastrous. Please forgive me. I behaved like a boor. How could I expect you to stop my Father from meeting me at the station? When I know how single-minded he is, how determined he is to get his own way.

I am sorry I was such a selfish bastard. All I wanted was a brief respite from the war, some time pretending it didn't exist. I thought it would just be simple to pick things up with you all. But of course I am so far away from your life; I forget that small children don't quite behave like that. Of course Will wouldn't recognise me. Of course Evie would be scared. Didn't I do the same when my father came back from his war? Of course my parents would interfere with all our plans the minute I arrived. I was wrong, quite wrong to take it all out on you. I am so sorry my darling, please can you forgive me?

I feel that this rotten war has poisoned the one place in my head where I was at peace. I know I don't deserve it, but I will not be at peace again till you tell me we're alright. You're the only one, the only person in the world who truly knows and understands me. Keep faith in me now, won't you, old girl?

Write soon, and I will write sooner,

Your loving husband Jack xxx

PS And don't sit under any apple trees, or Else!!

The letter makes up for everything. It is the only one she's ever received that hasn't been inked out and pored over by goodness knows how many curious eyes. What type of person works in a censor's office anyway? The kind of kid who likes looking up girl's knickers, probably. She has already sent her reply, letting him know she understands, without going into too much detail. She hopes he'll be able to read behind the words that might be publicly consumed, to understand her real meaning.

Leah's knock catches her by surprise. It is nearly nine o'clock. Oh Lord, now she's for it. 'Coming,' she says, checking herself in the mirror. Her face is too pale without blusher, but she hasn't much left, and Jacob is bound to disapprove.

Leah glides downstairs in front of her. Since the party, she's had very little to say to Elsie that isn't absolutely necessary, and has spent more and more time in her suite of rooms upstairs. Sometimes, when Elsie is cleaning, she finds her mother-in-law in Henry's bedroom, caressing the suits left behind in the cupboards, burying her face in the smell of his shirts. Or standing on the landing, staring at the photographs in the corridor, whispering words that are impossible to hear. It is odd, unsettling; Elsie is always relieved when she vanishes back to her bedroom.

Most Sundays the family worship in the village church, but once a month Jacob fulfils his duty as a lay preacher in the Bryngraean chapel. Today being chapel day, Leah is more communicative than normal: a blessing of sorts, because chapel days are always hell. The penny catechism Elsie grew up with has much in common with the mores of her parents-in-law: sin, judgement and repentance feature in both. Yet it strikes Elsie that the God Leah and Jacob worship is lacking in some fundamentals – forgiveness, kindness, love. Chapel days mean a bumpy cart ride, often in the cold and rain, followed by a sermon by Jacob that terrifies the children. Today, there is a surprise; Jacob has to collect some papers from the office, so much to Will's delight they are taking the Bentley. The children clamber over the red leather seats, Elsie trying to restrain their too-enthusiastic bouncing. At least Leah is sitting in the front; she is less likely to admonish from that position. Jacob turns the car out of the drive, taking the vertiginous road to Bryngraean. It is a clear, sunny day. The road is lined with beech and oak trees dressed in autumnal colours, their branches unsettled by the gusts of wind that sprinkle leaves around. The chilly air is turning their faces red with cold, but the children are too happy to care.

They drive up the steep slope, passing the tramway to the left, the huddled houses to the right, till they reach the north-facing chapel. Tiny arched windows decorate the grey-stone walls. The roof is tiled with slate dug from the Flint quarry. A small bell hanging from the gable rings the worshippers to prayer. A trickle of people is approaching the chapel; the village population had dwindled even before the war. With many of the remaining men away, it is only the old and the young who attend the Sunday service now.

Even on the sunniest days the interior is cold and dark; the lights are needed all year round. Today, as she sits down, the air is icy. Elsie wishes she'd brought a warmer coat. The service begins with a hymn, one of Leah's favourites. She sings with fervour.

> *O'er the gloomy hills of darkness,*
> *Cheered by no celestial ray,*
> *Sun of Righteousness, arising,*
> *Bring the bright, the glorious day.*
> *Let the morning*
> *Of Thy blessed Gospel dawn.*

Elsie doesn't like this hymn; the later verses celebrate a colonialism she finds distasteful. She concentrates instead on making sure the children speak in whispers, that Will at least pretends to be reading the Child's Bible she has brought. Her head is so full of her letter she loses the thread of the service. It is a surprise to see Jacob has begun his sermon. She shifts in her seat, hoping he hasn't noticed. It is a faint hope; he holds his gaze on her the whole time, his cold grey eyes boring into her.

'From that moment in Genesis, when God took the rib of Adam to create Eve, He set in motion the path that it is ordained for us. Bone of bone, flesh of flesh, a man leaving his father and mother to be with his wife, so that they might become one. The Book of Proverbs, chapter 18, verse 22 tells us, "If thou findest a good wife, thou findest a good thing."'

Jacob leans forward in the pulpit. 'Of course, in the first Letter to the Corinthians, chapter 7, verse 9, St Paul is right in saying that the single life is the purest, the closest to God; but if we cannot control our lusts, "It is better to marry than burn." It is Paul, too, who reminds us that fidelity to God means fidelity between husbands and wives. For without fidelity, a marriage is NOTHING.' Jacob bangs his hand down so hard on the pulpit, the children jump.

'So, brothers and sisters, I ask you to examine your hearts and minds. Before God and your conscience, to ask yourself what state your marriage is in. Husbands! Remember the warning in the Book of Revelation, chapter 2, verse 20: Jezebel is waiting for you, always ready to lead you astray. Wives! While your husbands are away from you, do not be tempted to behave like the woman in Proverbs chapter 7, verses 6–23: the one who behaved with such wickedness, seducing young men with scents and fine bedding.'

Jacob pauses, looking directly at Elsie. She gazes back at him, trying not to blush at his unwanted attention. 'And so, brothers and sisters, I say this to you. Be faithful to one another, and to God. Be faithful like the Israelites were faithful, each tribe ensuring they did not take foreign wives. Be faithful like the daughters of Zelophehad, who followed the law and married only those of their tribe. Be faithful to each other and to God and your marriages will be blessed, and your homes will be happy, flesh of flesh, bone of bone, man and woman becoming one.'

He steps down from the pulpit, rejoining them in the pew as the congregation sings 'Guide Me O Thou Great Redeemer'. He doesn't look at Elsie, and yet she is sure he had meant her to pay attention to every word.

Jacob does not mention the sermon as they leave the chapel. He herds them into the car, driving up the broad slope to the offices at the top of the hill. When he emerges clutching some ledgers and a box of papers, he notices Will looking at the tram tracks.

'This place will be yours one day, William. It is high time you had a look.'

'I think he's a little small to be going into the quarry,' says Elsie.

'Nonsense. My father took me down when I was his age, as I did my sons.'

'He is too young.' Elsie looks towards Leah hopefully. 'Don't you think so?'

'Mr Flint always knows best.' There is always a hint of resentment behind the older woman's compliance, yet she will never publicly contradict her husband.

'I want to go.' Will can barely contain himself.

'You see, the child is eager to come.'

185

There is nothing for it but to follow them to the edge of the tramway, where even on a Sunday a small group of men are unloading large slabs of slate from the trucks. The wartime schedule is no respecter of the Sabbath. The driver unclips the tram-horse from the end of the wagons. It stamps and snorts as he leads it to the other end, refastening it so it can return down the slope.

'Come up, son,' the driver calls.

Jacob lifts Will onto the cart, following behind. The driver cracks his whip and the horse is away, Will dwarfed in the seat between his grandfather and the driver. Elsie can hardly bear to watch. The trucks dip down the slope, the little boy turning for one last glance, like Persephone descending into Hades, and he is gone.

The women stand in silence for a moment. Evie tugs at Elsie's skirt, wanting to explore the top of the slope. Leah returns to the car as Elsie and her daughter clamber over gravel and shale. At the top of the ridge they find a pool, its clear waters reflecting the sun and sky in a perfect mirror – azure blue, sycamore yellow. It takes her breath away to find such beauty here on the scarred hill-side. Evie scampers about, throwing stones at the water.

'Careful, darling, not so close to the edge; that water is very deep.' Elsie tries to avoid looking at her watch. She hopes Jacob is right, that Will's trip to the quarry will not terrify him, as it once did his father. Twenty minutes pass; it must surely be time for them to return. But when she wanders back down to the tramway entrance, there is no sign of them. The wind blows up the valley; Evie is cold and tired, so Elsie leaves her in the car and returns to the entrance of the tunnel. Still no sign of the wagons. Where are they? To distract herself from her nagging fear, Elsie closes her eyes, letting her mind return to those last few precious hours with Jack . . .

After making love, they had lain in the darkness, etching the moments in their minds, imprinting themselves on each other. At six, driven by hunger, they had tiptoed down into the kitchen to spend the last hour watching the grey light of dawn sneak through the blue-black clouds. Elsie rustled up breakfast, a mush of powdered egg, potato and onion – a pale imitation of the boarding-house fare she'd once provided.

'It doesn't matter,' Jack said. 'It's better than mess food any day.'

She sat down beside him and began to eat. The sky brightened to a clearer blue, suggesting a better day ahead.

'I say, Jack, what was all that about yesterday, with your aunt's dress?'

'Old arguments.'

'About what?'

'I don't know exactly. Mother and Aunt Rachel . . . they fell out.'

'And it's not forgotten? Not even in death?'

'Not even in death.'

'How sad.'

Jack finished his meal, pushing his plate away. 'I won't, you know.'

'Won't what?'

'Do what my father says.'

'Won't you?'

'No.' He leant towards her, taking her by the hand. 'No. Honestly. I hate that bloody quarry. It can be sold, taken over. I don't care. When this war is over, I'll come back for you. We'll go back to Liverpool. I'll set up a new practice. We'll start again.'

She squeezed his hand tight. He kissed her on the lips, an intense kiss full of love, longing, the imminence of departure.

'I hate to leave you.'

'I know.'

'You'll never leave me, will you, Else? I couldn't bear it if you left me.'

'Where on earth would you get that idea?'

'Oh, don't mind me, it's just sometimes, the lads in the mess, they'll tease us old marrieds about what our girls get up to in our absence . . .'

'Not me.'

'I know that, really I do.' He danced her round the kitchen singing, 'Don't sit under the apple tree with anyone, Else, but me, anyone Else but me . . .'

She laughed at the way he personalised the song, joining in till they finished in unison, 'You're my L-O-V-E' before collapsing with giggles back in their seats.

★   ★   ★

188

The clip-clop of the horse's hooves breaks into her thoughts. She looks up to see a tiny light coming towards them as the cart emerges from the quarry. Will's face is ash white. He is shivering. His grandfather sits beside him, his back rigid with anger.

'It was a little strong for him,' says the driver, as he lifts Will down.

'It's alright, darling, it's alright.' The little boy trembles in Elsie's arms. 'I said he was too young.'

'He's a milksop, just like his father. He'll need to toughen up if he's to run this quarry one day.' Jacob climbs down from the truck. 'Let this be the first lesson.'

He strides off down the hill, leaving Elsie to comfort her distraught son.

'I hate that quarry,' says Will, when he has recovered sufficiently to return to the car. 'I'm never going to work there. Never.'

'It's alright,' says Elsie. 'I'll make sure you never do.'

DANIEL 4

'This is not the end. It is not even the beginning of the end. But it is, perhaps, the end of the beginning.' Churchill's words fill Daniel with disgust. He switches off the radio, kicking the kitchen table in his rage. How many thousands have died without an end in sight? How many more will die before it is over? Only yesterday he read of a bombing raid in Liverpool, in the old neighbourhood; 10 dead and 30 wounded. He wondered if it was any family they knew. And Jack is over in Germany somewhere, delivering the same to the other side . . . None of it is any good, none of it. He looks out at the garden. The trees are leafless; their debris litters the lawn in brown decaying piles. He should have raked them up when he had the time at half-term, but since June left he has been unable to muster the enthusiasm. It is just after four; the sky is already beginning to darken. He hates this time of year. When the days are this short, it feels like night has fallen before he's had time to take off his coat. Tomorrow is Armistice Day. He hates that too. He glances over at his only photo of his parents. He remembers his father talking about Remembrance once, not long before he died. How it should be conducted in a spirit of regret, the hope of war no more. Now it seems to Daniel that the ceremony has been twisted, forcing the nation into a jingoistic celebration of the glory of battle, the noble soldier, the righteous cause. He will go through the motions at school tomorrow, observing the silence as is expected, but all the while he will seethe with rage.

This is no good. If he stays in this mood all evening, he will be in a terrible state by bedtime. He must get out of the house. He pulls his coat back on, marches out of the front door before he can change his mind. The wind is cold, forcing him to pull his collar up. Uncertain which way to go, he finds himself heading for the war memorial. Tomorrow, he will join the villagers in laying their wreaths; he doesn't doubt their sincerity, but he'd rather mourn the dead alone tonight. He arrives at the stone cross, staring at the familiar names: Jones, Edwards, Clark, Thomas, Davies. Tommy Davies, old Mrs Davies's husband, killed on the Somme without ever meeting the son who shared his name. Peter Edwards died on the morning of the Armistice, as the ink dried on the ceasefire treaties; the generals refused to abandon their fight till eleven o'clock, condemning several hundred more men to an unnecessary death. His mother, Heather, never recovered from the shock, leaving the raising of Peter's younger siblings, Alfred,

Sarah and Henry, to her sister-in-law. There are already six new names waiting to be carved when this war is done, and who knows how many more? They'll include Alfred Jones, who'd escaped the last conflict only to be drowned in the flight from Dunkirk; George Thomas, Geraint's only son, killed on the frontline in Italy; and, of course, his cousin Henry, sunk when his ship went over a mine in the Thames. How could one tiny place stand so much loss? And what right has he to feel so sorry for himself, when he is safe and well? When he is too scared to be the man his father was and stand up for what he believes?

He is beginning to feel cold; above him, the night sky is darkening, the evening stars beginning to emerge. He checks his watch; the pub will just be opening. He might as well call in for a pint before supper.

As he is turning back to the road, he is startled to see someone standing a few feet away in the gloom.

'Hello?'

His question elicits no answer. Approaching the still figure, he recognises his aunt. She is dressed in black; her eyes are blank. How long has she been there?

'Evening, Aunt Leah.'

'My son is dead.'

'Aunt Leah? Is something the matter?'

'One son is dead. The other fights to defend us. While you . . .' She spits the words out. 'You hide among women and children, just like your father before you.'

'I can't fight, Aunt Leah . . .' He hates this lie, but to be safe, he has to maintain the fiction. 'Because of my ankle, remember?'

It doesn't matter; she doesn't appear to hear him. 'You are like your mother. You can't be trusted . . .'

'Why don't you come round to my house? Have a glass of water?'

'You should leave us.'

'Sorry?'

Suddenly his aunt rouses herself; she pushes her face close to him. 'You can't be trusted. Nor can she. You should leave us alone.'

'I don't know what you mean.'

But she cannot be appeased; an implacable Fury, she continues to hiss her rage and spite. There is no point standing here, listening to it. He make his way down the hill, slightly unsettled by the encounter.

The Whetstone Arms is cold. Ellen Morgan will not be using her precious coal for another two weeks at least, but Daniel's glad to be out of the wind. The pub is empty except for Geraint Thomas and Harry Evans, who are already sitting in their usual spot by the empty fireside. They acknowledge Daniel without inviting him to join them. He doesn't mind, after his meeting with his aunt; he'd rather drink by himself. He steps up to the bar, orders a pint of beer. The brown liquid fills the glass till it froths over. Ellen leaves it to stand as she collects his payment.

193

'Terrible news about young Tommy Davies,' she says, giving him his change.

'I hadn't heard.'

The froth on his beer dies down. Ellen tops it up before handing it to him. 'They received the telegram this morning. Killed in a sortie.'

'Where?'

'Some place with a funny name. In Tunisia, I think. I thought you'd know all about it with your connections at the hall.'

'I only visit occasionally,' says Daniel.

'I thought you and young Mrs Flint were pally.'

'I only visit occasionally,' Daniel says again, with a firmness he hopes will end the conversation; he is keen not to provoke gossip. He takes his pint and sits in a corner as far away from the door as possible, hoping he has found the warmest spot. He pulls his coat round him. Young Tommy Davies, dead! Poor bastard. He sips his beer. It is warm and bitter. He rolls it round the tongue. Once, he and Jack drank ginger beer with Tommy in the woods. They'd sat round their camp fire, pretending they were grown-ups, mimicking the men they'd watched through pub windows. Tommy was knock-kneed and big-eared. He, too, was fatherless, though he never let Daniel forget his dad had died a war hero. And now, he's gone, leaving another pregnant widow behind. How will his wife bear it? How will his mother? What a bloody waste. What a bloody, bloody waste. He drinks his beer, deciding not to have a second. There is no point sitting round here in the cold, getting drunk and maudlin. At least, unlike Tommy, he has the luxury of life, and a chop to cook for tea.

The thought of tea reminds him that tomorrow is shopping day. Elsie will be coming and, because of Armistice Day, the school will close early. His spirits rise at the thought of seeing her; she's the one person guaranteed to cheer him up.

He is not disappointed; the following day she bursts into his tiny hallway chatting excitedly, 'We've had a splendid time in Sandstown. I'm sick of running my life to Leah's timetable. I decided to make a day of it for once.'

'We had toffees,' says Will.

'I saved coupons,' Elsie smiles. 'And we saw a brass band.'

'I'm going to play the tuba when I grow up,' says Will. 'I don't like the quarry.'

'How do you know that?' asks Daniel.

'Jacob took him after chapel,' says Elsie. 'I knew it would be a disaster, but he insisted; you know what he's like.' She takes off her green hat and gloves and lays them on the kitchen table. Then she finds some paper for the children, who start scribbling immediately. 'Do you want a hand with putting these away?'

'I can do it later. Why on earth would Jacob put Will through that?'

'Insurance, I expect. Jack made it perfectly clear he'll have nothing to do with the wretched place, so he thought he'd prepare the next generation.

Silly old fool.' Elsie grins. 'It backfired on him – one trip and Will's been put off for life.'

'You're in a good mood.'

'It was fun, being out of the house like that. I should do it more often. The news seems a bit better too . . . I can't help feeling that perhaps the war's going our way at last.'

'Perhaps.'

'Mind you, it was terrible about Walker Street. Did you read about it?'

Daniel nodded.

'And poor Megan Davies. Annie Thompson always delivers her post to us, so I had to bring it round to her.'

'How awful.'

'It was. She didn't want to take it at first. It was almost as if she thought the news wouldn't be real until she opened it.' Elsie shuddered. 'But you know what was worse . . .'

'What?'

'Leah didn't say it, but I saw it in her eyes when Annie told us. And I know we both felt it. The thought we shared: *Thank God it wasn't Jack*. Is that too terrible of us?'

'It's quite understandable.' Daniel paused. Should he mention Leah's behaviour the previous night?

'Mind you, it's one thing sharing a single guilty thought with her. It's quite another trying to get along. She's been unbearable lately.'

'More than usual?'

'Actually, she's been a little odd. I catch her staring at me sometimes, it's quite unnerving. Some days she stands in the hallway mumbling to herself, but I can never work out what she's saying. It's very worrying.'

'She crept right up behind me at the war memorial yesterday, without saying a word. I suppose she was there for Henry. When I spoke to her, she kept saying I was hiding here while one son was dead, the other fighting.'

'That's hardly fair.'

'No, but . . . some of the things she said seemed to suggest she thought that you and I . . .'

'That's ridiculous!' Elsie all but stamps her foot.

'I suppose because June's gone, people are talking.'

'There's nothing to talk about. People are so sordid . . . Oh Lord!' Elsie puts her hand to her mouth. 'That's what Jacob meant by it.'

'By what?'

'Last Sunday. His sermon . . . The importance of fidelity. I was sure he was directing it at me, but I couldn't think why. It's because he thinks . . . That's so stupid . . .'

'It is.'

'What are we going to do?'

'I don't know.'

'I can't bear the thought of not seeing you. You're the only real friend I have here.'

'Perhaps we could meet somewhere private.'

'But where can we go without the gossips looking?'

'Down by the river?'

'Too many people . . .' Elsie thinks for a moment. 'Arthur's Stone. Do you know it? Hardly anyone goes up there but me.'

'That's perfect.'

'That's it then. We'll meet there. On Saturdays, at two o'clock?'

Daniel nods.

Elsie is nearly out of the door when she stops with a cry. 'Oh, I nearly forgot. I bought you a birthday present. I know it's a few days early but . . .' She searches in her bag and brings out a book. 'It's a first edition. I was so chuffed when I found it.' She hands it to Daniel.

'*A Farewell to Arms*. How marvellous,' he says, inspecting the blue and orange cover. 'I remember the excitement of taking this out of the library. I must have renewed it 10 times before I took it back. It's very generous of you.'

'Don't be daft – I found it at the flea market. It's to say thank you, too; a reminder of old times.' She gives him a peck on the cheek as she leaves. 'You're so good to me, Daniel. I don't know what I'd do without you.'

After she has gone, he sits at the table, gazing at the front cover: the lovers coiled with passion, yet somehow apart. A reminder of old times: those old times in her father's house, when the three of them would talk about the rise of fascism, the war in Spain, the hope that peace might still be possible. Jack wasn't interested in books; Elsie had reserved those conversations for Daniel alone. He'd always had a little frisson that they shared something his cousin couldn't understand, and he'd savour every moment. Was it then that he'd fallen in love with her? Or did it stretch right back to that first day, when she'd opened the door and he and Jack felt an angel had answered their prayers for a decent set of lodgings? He puts the book down. None of this is any good, none of it. He lost her years ago, that day in Southport, and if he'd been a wiser man he'd have left her with Jack, and broken free. Yet he never had been quite able to do that, even though he knew it was hopeless. When her father died and Jack was vacillating, was it some kind of masochism that had urged him on? *You can't leave her*, he'd said, *you can't*, while Jack trotted out his pathetic excuses: *I've still got exams. What will we live on? What will my father say?* Daniel had knocked them down, one by one: *She'll support you; you've got enough for a simple life; sod your bloody father for once.* So Jack had sodded his bloody father for once, taking Elsie away forever, leaving Daniel locked in this endless conflict between friendship and desire.

He picks up the book again. The woman on the front cover lies sensuous, her arms stretched back to the man who bends his head towards her with a mixture of ecstasy and agony. Daniel considers what Jack has done for him, keeping him out of the war, not berating him for cowardice – even now, with the fighting as bad as it is. The only repayment he's ever asked is that Daniel take care of Elsie, keep her safe, offer sanctuary from his parents. She needs him alright, but as a friend, not a lover. If he is going to hide away with the women and the children, the least he can do is fulfil this obligation to his friends. Their Third Musketeer, offering all he had for them, as they would for him.

It is the least he can do. For old time's sake.

ELSIE 5

'Can I bring my aeroplane?' asks Will, waving a Meccano creation as Elsie pulls on his wellington boots.

'You might lose it.'

'I won't, I won't, I promise.'

Elsie is about to insist, but Evie wants the toilet. By the time they have returned, Will is halfway up the garden path, carrying his plane aloft. She lets it go, not wanting to return to the house. Though the kitchen is clean, lunch prepared, the laundry done, it would be better not to bump into Leah, who is bound to find another task for her.

Outside, the sky is slate grey, threatening rain. Jacob is by the flower beds talking to the gardener he has hired from Sandstown to clear the leaf fall and cut back the dead foliage. He hails them as they pass. Instinctively Will shrinks behind his mother. Elsie squeezes his hand in reassurance.

'Going for a walk?'

'Yes.'

Jacob pauses, then addresses Will. 'Are you ready to redeem yourself, young man?'

Will looks at his grandfather, puzzled.

The old man adds, 'I am visiting the quarry tomorrow. I think you should accompany me.'

'It is clear he is too young,' says Elsie.

'The only way to overcome fear is to conquer it,' says Jacob.

'Or deal with frightening things at a more suitable age.'

'If you spare the rod, you spoil the child.'

'I have to disagree,' says Elsie. 'I'd ask you to respect that. Or shall I write to Jack for his views?'

Thankfully this is enough to silence him; he resumes his discussion with the gardener. Once out of their grandfather's presence, the children scamper ahead to the woods.

'Be careful,' says Elsie. 'It's going to be slippery.' The last two days have seen heavy rain; she dreads to think what the paths are like.

The outer trails are slightly soft, but as they enter the heart of the wood, the mud thickens. Before long they are glad of their boots. Will laughs as his feet sink into the black goo, enjoying the squelch as he pulls them up. But the bogs are too much for Evie, whose short legs seem to disappear into the deep mud. At one point her foot sticks so hard they have to wrestle with it for ages till Elsie can get it free. The little girl is so upset she refuses to walk any further, forcing Elsie to carry her. They make slow progress. A couple of times, Elsie nearly slips, bringing them all over, but as they reach the edge of the woods the paths begin to dry out, and Evie is able to walk unassisted again. They emerge onto the rocky path leading to Arthur's Stone. The wind is beginning to blow stronger, the clouds moving fast in the grey skies above them. With any luck the rain will hold off. Above them a kestrel circles in the sky; in the field below, a sheep bleats. They begin to make their ascent.

It is a strenuous march to the top. The children don't seem to mind, and at least it keeps off the cold. Just as they near the rocks, they see Daniel laying out a picnic blanket; for once, his leg doesn't seem to be bothering him.

'You've come prepared,' says Elsie as she looks at the blanket, the shortbread, the flask of tea and the cigarettes.

'I thought the children might be hungry.'

They sit on the rug, the children delighted with their biscuits.

'Your leg doesn't seem to be giving you gyp today,' says Elsie.

'Some days are better than others.'

Elsie lights a cigarette. She gazes out at the valley. The bracken has died back, leaving brown patches across the green hills opposite. Small trees huddle on the slopes, providing shelter for sheep. Even though the colours are duller than in the summer, there is something beautiful about the landscape.

'I love this view,' she says, 'whatever the time of year.'

'I know what you mean.'

'Mind you, the first time I came it was night,

so we couldn't see anything but the sky. That was the point – Jack wanted to show me the Perseids. It was magical.' She takes a drag from her cigarette, her face glowing in remembrance. Then she catches Daniel's gaze. 'I'm sorry, you must still be feeling a bit raw after June. I didn't mean to rub it in.'

'Life goes on . . . Did you know, this is where my parents used to meet? Dad proposed on this very blanket.'

'How romantic.'

'It was . . . They were.'

'You never talk about them much.'

Daniel pauses, stubbing out his cigarette. 'They were very happy together, but they were unlucky, too. They died too young.'

'Tell me about them.'

But Daniel shakes his head and won't be drawn. The children finish their shortbread; Evie clambers across the rug and climbs on Elsie's lap. Will jumps up with his Meccano aeroplane.

'Can I play now?'

'Stay near the stones – don't go too far,' says Elsie. She turns back to Daniel. 'If you ever change your mind . . . I'm a good listener. And I do understand a bit, I think. I feel that way about Mum. Dad, on the other hand . . .'

'He wasn't the easiest of men, was he?'

Will runs up and down beside them, throwing his plane, chasing to see where it lands.

'Too right. When he died, I thought I'd escaped

for good. But since the war, all I've done is exchange one tyrant for two.'

'Oh, Else.' He puts out a reassuring hand. The pressure is pleasant, calming. Maybe a little too comforting. She pulls her hand away. 'Don't pay attention to me, it's not that bad really. I'm feeling a little put out because Jacob's still harping on about Will going down the quarry.'

'You're not going to let him?'

'Over my dead body.' Elsie glances up to where Will had been standing a minute ago. 'Where's he gone?'

They stand up. It is Daniel who spots him first, running down a dip in the hillside. Elsie yells a warning. 'Will, come back up here at once! I told you not to go too far.'

The little boy looks at them and grins. Much to Elsie's relief he turns back towards them. She sits back down and pours some tea.

Suddenly Daniel jumps up. His ankle seems to be functioning perfectly, but there's no time to wonder at that because Will is shouting and when she turns round, she can see he has slipped over and is beginning to tumble down the hill.

Before she can do anything, Daniel is running, properly running, and is just in time to stop Will toppling over the edge. He grabs the boy, carries him back up to where Elsie is standing. She stares at Daniel. At his ankle, at his face, then back at his ankle. She knows she should thank him, but she can't stop staring.

'It's not how it looks,' he says.

'Isn't it?' She is too angry to say anything else. She gathers the children up and marches down the hill.

How could he have lied to her? And for so long? How could he? When Jack and so many others were fighting and suffering? What a coward, what a ruddy, ruddy coward. She should go straight home and report him to the authorities. Then he'd see.

They reach the wood and are just navigating the muddy swamp when Daniel catches up with them. Evie is in a panic again and Will is cross with her for leaving Daniel, so there is nothing Elsie can do but accept his help. Once back on firmer ground, she tries to ignore him and walk away, but he grabs her by the arm.

'I can explain.'

'Can you, indeed? I'd like to know why you're pretending you have a gammy ankle? Why you are skulking among women and children while real men are dying on your behalf?'

'Jack knows . . .'

'That his cousin is a coward?'

'He helped.'

'I somehow doubt it.'

'You've got to believe me.'

'I have to believe nothing.' Daniel opens his mouth to say something, but thinks better of it. 'You know the worst thing?' He shakes his head. 'Leah and Jacob have been right about you all along.'

'Please let me explain.'

'There's nothing to say. I'm done with you.' They have reached the bridle path to Echo Hall.

'Come again next week, so we can talk.'

'No.'

'I'll wait for you.'

'You'll wait in vain.'

This time, he lets her go. As she strides back home, she realises she can't rat him out, but also that what she said is true: she is done with him. Leah and Jacob were right, after all: he's no good, never has been. It is a bitter truth. It means she has lost her only friend. She is on her own now.

And yet, as the week passes, she cannot shake Daniel from her mind. She finds herself remembering evenings in her back parlour in Liverpool, reading Dickens and Shakespeare, listening to his accounts of the sadnesses and joys of the Brontë sisters. Daniel on the beach, that happy day in Southport, taking her arm, and joining in the laughter as they posed for the photograph. Daniel's comforting hug at the graveside when they buried her father, his warm embrace on her wedding day. He has been part of her life too long for her to abandon him now. How many times in the old days did he console her when she'd suffered the after-effect of one of Dad's benders? How many times in the past couple of years has he consoled her through Jack's absence, providing company, intellectual stimulation, an escape from Leah and

Jacob? She finds herself wishing she could take back her ugly words, wondering whether she should reach out and offer forgiveness instead of condemnation.

But then another picture comes to her mind. Megan Davies's pale face the day she and Annie Thompson knocked on the door of the coach house. Her hesitant hand refusing the telegram that she knew could only contain bad news. How, at last, she was persuaded she must, and how they watched her read the words, not seeming to comprehend their full meaning. How, after Annie left, it was Elsie who took her through into the back kitchen, boiling the kettle to make a useless cup of tea that could never assuage the grief the other woman was feeling. All the while wondering how Megan was going to bear it. Her baby was due in four months; how was she going to raise it alone? And how would old Mrs Davies bear the loss of her only son to add to the loss of her own husband all those years ago?

When she thinks of Megan, Daniel's behaviour fills her with fury. What right does he have – single, childless as he is – to be sitting here safe, when widows were being made, when children were being orphaned? The bitter thought forms: what right does he have to be here, when Jack is not? Why couldn't he be on the frontline, keeping Jack at home with his family? And yet . . . he said Jack knew everything. He said Jack helped. Was that true? All week the argument rages in her head

– whether to forgive or to condemn – until she is almost driven mad by it. And then on Friday, when Annie brings the post, there is a surprisingly large packet for her. For a moment, she thinks it is from Jack, but then she sees the flourishes and curls on the E and the S that mark out Daniel's handwriting. She hurries upstairs so that Leah won't see, hiding it in her room till bedtime. The day passes slowly, tempered with crotchety children, domestic tasks, family dinner and prayers. At last she is alone, and able to open it. Inside she finds a pile of letters. The top one is from Daniel, but the others are in handwriting she doesn't recognise. She picks up Daniel's letter up and begins to read.

School House
Main Street
Whetstone
19th November 1942

Dear Elsie,

I know that I am the last person in the world you wish to speak to at the moment, and I cannot blame you for that, but nor can I leave things as they are. I know I don't deserve your friendship and if I have lost it, I have only myself to blame. But I also know how fair-minded you are, and I can only hope that you still have enough affection for me to hear me out. And that once you have done so, you will better understand me.

The only way I can explain this is to tell you a story. of my mother Rachel and my Aunt Leah, who were once known as the 'Porcelain Sisters'. It was a name that captured my imagination when I was little. Because they reminded me of a pair of china dolls, so fragile they would break at the slightest touch, I assumed it referred to their looks. But as I grew older and put childish things behind me, I discovered the truth was less romantic. My grandfather, Geoffrey Walters, was a skilled potter, who made a name for himself by dint of craftsmanship, ambition, and sheer hard work. Eventually, he was able to establish his own business, which proved to be highly successful. By the time he was 50, he had factories all over the Midlands, producing china that furnished every dining room in the country. This earned him the name of the Porcelain King and his daughters the nickname that so enchanted me.

I never met my grandfather. For years, I failed to understand why. All I knew was that, after his break with my mother, he refused to entertain the idea of her continued existence, let alone mine. It was not until after his death that my presence was even acknowledged through a codicil to his will. But, though I never met the man, in time I came to know his house intimately. Whenever he was out of town, my grandmother would secretly entertain us. While she sat in the drawing room talking to my mother, I'd roam his suite of rooms, searching for clues, forming an image of him from the traces he left behind – a silk dressing gown, bottles of hair dye, the smell of stale cigars. When we returned to whatever seedy boarding house we were living in at the time, I would take his picture from our bedside table and stare it. The photograph was taken shortly after the family moved to Sandstown. My grandfather stands on the lawn in front of the house beside the cedar tree, smoking a cigar. I have studied this picture for hours, trying to understand how such a genial-looking man could have acted the way he did. But the photograph holds no answers. Its subject is long dead. For years the photo was all I had. It was not until my 21st birthday, when my mother's friend Sandra sent me their extensive correspondence, that I learnt the story behind our family feud.

I am sending these to you, as I believe they will provide you with all the information you need. I have selected the most relevant, and have annotated them on occasion to clarify an issue or cover a period of time that was not particularly significant. It is my hope that when you have read them, you will have some sympathy for the choices I have made.

The letters span 13 years, from 1911 to 1924, just before my mother's death. They begin the summer the new king was crowned, the year of unbearable heat, the year my grandparents moved to Sandstown.

Daniel

THE PORCELAIN SISTERS

1911–1924

My Dear Sandra,

I must apologise for the long delay since my last letter. My poor excuse is that the upheaval of moving has thrown us all into disarray. It is only now we are firmly established in our new home that I have the energy to take up pen and paper to write. I cannot begin to imagine how you managed to move continents with such ease in the spring. Birmingham is a mere two hours' train journey away, and yet I feel my whole life has turned higgledy-piggledy ever since we left. I am not sure I will ever get used to it.

As you know, it has long been Father's dream to leave the city; so, not surprisingly, he has settled in like a pig in clover. Mother has always supported his every venture (whatever her own feelings might be on the subject) and Leah, of course, was never fond of urban living. So I appear to be the only person in the family who is not yet comfortable. Already I am missing the company of old friends, the delights of balls, concerts and parties. Sandstown has been *interminably* dull so far – no theatre, a tiny Assembly Rooms and, since we have yet to be launched on the social scene, no interesting people to entertain us (this may be rectified tonight – but more of that later). The one bright spot is that there is a half-decent department store – Broughtons – in the centre of town. Though it is nothing like as magnificent as Selfridges, the staff assure me they always have the autumn collections the moment they are out. So, even though I am out in the sticks, come September I won't be dressed like a country bumpkin.

Oh dear! I have just read back these opening paragraphs, and all I have done so far is complain. I must hasten to add that it is not *all* bad here. The house is rather lovely, and I have made sure to bag the best bedroom – fortunately Leah doesn't care about such things. Right at this moment I am sitting in my favourite spot on the windowsill. It is deep and lined with comfortable cushions, the perfect place for reading a magazine, watching the comings and goings of the household, or writing a letter. Today is so hot, it is the coolest place I can find. The windows are open, and the shade from the privet tree offers some protection from the intensity of the sunshine. Looking out, I can see Father standing underneath the Lebanese cedar, smoking a cigar, surveying his new empire with pride. I've heard him boast so much about his recent acquisition, I can imagine that he is taking a moment to revel in the perfections of our new home: the house is large enough, beautiful enough, modern enough to impress his fellow capitalists in town. What's more, its situation is ideal. It is close enough to the town shops to satisfy Mother and yet backs on to farmland, providing the illusion that we are living on the country estate he has long desired. It thus provides the perfect matrimonial compromise.

He has finished his cigar. I'm watching as he throws it on the browning pine needles under the tree, crushing out the remaining sparks with his foot. He stops on his way back to the house . . . I can hear him telling the gardener to deadhead the roses – a wilting flower or two cannot be allowed to blemish the flawlessness of the garden. I can see Hodges nodding his head. Is it my imagination or is he a little impatient in his response? After all, doesn't my father pay him to take care of the gardens? He has his shears beside him; perhaps he was just about to do the job when he was stopped. It's no matter, I suppose; the flowers will be deadheaded, the gardens will maintain their perfection, and father can enter the house satisfied. In a moment I will hear him ascend the stairs and turn to his dressing room, where Peters is preparing the wax for his moustache. For tonight my parents are hosting their first dinner party and he will be keen to impress.

Here are his footsteps now . . . he passes down the corridor. I hear the door of his room open, Peter murmuring greetings. We will not see him for a couple of hours, when he will emerge in his dinner suit, moustache and hair oiled, the image of the country gentleman he aspires to be.

Next door Mother is turning in her bed, worn out by proceedings before they have even begun. As you know, she is easily exhausted, and the excessive heat has confined her to her bed in a darkened room, a damp cloth over her brow. Even though Mrs Paterson, the housekeeper, has everything under control, Mother will be worrying whether the cutlery is polished, the Watermeadows china collected, the black and white tiles in the hallway sparkling clean. I will have to pop next door in a minute to reassure her that all is well. I will remind her that Mrs Paterson is an able housekeeper and that her new chef M. Bertrand has created an intriguing menu that is bound make her mark on the Sandstown dinner-party circuit. Mother likes to shine at the dinner table; and since she has few other opportunities to show off her talents, who can blame her?

Mother is calling, I must finish this letter and go and see what she wants. Then Leah and I must make ourselves ready for the evening ahead. Let's hope our preparations are worth it.

Your loving friend,

Rachel x

Harmony House
Sandstown
15th July 1911

Dear Sandra,

Thank you so much for your lovely letter. I am glad to hear that you have settled into a lively social circle and have begun to make friends. I'm pleased to say I too can report that in the last month I have developed a congenial group of acquaintances and am much more reconciled to Sandstown life. In fact, I have been so busy with engagements this is the first moment I have had to write to you.

This change in my circumstances can be traced back to my parents' dinner party, which has resulted in a friendship that I hope will be long-lasting. The evening began well, because, as you know, getting ready is my favourite part of the proceedings. There is nothing quite like the delicious pleasure of pulling silk stockings up my legs, or letting Ginny pull my corset tight and help me into my dress before arranging my hair. (As you know, I love playing with different styles; that night I opted for an imitation of Queen Mary – I do love her elegance!) And there is no greater delight then trying on a new gown for the first time. I wish you could have seen me in my latest purchase! It is deep-blue silk, with an empire waist, an outer gauze jacket, decorated with Belgian lace. I looked divine in it.

Leah thinks I am vain to admire myself in the mirror as I did that night, and I maybe she is right to call me shallow. Yet I cannot always help myself. I love to look pretty – is it so terrible to celebrate the fact? Of course, Leah finds the whole business of dressing up rather sordid. However, she has come to the conclusion recently that it is a necessary evil: the means by which she will find the husband she desires. So that night she abandoned her usual dour greys and browns for a charming pink silk, and it was a fine pair of lovelies that descended the staircase.

Oh! But it was stiflingly hot in the drawing room, even with the French windows open. It was tedious to wait in such uncomfortable conditions, and initially we were grateful that the Flints arrived promptly at eight o'clock. There are three of them – Mr Aaron Flint, and his sons Reuben and Jacob; they run a quarry over the border at Bryngraean. Though Father has not been explicit on the subject, it was clear from the moment he presented us what manner of transaction was taking place. After all, wasn't this the means by which he and Mother were brought together? Leah, clearly, had no qualms about being paraded before the young Flints as an item for purchase; she wanted to examine them too. I was less keen.

I imagine Father and Mr Flint have already discussed the matter, and the plan is to unite Leah with Reuben, the eldest, but I could see straight away that it was Jacob who caught her eye. I can understand why; he has the seriousness she needs. He was dressed in black, his face solemn, his grey eyes direct. She told me later she felt they were staring into her soul. Personally, I found them quite chilling – they reminded me too much of the sea in winter: cold, dark, unfathomable. But we always have had different tastes. I agreed with her judgement of Reuben. When I shook his hand I had the sense his eye was cast on some far horizon; I do not believe he will fulfil his father's hopes by proposing to either one of us. And to be honest, the thought is a relief to me. I am not too keen on the idea of our parents choosing our life partners for us. What is wrong with us deciding for ourselves?

After our introductions, the Flints sat down so stiffly they reminded me of a row of gravestones. And the conversation that followed was equally deadly: slate orders, transport and union problems. It seemed to go on for hours, but was in fact only 20 minutes, and was thankfully interrupted by the arrival of the Earnshaws, which immediately livened things up. Mrs Earnshaw and her daughter Kitty are gorgeous creatures; they darted around the room, chattering about their recent trip to London while Mr Earnshaw beamed jovially. Immediately, they seemed a much better bet than the dour Flints, and so it proved at dinner time.

While Leah was making the acquaintance of Jacob Flint, I set out to discover a little more about Kitty Earnshaw. What a lovely woman she is! And so interesting! Her parents seem to have given her free rein in all things – she has studied Latin and Greek at a local college. She has attended socialist meetings and thrillingly professes to support the suffragettes: a piece of information that might have remained between us, if Father's bullishness hadn't brought it out into the open later on.

He was drinking heavily all night; and, after we had finished with dessert, launched into a long monologue about the deplorable state of the Navy. I could see Mother raise her eyebrows in warning: that discussing the government's war preparations was not suitable dinner-time conversation. It was no use; he was oblivious to her. So she tried another tack, inviting Mrs Earnshaw to support her assertion that men dwell on politics too much. Instead of agreeing with her, Mrs Earnshaw declared that giving women the vote might make such conversations less tedious. Father laughed at this, arguing, as usual, that we women are too weak and foolish to be given such a responsibility. Then gloriously Kitty entered the fray. I was so taken with what she said, I can almost repeat it word for word. 'Who says we are foolish?' she cried. 'Men. Who says we cannot understand complexity? Men. And who denies us the right to vote? Why, men again.'

This time, Father picked up on Mother's cue and attempted to end the discussion, telling Kitty that she would learn in time that the views of her elders were based on sound common sense. To my delight, she answered him back, stating this would never happen, and that one day we would see women in Parliament.

Of course, Father would have been horrified if Leah or I had expressed such an opinion, but I could see he found it rather charming from the mouth of such a good-looking young girl. It left him speechless; and while he was trying to think of a witty riposte, Mother seized her moment. She rose from the table, leading us out of the room. I grabbed Kitty's arm, and spent the rest of the evening by her side. Since then we have become firm friends. She has introduced me to some other families – the Fortescues, Lyndhursts and Elliots – and all of a sudden I find myself invited every-where. As a result, life in Sandstown has improved considerably.

The evening was a great success for Leah too. On discovering that Jacob Flint is a lay preacher at the chapel in Bryngraean, she managed to wangle an invitation to visit. Of course, I had to accompany her; and since then she's managed to volunteer us to help out at his mission, which is a terrible chore. But I'll do anything for her happiness – and if this will help win his hand, it is probably the least I can do. Talking of beaus, do write soon about the inter-esting gentleman you mentioned in your last!

Your loving friend,

Rachel x

Harmony House
Sandstown
8th August 1911

Dear Sandra,

Thank you so much for your lovely long letter. I was quite taken with your account of hiking in the Canadian Rockies. How exciting! And to have actually seen a grizzly bear . . . I doubt that I'll ever experience such thrills in my own life, so it was wonderful to receive your lively account and enjoy the experience vicariously. I am also greatly interested in your developing friendship with Mr Franklin. He sounds charming and I hope to hear good news on that front in the not-too-distant future.

We have had a very busy summer here too, though somewhat less thrilling. Sundays are taken up with visits to Jacob Flint's mission. Oh the things I do for my sister! These afternoons are so dreary . . . We arrive at three o'clock, in time for the opening hymn – usually Leah's favourite, 'O'er the Gloomy Hills of Darkness', which given the chapel's setting in the shadow of the hillside is particularly apposite. After the hymn is finished, Jacob Flint leads us in prayer. We stand, eyes down, hands together, united in preparation for the important work we are about to commence. It is all so terribly solemn I often find myself trying to suppress a giggle. It is a fatal flaw in my character that I want to laugh in the most inappropriate of circumstances, so I have to bite my lip very hard and pretend piety with the rest, or else Leah will never forgive me.

Prayers and hymns done, we line up at Jacob's table while he gives us each a list of addresses, a pile of paper and stamps, and we retreat to our desks where we set about writing our letters of appeal for the Missions. The only sound is the scraping of pens, and the quiet 'Thank you' from Jacob as we finish our allotted pile and take the next one. Leah is assiduous; she writes with twice as much care as I do, yet somehow manages to produce double the amount of letters. She always has had much more self-discipline than I – though of course it is not just the cause that inspires her so. Since the dinner party she has developed the strongest of feelings for Jacob Flint and I do believe this could be a good match for her. He is sober and hardworking, deeply religious and sincere. They seem to me to be ideally suited, and yet I must confess to a slight anxiety about it . . . I know I am a vain little peacock, but it is not unusual for men to show more of an interest in me than Leah, and I can often tell the signs. I do not think I imagined him blushing when I brought my letters to the table yesterday, nor the firmness when he pressed my hand as we left. I daren't tell

225

Leah and I do so hope that I am wrong, for she rarely exposes herself like this. She feels things so deeply that I would hate to see her hurt. For my part, I am taking very great steps to praise her at every turn and ensure that he has no cause to think I have any special regard for him. For even if I am right, surely he will quickly see that I am far too slight a creature for a man so serious?

Thankfully Sunday is only one day of the week. The rest of the time Kitty Earnshaw is on hand to ensure my constant entertainment. We see each other every day. We wilt at tea parties alongside the cucumber sandwiches following exhausting games of tennis. We escape the summer heat to wander in the cool of the art gallery, where she educates me on the finer points of the Impressionist movement. At night-time we slip outside the stuffy ballrooms to talk about politics and literature while we gaze at the stars.

I like her enormously, and know you would too. She has your adventurous spirit, and is bringing it out in me. While it is nowhere near as challenging as a visit to the Rockies, she has dared me to attend a suffragette meeting with her in a few weeks. You may remember that last time I attempted such an enterprise Leah stopped me in my tracks as I was sneaking out of the house. On that occasion she persuaded me to stay at home, pointing out that Father would be horrified and Mother would be embarrassed. It was enough to make me lose my nerve. But I feel bolder with Kitty beside me, bold enough to face their wrath if I am discovered. Though I hope that won't happen; this time I have made Leah promise not to tell.

Your loving friend,

Rachel x

Harmony House
Sandstown
25th August 1911

Dear Sandra,

I woke early full of the events of last night, and am bursting to tell someone. Alas! This is something I can't share with Leah. I am glad I can write to you instead!

I left at seven, having told my parents that Kitty and I were going to a concert at the Assembly Rooms. Jamieson dropped me at the Earnshaws' and we walked into town from there. The air was heavy and thunderous as we passed the cathedral. It really is a magnificent building. I love the animals that decorate the buttresses – the fox, kitten and spaniel are particular favourites. We hurried on to the Shire Hall, as rain looked imminent, and we were astonished at the crowds pouring in. Mabel Henry is clearly a popular speaker!

The hall was packed with women. To my surprise, there were some men too, and as we were looking for seats, one of them rose and offered me his so Kitty and I could sit together. I was very grateful; it was hot, and I was beginning to feel faint. I glanced up at him, nodding my thanks, glimpsing a tidy moustache, a round soft face, black curls. He stood by the wall just behind us, waving his pamphlet up and down. Had Mabel Henry not stood up at that point I might have been tempted to turn round for another look.

She is a fascinating woman, so slight in build; at first glance, I wondered how she had the strength to resist the police. But when she began to speak, her ability to command a situation became apparent. She was mesmerising. I wish you could have heard her. She talked of the progress the movement was making, the inspiration of the Pankhursts, the challenges to come. As she reached her conclusion, announcing a forthcoming march in London, the storm broke. There was a crash of lightning and the rain drummed on the roof as if in tumultuous applause. There was a marvellous moment where the whole room rose to their feet, including me. For an instant I was seized by the wild idea that it would be a wonderful to be part of this, that I *must* make plans to join the march. Then the applause died down; people began to sit, or move forward to sign up, and the feelings drained away. It is one thing to sneak out of the house and attend a meeting, but the idea of going to London without Father's knowledge! I think perhaps it would be easier to write to my Member of Parliament instead . . .

Kitty has no such doubts, but then her father is of a different breed entirely. He *approves* of her being involved in the suffrage movement, can you imagine? She dashed to the front to put her name on the list and express her gratitude to the speaker. I sat down to wait for her. To my dismay I caught sight of the Lyndhursts, making their way across the room to the exit. It wouldn't do if they spotted me, so I stared at my lap for as long as I could until I was sure they had passed out of the hall. When I glanced up, I found myself gazing straight into the face of the nice young man. To my surprise, instead of succumbing to my usual shyness, I was bold enough to thank him for offering up his seat.

He introduced himself as Joseph Clarkson, a teacher, formerly from Yorkshire. When I expressed my surprise that a man might attend such an event, he claimed that, as a Quaker, it was his duty to fight unpopular causes. That made me smile, as did his assertion that he taught history, geography and the decline of the British Empire. Apparently he has recently taken up a position at the grammar school after he was asked to leave his previous post. When I asked why, he explained that he taught that the Boer War was an unnecessary foreign adventure, the last gasp of a dying kingdom. He said that the concentration camps and the messy peace would cause no end of problems in the future, which was always the way with war. No wonder the governors asked him to leave! He claims that he has seen the error of his ways and these days teaches by the book. But I cannot tell if this is the truth or not, because it was all said with a twinkle in his eye and a charming smile.

Kitty returned, and though she was unable to persuade either myself or Mr Clarkson to attend the march, she somehow managed to invite him to join us in the park on Sunday. She also forced him to compliment me in such a way that my cheeks burned with embarrassment. I could have cheerfully killed her until I reflected that he is, after all, a pleasant young man, and at least it will provide me with an excuse to escape Jacob Flint's miserable sermons. With the arrangement agreed, he bowed low to us before setting off into the crowd to greet some friends. Kitty took my arm as we left the building.

Of course, Kitty being Kitty teased me all the way home about my new beau, even though I assured her that I am not in the husband market yet. I am not averse to meeting Mr Clarkson again – he has a very lovely smile – but I am too young to consider romance!

It was past eleven when the Earnshaws' chauffeur deposited me at my front door. Thankfully the whole house had retired and I was able to reflect on the evening on my own. I will have to keep so much of what passed hidden that it was a relief not to have to face questions about the concert programme, and the quality of the pianist. But once in my nightgown I was far too stimulated to sleep. So I wrapped myself in an eiderdown, climbed into my window seat and gazed out over the lawn. In the beauty of the night I felt for a moment that anything was possible. Do you ever experience that sensation? That somehow there is a realer, more vibrant life, beyond our immediate experience, and that if one could only reach out and grab it, things might be quite different. Perhaps it's just whimsy, but for a few seconds, I felt as if another future was entirely within my grasp. And then the moon went behind a cloud, and the feeling faltered in the darkness, and I was tired all of a sudden, more than ready to climb into my bed.

In the cold light of day that fancy seems a bit foolish now, but I do believe last night will have an effect on me for a long time to come. It seems to me that for too long I have accepted the assumptions that have surrounded me from childhood. That it is my duty to follow the edicts of my Father, marry where he suggests, and then to comply with the rule of the husband chosen for me. Today, I find myself asking – as others do – what right men have to rule the world with such confidence? Shouldn't we all have a happier, more harmonious existence if the sexes could find a way to live as equals? Do you find yourself having similar thoughts, Sandra? Or has a night among the suffragettes turned my head?

This is far too serious a train of thought before breakfast, and now it occurs to me that I am faint with hunger. I will pop this in the post bag right now, and bid you farewell, for my mind is set on bacon and scrambled eggs.

Your loving friend,
Rachel x

Harmony House
Sandstown
25th September 1911

Dear Sandra,

I received your letter this morning and was so excited by your news that I had to respond immediately and offer you my warmest congratulations. It sounds as if Mr James Franklin is a kind and thoughtful man, who is utterly worthy of your affections. It is encouraging to hear that he, like Mr Clarkson, is a supporter of the suffrage cause. It gives me great hope to think that, among our generation, there are men willing to align themselves to women and have more enlightened views then their fathers.

In answer to your question, I have seen a great deal of the aforementioned Mr Clarkson since I last wrote, and yes, I do like him *enormously*. Kitty and I have continued to meet him in the park each Sunday and the three of us have such an interesting time. Both he and Kitty have seen so much more of the world than I have, so our conversations are always stimulating, particularly on matters of social concern. Kitty, for example, has opened my eyes to the evils of the garment industry, and the sweatshops in London, where young girls sew for a pittance. She recommends buying from the more fashionable stores only, as at the higher end of the market the seamstresses are likely to be paid a reasonable wage for their efforts. Mr Clarkson, meanwhile, has been telling me more about the actions of our military leaders during the Boer War, and I am afraid it does not cast our nation in a favourable light. I have always believed it is a fine thing to be born British, to be part of the Empire. I remember how proud Father was when Lord Kitchener commissioned him to design a dinner set commemorating the South Africa campaign, but now I wonder whether all was as glorious in that war as we were led to believe.

And yet, sometimes, I feel the pair of them are too serious altogether, and need a little levity in their lives. So when I have had enough of politics, I force them to sit down on a park bench with me and observe our fellow promenaders, making observations on their outfits and mannerisms etc., until we are in paroxysms of laughter. So our afternoons are very agreeable and we are all three of us becoming the firmest of friends – the Three Musketeers – all for one, and one for all.

Leah was cross when I stopped going to Bryngraean, but she cannot complain as she can still attend with Ginny as a chaperone. I have a feeling that this is as much a pleasure for Ginny as for Leah; I detect she has more than a passing interest in the Flints' coachman, Davies. Of course, I have had to give Leah an excuse for not visiting, so I've told her I am helping Kitty with the Methodist poor boxes. It's not entirely a falsehood; we do sometimes pop into their hall on the way home (and I am certainly more inclined to help there, where we can do some real good, than write any more fundraising letters for Jacob Flint's missionaries!). But it's not the full story. I had intended to take her into my confidence, but I'm afraid we had a falling-out just after my visit to the suffragettes, which has made me trust her less. An argument that arose because, despite her promise to keep my secret, she revealed it within 24 hours!

Two days after our evening with Mabel Henry, I came into breakfast to a decidedly frosty atmosphere. When I asked what was wrong, I was confronted with my actions. There was no point in pretending; knowing Father, denial would only make things worse. I have learnt over the years that the only possible response to misdemeanour is the appearance of docility and remorse. I appreciate it is duplicitous, but sometimes duplicity is the only way to avoid his rages, and, as usual, it worked. Gradually, he softened his stance, particularly when Mother intervened. Fortunately she thinks highly of the Lyndhursts, so hearing they were there helped persuade him that my behaviour wasn't completely beyond the pale.

I suppose I should have mentioned Joseph Clarkson then, but it seemed too difficult at the time. Father has made it absolutely clear that he expects

Leah and I to marry wealthy men. The introduction of a young male school teacher as my newest acquaintance will take careful preparation. And besides, I am not sure quite what my feelings are about the young man in question, so why cause upset unnecessarily? I said nothing and steered the conversation to less dangerous subjects. Breakfast ended with Father in good spirits again, as he was off to meet the owners of the new hotel, who are keen for him to supply them with china.

Things were less straightforward with Leah. I was livid with her, and, once my parents had gone, said so. She made no attempt at contrition, claiming that she couldn't help herself. Apparently Father had been berating the suffragettes all evening. When he declared that I was the epitome of womanhood for attending a concert rather than Mabel Henry's talk, something snapped and she blurted it out. This infuriated me all the more, and I was about to explode when she said in a rather sad voice that I needn't worry, he'd forgiven me as he always does. She added that as his favourite, I can never do any wrong really, whereas she is always on the outside, always ignored. I had no idea she felt like that, and the minute she said it, my anger dissipated. I have to admit there is some truth in what she says; Father has always indulged me more than her, and that isn't fair of him. So I have resolved to be kinder and to try to ensure Father gives her praise where it is due.

And yet, since then, I have felt unable to trust

her completely. It's not just that she betrayed me. I don't think that she would approve of Joseph with his lowly occupation and unorthodox ideas. Besides, if she were unable to keep one tiny secret, I doubt she could keep this bigger one. So I have continued to meet him privately, while I decide whether the friendly feelings I have for him might perhaps develop into something deeper. I am not exactly proud of it, but I think it is better this way for the time being.

Your loving friend,
Rachel x

Dear Sandra,

Thank you for your letter and excellent advice, which is most helpful. I know you are right – I *should* tell Leah about my trips with Kitty and Joseph, but I can never seem to find the right moment. Part of the trouble is that she has been distant with me since the summer, and is spending so much time doing good works to impress Jacob Flint that she is rarely in. When she is home, all she wants to talk about is Jacob, for she is convinced he will propose soon, so I never have a chance to speak myself. Worse still, I fear she may be heading for disappointment in that regard, and have no idea how to broach the subject with her. I have a horrible feeling Jacob may be developing feelings for me. I may be wrong, but if I describe our recent visit to Echo Hall, perhaps you will see why I am worrying . . .

It was a foggy night, and had Father not been so determined not to offend the Flints, I think we would have avoided the journey. Jamieson is a careful driver, but even so the road to Whetstone felt perilous and we were glad to reach

239

our destination in one piece. Leah was enchanted by Echo Hall, but my first thought was that was a gloomy place to live. The house is approached up a steep hill, past a row of fir saplings on the edge of a dark wood. Its grey walls and large windows offer no welcome to visitors, and its location is as cold and bleak as its owners. It had an air of such misery I wanted to leave as soon as we arrived, but alas! There was no chance of us being able to escape.

The party was a small one – just us, Jacob Flint and his father. There was no sign of Reuben, nor any mention of him till we were halfway through dinner, when it emerged he has left England to work in the colonies for a mining company. My mother was horrified at the idea that Jacob had let his son travel to the other side of the world. She was not at all persuaded by Mr Flint's assertion that this was God's will and that Jacob could take his place at the quarry.

Jacob's change in fortunes has served only to increase his attractiveness to Leah. Though he has agreed to abandon his dream of being a minister, he will continue as a lay preacher at the Bryngraean chapel. But, more importantly for Leah, he will now inherit Echo Hall. He is all she has ever wanted – a man with a rich spiritual life and a large establishment; how could she not fail to love him?

It is unfortunate, therefore, that she did not appear to notice how often his eyes would focus on me when he thought no one was looking. How he pressed my hand a second too long when making a point about the problems unions caused. How quick he was to put on my cloak when we left. I would like to hope it was my imagination, but I don't think it was. And so, at bedtime, I tried to warn her in the gentlest way possible not to get too fond of him. It was no use. I simply prompted along speech about his kindness, his appreciation of her assistance and admiration of her good works. She is convinced that his invitation for us to visit the quarry means he is nearly ready to propose, and I cannot persuade her otherwise. I fear this will not end well.

Speaking of marriage – a spring wedding sounds splendid. I only wish you were not so far away, so we could come. I look forward to hearing about all the preparations in the meantime.

Sending you so much love,

Rachel x

Harmony House
Sandstown
30th November 1911

My Dear Sandra,

How lovely it was to return home to your letter and read about your wedding plans. I love the sound of your dress – lace over silk with a long train is exactly what I imagined for you. You will look divine!

We have just come back from a visit to the Flint quarry. I would have done anything to avoid such an outing, but Leah was determined to go; and when Ginny fell sick, I had no choice in the matter. The place is as grim as Echo Hall – no: grimmer. There are no luxuries for the inhabitants of the ugly slate cottages, who live surrounded by machinery, gravel and dark hills. As we arrived we saw a gang of men loading slate onto the train. I felt so sorry for them. It was pouring with rain and they had no protection while they worked. I was extremely conscious of the fact we had arrived in a fine car, and were fortunate to have Jacob there to usher us in out of the cold. I would have been grateful had he not taken my hand first, squeezing it firmly. Thankfully Leah didn't seem to notice.

We sat in Jacob's office as he arranged for cocoa to be brought to us. It was warm and dry, but I found it hard to relax when I could see the workmen still hard at work. Jacob seemed indifferent to their needs, however. When I asked if they would have a break soon, he said they wouldn't, but it didn't matter as they were used to it. I bit back the comment that that was all very well for him to say that, but he was sitting in the warm, drinking chocolate; I must say, Joseph Clarkson, with his passionate support for union men, had never seemed so charming. Leah had no such qualms about Jacob. She gazed at him constantly, seemingly unaware that he was casting furtive glances in my direction. If only I could have warned her of the danger she was in, but Leah is so stubborn! Once she believes something, it is impossible to dislodge that belief and it always ends in heartbreak.

When the rain had stopped, Jacob was keen to show off his empire. We emerged from the hut as the slate-filled train puffed past us and the workmen moved on to the next task, winching the empty trucks back up the hill. Another group pulled them to the quarry mouth and loaded them with more slate. There we found a horse hitched to two carriages. As we climbed on board, a young man – no, a boy; he couldn't have been more than 14 – dropped a block of slate. It shattered into several pieces. The foreman strode over, clipping him on the ear. The boy began to pick the pieces up, grinning ruefully at me; we turned the corner, and he fell out of sight.

We descended into darkness, the only light the tiny electric lamps on the wall. It was such a miserable journey! I felt like Persephone descending into the underworld. The cold made me shiver and I cursed Leah inwardly for persuading me to come.

As we approached the bottom of the shaft, we could hear the sounds of men shouting to each other as their chisels hit the rock. The horse came to a halt at the base of the slope, which led into a huge gallery, tunnels radiating from its centre. Men were hard at work prising slate away from the surface of the rock, which would be later loaded onto trucks and taken to the surface.

It was a lot to absorb all at once. It had never crossed my mind before to wonder about the work these men undertook. I watched in horror as two workers balanced on tiny ladders at least 40 feet up. It seemed such a dangerous occupation to me, and yet Jacob Flint appeared quite unperturbed at the thought that his workforce might suffer injury, or even death. I turned away. How could he stand to come down here, knowing people worked like this, and be comfortable with it?

Leah, of course, was convinced of his virtues. Even if the men are not unionised, she was happy to believe the Flints generous employers. I tried to smile and listen politely as Jacob explained how slate began. How the rock formed from mud flowing deep underground; how pressure and stress forced the crystals together, so they aligned into straight lines, hardening into rigid grey stone. But all I could think of was how soon we would get back to the surface. It was such a relief when he said it was time to go!

Leah was invigorated by the experience. She shook Jacob's hand warmly and was effusive in her praise for his work. He gave a stiff bow before grasping my hand, and thanking me for coming. His gaze was so intense, I couldn't possibly misinterpret his feelings. I don't know how Leah can't see it, but it is clear to me he is in love with me, which will mean upset for all of us. I fear the next few weeks will bring all kinds of unpleasantness but unfortunately I cannot think of any way to prevent it.

Much love,
Rachel x

Harmony House
Sandstown
23rd December 1911

Dear Sandra,

Christmas is just round the corner; we should, by now, be finalising preparations for the big day. But alas! Jacob Flint has put paid to that. Yesterday I glanced out of the window to see him walking up the path. He was dressed in his Sunday best, which immediately raised Leah's hopes. I tried to persuade her he was here on business, but to no avail: she was convinced he was coming to propose to her.

Once he was safely in Father's study we slipped downstairs to the drawing room. I stoked the fire as Leah paced the room; I'm not sure who was more nervous. Presently we heard footsteps in the hallway, the bang of the front door, and then Ginny entered saying Father wanted to speak to me. Of course, Leah declared she must be mistaken, but Ginny was adamant. There was nothing I could do but follow her. And though I tried to reassure Leah all would be well, I knew that I was about to break her heart.

Father, of course, was all smiles as he told me that Jacob would like to propose to me. He assumed

I would immediately say 'yes' so he was less than delighted with my response. Knowing the power I hold over him, I chose my words carefully, pointing out how little I know Jacob Flint, how unready I was for marriage. He was insistent that he thought this a good match for me, but I resisted as best I could. At last, I was able to extract a promise that I could have a few months before giving my final reply. It was the best I could do in the circumstances, but it was not enough to satisfy him. It was even less satisfactory for Leah. She refuses to believe that I have done nothing to encourage Jacob Flint and that I haven't been plotting this from the start.

Christmas is two days away but this house is far from harmonious. Father is not speaking to me and Mother has retired to her bed in despair. Worse still, a crack has appeared in my relationship with Leah, a crack that I am afraid may never be fully repaired.

Your loving friend,
Rachel x

Dear Sandra,

Many thanks for your latest most interesting letter. Your visit to the Indian reservation sounds fascinating. And I am so pleased that your plans are well advanced for your nuptials. I fear my recent letters have been very dull in comparison, but in truth there has been little to tell you. It seems that in winter the inhabitants of Sandstown hibernate like dormice, and no amount of cajoling will persuade anyone to have a dinner party or attend a concert for fear of catching influenza!

The first thing of note is to say that Leah and I have reconciled with each other. My parents, as you know, quickly forgave me, but she has been giving me the cold shoulder for so long that it had become quite tedious. Despite the state of affairs with Jacob Flint, she has continued to help him at Bryngraean each week, though she never discusses him with me now. In fact she has only spoken to me about domestic matters, and that only when absolutely necessary. At last, after several weeks of this, I could stand it no more. I decided to confront her one afternoon when I

248

found her sitting alone in the drawing room watching the trees blowing in the wind. I told her that I done nothing to encourage Jacob, and was convinced that he could never make me happy. I said that I didn't understand what he saw in me, other than the fact that I am so different from him.

She turned on me then, saying that by 'different' I must mean more beautiful, more charming, more precious than her. She practically spat the words out. Though I was startled by her vitriol, it made me more determined to try to make the peace.

So I tried again, explaining my belief that Jacob's interest in me is likely to be fleeting. He is so very serious that perhaps my light-heartedness seems attractive at the moment. But how could it possibly last? He has no time for dancing and entertainments; he has no interest in fashion. I am far too frivolous for him. We have nothing in common; I am sure it is just the idea of me that has caught his attention. The real me, the woman who finds chapel tedious, who likes to buy clothes and wear jewels, will only disappoint.

Thankfully, this seemed to have some impact. Gradually, the poison left her voice, her wavering smile indicating a forgiveness of sorts. So things have returned to a kind of normality. I think she has recognised that I have gone out of my way *not* to see Jacob Flint and so she is beginning, perhaps, to believe that I did not encourage him as she had first thought. I know that I could have made it easier on her if I had told her about my meetings with Joseph Clarkson, but I have been so angry with her, I haven't felt inclined. And when we had put our argument aside, I found myself unsure how to begin. While I hesitated, she was called away to assist Mother, who was feeling unwell, and the moment of opportunity passed.

I have, since then, been considering whether it is time I braved the inevitable upset to explain this friendship to my family. Before Christmas, I really wasn't sure enough of my feelings for him to think it worthwhile. But lately, I find myself thinking of him all the time. When I am not with him, everything feels duller; when I am about to meet him, my heart races 10 times as fast. I picture his face as I sit reading, think about him at dinner parties, dream of him at night-time. Is this how you feel about your James? Is this what love is like? If it is, I really should say something; but I have, as yet, had no indication from Joseph that he feels the same. Perhaps I should wait and see before I risk another family quarrel.

Your friend,
Rachel x

Harmony House
Sandstown
23rd March 1912

Dear Sandra,

I have the most exciting news to relate. I am engaged to be married! I am sure this news isn't entirely unexpected, given the tenor of my last letter, but let me tell you how it came about.

Yesterday Kitty had invited us to the Methodist picnic. It's an annual affair: after Sunday service the entire congregation sets off in charabancs for a ramble in the Welsh hills. For once I didn't feel too dishonest as I climbed onto the back seat alongside Kitty and Joseph. As we set off, a group of parishioners burst into a chorus of 'Let Me Call You Sweetheart'. Joseph and I joined in, and when he turned and smiled at the end, I knew he was singing to me. I smiled back, hoping to convey the same message. Shortly after we arrived at our starting point and spirits were high as we began the ascent of the hill.

As the morning wore on, the walkers began to spread out: the young and healthy at the front, the old and frail taking their time. But by lunchtime we had all made it safely to a plateau halfway up the hillside. We laid out our blankets, sharing a fine feast of ham and cheese sandwiches, pickled eggs and Dundee cake, washed down with cordial. Afterwards Joseph suggested a march to Arthur's Stone, a well-known beauty spot, where legend has it Arthur and Guinevere met and declared their love for each other. (Later she was said to have met Lancelot there too, which begs the question – why isn't it called Guinevere's Stone?) I was keen but the others all complained it was too steep, so in the end it was just the two of us that made the trip.

The path was sheer in places and a couple of times I slipped on the shale. But he was always there to clasp my hand, steering me safely to the top, where the view was as beautiful as he said. Below us the stone path continued down past the burial chamber on our right. Though it was rocky, the descent was easier than it looked, and we quickly reached our destination. Joseph took a blanket out of his bag and we sat down, testing out the natural echo chamber with our shouts of 'HELLOOOO, HELLOOOO.' The words returned from the valley: 'Hellooo, helloooo.' We both laughed, but I stopped mid-laughter as I caught sight of a horribly familiar spire almost buried in the fir trees.

I asked what village it was, though I knew before Joseph said the name: Whetstone. He wondered why, so I explained that behind those fir trees lay the home of the man I was supposed to marry. That my Father felt such a marriage would be good for business: the Flints' slate would build houses; the Walters' porcelain would decorate them. I told him how I'd struggled to say no when it was something my Father wanted so much, and yet how could I marry a man I detested, particularly when it would hurt Leah so badly?

He listened carefully. Then he took me by the hand and asked, 'Suppose you had an alternative?' Gazing at him, I realised how fond I had grown of his face: such a contrast to Jacob Flint, so grim and unbending. I replied that if that were the case, I would tell my father I was spoken for. He leant over and kissed me. I don't need to tell you how delightful it was to respond! We lingered on the hillside as long as we dared making the most of our time together. Just before we left, we entered the chamber, where Joseph took out his pocket knife and carved *J loves R* on the stones. According to local legend that means our love won't ever die. Isn't that romantic? After that we made haste back to the meeting point, so as not to miss the departure of the charabancs. We arrived only just in time just as the others were beginning to board.

It was getting dark when we reached Sandstown. Normally Joseph walks us to Kitty's house and the Eamshaws' chauffeur drives me home. Tonight, she showed no surprise when Joseph suggested he walk me himself. We took our time, savouring these first moments as lovers, our only interest each other. As we neared home, it occurred to us both that we should keep our engagement secret for

253

the time being. This will enable me to prepare Father in particular for the idea of a school teacher as husband. I was going to make an exception with Leah, but when I returned, she was in a scolding mood. She berated me for walking through town with a muddy skirt and messy hair, and would not hear my excuse that it had been a blowy day. So I shrugged and went to bed. I will find a way to tell her in the morning. But in the meantime it is delicious to share this wonderful news with you . . .

Your loving friend,
Rachel x

Dearest Sandra,

Well I'm in a pickle and no mistake. I suppose I have only myself to blame. I should have been more honest from the outset. My desire not to upset anyone has created worse upset, and now my entire family has stopped speaking to me. Worse still, I have been banished from the house.

Last night I returned from a meeting at Kitty's where we had been discussing the possibility of opening a suffrage chapter in Sandstown. My mind was full of the conversation and the news from London of the constant harassment of activists. So when I entered the hall, and Ginny said my Father wanted to see me, I thought nothing of it.

It was only when I entered the drawing room that I realised something was wrong. My parents and Leah were sitting stiffly side by side on the chaise longue, as if they had already passed judgement on me. Father looked stern, Mother stared in her lap, and Leah avoided my gaze. Before I could say anything, Father asked whether it were true that I was engaged to a 'mere' teacher. I said it was, and that there was nothing 'mere' about

Joseph. After all, am I not the granddaughter of a greengrocer? There's no shame, surely, in the daughter of a self-made man marrying an educated one, even if he is not wealthy? This sent him into a fury. Unfortunately, he looks like an angry walrus when angry, and I had to fight hard not to laugh despite the seriousness of the situation. I tried to explain that I had never tried to encourage Jacob Flint; that I had grown enormously fond of Joseph in the last few months and had not grown any fonder of Jacob.

This made him more furious still. He berated me for my deception and said I should be ashamed of myself. Well, I am, and I said so repeatedly. I tried to explain why, but it was to no avail. He claimed that my behaviour was disgraceful and I was a severe disappointment to him; in marked contrast to my sister, who had never given him any trouble. I happened to catch Leah's expression at that moment, and was disconcerted to see a satisfied smile on her lips, which soon turned to a disapproving frown as she nodded along to his condemnation of me.

I was further startled to discover that she was the cause of my undoing.

It seems that she saw Joseph and I that night we walked home. She was horrified by the sight of us kissing under the lamplight, and when I neglected to confide in her (oh silly, silly me, why did I let my irritation that night stop me?) she took it upon herself to look for evidence of our relationship. It appears that every time I have left the house, she has been searching my room, and yesterday finally found the proof she was seeking – a lovely letter Joseph sent after the picnic. She took them straight to Father, and that was that.

Father made it clear that the only solution was for me to break off the engagement, to save us all considerable embarrassment (I swear this is more of a consideration than my deceit!). He refused to listen to my apologies and gave me an ultimatum: give up Joseph, or leave. At first I couldn't believe he meant it and had to stifle a giggle at the sheer ridiculousness of the idea. It's all so stupidly Victorian. But when I glanced across at Mother and saw her staring into her lap, not daring to look at me, I realised he was absolutely serious.

There was nothing to do but take my letter and a carpet bag to the Earnshaws'. My state of distress was extreme – I could not believe that Father had acted in such a cruel way, that Mother and Leah had just stood by, that they had let me go. The Earnshaws welcomed me in immediately. They are as shocked as I am by Father's behaviour. They are kindness itself and have said I can stay for as long as I want. So, I will remain here tonight, and hope that Father will see sense tomorrow. Once he realises how happy Joseph makes me, surely he will forgive me?

Your loving friend,
Rachel x

Greenacres
Sandstown
15th May 1912

Dear Sandra,

Thank you for your last comforting letter. Hearing all your news about your wedding plans provided a welcome distraction from my sorry situation, and I appreciate your kind words on that subject.

You asked if things have improved since my departure from home. Alas! I have to report they have not. I was convinced that Father would not be angry for long, but when, the next day, I went to try to put things right, I was shocked to be refused entry at the door. The following week, at Mother's insistence, he agreed to let the Earnshaws come over and collect my remaining possessions, as long as I came nowhere near the house. Since then he has returned my letters unopened and, according to Mr Earnshaw, has told the members of his club that he has only one daughter now.

Mother and Leah are no better. Mother has never has been able to stand up to him, and so she silently supports his actions, even if she might not agree with them. As for Leah, I regret to say that she appears to have let all her former resentment dictate her behaviour to me now. She too returns my letters, and has joined the rest of the town in cutting me off. It is bad enough that my friends exclude me from social invitations, but when my own sister shuns me in the street – well, that is hard to bear.

Despite these setbacks, every moment I spend with Joseph makes me more determined than ever to marry him. He is kind, funny, patient. He respects my opinions and challenges my thinking. He always wants what's best for me – even to the point of suggesting that he withdraw from the engagement so I can return to my family. I said no, of course, but appreciated the gesture. It is such behaviour that convinces me that I have found a man who will make me happy – even if such happiness comes at a cost.

And it is quite a cost . . . We are currently planning our wedding, but I fear it will be very different from the one I dreamed of. Do you remember? I always longed for a perfect summer day. The sun would be buttercup yellow, no cloud would sully the azure-blue sky. My dress would be cream silk, my veil Belgian lace. I would wear orange blossom in my hair, be accompanied by four young bridesmaids, with Leah as their chief. Father would take me to the church in a shiny black landau, decorated with gold roses, identical to those in my bouquet. I would enter the church to Mendelssohn, leave to Handel. The wedding breakfast would be held in the best hotel, the food served on the finest Walters porcelain; afterwards my husband and I would depart for a honeymoon on the continent. All entirely possible for the daughter of Geoffrey Walters, but far beyond the resources of the fiancé of a school teacher. Fortunately Joseph is a practical man, and his proposal that we opt for a simple Quaker ceremony, with a party at the Earnshaws' afterwards, is really the only possible solution. After all, it is the marriage, not the manner of it, that matters isn't it?

So we have settled on a date in August and have begun writing the invitations. And though I am sad that Father won't give me away, Mother won't be there to weep for me, Leah to support me, I hide it from Joseph. It is not his fault that I was dishonest with my family, nor that they are so unbending. Strangely, I am discovering underneath my spoilt softness that my nature is more pragmatic than I'd ever realised. I can't change what has happened, and I am coming to the conclusion that the old adage is right – there really is no use crying over spilt milk. So I won't.

By the time this letter reaches you, you will be a few days off being married yourself. Joseph and I have despatched a small gift, which I hope will arrive around the same time. It is not as fine a present as you both deserve, but it comes with all our love and best wishes for a very happy day and many blissful years to come.

Your loving friend,

Rachel x

Post Script I was just about to seal this when

Kitty burst in with the most surprising news. Leah is to marry Jacob Flint! According to the town gossips, my behaviour brought him very low. In the days after my engagement became public, he absented himself from the quarry and chapel. No doubt he was pacing the corridors of Echo Hall brooding on the pain I had caused him. Leah took it upon herself to take care of his missionary work, and visited him every day with broth and comforting literature. It seems to have been a successful strategy. Jacob recovered from his heartbreak remarkably quickly for one who was previously so attached. So quickly in fact that the wedding will take place in the summer, shortly before ours. I always believed his feelings for me were superficial, so I am glad for both their sakes that I was proved right. And who knows? Perhaps, now Father has the marriage and Leah the husband they both desire, they will find it in their hearts to forgive me.

Chapel Cottage
Sandstown
14th August 1912

Dear Sandra,

By now you should be back from your Grand Tour and be able to receive correspondence again. I have so enjoyed your postcards from around the United States, and I am looking forward to a long missive where you can describe your journeys in more detail. Thanks too for the beautiful eiderdown you sent. It has pride of place in our bedroom.

It is two days since Joseph and I tied the knot, and I can quite honestly say that they have been the happiest days of my life so far. Even though I miss my family, I find that being Mrs Clarkson is a distinct improvement on being Miss Walters. And though the sun didn't shine for us, not even the rain could dampen my spirits!

Given the miserable summer we have had, it was no surprise to wake to grey skies, and no wonder that rain followed soon after. By the time I stepped out of the Earnshaws' Daimler, it was pouring, and I was forced to dash up the path to meet Joseph at the door. We entered the Meeting House together, as is the Quaker custom. It was a small gathering: 20 members of the Sandstown meeting, a handful of aunts and uncles from Joseph's family, and the Earnshaws. Right up until the last minute, I couldn't stop myself from checking the wooden doors at the back, just in case my parents had changed their mind. But the clock struck two, and there was no sign of them; so I focused my thoughts instead on the man sitting beside me. The clerk of the meeting introduced the service and the room fell silent. I was glad then that there was to be no giving away, that we would give ourselves to each other; it made my family's absence a little easier to bear. When the moment came, we stood up together. Joseph took my hands in his, promising to love and care for me. He placed the ring on my finger, and I saw as if for the first time: that all the finery and all the wealth my father offered was nothing in comparison to this. It was easy then to return his pledge and know that Joseph is everything I need.

So we are married. I have made my choice. Joseph is my husband, and I his wife. As I sat back down holding his hand, listening to the elders of the community bearing witness to the years of their own marriages, I knew without a doubt that whatever heartache it has brought me, this was a choice I will not regret. That, given time, I *will* be able to persuade Father of Joseph's virtues, that I *will* bring him round, and be reunited with my family . . .

Although we were a small party afterwards and,

unlike Leah and Jacob, could not afford the grandeur of the new King George Hotel, I dare say we had just as merry a celebration (no – a merrier one – they are too serious a pair for jollity!). The Earnshaws hosted a splendid buffet; there was dancing, conversation, charades; we were altogether tremendously cheerful all evening. We left at eleven to walk through the town to our new cottage, which is situated at the top of a small hill on the edge of town.

The rain had stopped; the evening warm. We were both too awake for sleep, and it was such a lovely night, so we sat out in the back garden stargazing. To my delight, the skies were clear enough for us to catch the Perseids – the annual meteor shower. Have you ever seen them? They are quite magical – silver darts of light criss-crossing the sky like fireworks – the debris from a comet on its annual journey round the galaxy. I know the display is simply an astronomical phenomenon, but it felt as if they asteroids had appeared just for us, as if nature was blessing our wedding. I leant my head on Joseph's shoulder, and was content.

Your loving friend,
Rachel Clarkson x

Chapel Cottage
Sandstown
14th September 1912

Dear Sandra,

The summer, such as it was, is coming to an end. The stubble is burning and autumn is already chilling the air. After a wonderful fortnight in the Lake District, duty beckoned and we returned to Sandstown so Joseph could prepare for the beginning of term. We had a few days of late starts and leisurely days, which were pleasant while they lasted. But, alas! Now term has begun, Joseph leaves early and returns late in the afternoon with piles of marking that keep him occupied till the evening. I remain here alone apart from Alice, our housemaid, and Mrs White, the cook, who comes at four to prepare dinner.

I am supposed to be in charge of our little establishment, but I fear I am quite hopeless at it. I should have paid more attention when I was younger, as Leah did, and watched how my mother managed things. It all seemed so boring and unimportant at the time, and I was sure that, when I finally did get married, Mother would be on hand to teach me everything she knew. I never imagined I would find myself in this situation, estranged from my family and with no one to advise me. I could ask Mrs Earnshaw, of course, but I feel I have asked too much of the Earnshaws altogether. And so I am muddling my way through Mrs Beeton (a wedding present from Joseph's aunt) and hoping for the best. I think it would be a lot easier if I could work out how to manage Alice, but it is beyond me at present. She's perfectly pleasant when Joseph is in the house, but with me she is insolent and lazy. I'm not very good at telling her what to do, I'm afraid, and I find that when she has gone home, she has left many tasks undone. I try my best to finish them off, but I am not very good at polishing and cleaning, so the house isn't as spick and span as I would like. Luckily, Joseph is fairly oblivious to his surroundings, and his main concern when he comes home is a decent dinner. At least Mrs White is a good enough cook and seems to make the most of the ingredients I buy from town each day. I suppose it is early days, and hopefully I will improve, but at the moment I feel that I have a lot to learn. Any helpful thoughts about how to manage a household (and better still, recalcitrant servants) will be gratefully received!

Other than that, married life is as blissful as I hoped it would be. After Joseph has finished his work, we dine at seven and share the day's news. He seems to enjoy my accounts of my domestic mishaps (buying pork instead of lamb, forgetting to instruct Alice to change the bedding, putting coal in the ice box), and is very encouraging about my progress, such as it is. In turn he tells me stories about his pupils and describes his teaching methods to me. Given past experiences, he is careful about what he teaches, of course, but I like hearing how he challenges their thinking by asking them to imagine alternative outcomes to historical events, and to argue different points of view.

On some evenings, we entertain. Kitty and her parents are frequent visitors, of course, as are friends from the Meeting House and those Methodists who still speak to me. I enjoy hosting such occasions, but, I think, what I enjoy most is when it's just the two of us sitting in the parlour reading together after dinner and Alice and Mrs White have gone home. It is at such moments that I feel very blessed indeed.

I'm also glad to report that I have some good news with regards to my family. I wrote to Leah in the summer, wishing her and Jacob well, and sending them a small present for their wedding. It seems that at last she was touched by this further attempt at reconciliation. Perhaps, because she has finally gained everything she has long desired, she can now afford to be generous. Whatever the reason, she has agreed to meet me, and we are currently trying to work out a suitable date. Although I am nervous, I am very much looking forward to it. I have missed my sister; it will be good to be friends with her again.

Your loving friend,

Rachel x

My Dear Sandra,

How marvellous to hear that you and James are expecting a happy event in the spring! And how strange that our lives seem to be operating with such synchronicity. For I too am pregnant – our baby is due in May, and so is Leah's! I made this delightful discovery when we met for lunch. How pleasing that we will discover the joys of mother-hood together.

I met Leah at the King George. Since I wasn't invited to her wedding, it was my first visit, and I have to say it deserves its reputation. Its black and white rafters are the height of modernity and inside everything is brand new and sparkling. So much so that I felt as if everyone was looking at me as I sat down. It was hard not feel ashamed of my old gown among the women dressed in the latest Doucets and Paquins and the smart young men debating the Irish Question. The sight of father's crockery on every table served only to remind me of my outcast status.

My unease wasn't helped by Leah being so late that I began to wonder if it was deliberate. It was bad enough feeling that everyone's eyes were on me, but I was even more humiliated when the Fortescues arrived. They swept past me without a word, even Lily. I am used to it by now, of course, but it still hurts that, only a year ago, she declared we would be friends forever; today she couldn't look me in the eye. Thankfully, Leah arrived shortly after. Apparently the car – a wedding present from Jacob – had got stuck in some mud, and it had taken some time to release it. I had to accept her apology at face value, but nonetheless, we were terribly awkward with each other at first. I was beginning to wonder if we'd ever speak to each other properly again when Leah suddenly commented on the appearance of our waitress. She looked just like the doll in a Beatrix Potter tale we'd loved as children, and the simple mention of it was enough to break the ice. So very soon, we were sharing news and having the merriest time.

A few months ago, I would have been envious of her trip round Europe, but once I had heard her account of it, I was glad we went to the Lakes. Jacob and Leah seem to have spent their time rushing from one capital to the next, and though she said she enjoyed it, it sounded rather like they were doing Europe by numbers. They had originally intended to visit the Balkans, but because of the recent troubles they gave it a miss. Leah says Jacob thinks it will soon blow over, but I am not so sure. Perhaps I am overly influenced by Joseph, yet I believe he has a point when he says that the treaties of great nations are piled like a pile of china plates. One false move and the whole lot will come crashing down. He says the governments across Europe have been buying arms for years, each trying to outdo the next; that the generals are like children, desperate to take their new toys out of the box so they can play with them. But of course, when they do so it will create mayhem across the continent.

Leah dismissed my anxieties. 'How can war break out in a world as peaceful as ours?' she said with an airy wave of her hand. Maybe she is right; in a room full of laughing diners, lulled by the pianist playing *Für Elise*, war didn't seem possible at all. Yet I can't help thinking how my life has changed beyond all recognition since last summer, when I'd had the self-same thought. I tend to agree with Joseph; we can't rely on the old certainties any more.

We parted company shortly afterwards, after I politely declined a lift home. Leah insisted on paying for dinner so I'd had enough of her charity for one day. Besides, I like nothing more than a brisk walk in the chill autumn air. The leaves are beginning to fall as the year begins to draw to a close. We often think of autumn as a sad season, as the trees bare their branches and the vegetation dies around us. And yet, surely, it is a hopeful time – the seeds spread by wind and bird will already have taken root. Come the spring, life will begin anew.

Your loving friend,

Rachel x

Chapel Cottage
Sandstown
11th November 1912

Dear Sandra,

I am writing in our little parlour at the back of the house. It is chilly, because although I have managed to get a small fire going, it is not a vigorous one. I am waiting for Joseph to come home from school and revive it. He is so much better at these domestic tasks than I am! I have just returned from an afternoon with Kitty to discover that Alice has taken the afternoon off. I really must take her in hand; this is the second time in a month. As it was, I was left to clean the grate and set the fire as best I could, which, as stated, is not very well. Still, I managed in the end. You'd have been proud, seeing me lift the coal and set paper alight as I have seen Joseph do. But it seems too much of an effort to toast teacakes now. Maybe I will, when I've finished this letter. Although I am beginning to feel a little strange, so perhaps I will have a lie down instead.

Note: it appears that this letter was never sent. I found it in my mother's papers after she died. My father returned that afternoon to discover she was

271

having a miscarriage and rushed her to the cottage hospital. Her life hovered in the balance for several days and, though my father was in constant attendance, and though Leah visited regularly, her parents never came. DC

Chapel Cottage
Sandstown
8th February 1913

My Dear Sandra,

I am sorry that I have not written to you since my miscarriage. Thank you so much for continuing to write despite my silence. Please do not think for a moment it is because I cannot bear to hear about your ongoing pregnancy, as you suggested in your last letter. Let me reassure you on this point: your letters have provided nothing but comfort and delight these past months. My lack of response has not been due to offence, but simply the desperate sadness I have felt for the loss of our child, and the difficulty in putting that emotion down on paper, rather than anything you have said to me. Now some time has passed, I feel more able to write and explain how things have been.

After the worst was over, I stayed at the hospital for a couple of days before returning home, weak and unfit for anything. Of course, Joseph was extremely thoughtful; he hardly left my side during the dangerous time, and employed a nurse to take care of me during my recovery. But as my physical condition improved, I found myself increasingly low in spirits, and unable to explain to him why.

The doctors have said there is nothing to stop us from having a successful pregnancy in the future. Though I was sure they were right, I couldn't think about it at the time. So when Joseph reiterated their message in an attempt to make me feel better, all I could do was snap back at him. Worse still, I was unable to admit to him the ridiculous thought that I lost our child because I had been cleaning the grate, an indignity Leah would never have to endure. It was hateful of me, but watching her stomach swell filled me with a jealousy I could not control. I resented the fact that she could rest whenever she wanted, the birth would take place in the most expensive nursing home in Sandstown, and our parents would be there if anything went wrong – particularly once the arrival of winter exposed all the flaws of our little cottage. Pretty as it is in the summer, its exposed position meant every window rattled in the gale, cold air blew through every corner, and I was rarely warm.

Joseph never seems to need much in the way of comfort and appeared oblivious to me shivering every night, wrapped in every item of clothing I had. And so I found myself resenting him too, while he in turn became taciturn and withdrawn. We tried our best to create a festive spirit during the Christmas season, but our attempts fell flat. The days passed slowly, with little conversation and even less cheer. I was actually glad when he returned to work after the holidays. Though I was often lonely, it was preferable to the evenings huddled by the fireplace as we struggled to recapture the light-hearted atmosphere of the first weeks of our marriage.

Thank goodness for Kitty! She has made it her aim to take me out of myself, and has been dragging me out to coffee mornings, women's meetings, visits to Sandstown's limited tourist attractions: the castle, the art gallery and the folk museum. I have tried my best to respond, but it took her bombshell today to rouse me from apathy. She has decided to move to London, to take part in the Great War for Suffrage, as she calls it. She is prepared to do anything, she says, even if it means prison.

My face must have revealed my feelings because she was quick to add that I mustn't worry; she intends to take good care of herself. She urged me to do the same. She thinks it is time for me to stop brooding, and consider trying for another child.

I broke down at this point, describing to her the true state of affairs between Joseph and I – barely talking, distant from each other. I told her how worried I was that seeing what a poor wife I was, unable to manage the house or carry his child, he might be having second thoughts. Kitty, of course, was having none of it. She told me I was being ridiculous; she had seen how anxious he was when I was so ill. He was grieving, that was all. We both were, she urged me to be open with him so we could share our loss and build for the future.

She was right, as always. Later, when I walked back up the path to our cottage and saw Joseph through the lighted window, it became obvious to me. He was sitting with a book, but clearly wasn't paying it any attention. Suddenly, I saw how desolate he was, how much he was suffering. It was easier then to enter, to take his hand and offer consolation and comfort. Of course, the loss of the baby will always mark us. But once the words were spoken, we found our way back to companionship. And for that, I am truly grateful.

Your loving friend,
Rachel x

Chapel Cottage
Sandstown
26th March 1913

My Dear Sandra,

It is a year since I wrote to tell you Joseph and I were engaged, and now I am writing with more wonderful news. I have been to the doctor and he has confirmed that I am expecting again. We are delighted, and this time round, Joseph has said he is taking no chances. He has sacked Alice and employed a new maid, Maxine, who works longer hours and is much more efficient at her duties. He has taken on extra tuition so that we can afford this luxury, and since I mentioned the importance of home comforts, has insulated all the nooks and crannies to keep off the chills – though of course, now we are into March, the weather is, thankfully, much warmer.

I love this Easter season, don't you? We had a joyful service at the Meeting House on Sunday and, since Joseph is on holiday, several pleasant walks since then. Spring is upon us; new leaves have sprinkled the branches green, lambs have begun to appear on the hillside and I am feeling altogether more cheerful. Even Kitty's departure hasn't dampened my spirits too much. Although she has been my greatest friend since I came to Sandstown, in recent months I have made others: Louisa Heatherton and Eppie Partridge from the Meeting House, and several more from our women's suffrage group, so I am not entirely alone. And she writes so happily from London that, even though I fear for her wellbeing, I believe she is in the right place, and doing what she must.

Your loving friend,
Rachel x

Chapel Cottage
Sandstown
15th May 1913

Dear Sandra,

This is just a short note to congratulate you on the safe arrival of young Barnaby. We were delighted to hear your news and that all is well with you. A small gift accompanies this letter, which I hope will be of use!

Leah too has recently given birth to a son, Henry, who arrived at the beginning of May. I hope it is not a bad omen that he bears a strong resemblance to his father! I have not seen Jacob, as Leah has made it clear my presence would offend him, so I visit when he is absent. I cannot imagine a man as severe as him enjoying fatherhood, but she claims he is as loving a parent as she; she seems so happy that I will take her at her word. And it is delightful to see her playing with baby Henry, realising I will soon have that joy myself . . .

My other news is less pleasant. Kitty is in prison. She was arrested for criminal damage a month ago. Of course, I always knew this might happen; but still, I hate the fact that she is there. She writes cheerful letters, forcing me to do the same, but it troubles me to think of her – lively, vivacious Kitty in drab prison uniform, forced to live in such hardship. Her parents are being immensely stoic. They have packed up their home to be closer to her, and as always support her in every way. Joseph too is more sanguine than I. He says that Kitty knew exactly what she was doing; that as Thoreau says, the only place in an unjust society for an honest man is prison, and that he would do the same in her shoes. I cannot imagine a set of circumstances in which that might happen, thankfully. I do not think I would be able to bear it.

All my love,
Rachel x

Chapel Cottage
Sandstown
23rd September 1913

My dear Sandra,

I am sorry it has been so long since I have written. Shortly after my last, we had a scare with the baby and I was ordered to take bed rest; it wasn't till the middle of July that the doctor pronounced me fit and well again. Joseph did not want to take any further risks, so he hired a cottage in Manorbier in Pembrokeshire for the summer. We spent our days there very peacefully, reading and walking by the beach, but somehow I have found even that exhausting, and failed to put pen to paper until now. Today I feel more energetic than I have in months, and so I am seizing the opportunity to write while I have the chance.

The baby is due in less than two months. Naturally my waist has expanded considerably and I have had to update my wardrobe. Alas! Our tight finances mean that I have been forced to shop in the drapers patronised by the milliners and factory girls, buying clothes I wouldn't have dreamt of wearing even a year ago. I know this means contributing to the sweatshops that Kitty so despises, but, as I wrote to her recently, some principles are only possible if you have money! Leah has been very kind and has passed on some of her own maternity wear, but I must admit to being a little loath to use it. It isn't just the hard cold hand of charity impressed on the silk and chiffon dresses; we have such different tastes. I hope I don't sound ungrateful, but I'd much rather wear cheap and cheerful clothes than Leah's dreary blacks and greys, no matter how expensive they are!

The only thing that has marred an otherwise happy summer is my parents' continued refusal to meet me. I had hoped my second pregnancy might move them, but Leah tells me they are implacable. I cannot understand how Mother, who was so horrified at the idea of Reuben Flint being on the other side of the world, is quite happy never to see me. And it hurts that Father – who used to boast how he had cared for me after my birth, when both Mother and I hovered between life and death – would not come near my bedside last winter. It is so hard to know I am unwelcome in their home. Sometimes, I can't help wandering across town to have a look at the place, in the vain hope that one day, perhaps, the door will open, and they will invite me in.

Yesterday, I arrived as Father happened to be out on the front lawn. He was examining the rose bushes with Hodges. It was the first time I had seen him since I left. He didn't look any different, still the same genial man he has always been. I stood by the hedge looking directly at him, but he seemed not to notice me. Presently he moved in my direction till he was a few yards from where I was standing. Which was when he saw me. I smiled, hoping for a smile in return, but he just turned round and marched back inside again.

I stood by the gate, willing the door to open to show he had changed his mind. But the only movement was Hodges, who continued to pile leaves in the wheelbarrow, steadfastly following his master's example and ignoring my presence. Eventually, I had to give up and return home. I suppose I might have to accept that he will never forgive me, and make the best of what I have. I should be grateful that at least Leah speaks to me, and of course I have many other blessings: a wonderful husband, a baby on the way, a roof over my head. That should be enough, shouldn't it?

Your loving friend,
Rachel x

Chapel Cottage
Sandstown
13th December 1913

Dear Sandra,

Thank you so much for your lovely present. The shawl is beautiful and keeps Daniel wonderfully warm. He is such a beautiful baby and gives us great pleasure. He is all the more appreciated after such a difficult labour and last year's sorrows. He feeds well, sleeps well and, although I find it hard work, I have taken to motherhood much more easily than I did household management.

Better still, today I met my mother! It was all very unexpected and ensured a day that began badly ended very well indeed. This morning I received a letter from Kitty. As usual, she made light of her situation, but it was clear she was suffering a great deal, and for once I could not be optimistic for her. On a whim, I decided to go and see Leah in the hope it might lift my spirits. But my grim mood was not helped by the sight of the draper's boy being beaten by his master as I passed by. Sometimes the world can be such a hard place, filled with unkindness. Even negotiating the hire of the dray was difficult. The owner was away; his hired man was surly and insisted on

284

a higher price, so I was feeling out of sorts when I climbed on board. The cart was uncomfortable and the wind cold as we jogged out of town past the road to my parents' house. As usual, I tried to ignore it, but it was hard not to think about the jolly Christmas they would have without me. Thankfully, though the carts usually go only as far as Whetstone, the driver took pity on me and took me all the way to Echo Hall. Not for the first time, I wondered as we climbed the hill how Leah could stand living here. It is so remote, so dark, so gloomy.

Ginny Davies opened the door (did I tell you she married her Tommy in September? They live at the coach house behind Echo Hall and seem extremely happy). She is usually pleased to see me, but today she seemed horrified; Leah, emerging from the sitting room, seemed equally shocked. It was only when I heard my mother's voice that I understood why. I pushed past Leah to find her seated on the sofa, sipping tea. Before she could protest, I sat down beside her and placed Daniel in her arms. He is such a bonny baby, she couldn't help but be taken with him; before long it was as if our estrangement had never happened.

So this Christmas already feels more joyful than the last, and I believe that it won't be too long before Father will finally come round. The year ahead will be a good one, I can feel it in my bones.

Rachel x

Note: after that, my grandmother resumed contact with my mother, allowing us to visit when my grandfather was away. By the spring of 1914, these visits were going so well, my mother began to believe a meeting with her father was imminent. How was she to know that this would be the year everything changed? That the death of an obscure duke in Sarajevo would bring the treaties of Europe crashing like a pile of china plates? Just over a month later, Germany invaded Belgium and England declared war. And had my mother but known it, the last chance for reconciliation with her father passed for good. DC

Chapel Cottage
Sandstown
28th July 1914

My dear Sandra,

Congratulations on the safe arrival of Emily! She sounds like a perfect poppet, and how lovely to have one of each. Leah's baby, Jack, has also arrived safely and is now six weeks old. After one visit, Daniel is already intrigued by a creature so much smaller than himself. I think he prefers him to Henry on the basis that newborns don't poke people.

Jack's arrival has also brought about a very happy turn of events. Some time ago, I extracted a promise from Mother that she would ask Father to forgive me. However, the months have passed without a hint that she has done anything to plead my cause. It has clearly been a case of biding her time, for she chose the night of Jack's arrival to pose the question. I suppose the fact he had had a glass or two of wine and was in a generous frame of mind, and she can be very persuasive when she wants, all contributed to him saying yes. Whatever the reason, he has agreed that Daniel and I can go to Sunday lunch when they return from their summer holiday. So I have that to look forward to; and, though I am slightly disappointed Joseph hasn't been invited too, I will at least have the opportunity to spend the occasion singing his praises. I can also point out that he is practically certain of being promoted to head of history when Mr Forster retires at Christmas; the headmaster has all but promised it to him.

The other piece of good news is that Kitty has finally been released from jail. She will be home on Thursday, so I will be able to visit her before we depart for a fortnight in Manorbier at the weekend. I will be glad to see her – not only because I am relieved she is free, but because I could do with hearing her perspective on the current international situation. The news is increasingly troubling each day and everyone seems to concur that the conflict we've speculated about for years is about to break out. War fever is everywhere; the general consensus in Sandstown seems to be that we will have to fight to save our nation. Everywhere except at the Meeting House, where the mood is sombre, and Joseph and his friends talk of how we might resist such a war. I suppose I shouldn't be surprised by the unorthodoxy of his views; it isn't as if he hasn't expressed such thoughts before. Yet now war is a real possibility, it makes me uneasy. All my life I have been brought up to believe our duty is to king and country, and though Joseph is right to say that I have shaken off a similarly strong belief about women's suffrage, this one is harder to dispose of. Particularly when on Sunday, as I was helping Mr Morgan, the Methodist minister, with the poor boxes, he spoke so passionately in favour of military action. He says that when war is declared, all the town clergy will come together for a public prayer for the safety of the nation. And so I wonder, how can my husband be right, when so many good and religious men disagree?

Much love,

Rachel x

Chapel Cottage
Sandstown
25th August 1914

Dear Sandra,

So, we are at war. We heard the news when we were in Manorbier, and I have to say, though we tried our best, inevitably it cast a gloomy shadow over our holiday and anniversary celebrations. It was a relief to come home in the end, where we found the town filled with patriotic fervour. There are bands and recruiting parades, and posters everywhere encouraging our young men to enlist. It's all very stirring, but also rather alarming; I find my opinion on the matter shifting one way and another, depending on my mood. When I hear reports about poor Belgium and the atrocities the Germans have committed, my blood boils and I'm all for joining up myself. But then Kitty or Joseph point out that the papers like to exaggerate these things so that we'll support the conflict. I think of what might happen to the young military recruits and I find my patriotism wavering.

Joseph, being Joseph, has not sat at home quietly, which is now the cause of considerable tension between us – particularly since did not tell me the full story at first. In fact, if I hadn't been shopping with Kitty in Broughtons, I might never have found out. We had gone in search of a dress to wear to lunch at my parents' house. It had been such a long time since I'd been there; I can't tell you what a pleasure it was to wander through the aisles touching the taffeta and silk dresses on display. Alas! My budget was limited to one, which made the choice agonisingly difficult. Eventually, I opted for a stunning gown with a red-gold brocade top, empire waist and a chiffon skirt, which I absolutely adore. As I was trying it on, I overheard a woman discussing the behaviour of her son's teacher. I might not have paid much attention, but then I heard her mention Joseph's name and that she'd be complaining to the head. I couldn't think what she meant at first, and then I remembered – Saturday's recruitment parade.

You see, on Saturday Joseph insisted on going to the parade to deliver leaflets. I begged him not to, but he said he had a duty to act on his conscience. He reassured me that it would be fine; there was nothing to worry about. And so, I told Kitty later, I had let him go, and now a parent had seen him, and would complain to the head-master and Joseph might lose his job. Being Kitty, she did her best to calm me, but I went home anxious and, oh Sandra, I was right to be! Last night we had such a quarrel! I can't imagine how we will resolve it.

I waited till Daniel was in bed before confronting him, by which time I was very angry indeed. Not only had he promised me nothing would go wrong at the parade, but he had failed to mention the problems that had occurred. How could he have behaved like that towards me? He tried to persuade me that it was a minor incident and there was nothing he could have done, but I couldn't accept that. I was unswayed by his declaration that I'd have done the same in his position. That if I'd seen the crowds cheerfully sending their sons and husbands to war, I too would have wanted to act. I, too, would have handed out leaflets, suffered being manhandled by the recruiting sergeant, endured the screams of the crowd. It was just unfortunate, he said, to have run into Mrs Arbuthnot and her son at that precise moment.

Unfortunate! That's an understatement if ever I heard one. I pointed out the damage she could cause us. She is the wife of the chair of governors, for goodness' sake. And, though he is convinced her threats are idle, I am not so sure.

If Joseph were another woman's husband, I might have admired the courage of his convictions. But I am his wife, and what good is his conscience if it means him losing his job and his ability to care for Daniel and I? What good is it if my Father gets to hear about it? And perhaps it is fickle of me to doubt him – but how can he be so sure he is right, when church leaders are exhorting us to support the war?

So we argued, waking Daniel, who spent the rest of the night crying and unsettled, unhappy with the discord between his parents. By the time he had gone back to sleep it was nearly midnight, and too late to resume the conversation. Joseph rose early and has gone to a meeting with his pacifist friends. So unusually, the matter still rests between us. I fear that it is likely to do so for some time to come.

Your loving friend,
Rachel x

Chapel Cottage
Sandstown
7th September 1914

Dear Sandra,

Thank you for your kind letter and encouraging words. I do appreciate you taking the time, particularly when you have so many things to attend to at home. I wish I could tell you that matters have improved, but I'm afraid to say that they have only gone from bad to worse. For the first time in our married life, I asked Joseph to sleep in the spare room last night. This morning I could barely look at him at breakfast; and now he is at work, I am pondering what I should do.

And yet yesterday morning we were so happy! After our recent argument, we had a long conversation in which we agreed to put our differences aside. He promised he would consult me before acting in future, and I promised to try to understand his position more. We had heard nothing more from Mrs Arbuthnot so assumed her threat was just a threat, and were beginning to rejoice in the fact that I was finally going to be reconciled with my parents.

It was such a pleasure getting ready. For a moment I could almost imagine myself back in my old bedroom, preparing for a family dinner, as if we had never quarrelled. A quick glance around the room was enough to remind me of the reality of my situation; but a look in the mirror reassured me regarding the effect I wanted to produce for my parents. My skin may be less smooth, my hair less soft, my slim figure distorted by two pregnancies, but I can still pass for a beauty. It was petty, I know, to want to arrive at my parents' house triumphant in love and the life I have made for myself; nevertheless, when I stood back from the looking glass, I was satisfied they couldn't fail to see it. Joseph was impressed, at any rate. When I entered the room, he kissed me, saying he wished he could buy me fine dresses all the time. I replied that of course that would be lovely, but I'd rather have him and Daniel. A dress is just a dress, after all.

I was full of excitement when the car drew up. But instead of opening the door for us, Jamieson simply handed me a letter, said my father wouldn't see me today and went on his way. Puzzled, I went back inside, passed Daniel to Joseph and sat down to read. My father was short and to the point. He had heard through his club about Joseph's activities; he was not impressed. His conclusion? Daniel and I will never be welcome in his house while I remain married to Joseph. Oh Sandra! Can you imagine how that letter made me feel? Joseph was apologetic, of course he was, but how could I not be angry with him? It was not enough, I said, that by choosing him I had lost my father's good will. Not enough, that his recent actions had placed our livelihood at peril. But now, for the sake of his wretched conscience, I will lose my family for good.

We argued all day, going round and round in circles, until at last at bedtime I asked him to sleep in the spare room. I hardly slept at all, and I don't suppose he did either. This morning finds me sitting in the parlour, gazing at Daniel and wondering what on earth I am going to do.

Your friend,

Rachel x

Greenacres
Sandstown
19th September 1914

Dear Sandra,

For the second time in two years, I find myself staying with the Earnshaws, though this time it has been my choice entirely. I had hoped that after a day or two my anger would have abated. But as the week has gone on, I have found myself more and more furious with Joseph. This was not helped by the news he brought home yesterday. He has lost his promotion. Worse still, the governors have said his contract will not be renewed at the end of the term.

I was speechless when I heard, and retired to bed early. Today I couldn't bring myself to talk to him, until finally, while Maxine was at the shops, he begged me to join him in the parlour. He asked me to sit but I refused. He walked towards me, took my hand, forcing me to look at him. He spoke at length about his love for me, his desire not to hurt me and how it conflicts with his need to do the right thing. It didn't help; and when he said he wished things could be otherwise, I was all the more infuriated. I said that they could be, if he chose, to which he replied that if he could be otherwise, he would be. He again professed his love for me, but I concluded that if he cannot put me first, his love is not what I thought it was – that it was easier for him to buy me fine dresses than do the one thing I'd ever asked of him. That last point was unkind, I know, but I was beside myself with rage.

He waited for my anger to subside before pointing out to me that he has never pretended to be any other way. And it is true – he has never lied about his pacifism. I realised then that I am the one who has been pretending: that the differences between us don't matter, that love is enough, that we can put aside any argument between us. Joseph can no more give up everything he believes in to please me than I can give up my family to please him. And so we reached an impasse. My only option was to leave.

I packed my faded gowns in the self-same bag I'd taken from Father's house two years ago. Joseph watched in silence. I knew he was willing me to change my mind, as I was willing him to change his. But how can I? How can he? Our situation is impossible.

He walked me to the Earnshaws', pleading with me one last time to change my mind. Part of me wanted to, he looked so forlorn. But I couldn't, Sandra, I just couldn't. The Earnshaws were as kind as ever, and the evening passed pleasantly enough. As I was going up to bed, Daniel woke, confused by his strange surroundings. I paced the room, soothing him, and once he was calmer, sat in the rocking chair gazing out of the window. The storm clouds had cleared, and the bright moon lit up the garden. It reminded me of the night I'd seen Mabel Henry, how I'd looked out at the garden and felt that anything was possible. For a moment, I thought, all might be well. Then a cloud crept across the moon, and all was dark again. I placed Daniel back in the cot and climbed into bed – where, despite my troubles, I slept soundly till morning.

Rachel x

Greenacres
Sandstown
7th October 1914

Dear Sandra,

Thank you for your reassuring letter. You have such a knack for understanding and getting to the heart of the matter. Kitty has been kindness itself, but she thinks so highly of Joseph and has such similar opinions that she doesn't always appreciate my point of view. I am grateful that you see quite what a dilemma this is for me, and your suggestion that I don't rush to judgement is a helpful one. You are right, I need to consider things carefully. I love and miss my husband, but he asks a lot of me – perhaps too much. Now I am staying with Kitty, I am reminded of what I have given up for him. It is remarkable how easy it is to become used to soft sheets, maids to attend to me, three-course meals each night. Such luxuries remind me that if I left Joseph, my life would be *so* much more comfortable.

For instance, today I was able to take the car to see Leah instead of the dray, which was much more pleasant. Leah was all apparent sympathy but nonetheless, she was shocked by the stance that Joseph has taken. You will find no finer patriot than my sister, particularly now that Jacob has enlisted with the RAF. I should have found her response comforting, and yet I felt her dismissal of my husband's position a little irritating. I may not entirely agree with him, but his case is not without merit, as Kitty points out to me on a regular basis. Then again, I shouldn't have been surprised; Leah has always been black and white on moral issues.

The real reason for my visit, however, was not to elicit her pity, but to find out more about Father's state of mind. And there, unfortunately, my sister had nothing positive to say. Unless Joseph changes his views, or I leave him permanently, my father will not change his. Leah said she was sorry, and I think she is; but for a moment, I thought I detected a glimpse of something, a hint of malicious triumph. It went in a flash, and really it was unkind of me to even think it. Despite our past differences, in recent years she has been a great support to me. I can't imagine she really wishes me ill. So the visit ended, as usual, in warm embraces, and her promise she would do all she could to help. Sadly, I left with confirmation of the bleakness of my situation: I can have Joseph or Father, but not both.

So here I sit in my temporary bedroom, looking at the pile of correspondence I have received from the husband I adore. Letter after letter, begging for me to return. They are full of affection, and yet, caught between *Yes, yes* and *No, I cannot*, I am unable to reply. Reading his latest missive, I am filled with a desire both to see him immediately and to let him go forever. *I am sorry that I cannot be the man you want me to be. It may be selfish; God alone can decide that. But my conscience warns me this war can come to no good. That the boys in my care are in danger. So I can only be the man I always was. Please come home and be by my side. And I will do everything in my power to make you happy.* I know he would, but he asks such a price for that happiness!

I will have to make my mind up soon. I cannot keep presuming on the Earnshaws' hospitality, and the current arrangement is not fair on Daniel or Joseph. But I really, really don't know what to do. If I leave my husband, Daniel will lose his father; if I choose Joseph, I lose mine.

Your perplexed friend,

Rachel x

Dear Sandra,

How lovely to hear that you are pregnant again. I couldn't be more delighted for you. Three children will be quite a handful, I imagine, but you seem to have the stamina for it.

I have just returned from an evening with our suffrage group, which I do believe has helped me clarify matters. It was lovely to go with Kitty again and see her welcomed with such enthusiasm. Everyone was so excited to see her that it took some time for the meeting to settle so that Sophie Jenkins could begin. She started by saying that we are at a critical point in the struggle for suffrage. We have shown the country our courage and our sacrifice and won the moral argument. She argued that now we are at war, we must join forces with our former enemies in government to defeat Germany. She painted a graphic picture of the brutalities of the Belgian conflict, pleading with us to offer our husbands, brothers, cousins, sons. It is time, she said, to make sure they answered and for us to keep the home fires burning. For, she concluded, this was the way the battle would be won.

She is a powerful speaker and soon the room was abuzz with cheers and women calling out slogans of patriotic support. I could see some truth in what she said, yet I found this sudden outburst of fervour troubling. The energy of our little chapter usually inspires me, but this cheerful willingness to send men to war . . . Collective madness, Joseph calls it. Silently, I conceded his point.

Kitty, who is never one for being silent, leapt to her feet. As the noise died down, she spoke of her time in jail, her belief in the cause, and how she hadn't suffered only to support a war led by men. There was a smattering of applause, but the majority booed until Sophie hushed them into a sullen silence.

Kitty was so upset that we left before the final song. She strode ahead of me, making no attempt to hold back her tears. It was nearly dark as we crossed the cathedral square, past the empty marketplace. Leaves were beginning to drift off the trees and the desolation of the town fitted our mood perfectly. I can't tell you how sad we both felt about the change in our little group. Six months ago we were united in a cause; now war had come between us.

Later, when we were drinking cocoa, Kitty said she wasn't really surprised. She'd heard rumours that even the Pankhursts had fallen out over the war. When I wondered out loud whether it was worth it, if it helped us win the cause for suffrage, she was quick to point out that it was an extreme way to win. War, she said, leads to so much human suffering and only promotes the cause of the wealthy – something I've heard Joseph say frequently. I joked that perhaps he should have married her instead of me they seem so united in their beliefs. She laughed at that. Joseph, she said, is not her sort; besides, she reminded me, he has only ever loved me. I know this, I really do. She pointed out that it was time for me to choose. If I want a life of comfort and ease, over which I have no control, I should return to Father. But if I want to be with a husband who loves me, one who allows me the freedom to be who I want to be, I should return to Joseph. It was time, she said, for me to do the right thing.

The right thing. I have been pondering this ever since. What is that? I have spent the last half an hour looking at my sleeping child, thinking about Sophie's comments earlier. 'Now is the time for sacrifices,' she'd said. I picked up Joseph's letter again. *I will do everything in my power to make you happy.* If happiness is to be counted in hillside walks and evenings by the fireside, rather than dresses and soft bed linen, he has already made me happier than I have ever been. I lay down on the bed, my body sinking into the soft mattress. Father's house is full of such comforts. Turning my back on him means leaving my girlhood luxuries behind for good; becoming a wife whom Joseph can rely on, not a fragile creature who needs protection from the harshness of life. Since we can no longer rely on his income, I must become an equal, learn skills so that I can earn money. It is time that I become the wife Joseph deserves, not the one I have been.

I rose from the bed to finish this letter. At last I feel at peace. I will return to Joseph in the morning.

Rachel x

Note: my mother was as good as her word. Her decision to return to my father marked a permanent change in her. She no longer mourned the comforts she had lost, nor wasted time thinking of the parents who had rejected her. She may have had doubts about my father's stance on the war, doubts she told me of years later, but she knew that, in choosing him, she had to accept everything he stood for. With such acceptance came the knowledge that she must give up all thought of the past. She must develop domestic skills and find a way to contribute to the family income. Over the next couple of years, she discovered abilities she had never thought to possess. She took a sewing course at the technical college, taking in work from those Sandstown families who did not object too much to her scandalous past. She did not complain when Joseph took up a job in the bottling factory or when people spat in the street. And when, in 1916, the law changed so that married men would after all be called up, she knew immediately that my father had no option but to refuse. DC

12, Balmoral Mansions
Sheep St
Sandstown
29th June 1916

Dear Sandra,

It seems a while since I last heard from you. I imagine you have been overwhelmed with the house move and all the upheaval that entails. I trust that your new home is comfortable and the children are settling in? It must be pleasant to have more space; it was sounding quite crowded in your old place. I hope that now you are safely ensconced, all will be well for you as you approach labour. To think you will be the mother of four soon! What an Amazon you are!

My life, too, has gone through an upheaval, though alas! Not such a pleasant one; for yesterday, we received the letter we have been dreading since the beginning of the year. I was halfway through a pile of sewing when it arrived; I knew from the seal and the post mark what it signified. Joseph was on an early shift at the factory, so I had only a few hours to wait for his return, but those hours passed slowly. For once I was grateful that I had the distraction of stitching and cutting, to calm my anxious thoughts.

I was going to give it to Joseph when he returned, but he was full of an encounter he had just had on the street, so I forgot at first. A woman had spat at him, shouting for a full 10 minutes before laying a feather at his feet. Poor Joseph! Such events are commonplace. Whenever he walks through town, one of these harridans will scream abuse at him. I find it puzzling – the war is killing their sons and husbands; why blame Joseph for trying to stop it? It would upset me tremendously if it happened to me, and I am always astonished at the calmness of his response. The way he wipes away the spittle, bows low as if his accuser has presented him with a flower, and walks on. In the early days of the war, he would attempt conversation with these women. He did so with no hope of persuading them to change their views; only so that they might understand his. No one ever responded, other than to hurl even more insults. Now he no longer wastes his breath.

He is normally quite sanguine about these events but today's encounter seemed to bother him. With the billboards proclaiming heavy losses in the Somme, the cinemas filled with footage of the lunacy and the streets overflowing with the injured, why, he asked, was she wasting time condemning him? I know what he means; I cannot understand what makes people tolerate this carnage. And yet even Ginny Davies, recently widowed with a small child to raise, can't bring herself to condemn it. It's as if the only way to make sense of the grief and loss is to believe it is for some greater cause than scrambling for sovereignty over a few inches of a muddy foreign field.

Our conversation turned to Kitty, who had written to say she has a new beau, Samuel Blake – a Londoner and a pacifist. Fortunately for Kitty, he is both wealthy and unable to fight due to rheumatic ankles. As Joseph said, that makes him a very lucky pacifist! It was then that I remembered the letter. He sighed as he took it, we both knew what it meant. How I hope that the Canadian government does not do the same to you. Imposing conscription does seem to me one step too far. If a man chooses to fight, let him, but why should all men have to do so? Particularly if their consciences dictate otherwise.

As expected, it was a summons to the tribunal. We have been preparing for this, but even so it was hard to read. Joseph began to say he wished things could be different, but I hushed him and stroked his face. I know the resoluteness of his intent, and while I can confess to you that I do not share it absolutely, I will not abandon him again; nor will I let him see me troubled or anxious. He is my husband. This is my choice. I made it openly and freely and now there is nothing else to be done than support him. We knew this day was coming, so once it was acknowledged between us, there was nothing I could do but return to my sewing.

I wish I could be as sanguine now, as I sit alone

while Joseph is at work. I do not wish to worry him, but I am terrified about the outcome of the tribunal. I do not know how I will cope if he goes to prison and I fear that Leah – who already resents the fact that Joseph is not fighting – will judge us harshly.

Your loving friend,
Rachel x

12, Balmoral Mansions
Sheep St
Sandstown
14th July 1916

Dear Sandra,

Well, he is gone. And I, like so many other women, will have to learn to live without my husband. I suppose I should be thankful that at least I know he will be safe, but right at this moment I feel lost and desolate.

It has been hard to feel calm over the last fortnight. I have tossed and turned most nights, fretting about the outcome of the hearing. On the day itself, we rose early, breakfasted and waited till Louisa arrived to take care of Daniel. As we walked through town we passed the Shire Rooms, where we first met. I squeezed Joseph's hand. Who could have imagined that that encounter would result in this? Would I have been so keen to know him if I'd realised?

Many friends from the meeting were waiting for us at court. It was kind of them to come and helped me stay calm. As did Joseph's joke at the sight of the coat of arms inside – the right of kings has led many astray, he said. I expect it has.

The usher indicated a seat in the dock. Joseph

kissed my hand before sitting down. I moved to the public seats with the others as the tribunal members entered the room and sat down, backs erect.

They questioned him for a long time. Why did he refuse to fight? Wasn't it his duty to his nation and God? Why was he so cowardly? Why did he not to want to protect his wife and family? Joseph answered each courteously, as if he were at a dinner party: because his conscience forbids him from fighting. Because he believes God is against violence. Because he doesn't want to defend his family by taking the life of another father, husband or son. On and on the questions came, and each was answered with a polite smile and calm voice. I don't know how he stood it; I was sick with fear, trying to hide the useless tears from falling. I've known all year that we would have to face this; but, listening to their interchanges, it occurred to me that I wasn't sure I'd have the strength to cope with the consequences.

And yet, I thought, as we walked home – after we had received the predicted result: report to barracks or face arrest – what would the alternative be? If he chose to fight, I'd lose him anyway, and would run the risk of him never coming back. At least this way, I have a chance of seeing him again, unlike poor Ginny Davies. At least he was trying to do something, no matter how futile, to stop another Tommy Davies from dying. The tribunal gave Joseph a week to report to barracks, but we decided it would be better for him to hand himself in immediately. So yesterday we made the journey to the police station. Outside, Joseph took me by the hand, told me he loved me, urged me to be strong and kissed me one last time. I watched as he entered the building, the door clanging behind him. It did not reopen. He was gone.

And now, I am a single mother, waiting at home for my husband to come back to me. As I said earlier, I am luckier than most, knowing as I do that his return is certain; but still, I find myself thinking that this is too hard a trial. I am not sure I have the strength to survive it.

Rachel x

Dear Sandra,

How sorry I am to hear that the Canadian government has backed conscription. I had hoped that the very unpopularity of the measure would have made them see sense. I can only hope that James will be able to claim the exemption that was denied Joseph. I would hate for you to be separated by war or imprisonment, as we are.

Talking of prison, you asked what it was like to visit Joseph. I will do my best to describe a typical visit. I leave before nine, for the train journey is over two hours and involves a change at Crewe. I reach Manchester by midday, and, not being able to afford a cab, I walk along the dusty road to Strangeways, where usually a queue has already formed. It always takes a while to reach the entrance, so there is nothing to do but gaze at the building, wondering as always at its design. With its tall grey turrets, high windows and brown arched gate, it looks more like a fairy castle than a jail, though I doubt the occupants find it so pleasant. My feet are always sore after the trek from the station and I am usually hungry, but I have to keep half my pasty for the return journey. So I try not to think about food, but focus on the knowledge that I will soon be with Joseph. Sometimes, someone in the crowd will speak to me – usually a woman; visitors tend to be women. Most conversations are friendly, but occasionally, I encounter the kind of harridan who used to torment Joseph. Yesterday, for example, a chat about my clothes led to an enquiry as to what someone as well dressed as I was doing in a place like this. When I explained, she scowled at me, called Joseph a coward and turned away in disgust. Sadly, an all-too-familiar response.

At one o'clock, the door opens, the guard indicating that the first group can come in. The queue shuffles forward. It is about 20 minutes before my turn. I give my name and watch as the guard consults his list. I am always anxious at this point, ever since the visit last autumn when my name wasn't there. Luckily it hasn't happened since, and I am allowed to proceed into the waiting area, which is cool and dark.

The guard calls us to the visiting room. I wait at my table till Joseph arrives. It is impossible to embrace, surrounded as we are by guards; we smile at each other instead. Eventually, one of us will speak. Yesterday it was me, wishing Joseph a happy anniversary. He was quick to joke he'd spared no expense to celebrate – making light of things, as always.

We talk about our lives, each being careful to minimise the hardships so as not to cause pain to the other. I do not tell him that there are times when my sewing jobs dry up, and I have to rely on our friends at the Meeting House for money to survive. I don't mention the insults I sometimes endure when Daniel and I go the shops. Or the nights I go hungry to make sure Daniel is fed. Nor does he let on about his treatment, though I gather the beds are hard, the guards are hard and the work is hard. Instead, he tells me about the camaraderie he has found amongst his fellow COs, the prayer services they hold and the jokes they share to keep their spirits up. In turn, I share my news, currently the preparations for Kitty's wedding and my concerns for Mother's failing health. He is interested in the former and offers comfort for the latter until it is time to go. We drop hands. There is no time for a kiss, no desire for one with the guard's hand reaching for Joseph's shoulder. He says goodbye and leaves without a backward glance. I know it is always too painful for him to take that final look, yet it is such a struggle to watch his departing back, to see the door slam behind him knowing I can't follow.

Yesterday, after he had gone, a phrase came to me, one I had spoken on our wedding day, hardly thinking about the meaning: 'To love and serve you from this day forwards'. This then, was the service I had pledged: a life of snatched conversations, long train journeys, a home without a husband. I should be used to it by now. I should able to rise from my seat and leave him behind readily. Yet I am always the last to linger, last to be chivvied by the guard, last to pass through dark corridors into the bright sunlight. Perhaps it is impossible to get used to it!

After yesterday's visit the walk back to the station was wet and miserable. I missed my train, and had an hour to wait at the cold damp station. By the time I arrived back at the boarding house, Daniel was already in bed, and Louisa was tidying up. I was immensely grateful for her help; I was too exhausted for housework. After she had gone, I undressed, curling myself on the bed, clutching the covers, imagining Joseph there. When he first left, I used to lie there while Daniel napped, holding the bedclothes, drinking in Joseph's smell. But the scent soon faded. He is long gone, leaving only an imprint, an echo of himself lingering in my memories. And, though I have become accustomed to the fact of his absence, it is always harder immediately after a prison visit.

But after a good night's rest, when Daniel woke me, pestering me to get up, I found I was able to rise and see to his needs. The day passed, because days do, because they must. And the next one will, and the one after that. There is work to be done, a child to raise, an establishment, no matter how lowly, to maintain. I am discovering I am more like the Earnshaws than I had once thought. Now the unbearable is an everyday occurrence, I am finding that it can, after all, be survived.

Much love

Rachel x

Room 1
Forsyth Boarding House
Hawthorn Street
Sandstown
7th September 1917

Dear Sandra,

Thank you for your lovely long letter. I am so pleased that James's work with the government spares him from conscription. And it is good to hear the news of all your brood. I don't know how you manage to look after four of them. One is quite enough for me!

I have had a most delightful couple of days celebrating Kitty's wedding. The Earnshaws kindly invited Daniel and I to dinner on Friday night to meet Samuel and his family, and we had such a lovely time. He is a fine man and just right for Kitty. He has a calm and easy-going nature, which complements her passion and energy beautifully. I think they will be very happy together.

The next morning dawned bright and clear, which was a great relief after the unseasonal squalls this August. Daniel and I had stayed overnight so I could help Kitty and the other bridesmaids prepare. I particularly appreciated being maid of honour and being of assistance to Kitty, as I never had the chance with Leah. We had such fun getting ready – just like old times. And I can't tell you how exciting it was to watch her step out of the carriage, in her beautiful dress of white silk and chiffon. The Earnshaws had spared no expense for their only daughter. It was a marked contrast to my own wedding, yet I couldn't blame them, and Kitty, of all people, deserved this day. She looked so beautiful and it is wonderful to see her blooming with health again after the hardships she endured in prison. I was happy to walk behind her, though as we entered the church to Mendelssohn, my eyes filled with tears; I couldn't help feeling Joseph's absence.

The reception was held at the King George, where we stood in line greeting the guests. It took such a long time! The Earnshaws had invited every manufacturing family for miles. Though Leah came, my parents declined. Father has never forgiven them for siding with me; and now Joseph is in jail, he is even less inclined to attend a social gathering where I might be present. And though most of the guests shook my hand, I could see behind the polite smiles their opinion of me matched Father's. I was glad when it was time to be seated at the top table, where Daniel's needs for food and drink took over, and I could put aside the longing to have Joseph by my side. The dinner was magnificent – I'm not quite sure how they managed it, given recent concerns about food supply. I suppose the Blake family may have had something to do with it; I believe they have influential friends. Whatever the reason, it was a rare treat to enjoy several courses, including the freshest salmon and the lightest Pavlova I have ever eaten.

After the meal, Leah and I had a chance to talk. It has been a while since I've seen her as she has been taking helping Father take care of Mother. Because he is home most days, I have been unable to visit. Her news about Mother is rather concerning. The doctors fear she may have some underlying condition that is making her so weak, but they cannot yet find a cause. So they give her medicines that have little effect and encourage bed rest, when that is all she can manage anyway. It is so frustrating not to be able to see her; I was grateful I could pass a message via Leah.

Despite this, it was a wonderful day, the happiest I have had for months. Today the newlyweds are off to Scotland. I hope they have a marvellous time!

Rachel x

Room 4
Boothroyd Boarding House
Clark Street
Sandstown
25th October 1917

Dear Sandra,

I have had a wretched few weeks. First my beloved mother passed away, and shortly after that, I was evicted for being a day late with the rent. Consequently, Daniel and I are holed up in an even smaller room, in an even uglier boarding house, in the worst part of town.

As you know, Mother has been suffering for the best part of this year. The day after Kitty's wedding, Leah sent a note to tell me her condition had deteriorated and that the doctors did not expect her to live beyond the week. I immediately applied to Father for permission to see her. I think he might have denied me even this, had it not been for Mother's insistence that I come. Nevertheless, he was absent from home the day I arrived, and did not put up an appearance for the duration of my stay. I hadn't seen her for over a month; it was a shock to find her so shrunk and pale, her breath shallow and rasping.

She was barely conscious when I arrived. Eventually,

she opened her eyes, and seeing I was there told me then that she'd asked Father to forgive me, and to make provision for Daniel. I doubt that he'll pay any heed to her, even if it is a dying wish; but I appreciated that she had made the effort. I apologised for my part in the quarrel, and the pain it caused her. She smiled and sank back into the pillows, the effort to speak further being too much. Soon she drifted off to sleep; I sat with her for my allotted time and then at four I kissed her goodbye and left the house.

She died a few days later. Despite the inevitability of the event, the news still came as a shock to me. In the days that followed, I found it hard to think that she was actually gone. I don't know if this is a common reaction to death, but my mind was constantly full of images of her: a day at the beach, my fifth birthday, my coming-out party. The pictures repeated themselves over and over again in my head, as if my subconscious were terrified I would lose the memories as well as the person. What made it worse was that I had to deal with my emotions alone. Leah spent all her time supporting Father; and, though we met once, it was simply to pass on the message that I wasn't welcome at the funeral. It seems that, even in death, Father and I are further apart than ever.

After the first feverish days had passed, I sank into a deep lethargy, which would have defeated me completely if Daniel had not required my care. Without the routine of getting him dressed, washed, fed, I was in danger of allowing my loss to overwhelm me. I am grateful that I married a man as sensitive as Joseph. Even from a distance, even with communication restricted to a letter a week, he has managed to comfort me in these dark days.

Once the funeral was over and Father needed her less, Leah has thankfully been more supportive. And though I suspect she often entertains me out of a sense of duty, our grief unites us. I feel closer to her now than I have done in years.

Rachel x

Dear Sandra,

Thank you for your kind words about Mother. I can't tell you how helpful it is to hear your reflections about death and dying from your own experiences with your parents. And it is good to know of the impact she made on you as a child. You are right, she was a timid soul. Though that timidity caused me much sadness at one point, I am grateful that in the last years we reconciled and have enjoyed each other's company again.

I have just returned from visiting Leah. She has recently received word from Jacob that he is being transferred to the Middle East and she was not in the happiest frame of mind. Leah has always had a tendency to be dour: a characteristic that seems to have been enhanced by the years she has spent living in the damp isolation of Echo Hall. Now the knowledge that Jacob will soon be on the other side of the world has depressed her further. When the black mood takes her it proves hard to shift. This afternoon, she had been speaking for so long about her troubles I was running out of suitable responses, when who should walk in but Jacob? I stepped forwards, uncertain how I would be received. I haven't seen him since I rejected him all those years ago, and Leah has led me to believe he has never forgiven me. To my surprise, he took my hand and shook it firmly. He even said he would be pleased to meet Joseph one day. This was not the greeting I expected at all.

Leah was equally surprised and her face fell, taking on an aspect I hadn't seen in years. Fortunately he took the hint and dropped my hand before turning to compliment her. It seems that he will be home for a week before departing to Iraq to protect it from the Germans and Turks.

When Leah went to fetch the children, Jacob and I were left alone for a short while. Not knowing quite what to say, I asked about his experiences. To my surprise he opened up admitting that he was often frightened. He told me the story of a young flight sergeant, just married, with a new baby on the way. He was only just 20 and on his tenth mission when he was shot down. Jacob saw his tail catch fire, his plane spiral out of control and crash in woods above Dover. He said such incidents were hard to forget.

He spoke with such emotion that I was deeply moved. I've always found him such a cold man, with no thought previously of the men in his care. To think that he has feelings like everyone else!

I was about to offer some comfort when Leah returned with the children. Henry, always rather pompous, gave his father a well-rehearsed speech. Jack's reintroduction to his father was less successful. He is much more timid than Henry anyway, and initially hid behind Nanny's legs. When told to say hello to his father, he became confused, crying that it wasn't his Daddy – his Daddy was in an aeroplane. Jacob was furious, Leah boxed his ears and the poor child was sent to the nursery. It seemed a bit harsh to me; he is only three, after all.

I made my excuses after that. Jacob pressed me to stay but I felt too uncomfortable. On the journey home, I mulled over the visit. It was a shock to discover that Jacob held no grudge, and a worry to detect that some vestige of feeling for me might still remain. Yet again, I sensed that he let his eyes linger on me too long, that he paid more attention to my comments than to his wife's. Judging by Leah's caustic remarks, this time round his behaviour had not gone unobserved.

As the cart rolled towards Sandstown, an unpleasant thought occurred to me. Had Jacob wanted to meet me in the past? Had Leah prevented him from doing so? In which case, had she done the same with my father? Could Leah be so calculating, so cruel as to keep me and Father apart? I couldn't believe that of her. I reflected further and concluded that the uneasiness of the encounter was more likely due to the fact that the three of us had not been together since Jacob's failed courtship. It is not surprising that he would be curious about me, nor that Leah would be over-sensitive. Still, I decided, as we reached the outskirts of Sandstown with the first flakes of snow falling, that it would probably be prudent to avoid Echo Hall while Jacob is staying there. Leah deserves to have her husband to herself for a while, and he, the care of a loving wife.

Rachel x

Dear Sandra,

Belated Christmas greetings! I am sorry I didn't manage to write in time for the festivities, but Daniel came down with a cough. Though it gave us the perfect excuse to stay away from Echo Hall, it also prevented me from leaving the house. By the time he had recovered, Christmas was nearly upon us. So Leah had Jacob to herself, and I trust they have had a pleasant time. Unfortunately, I haven't been able to visit since he left, for after that we had so much snow the roads have been impassable.

Daniel is much better, thankfully, but we haven't been very comfortable. The temperature has been below freezing; we have to be sparing with the wood and are constantly cold. I am behind on work as a result of his illness, so we have had to make frequent trips outdoors this week, skating the icy pavements to collect sewing. We sit by the woodstove, our outdoor clothes steaming on the drier, as I sew and he plays with his toys. We go to bed fully dressed, shivering under the thin blankets, the chilly air penetrating our dreams. In the morning we scrape ice from the inside of the windows; the standpipe freezes constantly and our hands and feet are covered in chilblains. I long for the thaw, though I fear it will not be for some time yet.

Despite the cold and my continued mourning for Mother, I did enjoy Christmas. Getting ready for the day took me out of myself. I have had to save all year for Daniel's presents: a tiny tin drum, a jar of peppermints and an abridged version of *Alice in Wonderland*. Though they were simple, the memory of the sight of his face when he unwrapped them has helped me through the days when I am gloomy and sad.

It will be mid-January before you receive this, but nevertheless I wish you all the joy of the season. I hope you had a lovely Christmas together. And as always at this time, I hope that the Christmas message of peace will at last herald in a New Year that sees an end to this terrible war.

Rachel x

Note: for once my mother's optimism was well founded; for, although she had to wait nearly a year for the Armistice, at last, in November, peace was finally declared. It was a while before we were reunited with my father, however, for conscientious objectors were the least of the country's priorities. The soldiers, sailors and airmen returned home first to be greeted by brass bands and bunting. Only a handful of men had survived from the original crowd that my father had tried to dissuade in 1914, and only three of them were whole and hearty – a fact that he would frequently comment on when he was released from prison, six months after the last soldier was back. Even so, he was home long before Jacob Flint, who volunteered to remain in Iraq to protect the British mandate, and did not return till 1920.

For my aunt, this was the last straw. She had seen my uncle once since he left in 1917: she felt it was unfair that my cowardly father had returned before her husband and told my mother so. Once more the sisters quarrelled, airing resentments that had been set aside in the years they'd been each other's only support. Shortly after this, my father was offered a job in York, and my mother was only too happy to leave Sandstown and Aunt Leah behind. At first, I was sad to leave my cousins and school friends, but once we'd arrived in our new rooms in Bootham, I could see our prospects were much improved. We had twice the space and access to a strip of garden; I soon adjusted to my new home.

Within a year of moving to York, we were living in a three–bedroom house in Avenue Terrace. It was a far cry from the houses my mother grew up in, and there was no money left for servants, but she no longer needed them. The years of penury had forced her to master the domestic skills that had once eluded her, and now we had income from her sewing and my father's teaching; there was more than enough to live *on and she was content. And if, from time to time, my father had periods of gloomy melancholy or suffered from acute bronchitis in the winter as a result of the years in prison, she told me later that it was a small price to pay to have her husband restored to her. DC*

Dear Sandra,

Thank you for your lovely long letter. It was so good to hear your family news. And thank you too for the photograph. How the children are growing! You and James are rightly proud of such a gorgeous brood.

We had a wonderful evening last night as Joseph gave the annual Armistice speech organised by the local Fellowship of Reconciliation. It went down well, I think, and it is good to see him appreciated in this community after all the years we were pariahs. The talk was entitled 'Lest We Forget'. He began by asking what the words *sacrifice, courage* and *struggle* should mean. When we think of the brave soldiers who fought in the trenches and their suffering, the words seem apt, he said. But while the generals and politicians who sent them into battle argue that they did not suffer in vain, this is Owen's 'old lie'. It is not sweet and fitting to die for your country. We should remember struggle, sacrifice, courage. Of course we should. But we should also remember that the war cost the lives of millions of soldiers and civilians on both sides, leaving twice that number wounded. We should remember that after four years of fighting in the most appalling of conditions, the British Army advanced fewer than 100 miles. We should remember the sound of women weeping in the streets on Armistice Day. And we should ask ourselves, what was it all for?

There were some hecklers, who disliked such sentiments, but most of the audience were encouraging, and I was pleased when more than one veteran stood up to applaud him. Joseph concluded by urging us not to forget. 'For the sake of our children, and our grandchildren, we cannot let the unjust peace carved at Versailles ferment into another conflict . . . The world must find other ways to resolve its disputes. Because war is too crude, too bloody, too cruel a solution.' He sat down to huge applause, and the questions when they came were mainly sympathetic.

The event ended later than scheduled, so it was nine o'clock by the time we stepped out into a cold, cloudless night. I took Joseph's arm, Daniel taking my other side, as we walked out through Bootham Bar. It still gives me great pleasure to return home, to put my key in the lock, to enter our *own* hallway, knowing we have the luxury of several rooms, a tiny yard, an inside toilet. A pleasure, too, to see Joseph celebrated, not scorned, and to end an evening together as a family. Better still, he has been promoted to the position of deputy headmaster, which means a welcome increase in his salary.

And in two days' time, we will have an election. The first at which women will be able to vote. Not owning property, I will sadly not be able to put my cross in the ballot box, but I and several others will stand outside the polling booth in our suffragette colours, with banners saying 'Votes for *All* Women'. I am sure we will have full voting rights soon.

Christmas is not far away and already Daniel is getting excited about the season. I am sure there will be lots of excitement in your house too. Expect a small parcel from us soon!

Rachel x

12, Avenue Terrace
Bootham
York
4th January 1923

Dear Sandra,

Happy New Year! I hope you had as splendid a Christmas as we did. Kitty and Samuel visited with their children Sophie and Benjamin; and, although we were somewhat crowded, we had a delightful time. Kitty was full of joy at the fact that after all these years she'd been able to go into the voting booth and place her cross in the box for Labour. And though we were all disappointed that the Tories got in again, we celebrated seeing the back of Asquith and Lloyd George and their illiberal ilk. We had a merry time with them while they were with us, even allowing ourselves the rare indulgence of a bottle of Champagne on Christmas Day. I think the children were quite startled by our giddiness as Joseph raised glass after glass to all the great causes: women's suffrage, world peace, an end to empire; while Kitty declared that women would one day rule the world. And later the four of us danced round the living room till we collapsed in giggles on the settee afterwards.

We had such fun in the days that followed. We

played games, walked by the river, toasted teacakes by the fire. There was only one day when it all palled; I had such a severe headache that I wasn't able to join in a game of charades, but all in all it was a very happy time. They left a few days ago, and though the house seemed much quieter without them, we still rang in 1923 full of optimism and cheer. Daniel will be 10 this year – can you believe it? He doesn't need me nearly as much as he did, and so I have made a major decision about my future. I will enrol at teacher training college and get my certificate so I can teach needlework and domestic science. Once we have two decent salaries coming in, we should at last be reasonably comfortable, and finally we will be able to buy the house we've always dreamt of . . .

I had more to tell you, but I have just received a telegram from Leah – my father has had a stroke. Daniel and I are leaving for Sandstown immediately. I will pop this letter in the post on the way to the station, and write again when I can.

Rachel x

King George Hotel
Sandstown
10th January 1923

Dear Sandra,

As promised, I am writing with the latest news of my father. I am afraid that although up until today we had hopes of a recovery, I have just heard from Leah that he died an hour ago.

I had also hoped that this illness might finally be the means of bringing us back together, but sadly it was not to be. It was late the night we arrived in Sandstown and I was not able to speak to Leah till the following morning. Fortunately, she has had the foresight to install a telephone at Echo Hall, so I was able to call her from the hotel. I know you said that you had purchased one recently, but this was the first time I had used one. It was a strange experience – does it always sound so echoey? Still, it was extremely helpful as I discovered that Father had been moved to the cottage hospital and that she would be visiting that morning. She advised me not to come straight away, as he did not need any sudden upsets; we agreed to meet for lunch instead.

It has been three years since I last saw Leah, and I couldn't help but be shocked at the transformation in her when we met in the hotel lounge. Perhaps it was the privations I endured during the war years, or the fact that I undertake my own housework and walk everywhere that have helped me keep my trim figure. But goodness, I couldn't help noticing how large she has become in comparison to me. Her face was always rounder, but now it has doubled in size; fat wobbles from her cheeks and under her skin. She always was rather solemn, but now her features seem fixed in a perpetual scowl. Still, her embrace was warmer than on my last visit, and she appeared to have tried her best with Father when he regained consciousness that morning. Apparently, he said nothing when she told him I was here. He just turned his face to the wall and refused to listen to her anymore.

She promised that she would try again and urged me to be patient. And I have done my best. For five days, I have sent word to the hospital. Every day I have been told he was unable to receive me. And so today, I had decided, enough was enough. There was no point staying here, and I was beginning to worry about Daniel missing school. We were halfway through packing our bags when there was a knock at the door. It was Leah. There was no need for speech; Father's death was written all over her face. He died without saying anything directly about me, although apparently he has done what Mother asked and left a small legacy for Daniel's education, which Leah and Jacob will hold in trust for him. So I suppose that is something.

We unpacked our bags and will stay here another night. After that, we will have to move to cheaper lodgings. We have stayed here only to make the point that we are no longer living in poverty, but I cannot afford to pay these prices and buy funeral clothes! I have sent a telegram to Joseph, and Daniel and I have had a quiet supper. Now Daniel is asleep, I am sitting here trying to sift through my feelings. My father's death means there is no longer any possibility of reconciliation between us. It has been so long since I have seen him, his absence is familiar to me, and I have become accustomed to it. And yet, now this absence is to be permanent, I sense there is pain bubbling under the surface, and that the grief, when it emerges, will be stranger and more complex than when my mother died.

Your loving friend,
Rachel x

Dear Sandra,

Well, that is over, thank goodness! I have a splitting headache and my feet are sore, but I have done my duty by my father, even if he never did his by me.

I had hoped Joseph would be able to join us, but unfortunately the demands of his new role meant it wasn't possible for him to get away; so Daniel and I endured the occasion without him. The funeral was a grand affair – perhaps it will be the last of the old kind. The coffin was carried in a glass hearse pulled by six horses, the undertaker with his silk black hat and long frock coat marching slowly in front. It seemed as if the whole of Sandstown had emerged to witness the passing of the Porcelain King and my prodigal return. The years had not lessened the spite of the society hostesses; I could still see it passing from mouth to mouth behind the ornate orders of service. I tried to ignore them, fixing my eyes on the coffin, but I know my cheeks were pink, and I was glad that Daniel was by my side. He did marvellously, though I think he was somewhat confused by it all. He is only nine and a bit, an age when it is somewhat difficult to know what to make of the death of the grandfather you have never met.

Afterwards, a buffet was laid out at the King George Hotel. They all came to pay their respects – the women who cut me for so many years – the Lyndhursts, the Elliots, the Fortescues, only too ready now to shake my hand, offering their crocodile condolences. I returned their thin smiles with one that was equally false, longing for the function to be over. The only person I was glad to see was Kitty, who had kindly made the long journey up here, though she unfortunately had to leave early to see a sick relative. So we have arranged to have lunch tomorrow before she goes back to London.

By five my head was throbbing and I was overwhelmed with exhaustion. I snuck away into a quiet corner and closed my eyes. I was in the middle of a pleasant daydream of home when I was interrupted by Jacob Flint. I really wasn't in the mood to talk to him, but there was nothing much I could do about it. I listened to him as attentively as I could; though after a while, I rather wished I hadn't. After he had offered his condolences he began to talk about my father's last days. He seemed to imply that Leah had not worked as hard as she might have on my behalf. In fact, he hinted that she'd done very little to support my cause over the years.

I don't quite know what to make of this. Was he telling the truth? Before I had the chance to ask him, he glanced up to see Leah scowling across the room at us. Even now she does not like us to be alone together too long. So he made his excuses and left me hoping that I had either misunderstood him, or that he was making mischief.

It was a relief to get away from it all, and come back here to rest. We have two more days in Sandstown, visiting old friends, and then we will return home. I cannot wait.

Rachel x

Echo Hall
18th January 1923

Dear Sandra,

The worst crisis of my life is upon me. I scarce have the strength to tell you, but tell you I must, for I need all your love and support at this moment, and will do for a long time to come. Joseph is dead. I can hardly bear to write the words. But they are true. Joseph is dead, and I don't know how I am going to live.

I was woken at eight this morning (was it only this morning?) by a knock on the door telling me I had a telephone call. Puzzled, I dressed quickly, leaving Daniel alone in the room. I went into the manager's office expecting it to be Leah, but the voice on the end was unfamiliar to me. It was a policeman from our local station ringing to inform me that Joseph was knocked over by a tram yesterday. He was killed instantly. It seemed so unreal, I couldn't really believe it. I still can't. After that, time became distorted. I vaguely remember sitting down but then whole hours passed and I was unaware of them. Daniel must have come in at some point, for I heard the hotel staff whispering to him. Later still, I rallied enough to give them Leah's phone number.

We returned to our room, though I cannot remember how. Then, suddenly, there was Jacob Flint, organising porters to carry our bags, instructing Daniel to follow him, picking me up in his arms and taking us away to Echo Hall. The journey passed in a daze, and we had almost reached the doorstep before I realised quite where I was. Leah came to the door to welcome me, although there was no warmth in her eyes. Instead I sensed resentment that Jacob had placed her in this position and anger that I had accepted. Nonetheless, I observed the proprieties, thanking her as if she meant it, as I stepped over the threshold.

So tonight I sit in my new bedroom at the back of the house, wishing myself far away. But with my father and husband both dead, I have no choice. Though it's the last place on earth I want to be, for now Echo Hall will have to be my home.

Rachel x

Note: there followed a terrible time. Like my mother, I could scarcely comprehend that my father had been taken from us. I was suddenly transported into a new world, where children were considered the least of God's creatures, and were governed by the strict laws of our elders. Worse still, my mother withdrew into herself, hiding in her room for most of the day, unable to pay me much attention. And, though I enjoyed having two cousins to play with and the gardens of

Echo Hall to roam in, most days I felt as lonely and lost as my mother. It took over a year before she began tentatively to reconnect with us all, and by then, I was desperate for us to leave. DC

My Dear Sandra,

Thank you for yet another beautiful letter, and the book of Queen Victoria's life, which strange though it may seem I found rather wonderful. I am not much of a royalist, as you know, but her courage in facing the loss of her beloved Albert was remarkable and has taught me a great deal. I am so lucky to have friends like you and Kitty. You have both helped me through this dark time – the darkest of my life – and I am enormously grateful. Leah and Jacob have been kind in providing Daniel and I with a home, but they are not an affectionate couple and there are days when I long to be away from here.

I hope that doesn't sound ungrateful, for without their hospitality, I don't know where I would be. But nevertheless, I can't help but feel that it is hospitality laced with guilt and duty. In those first days after Joseph and Father died, it didn't matter to me, and I didn't notice then how Leah snubs me in subtle ways. She has housed us in the old butler's quarters at the back of the West Wing, apparently so that we can have some privacy, but in reality to keep us in our place. When her friends come to call, she has been quick to let them know what an object of pity I am in my widow's weeds, and how generous she has been to provide me with a place to live.

In those early months, the knowledge that Father died without forgiving me, that Joseph died without warning, that I was unable to say goodbye to either, was all-consuming. But gradually, as winter thawed into spring, spring melted into summer, summer faded into autumn, autumn froze back to the winter that has just been overcome by spring, I have found some sense of self returning. I realise I have become too accustomed to the comfort of Echo Hall, where meals are cooked, rooms and clothes cleaned without me having to worry about lifting a finger or how to pay the bills. It is remarkable how easy it has been to get used to it; particularly since Ginny has been promoted to the position of housekeeper and manages to ensure we are always comfortable. (Everyone else calls her Mrs Davies these days, but she will always be Ginny to me!)

In recent weeks I have found myself wanting to cast off my mourning black and take up the reins of my life again. For a long time now, I haven't had to worry about managing a household. If I leave Echo Hall, my life will contain hardship and suffering again. Without Joseph by my side, I am not sure I have the stomach for it; yet I can't imagine remaining here either. It has become clear to me, now my strength is recovered and I can observe my surroundings better, that Leah and Jacob are married in name only. They sleep in separate rooms, spend their days apart, and come together only at dinner, where they act like strangers. This is not a happy house, and I don't think it is a good environment for me or Daniel. Worse still, Jacob has begun to throw me the kind of glances he shouldn't, so my continuing presence is unlikely to improve matters.

Today marks 12 years since Joseph proposed. I have been thinking all day how happy we were together and the strength he gave me to take control of my own destiny. Since he died, I have lost that desire; but now I am beginning to feel more myself. I owe it to him, I owe it to us, to take control once more. It is time for me to start making plans again.

Rachel x

Echo Hall
4th April 1924

Dear Sandra,

Since I last wrote, I have not been idle. I have written to Kitty, and asked if we might go and stay with her for a while. I will apply for work at her local technical college and try to obtain my teacher's certificate while I do so. I will ask Jacob and Leah if we can use Daniel's trust fund to pay for him to attend Grove House, so that he can continue with his Quaker education, which I have seriously neglected.

I am glad that I have made such plans, for today I received a rude shock that confirmed I should leave Echo Hall as soon as I can. This afternoon, Leah and I took the boys for a climb up to Arthur's Stone. Everyone wanted to go further, but my head was aching so I stayed behind. It was pleasant to sit on the hillside with my memories, remembering the day Joseph proposed. It is fanciful, I know, but for a brief moment he felt close, as if he has never left me entirely.

Because I was thinking of Joseph, I wandered back underneath the roofed stones to the rock where we had once carved our names. It was cool and dark out of the sunlight. I traced my hand around the names of other lovers engraved in the stone. This was still a popular spot; several had come since we made our vows; perhaps they too had been separated by war and death. I found the inscription *J loves R* and pressed my lips against it. He had loved me, he truly had, and we had been happy, even if only for a short time. I owe it to him to try to live the life we should have lived together, not to linger here in a place that can only make me miserable.

I was just about to leave when I was surprised to encounter Jacob. He said he had left the quarry early and, hearing where we had gone, decided to meet us. Given how suspicious Leah is, I did not wish to be alone with him for even a second; but to my annoyance, he blocked my path and insisted on speaking to me. Oh Sandra, what I would have given to have avoided this painful meeting! As it was I had to endure a long embarrassing speech in which he told me how he loved me and despised Leah. How he was sure I must feel the same, and though it was against every moral code he possessed he was willing to leave her for me. Imagine that! The hypocrisy of the man. Worse still, he declared that he had always admired me for defying convention and marrying Joseph. He begged me to do so again and accept his offer.

I was furious. How dare he presume upon me like this? How dare he treat Leah that way? I told him exactly what I thought, and then pushed past him. We emerged from the rocks to bump into Henry, who was running full pelt down the hill towards us. Leah was following in his wake with the other two; I could see by her face that she was immediately suspicious. And who could blame her? Though I have done nothing to encourage Jacob, she will never believe me. The only thing I could do was reassure her I was no threat. I took her by the arm and, leaving Jacob to walk with the boys, I began to tell her about my plans to move to London.

I cannot stay here any longer; it will cause too much pain and embarrassment for all of us. I will start packing as soon as I have finished this letter. With any luck, I can be away from here by the end of the week.

Rachel x

Note: my mother's plans never came to fruition. That night, she suffered a seizure, and in the following days, several more. A specialist was called for, who diagnosed a brain tumour. My uncle and aunt told me she was not well and needed bed rest. I was allowed to visit once a day between supper and bedtime. I read Dickens to her while she told me stories about my father. I had no idea how ill she was, she seemed so lively most days, I imagined she would get better soon.

Then one evening, my aunt said I couldn't see her – that she was too weak – and I was sent to bed. In the middle of the night, I woke to hear doors banging and voices shouting. The noises alarmed me, and all at once I wanted to see my mother. When I entered her room, she was lying in bed perfectly still. At first, I thought she was sleeping; but then I saw the pallor of her skin and the stiffness of her body, and realised she was dead.

I was about to leave when I heard voices, so I hid behind a curtain. It was my uncle and aunt. To my surprise, he was weeping, while she told him this was God's will, he had sinned and now God had taken the temptation from him. When she had gone, I crept back to my room, shocked and puzzled by their behaviour. But the next day, they acted as if nothing had happened. As usual, she was submissive, he curt, so I thought for a long time that I had imagined the scene.

A week later my mother was buried in the churchyard at Whetstone. And after that I was sent to the Quaker school in York in accordance with her last wishes. I came back to Echo Hall in the holidays, enduring the harsh rules of my aunt and uncle as best I could. As the years passed, I observed the coldness that lay at the heart of their marriage, and was desperate to get away as soon as I could. I left once my education was complete, vowing never to return. DC

INTO THE VALLEY OF DEATH

1942–43

ELSIE 1

Elsie puts the collection of letters down, her head swirling. Jacob – upright Jacob – loving Rachel and not his wife. Being prepared to leave Leah for her! Poor Leah. Poor Jacob. And poor, poor Daniel, always the outsider – his father had made sure of that. Yet Joseph was brave in his own way; Rachel, too. And the way they had continued to love each other despite the odds. You couldn't say pacifists were cowards when you heard a story like that. She has been so absorbed in reading that when she looks up, she sees that she has forgotten to draw the curtains. She glances at the clock. It is three in the morning; it's unlikely there will be enemy aircraft out here in the country, but it's best to be safe. Outside snow has started to fall; it is already covering the garden with a light dusting. She closes the curtains, resolving to find a way to visit Daniel tomorrow. Her anger at his behaviour has been replaced with admiration. For having read the letters, she can see he is showing a courage of sorts by being here, in the place that made him so miserable. No wonder he'd been so private about his past. No wonder his aunt and uncle are so unhappy. No wonder Leah chose to think the worst of Rachel. Perhaps that's why she dislikes Elsie so much – perhaps she is too much of a reminder of the fashionable, partying sister she felt had betrayed her. Elsie resolves to be kinder to her mother-in-law, to both of them. Events have made them who they are; she can't change the past, but perhaps understanding it might make living with the constant barbs that little bit easier.

It takes a while for her to fall asleep, and when she does, her dreams are filled with episodes from the story she has just read. In one, a man with a wax moustache is asking her to choose who she will marry, Jacob or Joseph. In another, she struggles with the decision to stand by her husband. Finally she is on Southport beach with Jack and Daniel. Millie asks them to pose for a photograph, but this time it is Daniel who takes her arm first, Daniel to whom she leans while a voice is singing, 'Don't sit under the apple tree with anyone, Else, but me.' This is all wrong; she tries to move towards Jack, but he is receding from her, further and further into the distance. She wakes with a start as Evie calls from the next room. It is seven o'clock, time to get up. She takes the children downstairs where they are all excited to see the snow that has fallen in the night. She rushes through the household chores so there is time to play in it. They have a happy time building snowmen and throwing snowballs till Evie becomes too cold and they return to the house for watery hot chocolate and a change of clothes.

Annie Davies has not been able to drive her van up the hill today. Elsie offers to take the post bag into the village; it is the perfect cover for visiting Daniel. Once discharged of the mail, she hurries through the village to his house, taking care not to be seen.

'Elsie.' She can hear the relief in his voice as she shakes the snow off her boots and enters the hallway.

'I came as soon as I could . . . I've read the letters. I had to tell you that I understand, I think.'

'Thank you.' He puts on the kettle and they sit down for tea, returning quickly to their usual companionship.

'Can I ask you . . .' she says, once the drink is in her hand and they are both feeling relaxed. 'Do you blame your father for what happened?'

'Not exactly. With his beliefs, I can't see how he could have acted any differently. But he didn't see, as I did, the effect his actions had on my mother. She hid it too well. Perhaps, if he had been less absolute, she would have suffered less during the war years. Perhaps, if she hadn't suffered then, she would have had enough strength to return to York after his death.' He stands up and moves over to the window. The fir trees are lined with thick snow, like ermine.

'I suppose he did what he had to do. It was brave of him.'

'Unlike me?'

'I didn't say that.'

'You called me a coward before.'

'Before I knew your story. I don't think that now.'

'But you are right. I *am* a coward. Though perhaps not for the reasons you think. I believe in all the things my father did. But I cannot be like him. I cannot act out my beliefs, take the risks he did. My early childhood was poverty-stricken, full of pointing fingers and thousands of tiny humiliations. Then we moved beyond it, and I found life doesn't always have to be like that. I can't put myself through it again. I just can't.'

'I can understand that.'

'The thing is,' Daniel says, 'I'm not strong enough to go to prison, but I can't fight either. So Jack and I cooked up a plan. He found a doctor who made a few bob on the side helping people fake medical conditions.'

'How did that work?'

'I broke my ankle as a boy; it was on record that it was weak. Rheumatic ankles had worked for Kitty's husband, Samuel, so I thought it might work for me. The doctor made up some notes and that was that.'

'Jack was happy to help?'

'I swear. The only payment he ever asked was that I came here to teach. He wanted me to take care of you. I've tried, Elsie, I've really tried. But if you can't forgive me this, then there will be no reason for me to stay.'

'Of course you must stay. Where on earth would I be without you?' She puckers in school-marmy sternness. 'But you should have told me.'

'We didn't want to get you into trouble.'

'You both should have told me. You wait till I write to Jack.'

'Be careful . . .'

Elsie laughed. 'It's alright. I won't expose you. Jack and I have had plenty of practice in saying things prying eyes don't pick up on.'

Daniel joins her in laughter and it is easy then to embrace him, and feel that all is well as she leaves. She walks back as quickly as she can, not wanting to be late for dinner, but few people have passed up the hill and each footstep has to force its way through deep drifts. Snow keeps falling into her boots and her socks are soon sopping wet; her feet are icy cold. It is dark by the time she reaches the driveway of Echo Hall. The journey up the hill is slow and arduous. She slips several times, and by the time she reaches the top her clothes are soaked through.

Veronica opens the door to her knock. She was visiting friends in Whetstone the previous day and has been trapped by the snow, so she has been invited to spend the second night at Echo Hall. 'At least I've been able to help out with the children, Else,' she says.

Elsie winces; Jack is the only one allowed to call her that. 'That's very kind of you.'

'They're little poppets,' said Veronica. 'The pleasure

was all mine.' She casts a glance at Elsie's wet skirt and bedraggled hair, smiling as if to say, 'I would never let myself look like *that*.'

Elsie makes her excuses, heading for the nursery where the children are playing a game with Evie's teddy bears.

'Mummy!' They rush to hug her.

'I hope you've been good.'

'Aunt Veronica looked after us,' says Will. 'She's mean. She wouldn't let me play aeroplanes. I think she's a wicked witch.'

'Hush,' said Elsie, though she admires Will's astuteness. 'It was very kind of her to help Grandmother.'

She reads them a story, fetches pyjamas, oversees teeth brushing and settles them into bed.

'Is Father Christmas coming soon?' asks Will, as he lies down.

'Very soon.'

'Will he bring me that fort I saw in the *Beano*?'

'We'll see.'

She has just enough time to dress for dinner, though she is the last to arrive. Jacob and Leah are in their usual seats at either end of the long table. They are grim-faced as usual, but, for once, Elsie feels a pang of sympathy for them, knowing as she does now what they have lived through, what they have suffered. Veronica sits in the middle; Elsie takes the chair opposite. Even though the blackout curtains are tightly drawn, the lights are kept low; even a chink could alert an enemy bomber to their presence, though in the whole war, there's only ever been one enemy plane over Whetstone, and he, poor bugger, crashed to his death in the woods below Wright's Fields. Not for the first time, Elsie wonders why they can't just eat in the kitchen, which is brighter, warmer, more comforting. There is something about the dining room that sucks the life out of everyone.

'It's lovely to see you, Else,' says Veronica, as she passes the vegetables up and down the table. 'And the children. I'm sorry I can't get away more often.'

'The WAAF needs you more than us. You are doing the country a great service,' says Jacob.

Easy enough if you don't have children, thinks Elsie, though she smiles as if in agreement.

'How's Jack? Doing well?' asks Veronica.

'As far as I can tell. The censor gets most of it.'

'Yes, I remember.'

Leah casts her eyes down at Veronica's words, reminding Elsie of the need to be kind.

'How's Daniel? Have you seen him recently?'

'Not for a while.'

'I thought you two were very chummy.'

'He's busy with the school.' Elsie can feel Jacob and Leah's eyes on her, daring her to reveal some hidden feeling. She may understand it better now, but it still infuriates. Why can't they just allow her the one friendship that helps to keep her sane?

'I heard his girl had left.'

'I believe she's gone to London.' Why is Veronica

so fascinated with Daniel tonight? Her face across the dimmed room is friendly enough, but malice lurks underneath her pleasant tone.

'What happened?'

'I don't know. Perhaps you should ask him when you see him.'

It is enough to silence Veronica for now. The conversation turns to other subjects until it is time to gather at the radio for the news, Eden's speech uniting them in sombreness.

'From all the occupied countries, Jews are being transported in conditions of appalling horror and brutality to Eastern Europe. In Poland, which has been made the principal Nazi slaughterhouse, the ghettos established by the German invader are being systematically emptied of all Jews except a few highly skilled workers required for war industries. None of those taken away are ever heard of again. The able-bodied are slowly worked to death in labour camps. The infirm are left to die of exposure and starvation or are deliberately massacred in mass executions. The number of victims of these bloody cruelties is reckoned in many hundreds of thousands of entirely innocent men, women and children.'

Hearing such words, it is hard to agree with Daniel that all fighting is wrong. Surely he would concede, if he was here, that someone should do something to stop such evil? Jacob breaks into her thoughts with his night prayer; for once, his words are exactly right: 'Lord God Almighty, forgive them their iniquities, imbue in us, thy servants, the courage to do what is right.'

'Amen,' Elsie says with fervour. 'Amen.'

Tonight she is warm with her goodnights, grateful for this place of safety so far from the horrors of the world. Daniel's story is still fresh in her mind; her parents-in-law have both suffered so much. Perhaps they still do. She must make it her business not to cross them, not to cause them any more pain. She is young; she will not be here forever. In a world so lacking in tolerance, she at least can afford to be kind. She will start with Christmas, she resolves. After she has written Jack a carefully worded account of recent events, she will make it one they will all remember.

The next day she is up bright and early to keep her silent promise. She and Leah have already made the cake and the pudding, saving a year's worth of rations so there is enough dried fruit. Turkey may be in short supply, but the butcher has promised to keep a little one aside for the Flints. She is pleased to see the sun is up too; with any luck the road will be clear in a day or so, she will be able to get into Sandstown to pick it up. She even forces herself to invite Veronica and her widowed mother to lunch, knowing how much her mother-in-law will appreciate the gesture. It is a shame she can't extend the invitation to Daniel; she'll save him some turkey on the quiet.

Her plans keep her busy over the next week. Since Megan Davies left to stay with her mother

Elsie has had her hands full. Normally she resents the work entailed in keeping this massive house clean; but now she is determined the place will sparkle. She mops and polishes, ending every day with an aching back and chafed hands, but delighting in the result. The snow thaws, enabling her to collect the turkey. It is only 8 pounds, but it is still a turkey and, with the vegetable rations Veronica sends over, she should be able to stretch the food to give a semblance of Christmases gone by. She persuades Will it will be fun to cut up his old comics for paper chains. They have not had a tree for years – there is no one young and strong enough to cut down a fir tree from the estate. On a whim, she decides to create one out of twigs gathered in the woods. She and the children spend a happy afternoon in the kitchen painting the branches white. They make tree decorations from sweet wrappers and are delighted one day to come across a forgotten box of baubles in the butler's kitchen that improve their efforts considerably.

Her hard work does not go unnoticed. Jacob takes her aside the night before Christmas to thank her. Leah goes as far as to smile in gratitude when she receives Elsie's present, a leather-bound King James Bible, discovered in a second-hand book-shop. Will is delighted with his fort, not even noticing the corner has been knocked. Evie loves the knitted teddy bear Elsie found in a wool shop in Sandstown. All in all, as they gather by the Christmas tree at the end of the day for evening prayers, and Jacob reads 'Glory to God in the highest heaven, and on earth peace', Elsie is satisfied. The children go to sleep happy; Elsie lies down in her empty bed, more peaceful than she has been in weeks. Jack maybe far away, but all wars end eventually. All she has to do is preserve this fragile peace with Jacob and Leah, and she will survive till they are reunited.

DANIEL 1

Christmas blows in with a gale that wakes Daniel in the early hours to a dark, chilly bedroom. It is so cold he cannot get back to sleep; after half an hour of tossing and turning he has to rise, put on another pair of socks, grab a jumper from the wardrobe. He is reminded of childhood winters in the boarding house, when he shivered under bedclothes that were always too thin. Now, as then, the extra clothes don't help. At six he gives up trying to go back to sleep, and instead stumbles downstairs to the kitchen. He lights the fire, makes himself a cup of tea, watches the black sky turn gradually grey.

'Merry Christmas,' he says to the wall, knowing the day will be far from merry. *And whose fault is that?* he thinks morosely. If he hadn't thrown June over, he'd be getting ready to pick her up; he'd have borrowed Geraint Thomas's car to drive to the meeting in Sandstown, which would be followed by a feast with the other land girls. He can't blame them for not welcoming him this year, but he'll miss the good humour and raucous jokes. If he'd had any sense, he'd have accepted Aunt

Joy's invitation to spend the season in York. Instead he has lingered here, hoping Elsie might work some miracle and wangle him an invite at the Hall. Some chance. Leaving his Christmas present on the doorstep with a couple of mince pies was the best she could manage. He ate the mince pies last night, but in obedience to the dictum she scribbled on the brown wrapping paper – *Not to be opened till Christmas Day!* – has left the present on the table. He unwraps it now, smiling as he uncovers a leather-bound copy of Donne's poetry. She has inscribed it with a quotation from one of his favourite poems.

'The world affords few friends will bide
   the test'
Happy Christmas, All my love, Elsie

The book and the quotation are a sure sign he is forgiven, and that knowledge is enough to rouse him from his depression. He finishes his drink, throws the tea leaves down the sink and rinses the cup, readying himself for the day ahead. Since he is up this early, he might as well brave the weather and walk to Sandstown for the meeting. He makes slow progress: it is a hard, hard slog maintaining the limp, the wind is in his face the whole time and the rain rarely lets up. It is a far cry from Christmases past, particularly that last one with Jack and Elsie . . .

★   ★   ★

It was good of them to have him that year, it being their first Christmas as parents – their last, had they but known it, in peace-time. But they'd insisted, saying they wanted to share the season with their best friend; no one else would do. It was 18 months since Elsie's dad had died and Daniel had persuaded Jack to do the right thing by her – 18 months in which he'd learnt to suppress his feelings, to push back the pain of losing her to Jack. Now, as he spent these days in their home, he found being on the edge of her joy was enough to make it bearable. Motherhood suited her. Marriage suited her. She danced and laughed her way through the season; she'd never looked so beautiful.

One evening, a couple of days after Christmas, Jack was called out to a patient, leaving Daniel alone with Elsie for the first time since her marriage. Will was sleeping peacefully in the cradle upstairs, a fire crackled in the hearth, the lights of the tree sparkled: red, yellow, pink, blue and green. They were full after a delicious beef stew, and were making their way through a bottle of red wine.

'Careful,' she said, as he poured her another glass. 'I mustn't get squiffy – I've a child to care for.'

'I've poured you half a glass.'

'We'll save the rest for Jack.' She settled back in the rocking chair. 'This is nice, you and me together again. It's not happened for an age. I wish you were still in Liverpool – I miss our chats.'

'Me too.'

'Tell me, what have you been reading? It's Jack's one flaw – his lack of interest in books. I've been starved of a decent literary conversation.'

'Orwell – *Burmese Days*.'

'Is it any good?'

'I'll say. Tells the truth about the Empire – the one we're not supposed to see. Where the natives are always inferior and the British always cruel.'

'That's a bit harsh, isn't it?'

'Is it? I always think it's the Englishman's best-kept secret – behind the veneer of good manners and pleasant speech, a brutal tyrant lurks. Orwell knew it; he saw it. No wonder the book was banned.'

'Do you think they'll ever shake off the yoke, then? The natives, in India, Africa, Asia?'

'I don't doubt it . . . I hate to say it, but it'll probably take a war to shake things up. It usually does. And when it does, you can count on one thing.'

'What's that?'

'The world being rewritten. Look at the last one. The Ottoman Empire, Austro-Hungarian Empire, Russian Empire . . . they'd lasted for years. Suddenly all gone. We'll go that way too. It's inevitable.'

'All empires fall then?'

'Of course.' They hadn't heard the door open, heralding Jack's return. He is grinning as he enters the room. 'That's your thesis, isn't it, Daniel?

Though why in heaven's name you're talking about it at Christmas, I don't know.'

They laughed as he poured a drink and settled down on the sofa, pulling Elsie to him. She sat on his lap, resting her head under his chin, immediately destroying the illusion that Daniel had been secretly harbouring: that it was he who was master of the house, the sleeping child upstairs his own . . .

Well, that was a long time ago. No good comes of thinking about it now, he reflects as reaches the town. Though he is anxious to get out of the cold, he is careful to make his way to the Meeting House slowly in case he encounters anyone on the way. Once he arrives he is grateful to be greeted by Frances with a warm smile and a hot drink before the service starts.

'Merry Christmas!' she says. 'You're soaking wet! You've never walked all the way from Whetstone with your weak ankle?'

'I took it slowly. I couldn't have got here otherwise.'

'I call that very dedicated. Here, let me take your coat.'

She hangs it by the tiny electric fire; it steams by the light of the two red bars. He sits down, letting the drink warm his hands, getting ready for silence. As others gather, and the clerk announces the meeting open, the warmth steals through his body and he finds the early start, the walk taking its toll. Soon, he is nodding off . . .

He dreams he is back in Liverpool, sitting with Elsie in the living room. But in the dream, it his lap she is sitting on, his head she nestles against. Jack is consigned to the rocking chair in the corner, an envious observer of their marital cosiness.

'So I think, at this season, in this time of war, of the child born for us, the wonder-counsellor, Prince of Peace.' George's booming voice jerks him awake. 'And I rest my hopes in Him rather than all the might of Europe.'

Daniel pinches himself awake, hoping that no one has noticed his unintentional nap. He forces himself to listen to the silence, focus his thoughts on God and prayers for peace, rather than his selfish wanderings.

After the service, George wanders up to him. 'A bit tedious, was I, then?'

'What? Oh no, sorry, I was just awake early, and tired from walking . . .'

'Don't worry, Frances says I always go on to much. She also says you must come back with us – that is, if you haven't got any other plans?'

Daniel is about to refuse. Then he thinks of the cold journey home, the empty house; remembers his mother saying kindness was hard to come by – you should always appreciate it when offered. He accepts gratefully.

They are kind, George and Frances, and it's a better Christmas then he'd expected, but the days that follow are dreary. A heavy fall of snow just before New Year means the path to Arthur's Stone is impassable. There is no chance of meeting Elsie, and left to his own devices he finds himself feeling gloomy once more. On the last day of the holidays, he is restless and tired of being cooped up in the house. He steps out for some fresh air. The snow has melted as quickly as it came, but the brisk wind is cold and the grey sky threatens rain. Passing the churchyard, he notices the gate is slightly open. On an impulse he decides to enter. It is some time since he has visited his mother's graveside; he ought to pay her a visit. A small creature scurries through the bushes, but as he reaches the corner of the church, he is conscious of another sound. A voice murmuring. It is indistinct at first; then he can hear a name, spoken over and over again.

'Rachel, Rachel, Rachel.'

Daniel is sure he knows that voice; he presses through the gloom to be sure. He reaches the yew tree overhanging his mother's grave. Someone is kneeling by the graveside, his back bent. He is repeating the name over and over again, sobbing, 'Rachel, Rachel, Rachel.'

It is Jacob Flint.

Daniel steps back, taking care not to so much as break a twig. There is a wooden seat beside the far wall, hidden from sight by a holly bush. He makes his way there, sits down, shaking. He should feel sorry for the man, but he is filled with anger. How dare his uncle, how dare he? Wasn't it enough that he'd driven a wedge between Rachel and

Leah? That he'd allowed his feelings to overcome his sense of propriety, so the last weeks of Rachel's life were full of trouble? That he'd refused to bury her with the husband who loved her? She'd been dead 20 years, and yet he was still trying to lay claim to the woman who'd rejected him in life. The cheek of the man.

He watches the remaining colour drain out of the sky, trying to control his feelings, keep his breathing calm. Presently, he is aware that Jacob has stopped speaking. He rises from his seat, peering at his uncle from behind the holly bush. The older man is standing now, his back erect and stiff as usual. He touches the top of the grave, then marches away, as if the sobbing wretch had been some other person entirely. Daniel watches him pass out into the gloomy night, hears the gate squeak, signalling his departure. He is alone among the dead.

He steps out from behind the bush and returns down the path to the grave. Jacob has left a wreath of holly beside the stone. He has cleaned off the lichen, revealing the epitaph that had been hidden: *She passed through glory's morning gate and walked in paradise.* The fury that Daniel had pushed back resurfaces. This isn't the proper resting place for his mother. These aren't her sentiments. She should be with his father in the cemetery in York. And it isn't Jacob's place to be cleaning her grave or leaving her wreaths. She detested holly.

'Bloody Flints. Bloody, bloody Flints. They take everything.'

The rain starts to fall; he hardly notices in his rage. He picks up the holly wreath in disgust and begins to tear it apart. The points prick him so hard that he bleeds, drops of bright-red blood that fall on top of the gravestone. Soon the wreath is in tatters. He gathers up the leaves, throws them in the corner of the graveyard under a fir tree. Back at the stone, he traces his fingers over her name: Rachel Clarkson. He tries to recall her face, her voice, her smell. But she has been gone too long. All that remains is the snatch of a smile, blurred features, like an overexposed photograph. She can't help him now.

It is only when he stands up that it comes to him that he is wrong. The dead do speak. They always speak. All he has to do is listen to the memories resting inside him, the stories that his parents left behind. He can, if he wishes, be like Jacob Flint, giving into a hopeless, pointless passion that would destroy the people he most cares about, or he can be the kind of man his mother needed. A man to offer friendship, love and support, asking for nothing in return. Because that is all Elsie wants from him. It comes to him that he has yet to make a New Year's resolution, and it must be this – to be her friend, and just her friend, all thoughts of love and passion put aside.

ELSIE 2

Elsie knows she is dreaming but she cannot wake up, no matter how she tries. In the dream, she hears the plane, just as she did last autumn . . .

She was down in the village, walking back from the bus when she heard it: the noise of an engine that was definitely not British. Not wanting to alarm the children, she put on her brightest smile and steered them towards the churchyard, hoping it might be the safest place. Though in truth, when you are in the path of an enemy bomber, nowhere can be counted safe. She walked quickly, trying not to let the children sense her anxiety at how close the plane sounded.

Just as they arrived at the church, the plane shot out of the clouds . . . It trailed flame and smoke, orange-black; the flight-path was so low, they could see the pilot still on board, struggling to gain enough height to escape – or maybe to change course. Not understanding what they were seeing, the children clapped in excitement; petrified, Elsie stood still, unable to speak.

The engine cut out just over the water meadows by the stream. By now a small crowd had gathered, watching the plane plummet to the ground, the explosion echoing back across the valley. At first, there were cheers and laughter as the community united in the downfall of one of their enemy. Elsie whooped with the rest, thinking of Het surviving bombers like this every night, the ruins of Walker Street, the danger Jack faced every day. Then it occurred to her that perhaps the pilot had known he was crashing; perhaps he had been trying to avoid hitting them. Others seemed to have had the same thought, or maybe a sense of humanity was creeping back in, for suddenly people were rushing down the valley to see if they could help. It was only then that she thought he might have a wife waiting for him at home, a wife who would now be waiting in vain. She watched helplessly, unable to move, as a plume of black smoke rose from the crash site, an orange glow lit up the hill. The men fought hard to put the flames out, but it was no use. *Poor bugger bought it*, they said, as they came back up the hill. *Brave for a Jerry, wasn't he?* She found herself weeping for the widow left behind, the children who would lose their father; knowing that, one day, this could be her fate.

Now, in her dream, she sees the plane flying overhead. The pilot is signalling to her, begging for help. She can see he is trying to escape from the hatch, pleading with her to get him out. It is only as he takes off his mask that she recognises Jack. Through the glass he is mouthing *Elsie, Elsie, Elsie*, but there is nothing she can do. She watches, helpless, as his plane corkscrews through the sky, crashing into the valley below.

She wakes to a grey dawn, shaking. She stretches out to Jack for comfort; after four years she should be used to his absence – the untouched pillow, the empty side of the bed. Yet it is always a shock to find him gone, that she must face her fears alone. There is a yell from next door; it seems she is not the only one suffering from bad dreams. Evie is rigid with terror and screaming when she picks her up. Elsie takes her next door so as not to wake Will, rocking the child to and fro till her sobs subside, the nightmare recedes. She wishes, not for the first time, she had someone to do the same for her.

It is early, but there is no going back to sleep now. Together they creep down to the kitchen, where Elsie makes up some powdered milk, boiling it on the hob. She pours some for Evie, cooling it with half a cup of water, stirring in a little bit of sugar. The little girl sits on her chair, content with her drink. Outside the sun flames the horizon, sending pink and orange light across the kitchen wall. The sky turns from blue-black to pale blue; the day ahead looks promising. Perhaps spring is not so far away. Though, it being scullery day, there will not be much time to enjoy the better weather – Leah will expect the kitchens to be gleaming by lunch. She likes to wander through when Elsie is done, checking for signs of dust, remembering her days as a young bride when she had hordes of servants to do her will. Elsie sighs. It's not as if she's not used to the hard work; she always was a grafter. It's just that when she married Jack, she thought she was going to escape all that. She begins to make preparations for breakfast, the horror of the dream still imprinted on her mind, like the negative of a photograph. As she mixes the porridge, she tries to recall another image to overlay the terrors of the night. A picture comes to her of a September morning, eight years ago: the day her boys first knocked on her door. The day that everything changed for good . . .

She hadn't expected it to be anything other than a normal Tuesday. Cleaning bedrooms, driving the last of the round-faced sweaty salesmen from the house; avoiding their winks and knowing looks, the assumption that because they were close to the docks, she'd be prepared to offer more than just bed and breakfast. Dad was sleeping off the effects of another bender and she was just going to start on the kitchen when the doorbell rang. She had no expectations as to who it might be; they only ever attracted one type down here. Middle-aged men with greasy hair and lustful eyes: down on their luck, trudging through the streets with their pitiful wares. Jack and Daniel were a total surprise

– a sight for sore eyes, as her mother used to say. She noticed Jack first: tall, with broad shoulders giving a distinct impression of muscles underneath. Fair wavy hair, a lock falling over his face. Piercing grey-blue eyes, like the sea on a calm winter's morning. A casual confident charm. Daniel was taller, more diffident. Even then he stood back, as if in Jack's perpetual shadow. Well, she understood that better now. His was a different sort of attractiveness. A mop of dark curls, a vague, distracted air. A man who'd look after you whatever happened. They were so different from the usual punters she was almost lost for words.

Luckily, Jack, standing right beside the vacancy sign, was daft enough to ask, 'Do you have a room for rent?' It enabled her to retain her composure with, 'No, that's why we put the advert up.' They fell about laughing, and she welcomed them in.

Students – that was rare. They usually liked to live up in town by the university. They didn't explain, Daniel the teacher and Jack the doctor; just said the price was right, and asked to move in. Boy, could they! They didn't know it, but she'd have let them in at half the price. If it weren't for Dad snoring upstairs she'd have done it, too. She made do with a discount on the deposit, agreed a moving-in date and let them go; it was hard to tell who was more satisfied.

They soon settled into an easy routine. They were always out and about together: dancing, concerts, the flicks. The Three Musketeers, Jack always said; all for one and one for all. They were such a contrast to the men she normally encountered. She'd never known anyone talk about poetry and books like Daniel; she could listen to him for hours. He introduced her to writers, encouraged her first feeble attempts at criticism, gave her a glimpse of the university life Dad had denied her. And Jack – right from the start, she was drawn to Jack. It wasn't just the way he made her laugh, the tiny kindnesses that helped her through each day; right from the first, being in his presence made her feel safe, at home, as if she had known him always. Though it wasn't till that day on the beach that she'd realised how much he meant to her. Then, when Dad died, she knew she would always need him. That he'd always care for her, providing the perfect escape from the drudgery she'd lived with since Mum died.

Some escape this has turned out to be, she thinks ruefully as she hears Leah in the corridor, keys rattling round her waist like a jailor. She forces back the pointless resentment, wishes the older woman a good morning, doles out porridge in a bowl. There is no point being gloomy about her situation – life is what it is. There are people far worse off than her. She resolves to focus on the positive today. She throws herself into the day's tasks with enthusiasm, heartened by the news report on the radio that the Germans have been defeated at Stalingrad. Nothing lasts forever; the last war was over in four years. Perhaps the end of this one is not too far away.

Then comes the best part of the day: the noise of Annie Thomas's van in the drive, the crunch of gravel as her firm steps walk to the door, the thud of a letter on the mat. Elsie rushes to pick it up; she hasn't heard from Jack for weeks. And there is his flowing writing on the envelope. She rips the letter open, reads it straight away. Then, later, when all her tasks are done and the children are out in the garden, she sits and reads it over and over again, imprinting his words on her brain.

5th February 1943

Dearest Else,

Thanks for your letter. Sorry I haven't written sooner; this is the first time I've had the chance in ages. I'm writing in haste because I don't have much time to catch the post. I am glad you had such a good Christmas and that the children had such fun. You must have worked a bit of a miracle this year, because my father bothered to mention how much you'd done in his New Year letter. Well done, old girl. I'm so proud of the way you put up with living there. And I'm glad all is well with you and Daniel – that you've had that conversation. I hope you understand why I've respected his wishes and not talked about his past until now. It makes it bearable being here, knowing he is there to look after you.

I don't know when I'll get the chance to write again. I'm hoping it won't be too long. But then I'm always hoping this whole damn shooting match will be over soon. How about we start making plans for afterwards? Mine start with a hotel room with just you and me, a bottle of Champagne, silk sheets and the deepest, hottest bath you've ever seen. How about yours?

Must go. My love always, the kids, my parents, Daniel. But most of all to you.

Jack xxx

It's amazing how a few words make all the difference to her day – that he can, after all, comfort her from so far away. She smiles at his plans for the end of the war. She'll be in that hotel like a shot the minute peace is declared. Afterwards, they'll pack their bags and get as far away from Echo Hall as they can. Back to Liverpool, Manchester maybe, or why not even London? He'll start his practice, they'll buy a big house nearby, in a nice neighbourhood where the kids can walk to school. Of course, Daniel will have to come, too; they can't do without him. He can live next door, teach at the school, help out with the kids. They can return to life as it was, before it was interrupted by war and separation: dancing, concerts, flicks – the Three Musketeers, all for one and one for all. The thought sustains her for days and weeks, as the news of German defeats in Russia bring hope that perhaps the war is on the turn, and the grey skies of winter melt into spring blues. All she has to do, she keeps reminding herself, is to sit these years out. The war cannot last forever. It cannot.

DANIEL 2

Once more, tiny green buds are appearing on the branches. The land girls drive the horses through the brown fields, churning up the mud ready for planting. Lambs with wobbly legs begin to appear on the hillsides, gradually growing in confidence, throwing themselves about the fields with abandon. The air grows warmer; the skies are blue more often than grey. And with the lengthening of the days, Daniel finds himself full of renewed energy. Since his resolve by his mother's graveside, he has regained some peace of mind. Now Elsie knows all his secrets, now June has forgiven him enough to write chatty letters from London, he is discovering that he has, after all, the strength to continue. He has wasted the winter moping over the woman he can never have; now he finds himself wanting to make the best of things, just as his mother always did. He finds it more rewarding than he could have imagined. He throws himself into work, finding joy in the simple pleasure of watching children master a topic that once defeated them, their enjoyment in an after-school treat, the talents on show at the

Easter concert. He continues to meet Elsie as usual, and finds, with his mind so full of school activities, he has stopped fretting about her. Instead he enjoys the friendship he has – the company of an intelligent, sensitive woman – and finds that it is enough.

As May approaches, his days are full of preparations for the May Day procession. Although the choice of May King is straightforward – pick any boy so long as he doesn't object too much to the indignity of the smart suit and crown – the selection of the May Queen is full of complications. A balance must be struck between rewarding good behaviour and the need for the queen to be beautiful. Thankfully, this year the choice is easy. Nine-year-old Jenny Jones is pretty enough, good enough and popular enough anyway, but the recent death of her father cements her selection. Everyone agrees she is the perfect choice.

In the days before the war, the May procession was a grand affair. Nellie Evans would gather donations from the villagers to create a satin dress and lace train for the lucky queen, white cotton for the king, taffeta for the princesses, silk waistcoats for the page boys. The florist in Sandstown supplied bouquets. The king and queen were crowned in a special service in the church before being pulled through the village by the page boys for maypole dancing on the green; afterwards there was a grand spread in the village hall, the children feasting on sausages on sticks, cheese, crackers, biscuits, jelly, ice cream and as much fizzy pop as their parents allowed. War has brought many changes. The queen has had the same dress for four years, tacked and re-tacked for each successive child by the patient Nellie. The king's cotton suit has grown grubby, requiring an annual bleaching to give it some semblance of its former pristine condition. There simply isn't enough material left to clothe more than one princess and page boy. They walk spreading blossom behind the royal carriage, which is pulled by those boys who still possess a decent suit. The celebration party limits the children to one glass of squash and a few biscuits each. And yet it doesn't stop Jenny Jones beaming as Reverend Dawson places the crown on her head; being chosen as May Queen is still special. Daniel smiles as he watches, glad to see her happy; she has been sad too long.

The church service over, Daniel leads the procession along the high street. It doesn't seem so long ago that he and Jack were excited page boys hauling the royal carriage along the road. The sun shone as they processed through the village, cheered on by his mother, who even roused herself from her grief to support them. Aunt Leah was more restrained, of course, but she too had enjoyed the event. They were at the village green, too, applauding as he danced around the maypole, weaving the ribbons, red, green, yellow, blue, purple, orange, until they made a neat pattern around the wood. Today, the weather is less kind.

The grey cloud that greeted them as they entered the church has turned to drizzle by the time they leave, and becomes a full-fledged downpour before they are halfway down the road. The king and queen are protected by the hood over their cart, but everyone else is soon soaked. The procession marches quickly; no one wants to stay out in this. When they reach the hall, the children stampede inside, whooping and yelping. It takes some time to restore order, and for Daniel to notice that Elsie has not made it down, as she promised. Perhaps the rain has put her off. He has no time for disappointment, however; he is needed to supervise the king and queen taking their thrones on the stage so they can oversee the entertainment. The bad weather has put paid to the maypole, but there is country dancing, singing, a little skit to be performed. And afterwards, party games: blind man's bluff, musical chairs and dead lions. It takes all his skill as a teacher to prevent the whole event descending into pandemonium. By the time the last red-faced child has left and the last crumb has been swept up, he is exhausted, ready to go home and have a long soak in the bath.

It is only when he is locking up that Mrs Hunt, the caretaker, says, 'Are they alright up at the big house?'

'Who?'

'The family . . . I thought you'd know.'

'Know what?'

'They've had news . . . the worst kind.'

'Jack?'

'Shot down.'

He can feel the colour leech from his cheeks as he steadies himself against the wall. 'I hadn't heard.'

His heart pounds. *Elsie, poor Elsie.* Then, almost as an afterthought: *Jack. Poor blighter. I hope it was quick.*

He moves slowly, the news seeping through his body like damp through the walls of a house. He is reminded of the day of his father's death, when everything slowed down as if he were living in a dream. He must have said goodbye to Mrs Hunt, handed the hall key in at the vicarage, but he remembers nothing of it afterwards. He is halfway to Echo Hall before he is even aware that he is walking, that the wind has rendered his umbrella useless; his hair is wet, his jacket soaking. He isn't even quite sure why he is going up there. He knows there is no hope of welcome – they didn't want him when Henry died; they won't want him now – but he has to try, and Elsie will be glad to see him at any rate. His footsteps beat out a rhythm, *Jack's dead, Jack's dead, Jack's dead.* His brain can't take it in. Jack can't be dead. He passes the trees on the edge of the estate. An image of Jack flashes into his mind: grinning from the top of the branches, daring Daniel to join him. Though they both knew he wouldn't. Daniel's courage was reserved for other occasions – defying Jacob when his strictures seemed too unfair; taking the punishment for something they had both done. He'd been happy to do it; it balanced the times when Jack led him out of a mess with his mates. It doesn't seem possible that the man with whom he's shared so much can be gone. How can Jack be dead? How can he? He reaches the gravel at the top of the drive, his feet sinking into the tiny stones like quicksand. He lifts his fist to knock on the door. There is no answer. He knocks again. After several more minutes, Leah comes to the door. Her bloated cheeks are ash-white; her grey hair lifeless.

'I came as soon as I heard . . . to pay my respects . . .' His voice falters. She looks straight through him. 'Aunt Leah?'

Still she says nothing, then her lips open a fraction. At first he cannot make out the words; he has to concentrate hard to understand. 'All dead, all dead, all dead . . .'

'Aunt Leah, are you alright?'

'They're dead. Both of them dead. Why are you still alive?' She pushes her face towards him, her jowls wobbling in fury. She looks almost comical; for a moment he is tempted to laugh. He bites it back. He cannot afford to make this situation worse than it is already.

'I'm sorry. Can I come in?'

'You're nothing but a coward, like your father before you.'

'Shall I fetch someone for you? Elsie? Uncle Jacob?'

'Don't you dare come near me. You should be

out there fighting like they were. It should have been you.' She spits at him.

'I came to help.'

'Keep away from us.'

She closes the door. He remains on the doorstep, uncertain what to do. Is Elsie upstairs? Will she see him? Come down? He stares up at the house, but the dark windows stare back at him, like blank unseeing eyes. Still he waits on the drive, willing her to appear at the window, so she can see he is there, waiting, ready to offer her whatever she needs. She does not come.

Jack is dead. There will be no more parties to celebrate his homecoming. His death will be another statistic in a report of casualties that won't even make it to the front page. A fact unremarkable to everyone except for the people who loved him. They won't even have the comfort of a funeral – making do, like everyone else, with a service without a body, a name engraved in stone on the war memorial. Another life gone from the village, and what for? Water trickles down his collar, reminding him he is cold and damp. There is no sign of Elsie, but still he lingers. It is only after another half-hour in which he becomes thoroughly chilled that he admits to himself there is no point standing here getting wet. He must try to meet her on Saturday as usual – she will be relying on him to be there. He turns away from the house and limps down the hill through the driving rain. When he arrives home he is soaked to the skin. He is too tired for a bath now; instead he runs upstairs to put on dry clothes as quickly as he can.

After he has changed, dried his hair, hung his clothes in the kitchen, he enters his parlour and pulls out a bottle of whisky from the sideboard. He pours himself a glass, downing it in one, before opening the drawer, looking for the photo that Will spoilt last Easter. It is right at the back, buried under some bills, still marked with soot. He fetches a damp cloth to wipe off the black marks. He holds the picture, staring at the carefree faces, thinking of that day when war seemed impossible: sunshine, beaches, laughing children. Now the man on the left is gone for good. He pours himself another glass, another and another. He has never been teetotal like his parents, but he doesn't usually drink like this. The whisky burns his throat, making his head spin. He doesn't care. Anything to blot out the knowledge that is rising in him: his best friend, his last hero, has gone, never to return. He drinks and drinks till he reaches a point when he isn't even aware he is drinking. He drinks till his eyes become heavy, he sinks his head on the table, closes his eyes and sleeps.

It is dawn when he wakes: a grey, chill dawn. His clothes are crumpled, his breath smells foul and putrid. His throat is sore and parched. The photo lies on the table where he'd rested his head. He picks it up. The laughing faces gaze back at him as if to mock him, reminding him that the day before was no dream, but cold, hard reality.

ELSIE 3

When the telegrams had come for Henry and Tommy Davies, Elsie had known something wasn't right from Annie Thomas's footsteps on the drive. Their usual briskness had drained away to be replaced by a slow funereal stomp. The knock on the door had been heavy, and she'd only had to look at the postwoman's face to know the news was bad. But Jack's telegram comes without warning. The steps on the gravel are firm, the rap on the door sharp. Elsie rushes to open it; it's been a while since she heard from him. She's hoping for a letter today. It does not register at first that the stranger standing on the doorstep has anything of importance to say; it is not until she sees the proffered envelope that the truth dawns on her. Even then, she doesn't want to admit it.

'Where's Annie?'

'Sick. I'm covering her round today.'

'Oh.' Elsie finds herself, like Megan Davies before her, unable to receive the envelope.

'Can you take it, love? I've a busy day ahead of me, double the work, can't get behind.'

Elsie is brought to her senses. 'I'm sorry.' She takes the telegram, walks slowly to the kitchen, as if slowing the pace can prevent the inevitable. As she passes through the baize door, she hears the crack of the engine backfiring, then silence, followed by a chug, chug, chug as the woman revives the motor. The sound fades into the distance as she steps into the kitchen and sits down, ripping open the envelope. She reads it several times before the words fully register. Black capitals on grey paper, spelling out the message she never wanted to receive.

REGRET TO REPORT FLIGHT SER-
GEANT JACK FLINT, SQUADRON
367 KILLED IN ACTION. LETTER
FOLLOWS.

She is still staring at it when Leah enters. 'Was that the post?' she asks.

For a moment, Elsie cannot speak, her dislike for her mother-in-law overwhelmed by an immense wave of pity – for the intolerable pain she is about to inflict on Leah. She hands the telegram over silently, rising to make tea, the banal ritual of comfort. As if a hot drink can salve the wound that is ripping through her. Leah reads with glazed incomprehension.

As the kettle screeches to boiling point, she looks up. 'He is dead then?' Her voice is flat. 'Both of them dead. My brave boys killed in battle while hers cowers at home among women and children.'

Elsie winces. It is not long since she'd shared such sentiments; she knows it will do no good to point out that her mother-in-law is being unfair.

'Let's not think about that now.'

She pours the water into the pot, watching as the leaves turn it rusty brown.

Leah stares at the telegram, then places it on the table. 'I will call the quarry. Jacob must be informed.'

She spurns the tea, leaving Elsie to drink alone. It seems that in grief they are further apart than ever. The children are upstairs in the playroom; she must find a way to bring them this news. She swills her tea; it tastes bitter. Dregs swirl at the bottom of the cup. She tries to compose herself, to summon the right words so she can explain. As if any words can be right in the circumstances. When she has drained the last drop, she cannot put the moment off any longer. She climbs the stairs to tell them.

The children listen without apparent emotion as she tells them their father is dead; it is hard to know if they have fully understood. Evie seems more put out that they will miss the May procession – for Elsie cannot face people today. When she sees her mother is adamant on this point, she wanders off to the toy box. Will is more matter-of-fact. He wants to know the time of the mission, the type of plane, the place where Jack was shot.

But all Elsie has are 14 words, black capitals on grey paper that provide no answers other than to tell them the man they all love is gone.

At last Will gives up, launching into a new topic. 'We'll need a new Daddy now. Can we have Daniel?'

She glances away, not wanting him to see the tears form – if only life was that simple. Seeing that he will not receive an answer, he too drifts away to the toy fort he received at Christmas, setting himself to creating a battle scene full of noise and fury.

Leah calls Elsie to the hall. Jacob will be back later, but they need to inform friends and family and she is not up to the task. She does not stop to enquire whether Elsie will be able to manage it; she simply leaves the address book, and retires to her bedroom. Elsie picks it up. The only person Elsie wants to speak to is Daniel but he has no phone, and besides, he will be tied up with the May Day celebrations. There is no way of contacting him. Outside the sky darkens, forcing her to turn on the lights; the rain begins to drum on the windows as she starts dialling. Though the first call almost chokes her, she finds herself developing a patter that she can repeat effortlessly by the end of the morning. *I'm sorry to share the bad news . . . Thank you for your kind thoughts . . . We are all as well as can be expected.* Meaningless words that help keep the reality of black letters on grey paper at bay.

The rain continues throughout the afternoon. Perhaps it's the muted atmosphere or the knowledge they are confined to the house that make Will and Evie run up and down the stairs, shouting so loudly that Elsie has to tell them off sternly for fear of disturbing Leah. The day drags on. At last, at four o'clock, Elsie cannot bear being inside any longer. She forces the children into raincoats and boots, dragging them out for a muddy wet walk in the woods. They are cold and miserable when they return an hour later, arriving just as Jacob comes in from work. His face is grey and worn. He moves towards them as if in pain, putting his arm around Elsie's shoulder in half an embrace. She has never been so physically close to him; his arm is thin and hard, his clothes smell of dust. He holds her for a moment, saying, as he lets her go, 'You will always have a place here, daughter.'

'Thank you.' It is not the place of her choosing, but where else can she go now? This is still the safest place she can be. She has no money, and without Jack no hope of any, aside from a tiny widow's pension. It won't be enough to help her escape Echo Hall – not now, perhaps not ever.

Jacob turns to Will, who is clinging to Elsie's damp skirt. 'You must look after your mother now, young man.' Will nods, not daring to contradict his grandfather. 'You must *be* your father now. You are the last Flint left. The quarry will be yours one day.'

Will tries not to look terrified at the prospect.

Evie whimpers, her wet socks giving Elsie the excuse she needs to run upstairs. *Over my dead body*, she mutters to herself as she changes their clothes and dries their hair. Over my dead body.

The week passes. Elsie knows she is alive because the children need feeding, the house needs cleaning, the shopping needs buying. She knows she is alive because when Will wakes crying for his daddy in the night, she is up immediately to console him. She knows she is alive because she still burns her fingers when she lights the gas stove. She is alive because the smell of soggy cabbage still offends her nostrils: a smell forever associated with death and mourning since the day she couldn't wake Dad from his teatime nap. The cabbage had been boiling in the kitchen as she tried to rouse him; it had run dry by the time Jack had appeared. He used all his medical skill, but it wasn't enough. The heart attack had killed him instantly; there was nothing anyone could have done. And later, later, while she was concluding that the business had too many debts, that she must pack up and find herself a job, any job if she was to survive, Jack had proposed. He'd stood in her dingy kitchen promising her he would always . . . She can't bear to think about it. She forces her body through the days, because life goes on, because it must.

Daniel doesn't call or visit. It is strange, but perhaps he knows he will not be welcome. She doesn't dare go down to see him. If the wagging tongues of Whetstone were so active when Jack was alive, what will they make of her visiting him the minute Jack is dead? Perhaps Daniel is doing the same, hiding out at home to avoid the intrusive stares, as miserable as she is. All she can do is hold on till Saturday, hoping they can meet as usual. But when Saturday comes, bringing rain-filled skies, Will is reluctant to go out, not wanting to face another sodden walk. Evie follows her brother's lead, and the pair fill the nursery with whines and wails. This is no good. Leah is her only hope of escape.

'I need some fresh air,' she announces to the older woman, who is sitting in the living room gazing out of the window.

'It's raining.'

'I'll take a brolly. It's too wet for the children.'

'Very well. Leave them with me.' Leah's voice is a listless monotone.

'Thank you.'

Elsie exhorts the children to be good before departing up the familiar path. She is glad of the umbrella. By the time she reaches the woods, the rain is cascading out of the sky, creating large puddles on the paths, rivulets that rush down the hill. The way is thick with black mud; her feet sink, leaving deep imprints that fill with water the minute she moves on. It is slow work; by the time she reaches the top, her skirt is wet and mud-spattered.

Daniel is not there. The weather must have put

him off, too. Her efforts have been wasted: she is truly alone. There is no one to help. No one. The wind whips the rain into her face, driving her into the cave. The words from lovers, normally such a comfort, mock her now. *EF & JF*, a love that was supposed to last for years. She throws down her umbrella, falling to her knees, pounding the ground, shouting his name. 'Jack, Jack, Jack!' Useless words for no one. 'Jack, Jack, Jack.'

And then some arms are round her, and they are like Jack's arms, but thinner, not so strong. A smell of musk, like Jack's aftershave, but not quite so sweet. The man who is taking her into his arms is enough like Jack for her to want to believe it. Like Jack, but not quite.

'Else, oh Else.'

Daniel holds her closer than he's ever held her. Closer than she's ever let him hold her. And now, suddenly, it doesn't matter how much he is holding her, how close he is. Because the reason that has kept them apart is gone. She gazes up at the face, so like Jack's but so unlike. And suddenly, is he kissing her or is she kissing him? She wants this, she does not want this. She should stop, she can't stop. It is a curse, a blessing, a necessity. And it is the end of everything.

Afterwards, she picks up her discarded clothes, remnants of her once-fashionable past: the camisole knickers, the brassiere, cotton top, sodden skirt. She pulls them over her shaking body, not daring to look at him. They dress in silence. As she turns to leave the cave, she sees the rain has stopped; the sky is streaked with gold light as the sun tries to force its way through the clouds.

'I'm sorry,' Daniel says.

Does he mean for Jack? Or for this?

'We shouldn't have done that,' she says, walking away.

Now it is over, his face reminds her too much of the man who is dead. It is more than she can bear. She runs down the path without looking back. Once inside, she uses the excuse of wet clothes to run a bath. She stays in the water for as long as she can, scrubbing and scrubbing her body until her skin is red-raw and reeks of carbolic. But no matter how long she stays in the water, no matter how hard she scrubs, it feels like she will never be clean again.

DANIEL 3

Daniel watches Elsie running down the hill. He cannot blame her. *Bloody idiot! You bloody, bloody idiot!* He hadn't meant to do it. He'd followed her here with no thought but to offer comfort, perhaps to receive some. They'd both loved Jack. They'd both lost him. When he saw her kneeling on the ground, he'd intended only to give her a hug, to sit beside her, share her tears. He'd not meant to hold her so tightly, to look down at her at the moment she looked at him. Or move his face so close that the kiss was inevitable. He should have stopped then. He'd wanted to stop then. He couldn't. He was too weak, too foolish, too glad to finally have her in his arms. The irony is that after all these years of wanting her, the minute it was over, he knew it was no good: he's been chasing a will o' the wisp. She has always loved Jack, and always will, even in death. Daniel was never supposed to be more than a friend to her, and now that friendship is ruined. All those months he'd not given June a proper chance, wasting his time on a pointless fantasy. He feels sick.

403

He gazes down the path, following Elsie's tiny figure rushing towards the woods until she disappears under the dark-green canopy. In the distance he can see the road up to Bryngraean, beyond which lies the Flints' quarry. This is their country through and through. He has no place here; he never did. His parents may have made their vows at this spot, resolved to defy Geoffrey Walters and marry anyway, but Daniel can lay no such claim on the land. And if they were here now, what would they think of his behaviour? His mother – who sympathised with Jacob Flint even if she couldn't love him – might have understood, might have forgiven. But his father would never have acted like this: misusing the woman who loved him, taking advantage of the one who relied on him.

Daniel stands up, wanders back towards the stones, traces his fingers over the initials of the couples who've preceded him. At the back he finds *EF & JF*, undeniable proof that Jack and Elsie have been there. Of course they have. Hadn't she said it once? When she told him about the night of the Perseids? He recalls how happy she was at the memory. His fingers search for his parents' carving, *J loves R*. He touches the groove of the letters, remembering the day his mother showed it to him, the glow on her face as she told him how his father proposed. He remembers, too, the day his father returned from jail, the happy years in York, the night of the 1922 election, when he had watched his parents dance around the lounge. It is by such small things that you judge love: celebration, dancing, laughter. Not a moment of lust on the hillside that leaves you with a foul taste in your mouth.

His father would never have acted this way. But then his father would never have been here in the first place. What was it Elsie had said? 'Why you are skulking among women and children while real men are dying on your behalf?' She'd retracted the words when she'd discovered the truth, forgiven him for his absence from the frontline. But how can she forgive him this betrayal? How can he forgive himself? He lopes around the stones, trying to steady himself, to work out what he needs to do. It is warmer now the rain has stopped; the clouds have parted, creating a sliver of yellow-orange light that gleams over the valley. Raindrops hang on the grass blades, shimmering rainbows that decorate the hillside like jewels. Daniel cannot enjoy the beauty. Jack has died, bravely, horribly. And the first thing his cousin, his best friend has done is betray his trust. 'What kind of man am I?' he'd asked Jack once. 'The best of 'em,' the other man had replied. He wouldn't say that now.

What on earth is he going to do about Elsie? They will not be able to recover from this, to resume life as if nothing had happened between them. He must leave. But to go where? To do what? A kestrel flies overhead, wings outstretched, searching out its prey. He envies the ease with which it moves through the sky, diving at the sight of a small animal, capturing it in one movement. If only he could act with such confidence and determination. This inability to act has always been his trouble; and this one time, when he should have stopped himself, he has behaved with a recklessness that has ruined everything. He stumbles towards the path, making his way homewards; perhaps things will become clearer at home. His thoughts possess him to such an extent, he forgets his manufactured limp until he almost runs into Geraint Thomas coming in the opposite direction.

'Mr Clarkson.'

'Mr Thomas.' Daniel automatically rubs his ankles; has Thomas noticed?

'Clearing up nicely.' The farmer appraises him. 'Looks like you got caught in the rain earlier. Mrs Flint too. I just saw her running back to the big house.' There is too much curiosity in the man's eyes.

'Did you? I haven't seen a soul.'

'You don't let that ankle hold you back, do you, Mr Clarkson?'

Daniel is unable to smile in response. Geraint Thomas isn't a gossip, but his wife is. Suppose he mentions this encounter to her? The news will be all over Whetstone in no time.

'I am always careful to take it easy,' he says, continuing into the woods, emphasising his limp, hoping it continues to convince.

The tracks are thick with black mud, imprinted with the feet that have passed this way today – his own, the farmer's, Elsie's. He pictures her running in distress back to the Hall and kicks himself again for his weakness. The path to the village bends to the right, but through gaps in the trees he can make out the shape of Echo Hall, glimpsing the back bedroom where he watched his mother die. For years, he has used her suffering as an excuse not to act; but the truth is, she never regretted what happened. If she were here now, wouldn't she tell him so? Unlike his father, he has no entanglements, no wife and child to worry about. Staying for Elsie's sake was the last excuse left to him, and now he has trampled all over that. This will forever lie between them, poisoning the affection they've always shared. What they'd done. What they should never have done. They'll never recover from it. As he reaches the bottom of the hill, he realises that there is only one choice left. It is time for him to prove what kind of man he is. It is time, finally, to step out from his father's shadow, to live up to the ideals he has always professed. He must go down to London, confess his deception, refuse to fight and receive the punishment that is long overdue.

But Elsie – what can he do about Elsie? He can't leave her exposed, alone. Then he remembers June's friend Susie. She might help. The land girls usually have Saturday afternoons off; with any luck he'll catch her in. The sun is drying out the road. His damp clothes chafe his skin as he limps down to the Williams' house where Susie lodges;

he might as well keep up the pretence till the end. Though his resolve is strengthening, he isn't yet brave enough to declare the truth to this small community which has welcomed him. When they discover what he has done, realise he has lied all this time, he will lose every bit of good will he has gained here. It will be much better for him, much better for everyone if they find out when he is far away.

Susie is preparing to go out. She has just washed her hair, which is wrapped in a large towel, and is wearing a dark pencil skirt and a clean blouse.

'Daniel! What a surprise! Haven't since you in ages. Not since . . .' She doesn't finish the sentence, as she leads him into the back parlour where the Williams allow her to receive guests.

'To what do I owe this pleasure?' she says, sitting down and lighting a cigarette. 'Not crawling back to June after your broke her heart, you naughty boy? She won't have you, you know. She's having far too much fun in London.'

'I know. I'm glad for her . . . I treated her badly.'

'That saves me telling you off. I've been mad at you, I can tell you. She's one of the best, is June. You shouldn't have treated her like that.'

'No,' said Daniel. 'I am sorry, believe me. But that's not why I'm here. I've come to ask you a favour. It's not really for me . . .' Seeing her frown, he adds, 'It's for Elsie.'

'Elsie? Of course. How's she bearing up?'

'Not too good. It's horrible enough, but my aunt and uncle – they're not that easy to live with.'

'So I hear.'

'The thing is, I've been looking out for her, while I'm here. Jack asked me to. But I've got to go.'

'Why?'

'Family reasons. I don't like leaving her alone. With no one to turn to. No one to escape to when it all gets too much.'

'You want me to do it?'

'Could you?'

'Sure,' Susie drawls. 'I like Elsie a lot. I'll pop in on her tomorrow.'

'I can't thank you enough. I'll write a note, drop it to you before I leave.'

'Where are you going?'

'London, probably.'

'I hope you're not going to bug June.'

'I'll keep out of her way.'

'You'd better, mister.'

He nods goodbye.

He passes the graveyard on his way home, resisting the temptation to go in. He has made up his mind. There is nothing left to say. Nothing left to do but go home and pack. There is precious little to take with him. Most of the crockery belongs to the schoolhouse. His successor is welcome to it. He has his collection of books, a couple of drawers and half a wardrobe of clothes, his diary, some pathetic attempts at poems – mainly about Elsie; the photo of his parents, their letters and his father's writings. Not much to show for the last three years of his life.

He has nearly finished in the sitting room when he remembers the photograph from that day in Southport. He takes it out of the drawer, staring at the three of them laughing together on the day their fates were decided. He should have been a better friend to them both. He should have rejoiced in their love for each other, not harboured this secret infatuation all these years. He sighs, putting the photo in his pocket. It is all over now. He sits down at his desk and takes up paper and pen to write his letter of resignation.

ELSIE 4

Elsie lies in bed staring at the ceiling. She has been awake since five, too tired to move, her mind too active for sleep. She has watched the room lighten to another dawn, listening to the noise of the rooks, their cheerful chatter seemingly intent on mocking her. She replays the events of the previous day over and over again. Why hadn't she waited till she was calmer before meeting Daniel? Why hadn't she stopped him from kissing her? Why hadn't she stopped herself? How could she have done that with Jack not dead a week? And to do it where she and Jack had made love all those years ago? What was wrong with her? At six-thirty, she gives up any further attempt to sleep, throws off the bedclothes and makes her way down to the kitchen.

There is someone there already, the figure so familiar she gasps in recognition. It can't be; it's not possible. Hearing her enter, he turns; of course it is Jacob, not Jack. She'd forgotten how physically similar they were. In the early-morning light, he looks so grey and careworn she almost feels sorry for him. He has lit the stove and is boiling the kettle. She didn't think he knew how.

'Let me do that.'

'Thank you. You're up early.'

'I couldn't sleep.'

'No, I expect not.'

The sympathy in his eyes is unexpected. It adds to her guilt. What would he say if he discovered his previous ill opinion of her were justified? She deserves every harsh word. The two of them sit in silence as the kettle boils. It is almost companionable.

Jacob says, 'We will hold the memorial service for Jack at the chapel this Friday. I will preach.'

'I would have liked to have held it in the village church.'

'The chapel is more appropriate.'

'He preferred the church. He considered himself an Anglican.'

'It is my decision.'

'I was his wife.'

'And I was his father. He has left you under my care and protection, expecting you to abide by my decisions. We will hold the service at the chapel.'

She doesn't have the strength to argue with him, nor does she feel able to claim fidelity to Jack now. The children potter in, Evie still rubbing sleep from her eyes. Soon the ritual of the day takes over – breakfast, getting dressed, chapel, where the words of the visiting preacher wash over her.

The Sabbath should be a day of rest, but Elsie

still has chores to do. Leah and Jacob retire to their rooms leaving her to her thoughts as she works. Should she take the children down to the village to try and put things right with Daniel? But what can she say? What can either of them say to each other now? As she is finishing off cleaning the kitchen floor, she is surprised by a knock on the door. It is Susie Clark.

'Hello, Elsie.' The other woman hesitates, seeing her startled face. 'Is it alright for me to call?'

'I'm sorry, I don't get many visitors. Of course it is. Come in.' Elsie takes her outside to the kitchen garden. They sit on the stone steps as the children enact a complicated game behind them.

'I'm so sorry about Jack, Elsie. What a terrible thing.'

'You're very kind.'

'I've a message from Daniel.' Elsie hopes she isn't blushing. 'He's had to leave Whetstone.'

'What?'

'He gave me a letter for you.'

'He's gone?'

'He dropped it in as he left.'

'Where's he gone?' Elsie struggles to make the words sound normal.

'London, I think.' Susie's voice is soft and kind. She reaches over and touches Elsie's arm. 'He said that you needed someone. That he wasn't able to help that way anymore. He asked if I could.'

'Oh.'

'Would that be alright, Elsie? He said you could

use a friend. And to be honest, so could I. It's not been much fun since June went.'

'What?' Elsie is still trying to understand the news; it takes a minute or so to register Susie's proposal. 'Yes, of course, that's a lovely idea.'

'Can you make time on Saturdays? My afternoon off.'

'Saturdays. Yes.'

'Shall we say two o'clock?'

Elsie nods, barely listening. She fiddles with the envelope, uncertain whether she should tear it open or throw it away.

Susie, noticing her distraction, rises. 'Well, I'll be off then.'

'I'm sorry, I'm not at my best today.'

'I understand.'

Elsie sees her off and returns to the kitchen. On the lawn Will is chasing Evie, who squeals with excitement. She could just throw the letter away, accept Daniel is gone and be done with it. But the need to know what is inside is too strong; she rips the envelope open, pulling out the sheet of paper inside.

8th May 1943

My Dear Elsie,

I have struggled to find the right words to send to you, to undo the damage I have done. You needed a friend and I acted

414

abominably. I doubt that you can ever forgive me. I can't forgive myself. I fully intended to stay here to fulfil my promise to Jack, to be the friend you need me to be till the war is done, but I've ruined all that, haven't I? There's no going back from what we did. It was unbelievably selfish of me.

I've come to a decision. I'm no good to you here now. Jack's death has made me realise how brave he was. How cowardly I am. I think it's time I stopped running away, and did the right thing for once. I'm going down to London to hand myself in. All my life I have been too scared to be like my father. I realise now it is the only honourable course left – to try to become the man he would have wanted me to be.

I am so sorry, Elsie, for everything. I'd stay if I thought it would do any good, but we both know that it won't. I hope you'll remember me as fondly as I will always remember you, and that one day you might come to forgive me.

Daniel

She has driven him away. The friend who has been her anchor all these years. How could she have been such an idiot? How had she not seen he'd been so soft on her? Or had she always known, deep down, secretly enjoying the thought that she had another admirer apart from Jack? How selfish of her; how hellish it must have been for him. Yet he'd stayed all this time to help Jack, to help her. How could she have been so stupid as to let him kiss her, make love to her? She has ruined everything, and the actions cannot be undone. And, though she doesn't know what she will do without him, she knows Daniel is right – no good would come of him staying.

'Have you made a start on supper?' Leah's voice makes her jump. She has glided into the room without a sound. Elsie stuffs Daniel's letter in her pocket. At least his departure will make one person happy.

'I'm just about to.' Elsie stands up. 'Susie Clark called with a message from Daniel.' Leah stiffens at the mention of her nephew. 'He has moved down to London. He won't be coming back.'

Leah permits herself a small smile. She is about to say something when they are interrupted by a wail from the garden as Evie tumbles on the steps. By the time Elsie reaches her, her knee is gushing blood, her face is red with the effort of bawling. Will hovers beside her, anxious about his sister's knee but also clearly hoping he will not be blamed. Elsie picks her daughter up, speaking soothing words, holding her tight till they arrive at the kitchen where she bathes and dresses the wound. Gradually, Evie's sobs die down; the cut clean and covered up, she is eager to return to the game. Elsie watches enviously; if only adult woes could be wiped away so easily. *Oh, for goodness' sake*, she scolds herself, *don't be so maudlin. You've a roof over your head, your children with you. You'll just have to make do.*

As the week passes, she repeats her scolding a lot. Making do proves to be a trial. Veronica calls most days, having wangled compassionate leave, even though she isn't technically part of the family. Her eyes are always open wide with concern, her tongue smooth with sympathetic words; Leah appreciates her visits, but they give Elsie a head-ache. There is a constant stream of visitors at the house, paying their respects, telling tales about Jack: his aptitude for sports, his academic prowess, his bravery in battle. They create a war hero, an icon, a man she doesn't recognise. She wants to scream out loud: these people know nothing about him. While the house is full of guests, she and Leah maintain the façade of women united in grief, separating the instant the last visitor leaves. Leah haunts the landing, gazing at the photos of her dead sons, barely speaking unless to discuss domestic matters. Elsie takes care of the children and the house; it is all she can do.

After a week spent living in this fashion, it is almost pleasurable to go outside for the service, to breathe fresh air, to mourn Jack outside the confines of the Hall. The day is bright, the sun already hot by the time they enter the car. She wears the same black satin dress she'd worn when her father died. She holds Will and Evie by the hand as they clamber into the Bentley, Will's usual exuberance subdued by the black clothes, the sad grown-up faces. As they drive off, she recalls sitting in the black car with Jack and Daniel on the way to her father's funeral. She couldn't have got through that day without them. Now she has lost them both; she must manage her grief alone. A breeze ruffles the cornfields, creating wave after undulating wave. They pass the familiar roads, the hedgerows bursting with plants: grasses, butter-cups, campion jostling for space, topped by a canopy of cow parsley. On any other day, she'd think it beautiful; today, she cannot appreciate anything other than the slow passage of the car through the countryside to the service she has hoped never to attend.

The chapel is full when they arrive and take their seats at the front. Presumably most are here out of respect for the Flint family, who still maintain a certain importance locally. She thinks back to the day she buried her father, the huge church almost empty save for Elsie, Jack, Daniel, Dad's two drinking companions from the Prince Albert, and the priest with mournful eyes and a doleful voice who presided over the service. It was a miser-able affair but at least there'd been a coffin, a tangible sign that he had gone. A funeral without a body is no kind of goodbye at all.

It is admirable, in a way, that Jacob preaches, as he did for Henry. To be able to stand in public, preaching about God's love, when both your sons have been taken from you. Elsie can see that it takes guts, but she cannot agree with the sentiment of his sermon.

'Abraham took his son Isaac and was willing to sacrifice him for God. God spared him because of his goodness and because it wasn't part of His plan. But God has not spared us. God has asked us to sacrifice our sons again, and again. To what purpose? To resist the conquering evil of Germany, to save the widow and the orphan. This is God's plan, and we should follow it without question. We mourn the loss of our loved ones, but we should celebrate their life and courage. They died that we might live. There is no greater love.'

What kind of a God asks that of us? Elsie thinks to herself. She catches Susie's eye across the chapel and sees the same thought in the other woman's eyes. Hope rises a little. In his last act of friendship, Daniel has chosen well. The nightmare of war has come home to her, but she has her health, her children, and at least one friend. She must make do, make the best of things, till, perhaps in time, she will mend.

DANIEL 4

The newspaper report says the war is progressing well in Italy, but there little else to suggest the end is in sight. Daniel puts the paper down, swigs his tea, finishes his toast. He should make the most of his solitary breakfast; after all, it is the last meal of the condemned man. But he is too restless. He rises from the table, washes the plate and leaves it in the sink, takes a final look at the room that has been his home for the past four months. The room is as bare as the lodgings of his past: a narrow bed with a metal headboard; a dark-green rug that barely covers half the floorboards; a winged armchair made of tatty red leather, a hole on the right arm; a brown wooden desk that rocks unless a piece of paper is placed under one of the legs; next to it, a wooden chair. If he closes his eyes, he could be back in Liverpool, waiting for Jack to knock on the door so they could liberate Elsie from her skivvying, take her dancing – allies in the war of attrition against her drunken father. Or in Sandstown, playing with his toys while his mother sits sewing, waiting for his father to return from the factory. A knock on the door brings him back to the present. It is Charles Haughton, an old friend of his father's, who has promised to accompany him. Daniel glances around; simple as his living quarters are, tonight he will be sharing a room a third of this size. He grimaces. He doesn't want to think that far ahead. Now it is time, he wants to appreciate his freedom as much as he can.

Outside, the air is fresh, the stiff breeze heralding the approach of autumn. The lemon-yellow sun shines in the clear blue sky, its rays touching the tips of the sycamore and oak trees lining the road. The leaves are beginning to turn, flashes of yellow bursting from amid the green. On the way to the tube they pass hordes of people emerging into daylight, sleepy survivors of night raids, keen to embrace the open sky. After the quiet of the countryside, the air raids have taken some getting used to. He is grateful for his landlady's Anderson shelter at the end of the garden. It has been cramped, sharing with his neighbours, but he cannot imagine spending a night sleeping on a hard platform, crushed against so many others: the stench and the noise must be unbearable.

They take the escalator down to the platform. The station staff are cleaning up after the night's visitors; they are so efficient, you can hardly tell the station is used for any other purpose than transport. The two men have hardly spoken since leaving the lodgings. Daniel is grateful for the silence – that Charles, having made this journey too, senses his need to be alone with his thoughts.

As they board the train, Daniel says, 'Is it difficult? When they close the door?'

'At first, yes. I thought I might suffocate. Particularly at night, when it's dark, cold and damp. But . . . it's astonishing what you get used to after a while. And . . . of course . . . there were lots of us. We kept each other's spirits up.' Richmond prison. Daniel grew up on the tales of the men who survived solitary confinement, who nevertheless found ways to communicate, to pray together, who wrote messages of solidarity on the wall. 'Of course,' Charles adds, 'you might not be so lucky, being on your own. Still, like father, like son. You'll be alright.'

Daniel isn't so sure, but the words are reassuring, soothing his anxious thoughts. The tube rattles round corners, through lighted stations and blackened tunnels, before lurching to a halt at their stop, expelling them onto the platform. They pass through the jostling crowds, air-raid wardens going home after the night shift, shop girls on their way to work, casting their eyes over the weary soldiers and airmen back for a snatched leave. Daniel feels like an alien in their midst. If they knew where he was going, what he is about to stand up and admit to, would their genial camaraderie be replaced by fury? Or would they just take no interest, considering his actions pointless? For, after all, how can one man's actions affect the course of the conflict?

Perhaps what he is doing is useless, yet as they reach the magistrates' court, he hears his father's voice: *You don't just do things because people agree with you, or because you believe they'll make an iota of difference; you do them because they're right.* Daniel wishes he shared such certainties. Well, right or wrong, he is here now. To his surprise, a small crowd has gathered, and a couple of people bear a banner: *An eye for an eye makes the whole world blind.* And there, unbelievably, unexpectedly, is June. She beams at him as if the last few months hadn't happened, as if he hadn't treated her so abominably. It is more than he deserves.

'You came,' he says, hugging her. 'I didn't think you would.'

'Daft ninny, I wouldn't let you go through this without coming to say hello. Though I must say, deciding to go to jail is a fine way to reintroduce yourself.'

He laughs. It is too much to hope that she might have him back, yet he feels lighter just knowing she is beside him.

They sit in the outer chamber waiting to be called.

'I heard about Jack,' says June. 'Susie wrote and told me. How awful for Elsie . . .'

'Yes.'

'How's she doing?'

'Terrible. I felt bad leaving her alone with his parents.' Daniel's throat is dry; if there is to be any possibility of a life with June, he'll have to tell her one day, but not now. 'I couldn't keep it up anymore, June. Not after Jack died.'

'Poor old you. I know how much you loved him.' June gives him a half-hug. Before he has a chance to respond, the usher calls them in.

Daniel walks to his place in the dock. He stares up at the empty magistrates' bench, the Queen's coat of arms above it: the lion and the unicorn on either side of the shield, *Honi soit qui mal y pense* written around it. He can't quite remember what that means; something to do with thinking about evil, though the words at the bottom he can translate. *Dieu et mon droit* – God and my right. His father always used to quote it, adding that the rights of kings led many a country astray. It is comforting to think that his father sat just like this, gazing at a similar emblem. He is smiling at the thought as the magistrates enter, and the court rises.

The prosecution begins. The morning is spent outlining his misdemeanours. As he hears them laid out, his heart sinks. Who wouldn't want to make an example of a man who has not only refused to fight, but falsified his records? He glances at June, who gives him an encouraging smile. When the prosecution rests, the court breaks for lunch. Daniel is released for the time being. He rejoins the others in a small waiting room, where they share luncheon-meat sandwiches. The talk is deliberately light. No one wants to speak of how the day will end.

When they return, Daniel is called to the stand. He explains his actions as best as he can. As he finishes the leading magistrate stares down at him. 'Let me sum up, Mr Clarkson. You did not wish to fight, for, you say, reasons of conscience. But instead of coming before the magistrates four years ago, you found an unnamed medical practitioner who was willing to provide you with a false medical certificate. Correct?'

Daniel nods.

'And you used that medical certificate to exempt you from military action? Spending your time teaching in . . .' he consults his notes, 'the village of Whetstone. Correct?'

'Yes.' Daniel's throat is dry. Had his father felt like this?

'Can I ask, Mr Clarkson, why you behaved in such a fashion? I understand this to be a question of conscience, but surely hiding in a schoolhouse is nothing but an act of cowardice?'

Daniel swallows. 'You are right. I was afraid. Afraid of the censure that I had seen my father face, afraid that those around me would be hurt, as my mother was. I believe God doesn't want me to fight, but I was afraid of the consequences.'

'Consequences that would have led you here?'

'Yes.'

'And, what, may I ask, caused you to change your mind? Fear of discovery?'

'No. My cousin died. He was shot down and I realised . . . that I don't believe in war, but I loved him. He believed in what he was doing; he died believing it. And I thought, if he could die for his beliefs, it was time I stood up for mine.'

'I see. So we have falsified documents and refusing to fight, which carry severe penalties.' The magistrate confers with his colleagues. 'We will retire to consider our verdict.'

They leave the room. June and Charles stroll over from the public gallery.

'You spoke well,' says Charles.

'I don't know where it came from.'

'One never does.'

'I think you impressed them,' says June.

'Not enough to avoid jail,' Daniel says.

'No.' They laugh.

'All rise,' the usher says.

June and Charles return to their seats. Daniel tries to control the trembling in his legs.

The magistrate glances down at his notes. 'We have considered the facts seriously. On the one hand, you have broken the law twice, missing opportunities to present yourself to a tribunal for the best part of four years. Had you done so at the beginning of the war, your application for conscientious objection might have been considered on its merits. You did not. In addition, you have falsified documentation, and have refused to give us the name of the person who assisted you. By behaving in such a fashion, you have made matters much worse for yourself.' The magistrate pauses. Daniel's stomach churns. He is going to

426

receive a heavy sentence. 'On the other hand, the court takes note of the fact that you have not spent this time in idleness, but have continued to use your teaching skills for the benefit of your community. Nor did you abuse your position by trying to unduly influence the pupils you taught. We therefore sentence you to 18 months on each count, to be run concurrently.'

Eighteen months; he could have had three years. He has enough time to flash a smile at June before he is handcuffed and taken down to the cells. Was it his imagination, or did she whisper she would write?

He sits in the prison cell, his legs shaking. It is done; his war is over. There is nothing left for him to do. He wonders how Elsie is; he hopes Susie is proving a good companion. He thinks of Jack – four months have passed and he still can't believe his cousin is dead. But this is what war does: snatches the people you love leaving blanks in your life, like blacked-out sentences in a censored letter. Presently the Black Maria arrives to take him to Wandsworth. He sits in the back alongside the other sentenced prisoners. Nobody speaks much as they bump along the road, past bomb-cratered and dehoused streets. Daniel doesn't mind; the silence is like being in Meeting. It helps calm his mind, preparing him for what lies ahead. It takes a couple of hours to reach the prison, a couple more to pass through reception. It is strange, after the years of pretence, to be given a clean bill of health. At last he is through to the wing, clothed in the prison uniform, locked in his cell. There are a couple of other men already there. He smiles and says hello. They indicate the top bunk.

'Welcome to the Ritz,' says one. 'I'm Paul Allen.'

'Daniel Clarkson.'

'What are you in for?'

Daniel takes a deep breath; he's done with lying, but it's still hard to admit. 'I'm a conscientious objector.'

'A conchie? You refused to fight?'

'Yes.'

The man considers this. 'Can't say I blame you, mate. My brother's over in Italy and it sounds a right bloody mess.'

The other man sits up. 'It says something, dunnit? About the world we live in? When it's better to be inside than out?'

They all laugh, and begin to share stories of their lives. When they discover Daniel is a teacher, they ask for help with letter-writing; he is happy to oblige, and the evening ends with more warmth than he could have ever imagined. His father always said people were more understanding in prison than anywhere else. That if you put your head down, lived each day one step at a time, the days become possible. In the first few weeks, that thought helps Daniel through the misery of petty bureaucracy, the locked cells, the lack of privacy. The word soon passes round that he is a teacher. Though some are not as tolerant as his cell-mates, many value his writing and reading skills, and assisting his fellow prisoners helps provide a sense of purpose.

The first month passes surprisingly quickly; his mood is lightened even further with a letter from June. *Such wonderful news*, she writes. *Jack has been found.* He reads eagerly: Jack's plane had been lost in a battle in the fog. In the confusion, no one saw him parachute out and land in the sea, where his identity card was lost. When he was rescued he was feverish, unable to recall his name. His memory has only just returned. Daniel puts the letter down. Hope, his father had often said – no matter how bad it gets, there's always hope. He was right. Jack is going home. Elsie will be alright. If she has any sense, she'll not mention their disastrous mistake. They'll be able to put it behind them, pick up where they had been before the war. Daniel reads June's letter again. There is an unmistakeable warmth in her tone. Behind the accounts of life on the busy ward, he detects welcome. There is an opportunity for him there, if he wishes to take it. Perhaps there is hope for him too. He closes his eyes, remembering a sunny day at the funfair long ago: Jack and Elsie riding on the horses ahead, *red-gold, red-gold, red-gold*, leaving him far behind. Ride on, he thinks, ride on; at last, at long last, he is able to let them go.

ELSIE 5

J ack is alive. It is wonderful. Marvellous. Life is returning to Technicolor. Jack is alive. She hasn't lost him. And yet . . . Elsie doesn't want to think of it, let alone say it out loud . . . the knowledge that threatens her, that threatens them both. Watching the children scamper ahead of her, she aches to be so carefree, to let the good news thrill through her as it is thrilling them. But the knowledge is there, brimming on the edge of her thoughts. The knowledge she hasn't dare admit to herself, or anyone else.

The stubble is burning in the fields; the wind catches the smoke, billowing it around them, making them cough and their eyes smart. The air clears as they turn the bend to Susie's lodgings. Last summer Elsie and Will had helped out at harvest time, piling sheaves of wheat on the truck, the little boy jumping up and down from the vehicle squealing with delight. Last summer Daniel had joined them, his arm casually around June when she'd had the chance to take a break. Last summer she'd been happy, or as happy as was possible in the circumstances, because she'd just received a letter from Jack, and Will's pleasure infected her. The sun had shone all day, browning their skin, creating a thirst that was quenched by home-made lemonade drunk under the enormous oak tree at the bottom of the hill. Last summer was another world.

Susie answers at her first knock. 'Elsie! I just heard the news this morning. It's simply marvellous!'

'Yes.'

'We must do something to celebrate.'

'Maybe . . . later . . . We're just off for a walk. Would you like to come?'

'I'll just get my jacket.' Susie pops inside for a minute or two, returning in a green oilskin coat. 'Where shall we go?'

'Up the hill?'

Susie nods and strides ahead, vaulting the gate which she opens for the children to pass through. The footpath is dry and dusty. A few weeks ago, the bracken that bordered it was nearly at shoulder level, the vivid green fronds waving in the wind. Now it has already died back, withering at the stalk, the brown leaves thin as paper. Above them, the sky is grey, but the clouds are moving too fast for rain. When the wind blows it chills the air; the children's cheeks glow red. Halfway up, they reach a plateau. It is a good spot for Will and Evie to run around, so they stop. Elsie is exhausted.

'Don't fancy Arthur's Stone?' asks Susie, who is still full of energy.

'Not today.'

'Is everything alright, Elsie? Only you seem a bit down in the dumps for someone whose husband has come back from the dead.'

'Fine.' She'd love to tell Susie; the words form in her head, but she cannot say them aloud. For what can Susie do? What can anyone do to change her situation? 'It's just a bit overwhelming, that's all.'

'Maybe you're coming down with something. You do look a bit peaky.'

'I wouldn't be surprised.' The opportunity passes.

Before long they are heading home, where she finds Leah glowing with good news. Jack's wing commander has been in touch to say he can be moved in a fortnight. Leah has been a different woman of late. Daniel's departure and subsequent disgrace had already gone some way to pulling her out of her depression; now, the knowledge that her second son has survived has filled her with eager excitement. Now she can prepare for his homecoming, and she sets to work with a vigour that Elsie hasn't seen since Jack's last leave. She makes all the decisions, telling Elsie of her plans only afterwards. Jack is to have the study on the ground floor as his bedroom, the east sitting room as a day room. Leah organises everything: the moving of furniture, gathering of bed linen, provision of commode. A nurse is engaged from an agency in Birmingham. She is bringing her daughter with her and they will have the Davies's flat above the coach house. Occasionally Leah even laughs, providing a flash of the young girl in the photo on the landing. It is good to see her happy; her new enthusiasm is preferable to the old dour Leah, yet Elsie finds herself slightly wary. There are times when her eyes seem too bright, her laugh too hysterical, her activity too frenetic. The mood is too brittle to last.

Elsie is relegated to the position of lackey. Ordinarily she would have minded; now it suits her purposes. She has to hide her pregnancy till Jack is well enough. She has to trust that she can find the words to explain. That he will understand. She smiles, sweeps, moves furniture, keeping her head down. She wears baggy clothes to hide the changing contours of her body, trying not to think what will happen if he doesn't forgive her.

Two days before Jack's arrival, she awakes with a headache. She has promised Leah she will mop the kitchen floor, though how Jack will know whether it's clean when he's confined to bed, Leah hasn't said. After breakfast, she fetches the mop, fills the metal bucket with water and sets to work. *Splash, squeeze, wipe, splash, squeeze, wipe, splash, squeeze, wipe* . . . For a while she is lost in the rhythm of the task, taking satisfaction in the erasure of dust and dirt from the floor. But as the morning progresses, her temples begin to throb; when she touches her forehead, she discovers she has a temperature. Her legs are shaky. She looks at the clock; it is only ten. She'll stop for a cup of tea soon, then lie down. *Splash, squeeze, wipe* . . . She is finding it difficult to focus; the cracks between the flagstones dance before her eyes. The children are playing in the garden; their voices seem a long way away. The door opens. It is Leah. She is standing at the end of a long dark tunnel. Elsie is shaking, she needs to sit down. She stumbles against the bucket, banging it into the wall. It ricochets, water spreading out in every direction, soaking her skirt. Leah catches her before she falls over, sitting her down on the chair. 'I think we'd better get you upstairs.' Elsie nods, closing her eyes. She needs to lie down, let this fever take its course. The journey upstairs fragments; she stumbles, Leah catches her; she sits, stands up again, finally arrives at the landing without quite knowing how they reached it. The next thing she knows she is lying down on her bed, conscious that there is something she needs to stop happening. She can't remember why but she mustn't let Leah undress her. She mustn't. She can't remember why. Yet when she looks down, she is in her nightgown. The fever takes hold again. Jack leans down to kiss her. As she leans up to him, his face changes. She is kissing Daniel instead. His kisses taste dry and bitter; she struggles to free herself from his embrace. She wants, doesn't want this. She hears a voice singing, *Don't sit under the apple tree with anyone else but me*, over and over again. And then Jack interrupts. *You sat with someone, Else . . . How could you?*

When she wakes it is early evening. Her head is still aching, but the fever has abated. She looks around the room, puzzled; something is wrong. At this time of day, the red-gold rays of the setting sun should be streaming in, but all she can see through the window is the pale-blue evening sky. And the counterpane – that's wrong, too . . . hers is green, this one is gold. It is only when she sits up that it dawns on her. She is in the wrong room. This is the bedroom at the back of the house where Rachel used to sleep. This is the room where she died. Someone coughs. She turns to see Leah and Jacob at the door.

'What am I doing here?'

'I always knew we couldn't trust you. Either of you . . .' Leah's voice is hard.

'It wasn't like that.'

'Do you think us stupid? All that pretence that you were out walking with the children, when all the time you were off with your fancy man.'

'It was just talking.'

Leah snorts.

'Except for one time . . . but that's between me and Jack.'

'We will not have him distressed when he comes home.'

'It's between us.'

The older woman appears not to hear her. Jacob puts a hand on her shoulder and says, 'We have prayed while you were ill, and God has guided us in our deliberations.'

'And?' It is convenient how God always guides Jacob.

'My wife is right. Jack must not be distressed at this time. You have committed a grave sin, Elsie – you must suffer the consequences. You will stay here in this part of the house. We will say that you are ill.'

'Scarlet fever,' says Leah. 'We shall say you have scarlet fever.' She smiles, as if the thought is giving her pleasure.

'When it is time, I will take you to a charitable establishment in Birmingham,' says Jacob. 'You will leave the child there, return home, and sin no more.'

'What if I refuse?'

'You can leave the house today if you wish. You can keep the child. By doing so, you will revoke your rights to your children, and your husband.'

Elsie lies back on the pillow. She is weak, in no fit state to argue. She cannot believe that they really mean it. Or that once Jack is here, he will allow it. She nods. For the time being she must do what they say.

At the door, Jacob adds, 'You are in quarantine. The children, of course, cannot come and see you.' She opens her mouth in protest. 'Consider it your penance. You will need more space than this. We will block off the back staircase so you can have the freedom of the servants' quarters. Tonight we must lock you in. Should you need anything, you may ring the bell.'

They leave the room, locking it behind them.

This is too absurd, Elsie thinks. Surely they will

reconsider in the morning? Then she remembers the determination in Jacob's voice, the gleeful enjoyment in Leah's eyes, and is less certain. If they intend to go through with this, she has very little choice. Life without Jack and the children is inconceivable. She sinks back into her pillows, drifting off to a dreamless sleep.

The sound of banging wakes her in the morning. Somebody is hammering nails at the top of the staircase. They are serious then. Leah brings breakfast, allows her out to the bathroom and locks her back in. On any other day, Elsie would revel in this rare chance to rest; today she chafes at the constraints. Anxious to see the children, she stands by the window waiting till they have an opportunity to play in the garden. Will is taking care of his little sister with a tenderness that makes her heart ache. She wills him to look up, to see her watching him, but he is too intent on his game, and the children return to the house without realising she was there. The banging continues till teatime, when Leah returns to tell her she has the freedom of the servants' quarters. Keys rattle on the chain round her waist; clearly she relishes the role of jailor.

Jack returns the following day. Elsie stands at the green baize door, listening to the excitement generated by his arrival: the ambulance at the door, the stretcher through the house, the children calling his name. She strains and strains to hear his voice, but he must be too weak to speak. The noise dies down. The children return to the nursery, where she can hear them playing. She is tempted to call to them, but she is not sure what Leah has said to them; she doesn't want to frighten them.

The days pass, because they do, because they must. The world and the war seem a long way away, but the horror has come home. To pass the time she writes and writes. Sometimes diary entries; sometimes reworking old stories, myths that Daniel told her; sometimes letters to Jack. Each time, she tries to explain it, to apologise for the hurt that she will inevitably cause him. Each one is dissatisfying, as if she is trying to excuse the inexcusable. Each day, the baby moves inside her, her body growing to accommodate it. The time is coming when she will have to give it up if she is to have a chance of keeping her husband and her family. She doesn't know how she will bear it.

At nightfall she breaks the blackout, watching as the stars come out and light the sky. Each night the owl flies overhead, a mouse caught in its claws. There is something about the outstretched wings, the power and strength of its flight, that raises her spirits. She must hope, and pray, and she will endure. As she retires to bed, she reads from Jack's prayer book, tracing her fingers over the notes he has made in the margins. He has marked Psalm 23, which becomes her nightly prayer: 'Though I walk through the valley of the shadow of death, I will fear no evil; for you are with me.' The words comfort her each night, enabling her to sleep. In her dreams she dances with Jack; the ballroom lights sparkle off the colours of her dress, red-gold, red-gold, red-gold . . . they dance through the night. But in the cold grey dawn, she wakes alone.

JACK

You are hot, burning hot. Smoky flames flicker through the cockpit, swathing it in orange-black light. Everyone else has bailed now except Alex Smith, tiny Alex Smith, your tail-end Charlie who lies slumped in his seat, killed in the first assault. There is not much time, but there is one last thing to do. You lean towards the dash-board, grabbing the photograph, blackened with soot: a Very light to guide you in the dark. You run to the exit and jump.

You are cold, freezing cold. The life jacket you inflated carries you on the waves as the water seeps into your clothes, chilling you to the bone. Fog blankets the sea; you lose all sense of direction. Your left leg hurts like crazy – you must have caught some shrapnel in the firefight. You try swimming, but the injured leg drags with pain. Her face on the picture in your pocket pulls you home, forcing you to say strong, stay awake. You will survive for her sake.

You are burning hot. You are freezing cold. You are in the cockpit. You are in the water. You are floating through the air; the voices of a thousand dying airman are singing you to heaven. You think of Elsie, imagining her close: lavender perfume, a red ball dress, the softness of her hair. You say her name, over and over. You hear voices above you: *I think he's saying something, I can't work out what. A name maybe?* Elsie, Elsie; her name is the talisman that will save you.

You are cold, freezing cold. The ambulance has no heating, the blankets are too thin. You are glad they declared you fit to travel but the roads are uneven and each jolt sends shudders of pain through your body. Your left leg hurts like crazy. You don't care about the pain. Each bump of the road brings you closer to her. You must be strong, stay awake. You're still alive; you must remain so, for her sake.

You are in the cockpit. You are in the water. The voices of a thousand airmen calling you to your grave mingle with the hushed voices of concern above your bed. You are burning hot, you are freezing cold. You are waiting for the one voice that doesn't speak. Elsie, Elsie, Elsie: you call and call her name but she doesn't come. Someone says, *She can't. She's sick.* You clutch the photo. You burn. You freeze. You have made it this far. Elsie, Elsie, Elsie. Her name: the talisman that will save you.

AT THE CLOSE OF THE DAY

1991

CHAPTER 1

It was pitch-black. I waited for my eyes to adjust, but the room remained absolutely dark. So dark, it felt physical, as if the night itself was pressing down on my chest, crushing the life out of me. I could barely breathe. I didn't want to disturb Adam, but I couldn't sleep like this. I had to let some light in. I got out of bed, but the windows were in the wrong place. I was at the back of the house, not the front. And when I opened the curtains, letting in the moonlight, I realised Adam wasn't there. Nor was Phoebe. Then it dawned on me that I shouldn't be at Echo Hall at all. I had to get out. I turned to the door handle, but it was locked. I rattled it and shouted but no one came. I was trapped. Somewhere in the distance I thought I heard a cold laugh, and I realised three things: I was afraid, I was powerless and I was completely alone . . .

The wind rattling through the windows woke me from my dream. For a moment I was confused as to where I was. Then, as my eyes got used to the darkness, and I began to make out the shape of the armchair and Phoebe's travel-cot, I remembered. It was Christmas morning and I was staying with Nisha at Emma Goldman Farm. I'd left Adam when I discovered that he'd married me to inherit the quarry. And now he was in Iraq, I knew I had made the right choice. Not just because he'd lied to me once too often. Reading the diaries had confirmed for me that we didn't stand a chance. Unlike Rachel and Elsie I had never experienced real love; and if I stayed with Adam, I doubted I ever would.

I switched on the lamp. Elsie's diaries lay beside me on my bedside table where I'd left them last night. I'd had such high hopes that the end of her story might lie in their pages; it was frustrating to finish and not know what happened next. Still, at least I knew enough to put Jack's mind at rest about one thing – despite that one terrible mistake, she'd never stopped loving him. At some point, I must find a way to tell him that.

The rain drummed on the windows outside. Phoebe would be awake soon and it would be time to celebrate her first Christmas. Last year, engaged to Adam with a baby on the way, I'd woken full of excitement and hope. Now, all I had was a seven-month-old baby who relied on me for everything. I loved her absolutely, I wanted to take care of her, to ensure this was the first of many happy Christmases. But today, I didn't feel up to the task.

Nonetheless, I tried. When she woke, I sat her on my knee, unwrapping presents that Adam and I had bought just a fortnight earlier, feeling faintly ridiculous. She was totally oblivious to the importance of the occasion; what on earth was the point? The rest of the house was sleeping, and by ten, bored rigid by playing with bricks, I fetched Phoebe's buggy and took her off for a walk. A pale sun hung in the blue-grey sky, but the wind was still cold; the air was filled with the aroma of cow pats. The muddy driveway clogged our wheels and we made slow progress, so I was in a worse mood when we returned; particularly when I found that Nisha, who'd promised to cook, was only just getting up. It was five before we finally sat down to our lentil loaf and roast potatoes, by which time I was starving and distinctly lacking in seasonal spirit.

I didn't mean to be churlish. After all, I had somewhere to be on Christmas Day; but the home-grown kale and broccoli were no substitute for the turkey feast I might have had at Echo Hall. Even the exchange of gifts was a muted affair. No one had much money and, with half the house away, the rest had voted to spend what they had on drink, not presents, opting for a Secret Santa instead. My gift, wrapped in newspaper, was a diary made of recycled paper. It was a nice idea; ordinarily, I'd have felt pleased with it, but now all it did was emphasise what I'd lost. I faked a smile, drank a glass of wine and was grateful when it was time to put Phoebe to bed, so I could escape the jollity for a while. By the time she was asleep, I'd missed the *Fools and Horses* Christmas special, and a game of charades had started. It became increasingly chaotic as more alcohol was imbibed. I was feeling sick, so I reverted to orange juice and sank into the corner to watch everyone becoming more and more raucous. I was glad when it was late enough to sneak up to bed without anyone noticing.

After Christmas the days passed slowly, each more grey than the last. To my surprise, Adam wrote often, though as I read his letters all I could think of were the sarcastic replies I wanted to make to his face.

I miss Phoebe. I miss you. Of course you do . . . *I'm sorry I didn't tell you about the inheritance . . . I just thought at the time we were getting on well, Granddad needed me and you were pregnant.* Providing you with a chance to inherit the quarry.

I was thinking . . . It was time I got married, settled down; you were there, and I guess I loved you. You guess you loved me? *Phoebe's birth has been the best thing ever – I just love being her dad.* Of course you do. *I don't think I've made a very good job of it so far. I want you back, so I can try again – to be a better dad, a better husband.* And I'm supposed to believe that's true?

It was impossible to respond to them, and even more impossible to know what to say when he phoned. Over a crackly line, aware the army was listening in, there was no chance to talk about the things that mattered. We spoke instead in stilted sentences. He learnt only that Phoebe was pulling herself up on furniture; and I, that he was some-where hot. The call was over almost as soon as it had begun.

And yet, despite my anger, as the UN deadline approached I found myself increasingly anxious for him. Particularly the night the bombs started falling. We sat in silence, watching the explosions on the television; the American reporter squealing with excitement, 'It's like the fourth of July!' He was right, it was quite a spectacle: white lights flared across the green night-vision sky, criss-crossing each other like the Perseids Mark and I had watched the previous August. Except these fiery arcs of light weren't for our delight – they blazed across the darkness with lethal intent. In the studio, military pundits spoke in calm tones about accurate pinpointing, legitimate targets, minimal casualties, with the confidence borne of sitting in safety a long way away.

'Yeah, right,' said Nisha. 'I think that's as much as I can bear.' Annie and Erin looked up from the futon where they were curled up together. 'Goodnight, all.'

I followed her upstairs, wandering down the corridor to my bedroom where Phoebe was sleeping peacefully, her round face completely relaxed, her chest rising and falling with soft, even breaths, oblivious to the state of her parents' marriage, the fact that her dad was somewhere preparing to go into battle. However angry I was, I hated that he was caught up in this. Hated too the thought of those poor people in Baghdad. What must it feel like to have bombers going overhead while your children sleep? I hoped they had decent air-raid shelters, some place of safety, somewhere to survive the relentless onslaught.

This was no good; none of it was any good. There was no point keeping myself awake worrying; I had Phoebe to look after, and besides, tomorrow we were seeing Jack for lunch. I wanted to be at my best for him. I forced myself to relax, and gradually my eyes grew heavy. I slept.

I had arranged to meet Jack at the King George Hotel. It seemed appropriate somehow. I arrived a bit late to find him seated at a table by the window. He seemed smaller somehow, and frailer. When he stood up to kiss me, he was trembling. He was clearly more nervous than I was.

'It's good to see you,' I said, after the waitress had taken our orders; and I meant it. I hadn't realised how much I'd miss him when I left Echo Hall. 'I'm sorry about the way I left.'

'It's not your fault.'

That was generous of him. A peal of laughter from the centre table caused me to glance over at a large group of men in shiny suits. They were having a long lunch, ordering beer after beer in loud voices.

'Did you see the explosions on telly last night?' one asked.

'Brilliant, wasn't it?' another cried.

I shook my head in disgust. 'How are you?' I asked.

'Lonely, rattling about the place by myself. I've missed you.'

'I've missed you too.'

'I'm glad to see you. I've wanted to say for weeks how embarrassed I am by the way I behaved.'

'You needn't be.'

'The thing is, I was so shocked when Adam told me his plans. I overreacted. But over the last few weeks, I've had cause to think he might be right. The quarry's got no future as it is. If I want it to survive, if I want a lifetime's investment to mean something, perhaps we need to make some changes.'

'Oh.'

'I'd like to apologise to Mark, but I don't think I can on my own. Will you help me?'

I wasn't sure that I wanted to be drawn back into the Flint family, particularly if it entailed visiting Mark. But, since it was partly my fault that things had come to this, I agreed. The waitress came over with our food: soggy lasagne for me, steak and ale pie for Jack.

'By the way,' I said as he began to eat, 'I've had a chance to read the diaries.'

'And . . .'

'Daniel and Elsie didn't have an affair, but . . .' I hesitated, worried that I might upset him. 'They did sleep together . . .'

'So my parents were right.' He scowled.

'I don't think so.'

'You just said they slept together.'

'Once.'

'When?'

'After you were shot down. They thought you were dead. They were upset.'

'Funny way of showing it . . .'

'They didn't mean for it to happen.'

'There are no excuses.' Jack's voice was cold.

'There's something else.' This was harder than I'd thought. 'She was pregnant.'

He didn't say anything.

'It was a mistake. She was horrified when she found out, but . . .'

Still nothing.

'I do know one thing, though. Elsie loved you.'

'Really?' His tone was sharp.

'Really. Here. Read them yourself.' I handed him the diaries.

'I'll think about it.' He put the diaries in his bag, and began to play with Phoebe, clearly not wanting to discuss it further. I couldn't blame him for being angry, so I let the conversation turn to other matters.

Just as we were finishing our coffee, he remembered something. 'This came for you.' He handed me a letter. It was from the Australian Embassy.

I opened it. 'They've found Will!' I cried. 'They say if he gives his permission, they can provide his details.'

'Oh.'

'If he does, I could phone him, if you like?'

He hesitated, then nodded. 'Perhaps you could do me another favour?'

'What?'

'Would you think about coming back?'

'To Adam?'

'Yes.'

'I'll think about it.'

On the drive home, I pondered Jack's suggestion. Should I go back to Adam? Give him one more chance? But when I arrived home to see the others coming back from a vigil, I could hear his voice arguing that war was a necessity when the cause was just. I couldn't agree with that; weren't we better off apart?

Later, when we were sitting in Nisha's room drinking Barleycup before bed, she asked me how it had gone with Jack.

'He suggested getting back with Adam.'

'You're not thinking of saying yes, are you?'

'It's not just me I'm thinking of. There's Phoebe, and . . . I think I might be pregnant again.'

'Severe attack of déjà vu coming on. Ruth. Look what happened last time.'

She was probably right, yet somehow I still felt I owed him a chance. And it wasn't just that. Finding Will's address gave me another opportunity to discover what happened to Elsie. It seemed too shameful to admit it to anyone but myself, but I knew this was the most pressing reason for my return.

CHAPTER 2

'Hello?' The voice on the other end of the phone was clogged with sleep.

'Hello, you don't know me but . . .'

'Who the hell is this? Don't you know what time it is?'

'I'm calling from England.'

'I don't care where you're calling from – you don't call anyone at six in the morning.'

'I'm sorry, I thought you were eleven hours ahead.'

'That's during daylight saving. It's ten now . . .' The voice was getting angrier, all vestiges of pleasantness wearing away. 'Who the hell are you?'

'My name is Ruth Flint. I'm married to your nephew.'

'I don't have a nephew.'

'Yes, you do. He's called Adam.'

There was a pause. 'How did you get my number?'

'The Australian Embassy said you gave your permission.'

'I did no such thing.'

'I'm calling to let you know your father wants to make contact.'

'I don't have a father . . .'

This wasn't going as well as I'd hoped. 'He's sorry. He wants to make amends.'

'After all this time?'

'After all this time.'

'Tell the old bastard it's too bloody late.'

Before I could say anything else, he'd hung up.

I put the phone down in frustration. I'd felt so pleased with myself, tracking Will's number down. It hadn't occurred to me to wonder what his response might be. Oh, what was I thinking of, anyway? I wasn't even sure I was a Flint anymore – if I ever had been one in the first place. I wandered back down the hall. The rest of the household had gathered in the front room for the weekly community meeting. The others were back from Iraq, having been expelled from the country a week before. The farm was beginning to feel crowded, particularly with a new couple arriving soon. I'd have to start thinking about moving on.

As house guest, I was excused from the meeting, which initially suited me fine. Whenever I walked in on them, I was reminded of the intense discussions we used to have in my political days. At the time I'd been as passionate as the rest of them about the issues under discussion. But when our group fell apart in my post-relationship Armageddon, I'd walked away from it all. It was hard holding onto such beliefs when the two people who'd most inspired me had betrayed me.

It made me feel their whole value system was hypocritical. I wanted no further part in it. And yet, since I'd been at the farm and seen the urgency of these debates, I'd found myself tempted to join in. For years I'd resisted Nisha's calls to action, not wanting to be drawn back into that world – the frenetic energy, the blurring between the personal and political. Now, with the bombs falling on Baghdad, and even though Adam was on the side of the bombers, I could feel the pull again, the desire to want to take part, to take some action, no matter how small.

The feeling faded as I entered the kitchen to find a stack of dishes in the sink. As usual, I was the only one who seemed to care about the mess. Annie had been on cooking duty and seemed to have used every pot in the house, burning several in the process. I might as well clean them up while Phoebe slept, otherwise they'd be there all day. I scraped blackened lentils, rice and carrots into the bin, filling the pans with water to soak. The chopping board was piled high with rotting vegetable peelings and stewed tea bags. I wrinkled my nose at the pungent odour as I threw them in the compost. I returned to the sink and ran the water. It was quite pleasant to plunge my hands into the eco-friendly bubbles. To have a bit of time to myself. The trouble with communal living, I was finding, was that wherever you were, there was always someone in your space, even with half the household away. After the peace and quiet of Echo Hall, it was often overwhelming. It was ironic, really. Last year, I'd have given anything for a bit of company; now, I was always desperate for some time alone.

The sound of the meeting breaking up prompted me to put the kettle; the others drifted through to the kitchen. The talk round the table soon turned to the peace camp: those who'd gone shared vivid stories of encounters with families living in fear of bombs, and visits to milk factories blown to smithereens.

'Did it achieve anything?' I asked, thinking of Adam's view that the camp was self-indulgent. 'Was it worth it?'

'Solidarity,' said Liz.

'It showed that peace activists should be willing to risk their lives as soldiers do,' said Simon.

'Raising awareness that the other side are human too,' said Nisha. 'It was definitely worth doing that.'

The discussion turned to the war in general, as it did every night, and any thoughts I'd had of being involved in campaigning quickly dissipated. It was so full-on with them all; they talked of nothing else. None of them, not even Nisha, stopped to think that the constant conversation of bombs and battles might be adding to my anxiety about Adam. So I was grateful that I'd arranged to visit Mark and Helen the next day; it would be good to get away for a night.

★   ★   ★

Even though I had forced myself to abandon my feelings for Mark, I couldn't stop a shiver of anticipation as I walked up the path. I pushed it back, so that when Helen opened the door, I was able to respond to her warm hug without feeling too hypocritical. Nevertheless, as I sang Phoebe to sleep in the spare room, it was hard not to be aware of Mark next door, reading to his sons, and imagine for a moment that things were different. That there was no Helen downstairs, and that when the children were asleep we would have the evening ahead to ourselves. Then Phoebe smiled as I laid her in the travel cot, and I was reminded of Adam. I realised I had no right to think like this. I waited till she was asleep and Mark was downstairs before joining Helen in the lounge.

'It's wonderful when you have the evenings back,' said Helen, handing me a glass of wine. 'Particularly when it's his turn to cook.'

I smiled and sipped cautiously. What on earth were we going to talk about while Mark was in the kitchen?

'I'm so pleased you came over.' Helen's warmth was unexpected. 'I've been wanting to see you ever since Adam left. It must be so horrible for you with him being over there . . . and I gather things are a bit difficult.'

'Yes.'

'I can understand why. Having a baby is hard on anyone, even old marrieds like Mark and I. When you throw in a quick wedding, moving to a strange

458

place and your husband going off to war . . . Well, it's no wonder really.'

My eyes pricked with tears. I had no idea she could be this sensitive. 'There's a bit more to it than that.'

'There always is,' she said. 'Believe you me, there always is. Look, Ruth, I know we don't know each other very well, and maybe I'm speaking out of turn, but I do know Adam. He's a good man. He deserves another chance.'

I was prevented from responding by Mark calling us into dinner – a chicken casserole that was a welcome change after weeks of tofu and rice – followed by strawberry meringue.

'This is delicious,' I said. 'I didn't know you could cook.'

'One of my many virtues,' he replied.

'Which I intend to exploit much more, now work has calmed down.' Helen's gaze was affectionate. 'Don't you dare take on any more projects without my permission.'

'No Miss, promise Miss.' Mark saluted, and they both laughed. I was filled with a wave of envy, tinged with shame. For the first time since I'd known them, I realised that Adam was right. They clearly adored each other; I had no right to try to get between them. I never had. Still, it was a good opportunity to mention Jack; and, despite Helen's reservations about Mark's workload, they were soon enthusiastic about working with the Flints. I went to bed feeling at least I'd done one thing right.

The next day I drove back to Nisha's in a sombre mood. Jeremy and Gail aside, I'd always considered myself a good judge of character, yet I'd totally misread Mark and Helen's relationship. Had I misjudged my own, too? I mulled it over all the way back, and by the time I arrived I'd come to a conclusion: it was time to go home. I went upstairs immediately and began to pack.

Nisha entered when I was three-quarters of the way through.

'What are you doing?' she asked.

'Going back home.'

'Are you sure?'

'Certainty is a difficult concept . . . 50:50, maybe?'

'Your call, but I think you're mad . . .' She bit her lip. 'I wish you were staying. It's been nice having you both around.' Phoebe was sitting on the bed, propped up by pillows, playing with a music box as I worked.

'It's been great, but . . . I've got to give Adam another go. Besides, it'll be a bit crowded now the others are back.'

'You can always come back if you need to.'

I nodded, returning to my packing. Though I'd miss Nisha, I had a feeling that living with Liz would have posed a whole new set of difficulties.

A mist was beginning to form as I drove out of the yard. By the time I reached the Sandstown road it had become a thick fog. I drove cautiously, occasionally picking up a tail light for a few miles, till it turned off and disappeared into the darkening evening. As I left the main road, the clouds in the country lanes thickened, limiting visibility further. The villages took me by surprise – their stone walls leaping at me, the yellow lights of the houses muffled, pale beacons in the darkness. Sometimes, the fog parted, and I could just see the tops of skeletal trees arching over the road. I gripped the wheel tightly. Why hadn't I waited till morning? It was a relief when the sign for Whetstone appeared, and even greater relief to come upon the familiar slate houses, church, graveyard, war memorial. I took the hill slowly, the car's beams picking out the roots grasping the side of the hill, mosses and the remnants of bracken fighting for space on the black rock. And then we reached the entrance – the lichen-encrusted walls, the sentinel fir trees. I wondered for a moment if I was wrong to come back, but as I drove up the gravel driveway the mist parted and I saw Jack's light was on. I parked the car, walked over and gazed in through the window. He was sitting in his usual place, by the fireside, his face red in the fire's glow. He was reading a book, oblivious to my presence. At least, I thought, he would be pleased I'd come back.

And what about me? Was I glad I'd come back? Did my relationship with Adam stand a chance? If I was really truthful, the odds were even lower than I'd admitted to Nisha. But, I thought, as Mrs Davies opened the door, beaming with pleasure to see us, he'd said he was sorry – and he was the father of my child. If Elsie's story meant anything, it was that people should be given second chances. I owed him that at least.

CHAPTER 3

I wrote to Adam as soon as I could. I made no promises, and my tone was matter-of-fact. I acknowledged his apologies, agreeing it was worth trying again, ending on a conciliatory note with news of my pregnancy and the resurrection of the quarry project. It wasn't the warmest of letters, but it was the best I could do in the circumstances; I hoped it would be enough.

Jack was in the hall when I returned from the post box.

'I've been waiting for you,' he said. I followed him into his room. 'I've read the diaries.'

'And?'

'I was angry when you told me about Daniel and Elsie. Angrier still when I read what they'd done. But the more I read, the more I realised why it happened, and how much she regretted it. How much they both did. You are right. Elsie did love me. Knowing that really helps.'

'We still don't know what happened, though,' I said.

'Have you had any success with Will?'

'I phoned. He hung up. He is very angry still.'

'I can't say I blame him.'

'Why not?'

'What I did . . . It isn't something I'm very proud of. Please try not to judge me too harshly.' He didn't want to meet my gaze, focusing instead on a corner of the room.

'When I first came home, I wasn't aware of what was going on. I was delirious a lot of the time, reliving the details of the crash, the pain, the water. I kept asking for Elsie over and over again but they said she was ill and couldn't come. One day I woke to find the pain had lessened enough for me to pay more attention to my surroundings: the dark oak panels provided the evidence of where I was. I asked for Elsie, and at first no one said anything. Then, at last, my mother said she was dead. I refused to believe it at first. I had survived the firestorm with one thought – to get back to her. She couldn't be dead. But my mother repeated it again and again. *She caught scarlet fever. She died.* Until I had to accept the truth.' He sighed.

'I wanted to give up then and there, but my parents kept coming at me. I had responsibilities to them, to the children, to the quarry. I had come through the valley of death; now God had a new purpose for me. I refused to listen, saying I didn't think much of God's purpose, and turned my face to the wall. My mother spoke to my father, urging him to tell me the truth. I'd noticed that, since my illness, she seemed more in control, as if something had happened to banish the demons that had been tormenting her for years. He, on the other hand, seemed diminished, handing over authority that had always been his; which he was to do for the rest of his life. At my mother's urging, he told me that my precious Elsie was anything but; that she'd had an affair with Daniel. I tried not to listen, but their certainty frightened me. War does strange things to people. Elsie had been alone all these years. She wouldn't have been the first wife to stray. Had she and Daniel . . .? Had they really? My mother knew me well. She came back again and again, whispering in my ear, *Daniel Elsie, Elsie Daniel*, till I was going mad with it. As my strength returned, I found myself listening to her more and more. I realised I had to find out what happened. Which was when they told me Will could confirm everything.'

Jack paused, and looked at me. 'It's a terrible thing for a father to do what I did, but I had to know.'

'What did you do?' I asked, not sure I wanted to know the answer.

'I did what they suggested: I interrogated my son. I can still see him now, his tiny body stiff with fear: of me, of my parents, of saying the wrong thing. He was five years old, for Christ's sake, and I asked him. I asked him if he'd seen Mummy with Daniel, and he said yes, he had. I asked him where, and he said, they'd go walking together, that no one must know. Now, of course, I realise she must have said that to protect Daniel from

465

the authorities. But at the time, when Will said they did it every week, I began to listen to my parents. My mother stood at one ear saying, *Perhaps they were always . . .*; my father stood at the other, telling me *You need to marry again*; and Veronica kept showing up at the house reminding me *The children need a mother.* So I believed that Elsie betrayed me, and I stopped caring about anything. I turned my face to the wall and let them do what they wanted. I married Veronica six months later. Shortly afterwards I went to work in the quarry, in accordance with my father's wishes. I gave up on my own life, submitting to their will.'

Phoebe crawled towards him and he picked her up, placing her on his lap. 'The war ended eventually, changing the world as Daniel always predicted . . . India was given to its people. Palestine to Israel. The African nations rose in rebellion. And as the British Empire dwindled, so did ours. There was to be no post-war slate boom in 1945. This time my father was forced to keep the quarry alive by selling off the old Walter porcelain factories and by sending me touting for business across the damaged continent. And as the old certainties changed, I watched my children grow, indifferent to their progress. When I was married to Elsie I was devoted to them, but now I washed my hands of fatherhood, leaving Veronica to care for them. I sank into a world of dust and stone. I let myself harden with the earth, recreating myself in the father's image I had once rejected.'

Phoebe giggled at him, and he smiled down at her sadly. 'I'm sorry to say that the children were frightened of me, particularly Will. I wish I'd shown more sensitivity. I should have seen how Will hated his stepmother, how she was harder on him than Evie, who was a more biddable child. But when I looked at my son I was filled with doubt. Not only had he been present during Elsie's betrayal, but I was beginning to doubt he was mine. Evie's conception I could be sure of, but Will's was just after we were married, when Daniel had been a frequent visitor to the house. I began to wonder if they'd made a fool of me even then. So I gazed at my son, and instead of seeing the features that made him so definitely mine – the strong jaw, the long nose – I saw dark hair, and doubted . . .

'The years passed, each one drier and dustier then the last. Then one day, when Will was 12, he and Evie found the key to Elsie's room. Veronica had wanted to clear it out after Elsie died, but for some reason I wouldn't let her. I couldn't bear to go in there, but neither did I want her memory completely extinguished. So I made sure the rooms were locked and no one could get in. Once they'd found it, the children egged each other to have a look . . .'

'What happened?'

'It was Mrs Davies who heard the scream. She

ran upstairs to find Evie looking at her brother helplessly. He was rocking back and forwards, pale and sweating. We could not get him to speak. This was 1949; we didn't understand such matters then. We'd talk about people suffering from "nerves", not realising the impact of emotional trauma. So we sent Will away to a sanatorium for a while. When he returned, we continued the Flint family tradition of not speaking of things that made us uncomfortable. Over the next few years, Will had several episodes like that. Each time, he was sent away; each time he returned quiet and pale, and each time nothing was said. Until the last time . . .'

'The last time?'

'My father had just died. After the funeral Will had another turn, as we called them. He went away to the usual place, but when he returned, he seemed unusually agitated. One night he came to me, saying he was going away. When I asked why, he wouldn't say. I asked what he would do for money, and he said he would find himself a job. I asked how he would do that, given he was so inexperienced; he said he'd manage. I laughed at him. I shouldn't have I know, but he still seemed like a child to me. The idea of him leaving was preposterous. I think it must be this that made him react the way he did. He started shouting at me; once he started he couldn't stop. I was a terrible father, he said – I'd never loved him. I'd never loved Elsie. I'd killed her, so I could marry Veronica.

'I should have recognised how fragile he was, but I in turn became furious that he might think I would betray Elsie. Particularly when she was the one who'd had an affair, when all I wanted to do was get back to her. I told him, though I didn't mean it, that his mother was a tart, that he was a bastard and had never been a son of mine.

'"Sons should look up to their fathers," he said. "They shouldn't fear them. All my life, I have lived in fear. Not anymore." He left the house shortly afterwards. I haven't seen him since.'

Jack looked down at Phoebe. 'You know . . . when your children are born, you swear to love and protect them all their lives. You could never imagine that anything would make you act otherwise . . .' He sighed. 'The irony was that the minute I'd calmed down, I realised his whole attitude confirmed he was mine. He saw me exactly the way I'd seen my own father. He was more courageous, of course. He was prepared to stand up to me – he got that from Elsie. But at the moment I was denying him, he was absolutely the son I had sworn to cherish and love at his birth. I should have gone after him then and there, but I was too ashamed. I thought he'd come back with his tail between his legs, and we could start again. But he never did. And as each day passed it was harder to follow him, to find out where he went. By the time I'd built up the courage, he had gone, taken the boat to Australia, leaving no forwarding address.

'More years passed. My mother died, and then Evie, giving me the chance to try again with Adam. But my old habits were too ingrained; I repeated the same mistakes with him too. Then Veronica died, and you came, and showed me perhaps I could make amends for the past.'

'You could, I'm sure of it.'

'Will hates me, and with good reason.'

'If he knew you were sorry . . .'

'I'm not sure that'll make any difference.'

'We've got to give it a try.'

'You're very committed, Ruth, but I'm not sure even you could pull off such a miracle.'

I wasn't ready to give up yet. As I warmed up Phoebe's tea, I determined I would write to Will to tell him what happened. I was determined to make him see how much Jack needed his forgiveness.

I wasn't ready to give up yet.

CHAPTER 4

*D*ear Mr Flint, I know you have made your
feelings plain, but I think you will regret it
... I crumpled up the paper and started
again. It was hard to find the words that would
persuade Will his father was serious. In the end it
took 10 attempts before I finally sealed the letter.

I strode down to Whetstone, skirting round the
black puddles in the road, hoping the rain desperate
to burst from the low-lying clouds would hold off
before we returned. I walked fast, and was soon
at the village shop.

'A letter for Australia? We don't get many of
them.' Ivy gazed at the envelope as if it were an
alien object. She fiddled in the back, then returned
with a pair of weighing scales and carefully balanced
the gold weights until the pans were level. 'Airmail,
is it?' she added as she took my payment, ferreting
around for the small blue sticker. She glanced at
the address; no doubt by teatime the whole of
Whetstone would know I'd written to Will, but
there was nothing much I could do about that. I
said goodbye and pushed Phoebe out of the shop.

It had been ages since I'd walked through the

village. On the spur of the moment, I decided to pop into the graveyard. I walked along the slope and round to the back, pushing the buggy over the green mossy grass, past the lichen-covered stones, until I reached Elsie's. The flowers Jack had left last winter were still there, their stalks withered, and the few petals left bleached by the sun. Dead leaves had drifted over the mound, so I tidied it up, removing the flowers and placing them in the compost. I looked at her headstone. She was so young. What had happened that she had died so young? And there, behind, was the shallow trough, a marker in the ground noting that Rachel Clarkson had once been buried here. Jack had said that after the war, Daniel had exhumed her body and buried it in York. She too had only been young when she'd died. No wonder the back room at Echo Hall felt so sad; both of them gone before their time.

The task of clearing up the grave was more tiring than I'd imagined. By the time I was done, Phoebe was asleep and I needed to sit down. I pushed the chair to the bench; it wouldn't hurt to close my eyes for a while . . .

I must have dozed off, because when I opened my eyes it was raining. My collar was damp; my shoulders were beginning to chill. I was about to stand up when I saw that a funeral procession had entered the cemetery, and gathered round an open grave. Not wanting to intrude on their grief, I remained in my place. A small boy with dark hair stood on the edge of the group. He looked about five or six. He turned round and gazed at me with an expression of such sadness that I felt like grabbing him in my arms to comfort him. I wondered why no one was paying him any attention, why the adult mourners stood with ramrod backs facing the vicar, and why not one of them thought to hold his hand. It was only as he turned back to face the group that I noticed something strange about him. His jacket – it wasn't what you'd call modern; the collar was too stiff, the shorts that bit too long. I gazed at the grieving party, their clothing – the hats, the coats, they were all wrong. And come to think of it, who had dug the grave?

Phoebe's yelp caused me to look away for a minute. She was working herself up into a proper milk frenzy. I'd not expected to be out so long and hadn't brought any with me. I turned back to the group, wanting to apologise for my daughter's noise, but there was no one there. I shook my head. I must have been dreaming. I was thinking about Will; it was natural, sitting here in the graveyard after hearing Jack's story, that I'd think of Elsie's funeral. Nonetheless, the experience was unnerving. I pushed the buggy out of the graveyard and headed up the hill as fast as I could.

Jack was out when I returned, though the sound of hoovering from his room indicated that Mrs Davies was around. I sorted out lunch and then settled Phoebe down for a nap. As I left her room, I paused on the landing. Something had occurred to me. After she was imprisoned, Elsie had mentioned that she'd written Jack some letters. But I'd been through all the boxes with a fine toothcomb and not found them. Perhaps she had hidden them somewhere? I went to the back bedroom and sat on the bed. If I was going to hide letters in here, where would be a good place? *Think.*

I walked over to the skirting boards. They were firmly attached to the wall; the floorboards beneath were rigid and unbending. There was nothing there. Nor in the cupboard, or the desk. That left under the bed. I pulled up the covers and peered under the base. It was too dark to see. If I pushed it, I might be able to expose some floor. It was heavier than I'd expected; it took me several minutes to move it far enough. To my delight, in the centre I found two loose half-boards. I pulled them up. I was right. Underneath was a pack of letters, the envelopes faded yellow, covered in dust. They were mainly addressed to Jack, though there was one for Daniel, and one for her sister Het.

I rifled through them, checking the dates until I arrived at the last, written the day before she died.

Echo Hall
12th December 1943

My Dearest Jack,

Christmas is coming. For the first time in many years we are under the same roof. How ironic, then, that we are further apart then we have ever been. I know I only have myself to blame for that. But I long to see you, to hold your hand, to kiss you. Make you well again. I resent your mother usurping my role – having to rely on her for bulletins about your recovery, as I've had to rely on the news reports to guess your whereabouts for years.

It is still a while before they send me away. I have a little time before I will have to give up this baby if I am to have any chance of keeping you and the children. Perhaps this is why I feel so anxious. And this time round, I don't have you by my side to reassure me, as you did with Will, or write me encouraging letters, as you did with Evie. Well, I dare say I don't deserve it. You reap what you sow: isn't that what these farming folk say?

I miss the children. Each day I watch them from the window, playing in the garden with the nurse's little girl. They look happy from where I stand, but I hate the idea of your mother looking after them. I have protected them from her for so long; it is killing me that I can't protect them now. I have to believe that this is temporary. Once I've had this baby, given it away to strangers, my penance will be complete, and I can return to you. And then . . .

And then, I don't know what will happen.

Your parents want me to conspire to hide the truth from you. Perhaps they are right that past hurts are best left in the dark – life is better lived by moving forward. But I cannot believe that, not really. I have to have faith in us, faith in you. Faith that if I tell you, you will have the capacity to understand. Maybe, even, to forgive.

In the meantime, I will keep writing you these letters. Letters that I may never send. Letters to keep my hope alive.

Your loving wife,

Else x

There was nothing more. I could have cried with frustration. I don't know what else I expected, really. I walked across to the window; this was the view she'd had every day as she stood watching her children play. It must have been terrible to be so close, yet unable to be with them. I turned back to the bed, intending to pick up the letters to take down to Jack, when a sharp pain stabbed in my stomach, taking my breath away. Instinctively, I stroked my belly. The pain stabbed me again. I sat on the bed and then, as the pain intensified, I crunched up, foetal-like, on the mattress. I tried to convince myself it was just indigestion; I'd eaten too much at lunch. I closed my eyes as liquid trickled down my legs. I tried not to think what that might be.

I needed to do something. To call for help. But

I couldn't think. Somewhere in the back of my mind, I knew there was some way of calling for help. What was it? My stomach cramped again. This wasn't happening. It couldn't be. I hadn't even told Adam. The moment passed and my mind cleared enough for me to remember. The servants' bell. There was one in here, too. Elsie had used it. Perhaps Mrs Davies was still downstairs; she might hear me. I pulled and pulled and then lay back on the bed trying to pretend this wasn't happening. I'm not sure how long I was there before Mrs Davies came. She called Tommy and together they managed to help me downstairs so that he could drive me to the hospital.

He was very kind. He waited till I was admitted to A & E, and even offered to stay with me, but I sent him away; if Adam couldn't be with me, I didn't want anyone else. Afterwards, when it was all over, I lay on the bed waiting to be discharged, listening to the sound of babies crying in the nearby maternity ward. I drifted in and out of sleep, awaking to find myself stiff, sore and cold.

It was only when I was back in my own bed at home that it came back to me. The voice I'd heard, as I lay on the bed cramped with pain. It could have been my own voice, but I knew it wasn't. A woman's voice, calling in desperation. '*Help me. Someone. Help me, please.*'

CHAPTER 5

Phoebe woke me at six. I lay in the darkness, not wanting to move till she yelled again, more urgently. I picked her up from her cot and carried her downstairs. The kitchen light was on. I opened the door to find Jack making a cup of hot chocolate.

'Couldn't sleep? I'm not surprised.'

He added some milk to the pan as I placed Phoebe in the high chair, patting me on the shoulder as I passed him to fetch her cereal from the cupboard. I nodded, concentrating my energies on preparing my daughter's breakfast. Jack poured me a cup of cocoa as I returned to the table and began to spoon mushy porridge into Phoebe's mouth.

'Thanks.'

'I'm sorry, Ruth.'

'Me too . . .' I took his proffered hand. 'I'm not sure I can talk about it yet.'

'No, I expect not.'

Rain began to bang against the window, lightly at first and then, as the wind grew stronger, pelting angrily on the panes. The sky was covered in dense, black clouds that showed no sign of lifting. Daybreak wouldn't arrive for a while longer. I fed Phoebe another spoonful. She swallowed eagerly; I fed her another. Jack sipped his chocolate.

'With everything that happened yesterday, I didn't get a chance to say – I found some letters.'

'From Elsie?'

I nodded. 'You should read them. I think they'll help.'

'You're very good to do this for me.'

Phoebe laughed at nothing in particular, drawing us into her world of simple pleasures. Between us we maintained a flow of small talk, a shared appreciation of her antics. It was easier that way.

I passed through the week in slow motion, functioning because I had to. Since my return, I'd taken to sharing domestic tasks with Mrs Davies; the floors still needed mopping, the carpets hoovering, the shopping buying. Phoebe still needed attending to, though I changed her nappies, fed her, bathed her with less enthusiasm than normal. The only bright moment was Jack's reaction when I gave him the letters. I wanted to be pleased for him, but now his joy hardly touched me; particularly when the post brought a reply from Adam, delighted we were back together with another baby on the way. How on earth could I tell him that it was no longer true?

I was grateful when Nisha rang, asking if she could come over. I hadn't seen her since I'd left the farm, and I jumped at the chance, hoping she might cheer me up. But when I met her at the station, she was unusually subdued.

'What's up?' I asked, as we took the road out of Sandstown.

'It's just all so depressing.' She gestured to the brown fields, and the grey sky. 'Winter in the countryside. Eats into you somehow.'

'I know what you mean.' The land was bare, the ground clogged with brown churned-up mud. The clouds were low on the horizon, pressing down on the earth, readying themselves for rain. I glanced across at her. Her eyes were listless; her skin lacked its usual healthy glow.

As I turned onto the Whetstone road, she added, 'It's not just the weather.'

'Oh?'

'I read an awful article on the train. There was a bomb shelter in Baghdad . . . Four hundred people were sheltering in it. And we bombed it. Four hundred people. Jesus.'

'That's horrible.'

'I've thought of nothing else, the whole journey over. It makes me want to scream sometimes.'

'What?'

'People's indifference. Everyone here, just getting on with their lives, the war hardly touching them – it's all so far away, and not happening to anyone they know.'

'I'm sure most people don't think that.'

'Enough do. Though others are worse.'

'What do you mean?'

480

'The number of times I've been told to go back to my own country recently . . .'

'God, I'm sorry.'

She shrugged, gazing out of the window. I hadn't had a chance to tell her about the miscarriage. I felt even less inclined to now. We drove the rest of the way in silence.

'This is a hell of a place to live,' said Nisha, as we turned up the drive. 'How do you stand it?'

I glanced up at the grey walls and tall black windows. It did look particularly unwelcoming this morning. 'I dare say we won't be here forever.'

The clouds burst during lunch, streams of rain pounding the windows so hard we thought it would be set for the day. But, much to our surprise, it proved to be just a heavy shower. By early afternoon, the clouds lightened; we could even glimpse a patch of blue sky, a sight encouraging enough to prompt a walk up the hill. I'd just bought a new backpack for Phoebe and it was pleasant to hear her gurgling behind me as we climbed up the familiar path to the woods. It was damp and muddy after the recent rainy weather, the steep incline causing me to gasp. I was quickly out of breath.

'Are you OK?' Nisha asked.

'She's heavier than you think . . .'

'And of course, you're walking for two.'

I opened my mouth, then closed it again. The words wouldn't come out. Instead I turned up the path, pushing the pace. It was only when we'd arrived at the stones, spread out a rug, and Phoebe's pack was balanced safely on the ground that I could bring myself to explain.

'I'm so sorry, Ruth.'

'I suppose it's for the best. In the long run, I mean.'

'Do you really think that?'

'Trying to make do, I guess.'

She put her arm around my shoulder. 'Come on, let it out.'

'It's crazy, I know. The baby had barely formed. All the same, I was beginning to think about it, wonder whether it was a boy or girl. Imagine Phoebe as a big sister.'

'That's not crazy.'

'Have you got a tissue?'

Nisha handed me a pack from her pocket. I wiped away the tears, blowing my nose.

'How has Adam taken it?'

'He doesn't know yet. I don't know how I'm going to tell him . . .'

'You'll find a way.'

'Perhaps . . . How are things with you and Simon?'

'Not great. He's been different since Iraq.'

'What's happened?'

'You know how people say, "It's not you, it's me"?'

I nodded.

'According to him, it *is* me. Apparently, I'm a control freak. I boss him around. I speak for him.

As long as he's doing what I want him to do I'm nice, but when he wants to branch off on his own I'm a demon . . .'

'Ouch.'

'I'm not, am I?'

'Of course not, but . . .'

'What?'

'You do always seem to pick a type.'

'I do?'

'Yes. Nice. Sweet. Not much backbone. Perhaps you need someone a little more strong-willed?'

'Hmm . . .'

Thinking I might have offended her, I added, 'Are you still together?'

'Hanging on by our fingertips.'

'Maybe you can work things out.'

'Maybe. I'm thinking of moving back to London whatever happens. It's Liz, as well.' She rose to her feet and paced up and down in front of the rocks.

'Ah.'

'When I first met her last year, I thought she was amazing. She'd done all these incredible things. Resisted the Contras in Nicaragua. Lived in the shanty towns in Soweto. Had countless jail sentences round the world. And she's smart. She inspires people. When she said the community needed a new member, I jumped at it. But the truth is . . .'

'She's hard to live with?'

'If I'm a control freak, she's a megalomaniac.

She just can't handle people disagreeing with her. It's been worse since she got back.'

I smiled. 'She invited the wrong person home then.'

'You know what really makes me mad?' Nisha's feet stamped out her frustration. 'She didn't even start the community. Annie and Erin were there before her. She's lost sight of the original vision – to balance the activism with self-sufficiency. Margie and Pete, the founders, they had this idea that we're better campaigners when we've got other things to focus on. That digging the compost helps put our successes and failures into perspective. Liz says that's all very well in peace-time but war changes everything. Now Annie and Erin are off travelling, she's got everyone else agreeing with her, even Simon. They've been thick as thieves since Iraq. And in the meantime, if I don't turn the ground, there'll be no veggie boxes to sell in the summer, and no potatoes for us to eat in the winter.' Nisha stopped, her shoulders drooping in the cold. 'It's just so exhausting.'

'Do you want to stay here for a bit? Take refuge, like I did with you?'

'That's sweet of you . . . Thanks. But I'll be alright. I'm off to London tomorrow. I'll be away for a week – time to take stock.'

I stood up too. The sun had gone behind a cloud; it was getting cold. I picked Phoebe up, strapped her backpack on and set off at a swift pace. We had no desire to get lost, as we'd done last year.

Even so, the woods were darkening as we passed along the muddy paths, our boots squelching through the ooze. In the gathering gloom, the trees seemed to press in on us; I was glad when we reached the path at the edge of the estate. As I opened the gate for Nisha, I happened to glance back. There was someone standing by the sycamore tree at the top of the path. A woman; it was definitely a woman, though I hadn't heard anyone behind us.

'Help me with this,' said Nisha. Her coat had snagged on the gate.

When I looked back, the woman had gone. It must have been a trick of the light. What was it about this place that had me seeing things all the time?

We walked down the slope towards the Hall. In the greying light, the house resembled a death mask: the two bay windows on the first floor black, unforgiving eyes; the row of windows by the kitchen a stern mouth. Nisha was right; this was a hell of a place to live, and yet something drew me to stay. And despite our reconciliation, it wasn't Adam. Entering the house under the gables of Elsie's old bedroom, I knew that what kept me here was the desire to find out what happened to her at all costs. Nothing else mattered more.

CHAPTER 6

The crackle on the line was enough to alert me that it was Adam on the other end of the phone. He couldn't have had a better reason for ringing. The war was over. He wasn't sure when he'd be back, but it wouldn't be long. Unlike Elsie, unlike Leah, I wouldn't be waiting years to see my husband again. Though part of me was nervous at the thought of what lay ahead for us, mostly it was a relief to know he wouldn't be in danger anymore.

The news was enough to help lift my low mood. Knowing he was safe, I felt able to tell him about the miscarriage. And it was fun making plans for his return. I rearranged the furniture in our room and painted it a pale yellow to make it more welcoming. I was determined to make an effort, to ensure that this time round things would be better. Phoebe's progress was also a delight to me. Every day she was learning something new, whether it was clapping her hands, pulling herself up on furniture or making babbling sounds that were almost like words. For the first time in weeks, I felt almost happy.

And yet as March dragged on, and the weather didn't improve, I couldn't help noticing Jack's spirits drooping. He still went out for walks, but each time he seemed to return more quickly than the day before. He was in his sitting room more often, where he sat gazing into the fire. Quite often now, when I popped in to see him, he was dozing. If I disturbed him, he'd come to, confused as to where he was. Once or twice he called me Elsie.

One morning I was coming back from Whetstone with Phoebe when I met him on the drive. The wind was cold, chipping at our faces. My hands were chilled, even through my gloves.

'It's been six weeks since you sent your letter.'

'Is it that long?' With everything that had happened, I'd lost track.

'I thought it unlikely that he'd respond . . .'

'Never say never. He may be trying to work out what to say.'

'Perhaps.' He looked down the hill. 'I'm just afraid if he leaves it much longer, it will be too late.'

'Nonsense! You are so much fitter than when I first came here. You've got years in you yet.'

He didn't answer. Instead, he set his face against the wind and struggled back to the house: a hunched old man, fighting to keep his breath. I'd noticed his frailty when I returned in February, but I'd put it down to the harshness of winter. Now I observed him more closely, he did seem weaker than he'd been six months ago. I followed him into the house, hoping I was imagining it. I didn't like the idea of Echo Hall without him.

As I climbed into bed, I was conscious for the first time that Adam's absence meant I had no one to share my anxieties with. If he had been here, he would surely have put my mind at ease, told me that someone of Jack's age would inevitably be a bit breathless at times, get a little gloomy on occasion. That I had nothing to worry about. And then, perhaps, when I was reassured enough, he might pull me towards him, nibbling my neck the way I liked, in the way he used to before he disappeared, before Phoebe, before I discovered he'd lied. I found myself smiling because, for the first time in months, I had a feeling that when he was back in my bed again, I might just want him to do that. When I dropped off to sleep, my dreams were of sunshine and sand, and Adam's smile. And the sense that everything was going to be alright.

Something woke me at three in the morning. My first instinct was that it was Phoebe, but when I looked in her room, she was still fast asleep. There it was again: *bang, bang, bang.* It seemed to be coming from downstairs. The wind rattled the window frames. It was cold and I was tempted to stay in bed, but it continued: *bang, bang, bang,* an insistent knock that I couldn't ignore. With a sigh, I grabbed my dressing-gown from the end of our bed. The landing was pitch-black. Rain was pummelling the windows. I switched on the light, following the sound downstairs.

The gale was forcing its way through every crack and cranny, filling the hall with icy air. As I reached the bottom of the stairs I saw that the green baize door was open, and a yellow glow was spilling into the dark corridor. Someone must have forgotten to turn off the light. *Bang, bang, bang.* The sound was louder now. When I entered the kitchen, I saw the back door swinging open and shut. The wind was blowing rain inside, creating a puddle of water by the step. I was about to shut it, when I heard a faint sound outside, like an animal in distress. The night was black with thick cloud; the air heavy with water. I peered out of the window. I could hardly see the bushes. Then I heard it again. Something on the lawn was making a piteous noise. I craned my neck. Through the driving rain, I could make out a faint shape hunched on the ground, distorted like a blurred photograph. Was it a person? I couldn't be sure. To be on the safe side, I grabbed an umbrella and a couple of raincoats from the hall and raced outside.

The garden was gushing with water, soaking my slippers in seconds. The figure on the lawn was kneeling, face down, thumping the grass, oblivious to the torrents falling from the sky, the roar of the wind down the hillside. It was Jack, dressed only in rain-washed pyjamas that stuck to his skin. Water was flooding down the cracks of his face. The wind was whipping his hair, beating at his body. Yet he seemed unaware of anything but the ground in front of him. He pounded and pounded the earth with an astonishing vigour for a man in his seventies. As I reached his side, I could hear him above the wail of the wind, repeating one word, over and over again. 'Elsie, Elsie, Elsie.'

I rushed towards him.

'Come back inside.'

He didn't move.

I pulled at him. 'Jack, you must come back in.'

He turned to me, bewildered for a moment, then straightened himself up and took my arm. I led him back to his room, fetched towels and pyjamas, dried him down and helped him get into bed. He lay back on the pillows, his face grey.

'Thank you,' he said in a subdued voice.

'What on earth possessed you?'

He mumbled something I couldn't understand and then, a little louder, 'Sometimes, I . . . hear her voice . . . She calls . . . Jack, Jack, Jack . . . Tonight . . . I had to . . . had to . . . see . . .'

Who was I to judge him? The woman who heard voices and saw impossible reflections in the mirror? I just nodded and said, 'Take an umbrella next time, eh?'

He smiled a sad smile. 'Would you mind staying with me for a while? I don't really want to be alone.'

'Of course.'

I settled him back on the pillows, switched off the light and sat watching and waiting. Outside, the rain settled to a gentle tapping on the window. Jack's breaths rose and fell, heavily at first, as if the very act of breathing was a major effort. But then as he relaxed, he began to breathe more evenly, slowly drifting off to sleep. I sat for a while, just to make sure, as I sometimes did with Phoebe; thinking about what he'd said, the sight of him pummelling his grief out in the storm. As I left the room, I wondered whether I'd been stupid to write to Will, to raise Jack's hopes. He'd made it clear on the phone that he wasn't prepared to forgive, and without him, we might never find out what happened to Elsie. At the doorway I turned to make sure the old man was properly asleep. The light streamed in from the hallway, picking out the creases and folds of his skin. In the brief time I had known him, he seemed to have aged several years.

I suddenly had a horrible feeling that Jack was right. If I couldn't persuade Will to come home soon, it would be too late.

CHAPTER 7

My fears resurfaced in the morning when I went to check on Jack and found him feverish and confused. I rang the surgery, who advised fluids and paracetamol. The doctor couldn't come till the evening; they promised to send the district nurse instead. So Mrs Davies helped me drag Phoebe's playpen into Jack's room and I settled down beside him. His face was ashwhite, his breath was coming in short sharp bursts, his hands were clammy. Although his eyes were closed, he grabbed my fingers hard. He drifted between sleep and wakefulness, repeating Elsie's name. The morning dragged on. I made sure he kept drinking, gave him more paracetamol, held a cold flannel to his head, but he didn't appear to be getting any better. I was about to call the surgery again when Mrs Davies knocked on the door and ushered in the district nurse. I stood up to shake her hand, recognising the woman I'd met the previous year, when I'd just arrived at Echo Hall.

'Nurse Owen, isn't it?'

'Katie, please.'

She was an immediately reassuring presence. After a quick examination she concluded there was nothing to be done but to let Jack sweat it out.

'What on earth was he doing, going out on such a terrible night?' she asked, as I accompanied her back out to the hall.

'Long story.'

'This is a troubled house, isn't it?'

'What makes you say that?'

'Last time I was here I thought that it seemed familiar. Those fir trees, the driveway, the panelled hall. I've been here before.'

'Really?'

'My mother was a nurse. During the war, while my dad was away, she took live-in jobs. It was the easiest way to make ends meet. We must have stayed in lots of houses over the years. They all looked the same after a while, yet this place stuck for some reason. I checked with her after my last visit and she said yes, we'd been here. She'd looked after Mr Flint, while he recovered from his injuries. Funny isn't it, that we're both caring for the same man?'

I tried to keep my voice steady. 'When would that have been, then?'

'Let me see . . . I must have been about six or seven . . . 1942, 1943, maybe?'

'I hope you don't mind me asking, but do you remember anything else?'

'There was a boy . . . What was his name, now?' She paused for a moment. 'Oh yes . . . Will. He had a little sister, Evie. We used to play together. We didn't stay in the house, of course; we had lodgings in the coach house round the back. The family who normally lived there were away, I think. I do remember running around in the garden. It's enormous, isn't it? We used to play hopscotch on the paving stones at the bottom, and hide and seek further up.' She pulled her coat on. 'Why do you ask?'

'I'm researching family history.'

'They didn't seem a very pleasant bunch. Will's grandparents were terrifying. We kept out of their way as much as we could. If you made too much noise, or broke so much as a flower head, old Mrs Flint would appear from nowhere to give you a clip round the ear. Mr Flint was working a lot, of course, but sometimes he'd come home early. He'd never pass us without giving a lecture about our sinful ways.' She wrinkled her face. 'No, they weren't nice people at all.'

'Do you remember young Mrs Flint?'

'Wasn't she sick or something? Will could never see her because she was in quarantine – locked away at the back of the house. Scarlet fever, wasn't it?'

'So they said.'

'It wasn't that? How strange . . . No, I never saw her. Just old Mrs Flint and some woman who used to visit a lot . . . Veronica. She always seemed friendly, but there was something false about her smile . . . Too many teeth, I think. Will hated her.'

'How long were you here?'

'For a few weeks. Then young Mrs Flint died. We left soon after that.'

I tried to hold back a bubble of excitement. They had lived in the house when Elsie died. Katie's mother might know something. 'Do you know why?'

'Mother never said. It was the only time I ever knew her leave before the job was done. She wasn't that keen to talk about this place when I mentioned it. Just said the Flints were the nastiest people she'd ever worked for; that this was the unhappiest house she'd ever known.'

When I told her Jack and Elsie's story, she was only too happy to talk to her mother, whom she was due to visit in April. She promised to be in touch if she found out anything useful. After she left I returned to Jack. Outside, the rain fell against the windowpanes; inside, I repeated the treatment throughout the day, cooling his forehead, making him drink, giving tablets. Every now and then Phoebe needed a change or a cuddle. It was a gruelling day; the fever didn't break till well into the afternoon. As the wind and rain of the night finally died down and a ribbon of orange streaked across the sky, Jack sat up.

'What time is it?'

'Nearly four-thirty.'

'You've been here all day?'

'On and off.'

'You must think me an old fool.'

'Not at all. I'm just glad you're alright. You had us worried there.' I thought of telling him what

Katie had said, but decided against it. There was no point raising his hopes – or mine, for that matter. The chances were her mother didn't know anything anyway. 'Mrs Davies is cooking tea; do you fancy some?'

'Do you know, I'd love some scrambled eggs.'

I helped him get up. It was a bit of an effort, and just as well we'd kept his walking frame. I swung his legs round so he could stand up, then supported him as he shuffled across the room to the chair by the fire. It was good to see he was a bit stronger, the colour returning to his cheeks. After he'd eaten, I let Phoebe out of the playpen so she could have a bit of exercise. She raced round the floor in excitement, thrilled to be free, and then began her regular efforts at pulling herself up on the furniture. We watched as she managed to get halfway up the sofa, only to fall on her bottom with a puzzled look on her face. At last, after five attempts, she crawled towards us, pulled herself up on my chair and stood for 30 seconds or so. She was so excited she clapped her hands, which made her lose her balance and fall back to the floor. We all burst out laughing.

'Such a beautiful age,' said Jack. 'They learn something every day, don't they? I always remember the excitement of Will's first walk. Of course, I missed Evie's. Elsie said she just woke up one morning, toddled out of her bedroom and that was it.'

He smiled at the memory, his face was bright in

the firelight. He chatted for a while, enjoying Phoebe's meanderings across the room, but after a while I could see he was getting tired. I helped him back to bed. As he leant half on me and half on the walker, I was reminded of the night Phoebe was born, when we'd clung together at the bottom of the stairs. I smiled at the memory, but as he settled down in the bed, my anxieties returned. His breathing seemed irregular again, his body fragile, his face ancient. His hold on life seemed so slight.

When Phoebe was tiny, I'd had this fear – the sense that I shouldn't stop watching her, that every breath was so precious, there was a chance each one might be the last. I was grateful for the doctor's arrival and his brisk, reassuring prognosis: Jack was suffering from a severe bronchial infection. At his age, it might take some time to recover, but recover he would; we would just have to be patient. After he had gone, I returned to Jack's side until at last he drifted off to sleep.

I left Mrs Davies keeping an eye on him and took Phoebe upstairs, but after a day confined to Jack's room she was alert and giggly. It wasn't till nine o'clock that I managed to escape; when I came downstairs Mrs Davies had already gone to bed. She had offered to sleep downstairs in case Jack needed anything, and had clearly decided she needed an early night in case she was disturbed. I wandered into the living room and turned on the television. Though the news from Iraq was better – Saddam had accepted the ceasefire; the troops were coming home – I was in no mood for reality. I switched channels to find that *Men Behaving Badly* had just started. That's what I needed: a little light entertainment. I didn't begrudge looking after Jack, particularly when I knew this wasn't serious, but the scars of my mother's illness ran deeper than I'd realised. I'd forgotten how draining it was to care for someone you loved. I sat back on the sofa, grateful that Mrs Davies had stoked the fire. The red-gold flames crackled in the hearth, warming the room. I let myself be diverted by a mindless Harry Enfield sitcom for a while, but the combination of warmth and exhaustion soon had me nodding off. The laughter track on the television provided a backdrop to half-dreams in which I chased Katie down the corridor, asking for answers. When she turned round it was not her face I saw, but my mother's. 'I'm dead, dear,' she said. 'I can't help.' I shook myself awake for a moment before sinking back into another doze. Elsie was standing in the woods by the sycamore tree; she was holding a baby in her arms. 'It's alright,' she said. 'Will's coming.' In the background I was conscious of applause, the music of the closing credits, and another noise, shrill and insistent. It took a couple of minutes to realise it was the phone. I jumped up and ran out to the hall.

'Hello?'

'Is that Mrs Flint?'

I couldn't quite place the voice. 'Yes, who is this?'

'You're very persuasive.'

'Will?'

'We've booked our tickets.'

'You have?'

'My wife Martha has been nagging me for some time. She made me read your letter. She thinks I need to come. We're bringing the boys. We'll be with you by the end of June.'

'That's fantastic. I'm so glad you've changed your mind.'

'As I said, you're very persuasive. See you in June.'

I put the phone down and went back into the living room, very pleased with myself. All that effort had paid off. I couldn't wait to tell Jack in the morning. It wasn't till I went up to bed, however, that another more unwelcome thought crept into my mind. What was to say that Will's change of heart had anything to do with my letter? After all, he was bringing his wife and children under the roof of Echo Hall. If they decided to stay, he'd be fulfilling the terms of the inheritance, and Adam would get nothing. For months I'd had one single purpose: to help Jack reconcile with his son. If I were right, then all would be well. But if I were wrong, I had just started a chain of events that meant my husband arriving home to discover he stood to lose the thing that he prized the most.

CHAPTER 8

The storm proved to be the last gasp of winter. Within days of Jack's night-time outing, the buds were bursting into leaf. The trees that had been bare for months were sprinkled vivid green, the roadsides sprouted daffodils, the first shoots could be seen in the fields. The sky was blue more days than it was grey. The air was warmer. After months of mist and fog, the damp at Echo Hall was lifted by the spring breezes that flooded through the house. Inside, Phoebe was cruising round the furniture, seemingly determined to walk before she was one. Outside she chuckled at every new sight, babbling at me incessantly, pointing and clapping at the crocuses in the garden, the blue tits in the trees. A year ago she wasn't even born, yet here she was racing through each day, embracing life with enthusiasm and vigour. Jack's illness, however, seemed to have accelerated his decline. He rarely went out now; and, though Phoebe and I were welcome in his room, he tolerated us for shorter bursts of time. I developed the impression his grip on life was becoming less certain, and sometimes

I felt he might have let go altogether if it hadn't been for Adam's return just before Easter and Will's forthcoming trip.

Adam's homecoming was a quiet affair. One day I was alone, and then all of a sudden he was at Sandstown station, sunburnt, thin, looking like he hadn't slept in weeks. Though our recent letters had been warmer, the four-month separation had marked us; it was a while before we found it easy to converse about anything other than Phoebe and the plans for the quarry. And faced with the real man in my bed again, it was disappointing to discover that our love-making was as much of a struggle as it had been before he left.

But as the days passed and he returned to work, we drifted back into the routine that proceeded his departure. Though Jack wasn't up for long evening meals, they seemed more relaxed in each other's company. And gradually, as we sat in the living room after supper, he began to let slip the odd story from the war in Iraq. The terror of knowing a missile had been launched, wondering where it might fall. The fear in a child's eyes at the sight of an army truck. The wastelands created by Allied bombs. I, in turn, was able to talk a little about the miscarriage and together we were able to offer each other consolation. It felt enough like intimacy to make me believe that, if we kept working at it, our marriage still had a chance.

★   ★   ★

A fortnight after his return, Nisha invited me to another of Liz's talks. Although Adam raised a cynical eyebrow, he said he was happy to look after Phoebe. So I took the bus into town, amazed that the hedgerows, so recently barren, had burst into life; grasses and buttercups jostled for space on the roadside under a canopy of cow parsley. As the bus reached the outskirts of Sandstown, I glanced at the streets of black and white houses. I thought of Geoffrey Walters, imagining the roads as they must have been in 1911, when Rachel and Kitty set off on their fateful journey. I alighted at the cathedral. The sky above was dusky blue, a small sliver of gold light streaking the horizon. I walked quickly until I reached the Quaker Meeting House where Daniel and June had once listened to Edward Norton, and his parents had held their simple wedding service.

I arrived just as the talk was beginning and slipped into a chair beside Nisha, where I was once more gripped by Liz's oratory. I didn't like her, but you couldn't help but be affected by her stories of bomb craters and grieving families. I knew Adam would disagree, but her conclusion was compelling. The war might be over, but with Saddam Hussein left in power, the failure of the uprisings that Bush had encouraged and sanctions threatened, the worst was yet to come. 'Have we learnt nothing from history? From the Treaty of Versailles, from the carving up of empires after 1945? When we punish the loser, when we impose

502

an unjust peace, we sow the seeds for the next violent conflict, each one more horrific than the last.'

She sat down to loud applause. After the inevitable question-and-answer session, we stood chatting over cups of weak tea. Nisha was soon engaged in a debate with a young woman with ginger frizzy hair, leaving me slightly awkward on the side-lines. I scrutinised the posters on the wall, drifting in and out of the conversation. 'That Kuwaiti princess who said the Iraqis turned the baby incubators off? She was lying . . .' Yet again, the Greenham picture caught my eye. I remembered the exhilaration I'd felt, holding hands with my neighbours, how joyfully we'd sung when the base was surrounded and I'd felt part of something bigger than myself. 'Of course we approved sanctions during apartheid – the South Africans asked us to. This is different, sanctions will hurt ordinary Iraqis . . .' Even now, after her last few stressful months, Nisha still cared about this passionately; it was admirable, it really was. 'You know, Churchill threatened to gas the Kurds . . .' Listening to her, it occurred to me that perhaps I could get involved again. On an impulse, I picked up a leaflet about becoming a Quaker and stuffed it into my cardigan pocket.

Nisha was staying the night with me, and when we reached Whetstone we stopped off at the pub, where a young woman with greasy black hair was singing a Bob Dylan song by the bar. Her voice was thin and reedy and she missed too many chords. Nisha pulled a face. 'Think I'd prefer a bit of Bananarama, myself.'

Over drinks she told me that she had made up her mind. Now she and Simon had split up, she was leaving the farm and heading to India.

'Your fault, actually. Everything you're doing got me thinking about *my* family stories. My granddad joining the salt marches. The wife he left behind. Their parents who worked for the Raj. The horror of Partition. I'd like to understand it all a bit better. And it will be nice to be living where my skin colour isn't an issue for a bit.'

'Perhaps, when you come back, Liz might have gone, and you can return.'

'All tyrants fall and empires crumble – if you wait long enough.'

We both laughed; it was one of Nisha's favourite sayings.

Later, we staggered home, drunk and giggling. The moon was full, the black sky dense with stars. I gazed up at my bedroom window. I should feel happy that Adam was lying waiting for me; yet when I crept into the room and saw his sleeping face, I was filled with a deep sadness.

Nisha left in the morning, eager to get back to the farmhouse to pack her belongings. Part of me envied her. Spending a few months in India was the kind of dream I'd once had, before Mum got ill and needed me. But then Phoebe smiled at me, and I realised I was content with the adventure I had in front of me. I set about planning her first birthday.

We decided to keep it simple, inviting only Helen and Mark to join us. Nonetheless, I found making plans a useful distraction from my nagging doubt about the state of my marriage, and the fact I had not yet heard from Katie. And it was a relief when they arrived to realise that my foolish feelings for Mark had dissipated. I was able to welcome them both warmly, and enjoy the sight of their mutual affection.

We picnicked under the oak tree. Phoebe toddled round at the edge of the blankets, chasing Alice and her brothers and being chased in turn, giggling with delight.

'It's lovely to have you back, Adam,' said Helen, as he poured her a drink.

'Did you see much action?' Mark asked.

'Enough. But to be honest, they got the worst of it.'

'What do you mean?'

'After the ceasefire, the clean-up began. We were assigned into units to take on different sections. Clearing rubble, taking away vehicles, stuff like that.' He paused. 'We got used to the impacts of the American bombing. Those surgical strikes they like to boast about? Lots of them hit other targets. I can't tell you the number of bombed-out homes we saw . . . In some places, whole streets were flattened. But one day . . .'

The toddlers got bored with the boys, who were now shooting each other. They wandered back to us. Phoebe climbed onto my lap and I pulled out a picture book, turning the pages as Adam spoke.

'The newspapers called it "The Highway of Death". That was an understatement. We had to clear only one section, but it went on for miles. Cars, tanks and lorries strewn across the road. Every window blown into tiny pieces that sunk into the tarmac, which had melted in the bomb blasts. Charred bodies everywhere you looked. There were hundreds of corpses. Hundreds. This was no ordinary bombing raid – this was us sending a lesson.'

'Horrible.' Helen shuddered.

'The worst thing is, they were on the retreat. And not just that, there were regular cars going in both directions, civilians just going about their business. In one vehicle alone we had to remove the bodies of seven children, the youngest not much bigger than Phoebe.'

'How can that be justified?' I asked.

Adam shrugged. 'These things happen in war.'

I wanted to argue with him, but it seemed pointless. We weren't going to agree. He thought it was worth it to stop Saddam; I didn't. I didn't want a row about it, not today.

I turned the pages of Phoebe's book, letting the men drift into another conversation. The air was warm. There was no cloud in the blue sky. Down in the valley I could see sheep meandering across the fields. Above me a kestrel hovered. We were home, at peace. It should be enough, shouldn't it?

Helen and Mark had family coming, so they didn't stay late. They piled the children into the car with jokes and laughter, kissing and touching like newlyweds. I was glad they were so happy, and that my feelings for Mark had completely vanished: a ridiculous crush that had disappeared when I understood their relationship better. Adam and I went back into the house. We didn't touch or kiss, and it was then that it dawned on me. My foolish feelings for Mark had been a symptom, not a cause.

CHAPTER 9

Will arrived at the end of June, sweeping up the drive in a seven-seater Toyota that he and his wife Martha had hired at the airport. The back seats were piled high with luggage while their teenage boys, Ewan and Scott, sprawled across the middle ones. It was a warm day; I'd been sitting on the front doorstep with Phoebe, waiting for their arrival. Will emerged from the car: tall, like his father, his greying hair crinkled in the same waves. Any doubts Jack might have had about his son were clearly off the mark – Will looked like a younger version of him, one full of energy and bustle.

'So you're Ruth,' he said, his Welsh tones accentuated by an Australian twang.

'Thanks for coming.'

'As I said, you're very persuasive. Besides,' he added, as he introduced me to Martha, 'the missus has been trying to get me to do it for years.'

Leaving them to settle in, I sorted out Phoebe's milk and popped my head in on Jack. He was asleep; I didn't disturb him. When Martha and Will descended, they seemed to have decided something, because she quickly took the boys out to explore the grounds, leaving us alone in the living room. He paced up and down, unable to relax.

'Are you alright?'

'I can't quite believe I'm here again. I didn't leave in the best of circumstances.'

'Jack told me.'

'Did he? How he screamed I wasn't his son, sent me packing?'

'And how sorry he was; how he tried to find you and couldn't.'

'You found me.'

'Only because I wasn't caught up in pride and grief.' I paused, wondering whether I should ask the next question. I decided I must. 'He said that you accused him of killing Elsie. What on earth made you say that?'

'I had good reason to believe it at the time.' He stood at the mantelpiece, staring down at the empty fireplace. 'After years of useless treatment at that awful sanatorium, that summer I had a break-through. I began to remember things that had happened years ago – when I was about five or six. It was a horrible time. First they said Dad was dead. I hardly knew him then, so I wasn't sure what to think about that, but everyone about us was sad so it made me sad too. Mum stopped smiling. And my grandparents, who never smiled much anyway, just seemed to give up altogether.'

'Go on.'

'Then, sometime in the autumn, I think it was, we heard that Dad was alive after all. At first everyone seemed happy about it, but it didn't last. Next thing I knew, they told me Mum was ill and couldn't be disturbed. She moved into the back room upstairs, and only grandmother went into see her. Grandmother moved into Mum's room and kept an eye out for us, but it was horrible. I didn't want to go to her at night-time. She scared me.

'Then Dad came back. There was a nurse who came to look after him. She had a little girl who used to play with me and Evie – I can't remember what she was called. But we weren't allowed to see Dad either. He was too sick. So there we were, our parents both in the house, but neither accessible to us.'

'Her name was Katie,' I said, 'She's a district nurse now. She's visited your Dad a couple of times.'

'How strange.'

'Yes,' I didn't want to think about her then; it reminded me that I still hadn't had any news, and besides, I was keen to hear what Will had seen. 'Then what?'

'One night . . . I woke up to hear shouting, banging doors. I got up and went to the landing. The lights were on, but there was no one about, and the green baize door was open for the first time in weeks. I didn't hesitate. I rushed through, desperate to see Mum.' His hand gripped the mantelpiece. 'And . . .'

'Yes?'

'I entered the room. There was no one there but my mother. She was lying on the bed. I thought she was sleeping at first, but she didn't respond to my call. I climbed up to touch her, and her skin was waxy and cold. It was then that I noticed the blood. Somebody had cleaned her up, but her clothes were covered in blood.'

'What did you do?'

'Ran back to bed. Tried to forget what I saw. They must have told me she'd died the next day, but I don't remember anything much till the funeral.'

'It was raining. You walked behind the coffin.'

'How do you know?'

'Never mind. Why did you blame Jack?'

'Because they all said, forget Mum. Even he said it. And he wouldn't stop questioning me about her and Daniel. And married Veronica even though I hated her . . .' Will sighed. 'For a long time, I forgot the rest of it – the terrible night, the open door, the blood. When I finally did remember, I was sure Dad must have been part of it. Why else would he marry that old cow? How else could he tolerate staying here?'

'And now?'

'I'm older. Wiser maybe . . . Martha's been trying to persuade me that I'm wrong. After all, he must have still been sick when she died.'

'He was. You should talk to him. Hear his side.'

'I could go through that door and see my dad? Is it that easy?'

'You've come this far.'

He nodded. 'Alright then.'

He stood up and left the room. I heard his knock on the door, and Jack calling, 'Come in.' Will opened the door and closed it quickly behind him. It was up to them now.

It was a start. Though Jack chose to dine alone, Will didn't look too unhappy when he emerged from his room. Adam arrived home from work as we were all sitting down. Although he greeted Will and the others politely, he, seemed keen to show Will who was in charge. He pulled up a chair at the head of the table as Mrs Davies brought the soup in.

'So, you're running the quarry now?' asked Will.

'Yup.'

'How's it going?'

'Fine.' Adam barely looked up, concentrating on his soup.

The silence was suffocating. I felt for a moment as if time had rewound to our early days at Echo Hall, when Adam and Jack could barely speak to each other.

Martha made an attempt to break the ice. She turned to Adam. 'I've so enjoyed playing with Phoebe today. It's lovely to have a little one around.'

Adam managed a curt nod, forcing me to cover for his churlishness. 'I suppose you're busy in a different way these days,' I said.

Martha smiled. 'They don't look like it at the moment, but it's hard keeping up with them. You two are always on the go aren't you?' She smiled at the boys who nodded, slightly embarrassed at their mother's enthusiasm.

'We should take them up the quarry, shouldn't we, Adam?' I said.

'That sounds cool.' said Ewan. Scott smiled at the thought.

Adam looked horrified at the prospect. 'I don't think that's a good idea.'

Will laughed. 'I hope that stupid codicil doesn't make you think I've got designs on that quarry, does it?'

'Of course not.

'Well, I haven't, mate. Hate the bloody place and this house too . . . It never made my grandparents happy, or my parents, or step-ma. My sister seemed to like it, but she was the only one . . . I'm doing well enough for myself. I don't need anything else.'

'Oh,' said Adam. 'Well.'

'That's settled then,' I said. 'We'll take you up there and Adam can tell you about his plans for the place.'

We drove to Bryngraen the next day. In bright sunshine, under blue skies, the quarry looked almost beautiful. The grass running up the old tram tracks was filled with summer flowers: purple vetch, pink rosebay willowherb; the hillside was covered in white heather and yellow gorse. Once out of the car, the boys rushed ahead, keen to take the underground tram. I had no desire to revisit the quarry, even though Adam had assured me he'd fixed more lighting since my last trip. Will too declined to go, admitting, somewhat sheepishly, to a sense of claustrophobia.

'He's a right wimp about it,' laughed Martha.

We watched the others climb into the little train, then Adam swept it off down the track.

'Shall we walk?' said Will.

'OK.'

I pushed the buggy back down the slope as we wandered through the abandoned village.

'Your husband's got his work cut out. Redoing all this.'

'It will be worth it, though, don't you think? Reconstructing it as it was?'

'Maybe.' He paused outside the chapel.

'Do you want to go in?'

'To revisit memories of a slicked-up suit, an uncomfortable seat, my grandfather glaring at me from the pulpit, about to denounce me for naughtiness? Not really, but . . . Martha says I need to put the past behind me, or it will always control me. Here goes.'

He pushed against the door and we stepped into the stone chapel. It was cold after the warmth outside, and so dark that Phoebe whimpered in her buggy; I rocked her back and forth. Gradually our eyes got used to the shadowy light, and she calmed down. The electrics had long been turned off; we propped the door open to let in as much daylight as we could.

Will walked up the aisle past the dark wooden pews. He sat down in the front row, gazing up at the stone pulpit. I sat beside him. Remembering Elsie's diaries, I shuddered. 'A tough man, your grandfather.'

'Yes.'

'You weren't alone in feeling like that. Your mother, and your father too – he was hard on both of them.'

'My mother got the worst of it.'

'Jack suffered too . . .'

'Not as much as her. I was little, but even I could see how she had to spend her life pretending to be someone she wasn't. Get something wrong and she'd feel their wrath. Evil, they were. And . . .'

'I hope you're not going to say your dad's not much better. Because he is, you know. And even Leah and Jacob had their redeeming features.'

'If you say so.'

'I know so. I've read your mum's diaries. And Daniel's. You should read them; you'd understand everything so much better.'

'Perhaps,' said Will.

'Moving on. It will help with that.'

'Out!' Phoebe was beginning to experiment with words, and she could be quite imperious at times. We'd been there long enough.

'Come on,' I said. 'Let's go and meet the others.' We locked the past away and made our way back up the hill. The boys were full of their adventure in the darkness and chatted excitedly all the way home. Will barely said a word.

When we arrived back at the house, he turned to me. 'Alright, I'll read them. Where are they?'

'With your dad.'

'Of course they are.' Will grimaced.

'I can ask him, if you like.'

'Thanks. But . . . as you say: moving on.'

I watched as he knocked and entered, pleased to see that he stayed there all day. Perhaps I had done the right thing after all.

CHAPTER 10

Although reaching an understanding about the past didn't restore Will and Jack to an easy relationship, with each passing day they were able to tolerate each other's company more. Even Adam, once he'd seen that Will had no interest in the quarry, grudgingly admitted that the visit was doing the old man good. Yet I'd failed in one respect, the most important one: we still didn't know the end of the story. All we had was Will's version of Elsie's last night, the half-memories of a traumatised child; it was not enough to tell us what really happened. Not enough to bring Jack peace. The only hope left was Katie, but she hadn't been in touch for months. Just when I was beginning to think we'd not hear from her again, she rang, full of apologies. Her mother had been in hospital since April and had only just come out. She'd written Jack a letter, and Katie would bring it over as soon as she could.

She came a couple of days later. At Jack's insistence, we all gathered around his armchair in a semi-circle. Adam and I sat on one side, Phoebe on my lap; Will and Martha sat on the other. The boys were out in the woods. It was a warm day; sunshine streamed into the room, welcoming Katie as she entered. She shook our hands, embraced Will, then took out her mother's letter.

'Could you read it to all of us?' Jack asked. 'I think we all need to hear it.'

'Are you sure? Mother said it wasn't a pleasant story.'

'I'm sure.' Jack gripped my hand.

Katie took a deep breath, then began to read:

Dear Mr Flint,

You must forgive me for not having told you this before. I have often thought of contacting you, but I believed no good would come of me sharing what I knew. My daughter tells me that this may not be the case, so it seems to me that I should break my silence after all this time.

As I listened to her words. I closed my eyes. Remembering the voice I heard, I pictured a cold December evening, Elsie in the back bedroom writing her last letter to Jack . . .

Elsie is finishing a letter to Jack. Earlier she heard the children making their way to bed, their voices filled with excitement at the thought of Christmas. Leah has at least allowed her to choose each of them a present – *Just William* for Will, a rag doll for Evie – but it hurts that she won't able to see their faces when they open their gifts. She sighs, seals the envelope and places it under the floor-boards; only a couple more months and this will be over. Dragging the bed back is an effort – she won't be able to do this for much longer. It is as she straightens her back that her stomach cramps with a sharp tight pain. It can't be. She lies down on the bed, hoping that the pain is a sign of too much exertion. But it comes again. She yanks the bell. Another wave of pain shudders through her body. She rings again. It is another 10 minutes before Leah appears, by which time she is curled on the bed.

'I need to get to the hospital. The baby is coming.'

'It is too late to be driving in the dark.'

'I need help.'

'You are in God's hands now.'

'Help me, please.'

Leah leaves the room. The waves of pain return again, and again, pulsating through her body, each time stronger than the last. Elsie pulls the chain again. There is no answer. She rings again until her arms tire. She shouts instead: *Help me, someone help me, please . . .*

Downstairs Hilary Owen is vaguely aware of a bell ringing in another part of the house. She assumes Mrs Flint will deal with it. At the moment her patient is her only concern. The spike in his temperature after several days of improvement has

519

been worrying enough for her to have made up camp beds for herself and Katie in the room next door. Now, as she checks the thermometer, she is relieved to read 98.4, to observe his breathing is more regular. He is moaning less, and appears to be drifting off into a deeper sleep. She looks at her watch: midnight. With any luck she can grab a few hours' sleep. As she tiptoes out of the room, she hears the clanking of the bell again. It occurs to her it has been ringing for some time now. Why has no one answered the call? She hesitates for a minute, then decides to check in the kitchen. The room is in darkness, the clang of the bell echoing round its stone walls. Switching on the light, she jumps at the sight of Mr and Mrs Flint sitting at the table. Their hands are clasped in prayer. *Thy will be done*, says Jacob Flint. They do not look at her when she walks in.

'Why is the bell ringing?' Hilary asks, seeing the board indicating the back bedroom. 'Does Mrs Flint need some help?'

Forgive us our trespasses, as we forgive those who trespass against us.

She repeats the question, louder. 'Does she need some help?'

Deliver us from evil. Amen.

The prayer ends. Leah Flint gazes at her. 'She is in God's hands now.'

The bell jangles, once, twice, three times more and then stops.

'Why are you not answering her?' Hilary asks.

Jacob doesn't say anything. Now the prayer is finished, his body has lost its usual stiffness; he slumps on the table, head in hands. He doesn't look at her, or his wife, leaving Leah to respond. 'She is in God's hands.'

'Don't you think someone should check on her?' Hilary asks again, astonished at their lack of concern.

At first the pair do not reply. It is not until the third time of asking that Leah finally stands up. 'Very well. Come with me.'

Jacob remains at his seat. As they close the door, she hears him begin to pray again. *Our Father, which art in heaven, hallowed be thy name.* His voice fades into a murmur as they walk down the corridor, making their way across the hall. Whose stupid idea was it to block the back staircase? Hilary wonders. They'd have been up there in no time if it were still open.

As they reach the green baize door, they can hear the sound of a voice mewling in pain, *Help me, someone help me, please.* Leah takes the key and turns it in the lock. The door swings open, revealing a dark corridor. The older woman switches on the lamps; they light up slowly, casting long shadows along the corridor. Hilary squeezes past the piled paintings till they reach the bedroom at the end. They enter to see a young woman lying on a red-gold coverlet: her face is grey, her breath shallow.

Hilary rushes to the bed. 'She's in shock.'

Leah stares at the younger woman, a slight smile forming on her face, which vanishes the moment Hilary says, 'She needs warmth. Fetch some blankets from the cupboard.' Her voice is so authoritative that Leah obeys immediately.

Elsie's eyes are closed. She is whispering a name, over and over: *Jack, Jack, Jack.* Hilary reaches over to elevate her legs on a couple of pillows. It is then that she realises the red is not part of the fabric, but splashes of blood: patterning the counterpane, red-gold, red-gold, red-gold. And then she sees it: the cord between the legs – a bloody, mucus-covered child at the end. Her face is blue, her body is stiff. There is nothing Hilary can do.

'Why didn't you call me?'

Leah says nothing as she hands her the blankets. She puts them aside. Elsie's stomach is still contracting; she hasn't yet delivered the placenta.

'Get me some scissors, hot water, bandages, needles and thread.' She is too late to save the child, but the mother still has a chance. Leah does what she is told, returning quickly with the required items. There is enough time to cut the cord before Elsie gives a final shudder, delivering the placenta. Leah wraps the baby in a cloth. She stands back as Hilary treats her patient. She doesn't offer to help. The nurse bandages as tightly as she is able; sews up wounds, trying to staunch the blood, but it is no good: Elsie has lost too much. Her pulse slows, her breaths come further and further apart.

Soon she stops breathing altogether. At two o'clock Hilary gives up, closing Elsie's eyes. She cleans her as best she can and removes the bed covers.

It is three before the women go downstairs. Jacob Flint is standing in the hallway. Seeing the pile of bloody sheets in her arms he asks, 'She is dead, then?'

'Yes.'

'And the child?'

'Yes.'

'So be it. This is God's will.'

Hilary wants to retort it wasn't anything to do with God's will, that no God of hers would do something so wicked. This isn't God's will – just human cruelty and lack of sense. But she says nothing. These Flints scare her. If they let this happen to one of their own, what might they do to her? She decides she will hand in her notice in the morning. She doesn't want to stay here a moment longer . . .

I opened my eyes. Jack's face was ash-white; tears were flowing down his cheeks. Martha had her arms round Will, who sat with his head in his hands. Even Adam was crying. Katie continued to read, though her voice was shaking:

> I don't know what they told you, Mr Flint. I don't know what they told the world, or how they persuaded a doctor to sign a death

certificate. I just didn't want to be part of it. It did cross my mind that you might want to know the truth one day, but what good would it do? Knowing your wife had died like that, and your parents hadn't lifted a finger to help? I decided to let it be.

I am sorry if this was the wrong thing to do. My Katie says this matter has troubled you for years. I did what I thought was best at the time. I am sorry I wasn't able to save her. I hope the truth, even this late, is of help to you.

    Yours sincerely,
    Hilary Owen

Katie finished speaking. We sat in silence for a moment. Will stood up, walked across to Jack, and knelt in front of him.

'Dad,' was all he said.

Jack let go of my hand and put his arms round his son.

'I'm so sorry,' said Katie.

Will turned. 'It's OK. It's better to know.'

We sat in silence, each absorbing what we had just heard, till Phoebe's wriggling alerted me to the fact that her nappy needed changing. I took her out, and set her down for her morning nap. By the time I came back down, Martha was in the kitchen preparing lunch.

'Ugh . . .' said Martha as we entered the kitchen. 'To think they sat here and just let her die.'

I shivered. 'Horrible.'

After listening to Hilary's story, even the cold dark dining room seemed a preferable place to eat. But as we immersed ourselves in the simple task of preparing food, the horror slowly subsided. By the time we carried the sandwiches through to the dining room, I was even able to pose the question that had been troubling me. 'What about the baby? What did they do with her?'

'Bury her, perhaps?' said Katie.

'Oh,' I said, picturing a woman with a baby underneath the sycamore tree. 'I think I know where.'

The men took spades and dug where I told them to try. They found a tiny skeleton wrapped in the remains of a white sheet. It took several weeks of wrangling with officialdom but eventually we were able to move her remains and bury her in the same grave as her mother. Though Jack did not come, at his request we named the baby Hilary.

A few days after we found the body, Will and Martha took the boys to visit her relatives in Chester, and I took the opportunity to sit with Jack for a while. Since Katie's revelations, he had been quiet and thoughtful. Now he said to me. 'I want you to know that I've consulted my lawyer.

I've torn up the codicil. No one should be forced into a life they don't want. I've made a new will.'

'Can I ask?'

'Adam gets the quarry, Will gets the house. They'll both be happier that way. Will can sell the place – he's always hated it. And Adam can create the leisure empire he was always after.'

I smiled. 'He will be pleased.'

'It's all thanks to you, Ruth. None of this would have happened without you.'

'Don't mention it.'

'I'm leaving something for you too.'

'There's no need.'

'There's every need.' He grabbed my hand. 'If the time ever came when you needed to be independent, you wouldn't get far without money.'

'What do you mean?'

'I thought it was best if you and Adam stayed together. But I look at you now, and I wonder. If you should ever want to leave, Ruth . . . I want you to be free to do so. You understand? I want you to be free.'

CHAPTER 11

T he next fortnight was uneventful. The weather was warm that year, and we were kept busy with hillside walks, visits to tourist attractions and al fresco dinners. For a while, Jack seemed to have more energy, sometimes joining us for drives in the country; once or twice he sat with us till the sun went down and the owl flew overhead. It was so peaceful, and the atmosphere so congenial, that I was almost persuaded Adam and I were going to be alright; but then I realised we barely talked except in the company of others. As the time for our guests to leave drew closer, I found myself dreading the thought of the return to the life we'd led before. For months, my whole focus had been to discover what happened to Elsie. Now we knew, and Jack and Will were reconciled. What on earth was I going to do next?

It took another crisis with Jack to jolt me out of my introspection. Mrs Davies walked in one morning to find him collapsed on the floor. She and Will accompanied him in the ambulance; Adam and I followed in the car, while Martha stayed behind to look after the children. It was a bright clear morning; and though the road was clear, he was as hunched and tense behind the wheel as he'd been on that first foggy day the previous February.

'They've taken him to the stroke unit,' Will told us when we arrived.

We followed him down long grey corridors, the floor covered in linoleum. The smell of Dettol followed us everywhere: sharp, pungent, reminiscent of death. As we sat in the waiting area I was taken back two years to the cancer ward where Mum died. I hated hospitals. I wasn't sure I was ready for this again, sitting waiting for the inevitable bad news.

But when the consultant arrived, he was more optimistic than I expected. 'The stroke has attacked his right side. He's lost function in his limbs, and his speech. But he's stable. It's a question of wait and see.'

'Can we go in?'

'One at a time. He's asleep at the moment.'

I was the last to enter. Jack was lying with a drip in his arm. In the hospital gown he looked very frail. His face had the same waxy pallor my mum's had had just before she died. My stomach took a lurch as I stepped towards him, but he was breathing well enough, and when I grabbed his left hand, I was relieved to find his grip was still strong. I wasn't ready for him to leave us yet. I stayed for a few minutes before returning to the others.

'There's no point us all being here,' said Will. 'I'll stay for now. I'll phone you at lunch.'

We nodded, then drove back to Echo Hall in silence, our default mode these days. In the barley fields, little breezes ruffled golden waves across the undulating slopes. Above us the sun was high in a deep-blue cloudless sky. It was a perfect day, but I felt sick. I didn't want to say so to Adam, but I couldn't see Jack recovering from this. He seemed to be sensing my thought, though, because as we turned up the drive he put his hand on my knee. 'He'll be alright.'

'Hmm.' I didn't want to disagree.

It was unusual to have Adam at home during the day. I'd have suggested going for a walk, but neither of us wanted to be too far from the phone. In the end, we sat out in the back garden while Ewan and Scott devised elaborate hiding games for Phoebe, who ran around crying, 'Hide, hide!' and squealing with delight.

'Nothing like a one-year-old to lift your mood,' said Martha.

I smiled. Nothing like.

My gloomy predictions did not come to pass, however. Will rang at four to say that Jack was awake and eating; the stroke was not as severe as the doctors had first thought. He stayed on the unit for a week. When he came home, his speech slightly slurred, he went back to using the frame again and seemed bright and positive. We hired a nurse to care for him at night; life settled back into its normal routines. Martha and the boys, who'd deferred their departure, finally left at the beginning of August, as they needed to get ready for school. Will stayed on, spending hours in Jack's room, talking, playing cards. It was pleasant to hear the sound of their laughter as I passed their door.

By mid-August, it seemed the crisis had passed. We dismissed the nurse, and took advantage of Will's last fortnight with us to go on holiday, just the two of us with Phoebe. Perhaps it was naive of me, but I was hoping some time away would help Adam and I reconnect. I still had the picture of Elsie with Jack and Daniel in Southport; it looked as good a place as any, and it wasn't too far to travel. Remembering sunny days at the seaside with my parents, I thought it might be fun.

But it all went wrong right from the start. Adam and I had spent the last 18 months sharing our home with others. Now we were left to our own resources, the cracks in our relationship were exposed. Without Will or Jack or even Mrs Davies to join in our conversation, we found we had little left to say to each other. It was as if, all this time, we had been living the impression of a marriage, rather than the real thing. Neither of us spoke of it, but I could see it in Adam's eyes, too. Was this going to be it for the rest of our lives?

On our first day, we headed to the beach. The tide was in and the sea sparkled, Air Force blue. Family groups dotted the water's edge, as parents and children jumped and splashed in the waves, shouting with laughter. Further out, swimmers bobbed up and down, enjoying the unusually warm waters. The sea looked inviting, but Phoebe took one look at the water and screamed at the top of her voice. Whatever the reason, the immensity of the sea or the noisy crowds, we couldn't persuade her to come anywhere near it. We were forced to retreat to the promenade where she was only pacified by ice cream.

Far from being a happy holiday, the week soon descended into fractiousness. The bright mornings woke Phoebe early; the light evenings made it difficult for her to settle. Often, in desperation, I would walk down to the sea front, and pace up and down outside the cafes and arcades. Just when I was about to give up, Phoebe would suddenly fall asleep. I would wander back to the tiny bungalow and fall into bed, exhausted, without a word, ignoring Adam's hints about sex. The one time we did try, Phoebe woke up wailing halfway through; and when I returned to the bedroom, Adam was fast asleep.

We were both glad when it was time to pack our bags.

When we returned home, Will's face was grave. 'Dad's had a mini-stroke in the night,' he said. 'The doctor thinks he might have another one, but he's refusing hospital. Says he wants to end his days here.'

This time we hired two nurses and devised a rota between the three of us to watch and wait. A hush fell on the house. It was not unlike the hush that had heralded Phoebe's arrival; but now, as the days shortened towards autumn, Jack began to slip away from his life at the same rate she had rushed to embrace hers. Where every new day with Phoebe had been an adventure as she gained new experiences, each moment for Jack seemed to mark a steady decline. When she was first born, Phoebe was asleep as often as she was awake, but as the weeks passed, she wakened to the possibilities around her. Now, in his last few weeks, Jack became less and less aware, drifting between wake and sleep. Often he was somewhere else altogether: dancing, playing with his children, singing under his breath, *Don't sit under the apple tree with anyone, Else, but me.* Thankfully the stroke seemed to have stripped him of his nightmares: his dreams were all benign, and for that we were grateful. The world outside seemed remote: Nisha's plans for India, Helen and Mark's announcement of another pregnancy, world news all appeared as tiny images at the end of a telescope. Life was reduced to the passage from the kitchen to Jack's bedroom and back, sitting and waiting by his side. And Phoebe, normally such a lively child, seemed to sense it. In Jack's room she was quiet, watchful, still, responding to him only on the rare occasions when he had the strength to hold her as he lay in bed. There, she laughed and babbled at him in delight.

One afternoon it was my turn to sit with him. I could hear Adam in the study next door, playing a tape that would provide the backdrop for the installations in the quarry. 'Metamorphic rock begins to form deep in the earth, from mud. Malleable, flexible, the crystals begin to arrange themselves in different directions.'

The sun and rain had been fighting for control of the skies. Now at the close of the day, cloud and sunshine co-mingled, casting an orange-black light over the fir trees at the edge of the estate.

'Pressure and stress force the crystals together, squashing them into shape. They begin to align themselves in straight lines. They harden, become rigid, and slate is formed.'

Phoebe climbed on to my lap, clasping a picture book. I was reading to her quietly when Jack sat bolt upright.

'Elsie?' he said.

'No, it's Ruth. Can I get you anything?'

'Elsie,' he repeated, his voice stronger than it had been for some time. He wasn't looking at me, but at the end of the bed. His hand was stretching out as if he could see someone. He smiled and settled back down on the pillows. The dying rays of the sun glowed across his face for a moment, giving a fleeting impression of a much younger man. Then clouds rolled across the sky, extinguishing the orange light. Outside I could hear the sound of the rain, at first like a gentle rush of wind, and then more firmly tapping on the window. Next door, the tape concluded, 'The stone weathers in rain, wind and sleet. Rocks fall. The slate breaks up, smooths over, crumbles back to the free-flowing mud from which it came.'

Now the sun had gone, the room was dark. I stood up and turned the light on. Jack had subsided into sleep, breathing with a rasping, rattling breath.

I am not a praying person normally, but I noticed then that he had a prayer book beside him: a Catholic Missal. He must have asked Will for it earlier. I opened it. The flyleaf bore the inscription *Elsie Forbes 1935*. On the contents page, she'd underscored *Readings for the Sick and Dying*. I opened a page, and without thinking read out loud:

I said 'No more shall I see the Lord,

in the land of the living,

no more shall I look upon men

within this world,

My home is pulled up and removed

like a shepherd's tent.

Like a weaver you have rolled up my life,

you cut it from the loom.

For you, Lord, my heart will live,

you gave me back my spirit;

you cured me, kept me alive,

changed my sickness into health.

As I sat in the fading light, the words were comforting. Shortly afterwards, Adam came to relieve me. I touched Jack's hand before leaving. It was cold; I could barely feel the pulse. His face was a wax mask, as if he had already departed. The only sign he was still with us were his rasping, stuttered breaths.

By bedtime, Jack's condition hadn't changed, and I was exhausted. I left Will and Adam with him and went upstairs to sleep. And so I missed his final moment, a gradual releasing of breath, Adam said, as if he'd reached the end of a very long journey. In the morning, I entered his room to say my final farewell. His body was laid out under the bed clothes. But for the empty look in his face, the stiffness of his limbs, he might have been asleep. He looked more peaceful than I'd ever known him. As I stood up to leave the room, I knocked his pillow, dislodging a letter that was lying underneath. I picked it up. It was Elsie's last letter. *I have to have faith in us*, she had written, *faith in* you. *Faith that if I tell you, you will have the capacity to understand. Maybe, even, to forgive.* Looking at his calm face, I knew without a doubt, that he had.

CHAPTER 12

The funeral was over. The guests had come, eaten, drunk, shared stories about Jack, and gone, leaving Will, Adam, Mrs Davies and I with a pile of washing-up and a house cavernous with loss. We tidied away, sometimes speaking, sometimes not; all aware that, now the rush of activity had ceased, we were left with the reality of his death. Though I was glad he had died peacefully, restored to Elsie, restored to Will, every stone in the house seemed to ache with his absence. It was just as well he'd left the place to Will. The minute he had gone I knew there was nothing left to keep us there.

The day after the funeral, we began the task of clearing out Jack's rooms. There were clothes, papers, books, nearly 80 years of life to sort, separate, bag up and pass on to others. It was going to take us days. The collection of letters and diaries was still beside Jack's bed. As I rifled through them, I came across June's letter to Jack; she had included an obituary for Daniel. I read it, smiling. By all accounts, he'd had a good life – three children, five grandchildren; he'd become a headmaster, and

536

in retirement had played an active role in the peace movement. I was glad. Jack must have been, too, for he had underscored several of his cousin's achievements and added the comment 'Good!' in the margins.

'We should burn these papers,' said Will, looking up from a pile of bank statements and old bills. 'There are too many to bin.'

'Add these,' I said, pointing to Elsie and Daniel's writings. Now I knew how their stories ended, their diaries were just books, empty shells like Jack's body. There was no longer a need to keep them.

So after lunch we built a large bonfire, piled it high with branches and stuffed newspaper in the gaps to ensure there was enough dry material to set it alight. Phoebe ran around our legs, pushing twigs in holes, clapping at our exertions. Will lit the base, then we watched as the flames began to spread around the bottom of the wood, forcing their way through the branches, leaving trails of black smoke. Adam kept Phoebe at a distance as I picked up the diaries. I ripped out pages, throwing them on top, one by one, watching as the heat ran through them. The paper curled, darkened by the fire, which gradually blackened the words until they were obliterated, disintegrating into white ash that floated above us. It took 20 minutes or so for every page to burn, every word to disappear. When we were done, I stepped back, my clothes thick with smoke, my eyes red-raw from the smouldering flames, or with tears – I couldn't quite tell. We watched the flames shoot through the wood, till the last branch crumbled and all that was left was a pile of charred smouldering soot. Will threw water over the fire to put it out. It hissed and steamed, leaving only soggy charcoal behind.

We returned to the house, but I was restless, unable to settle. The house filled me with the same sensations I'd experienced when I first arrived – an oppressive choking feeling, as if the very walls were pressing in. I had to get out. Luckily Adam was in the mood to stay indoors and play with Phoebe. Will was popping into Sandstown; I fancied he needed some time alone, just as I did. I gave Adam and Phoebe a kiss, pulled a coat from the cupboard and strode out of the back door, up the familiar path to the woods. Autumn was all about me. Once more, the forest floor was filling with dead leaves: orange, yellow and brown that crumpled underfoot. The bracken was dying back. Through the gaps in the trees I could see formations of birds beginning the long journey south.

The sun was low in the sky by the time I reached Arthur's Stone, and the air was chilly. I lay a rug on the ground and gazed out over the valley. Jack and Elsie, Elsie and Daniel, Joseph and Rachel had all come here before me. Their lives had possessed me for months, giving me purpose and direction, but now their stories were done I was struggling to find my way once more. The day's exertions had tired me; I closed my eyes, listening to the ruffling of the wind in the grass, the sheep baaing on the hillside. Other than that it was quiet, so quiet I could hear my heart beating. And in the echo of that heartbeat I was drawn back to the women who had been here before me. To Elsie, overwhelmed with a mad grief that led her into the arms of the wrong man. Elsie, snatching the happiness of half an hour alone with Jack away from the prison of Echo Hall. My heart beat faster, and I was drawn back further, to Rachel, giving her life totally to Joseph, never regretting it despite the price she paid. For a minute, maybe 10, maybe 30, the lives of the women who had preceded me reverberated through my body. I felt their feelings, loved their loves, lived their losses. It took my breath away. The wind picked up, blowing colder. My heart rate slowed and I shivered my eyes open.

Grey clouds had covered the sun, extinguishing the remaining heat of the day. A pair of owls swooped over my head flying in the direction of Echo Hall. I sat up, putting my hands in my pockets to warm them. As I did so, my fingers came upon a piece of paper. It was the leaflet I had picked up at Liz's talk. I hadn't thought about it since that night, but now I took it out and looked at it: *Living the Quaker Way*.

I read the first couple of lines. 'Do you feel that something is missing in your life? Do you feel the need to live life more truthfully, more authentically?'

I found myself nodding. Joseph and Rachel had been Quakers; Daniel and June, too. It seemed to have provided them with a sense of purpose, of worth. Perhaps it might do the same for me. I turned the paper over. There was a number on it, and I decided to give them a ring. The wind blew even colder; it was time to go back. I folded the blanket up and put it back in my bag. And as I stood up, I realised that I had reached another, far more important decision. For the first time in a long, long time, I knew exactly what I had to do.

When I returned, Adam was still in Jack's room, staring into Jack's wardrobe while Phoebe sat on the floor, absorbed in a stack of bricks.

'I can't . . . I can't . . .' he said as I entered.

'Can't what?'

'Work out how to sort these suits. Which ones should go to Oxfam, which to the bin?'

'Oh, Adam.' I remembered feeling so overwhelmed when Mum died. I hugged him.

'Who'd have thought it?' Adam shook his head.

'What?'

'That . . .' The words came out in a wrenching sob. 'That I'd miss the old bugger so much.'

I held on to him until his tears subsided, and then, because I didn't think it fair to stay like that, I let go. I walked towards the window and looked out onto the trimmed lawn, the gravel drive, the fir trees standing to attention at the edge of the estate. The rooks gathered in the rookery for their afternoon convocation. It had started to drizzle.

I turned back to my husband and said, 'The timing's probably lousy, but if I don't say it now, I might never say it.'

Adam held my gaze. 'Say what?'

'Us.'

'We're doing alright.'

'No, we're not. And I don't think we ever will.'

'I could have done things differently, I know. But I've learnt a lot in the last few months. I could change.'

'No – you couldn't. And I shouldn't make you. I shouldn't have ever let you try. It takes two to make a mess like this. I was just as selfish as you.'

'But Phoebe . . .'

'Do you think I like the idea of her growing up with parents apart? We both know what it's like to live in families that aren't complete.'

'You'd still do it?'

'If there was a way we could be together, and be happy, I'd stay. But there isn't. We're too different. We don't believe in the same things. And I don't want her growing up in a house like this, full of unhappy women and bitter angry men. It's time to move on.'

'I want to be with you.'

'That's just grief talking.'

He opened his mouth to deny it.

'Take it from one who knows,' I added. 'Perhaps if I hadn't been so messed up after Mum died, I'd have thought this whole thing through.'

'You don't regret Phoebe?'

'I don't regret Phoebe.'

'Come here.' I thought Adam was still going to try and persuade me, but all he did was give me a hug, adding, 'I need to get on.'

'I'll give Phoebe her tea.'

As I moved to the door he said, 'You don't have to go straight away?'

'It'll take me a bit of time to sort myself out. I need to find somewhere to rent in Sandstown.'

'Take as long as you need.' He turned back to the wardrobe and began laying the suits carefully on the bed. I left him to it.

It took longer than I thought to plan the separation. I didn't want to leave immediately, not when Will and Adam had so much to sort out in the house. It took a month to clear the bulk of it, and for the solicitor to begin dealing with Jack's estate. Will left at the beginning of October, promising to return when the house was on the market. I was sorry to see him go, but once he was gone, there was no excuse left to stay. I set myself the task of finding somewhere to live, eventually choosing a two-bedroom terrace in the centre of Sandstown. The deposit ate up most of my savings and I was grateful that Jack had proved true to his word – a cheque for £20,000 was on its way. Adam had promised he would provide for us, but I felt happier having money of my own.

Telling people was the worst. Mark and Helen, caught up in the imminent arrival of another baby, were sympathetic, though I suspect they were relieved their relationship was stronger than ours. I told Nisha just before she left for Delhi. She refrained from being too obvious with her delight; she just hugged me and said she was glad I'd seen sense. Mrs Davies couldn't get over the upset of it. 'With Mr Flint dying and the old house being sold, it doesn't seem right,' she repeated again and again. I was glad that Will had promised to provide her and her son with permanent homes from the proceeds of the Hall; it was the least they deserved for a lifetime's service.

But finally, it was done. On a cold December morning, we loaded the car together. As I strapped Phoebe in the car seat, Adam carried out the last bag and put it in the boot.

'Lovely morning,' he said.

I nodded. The evergreens pierced the blue sky; the sun burnt pale yellow, its rays providing little warmth, but the air was crisp and fresh.

'You're sure about this?' he added.

'I'm sure.'

He leant into the car, kissing Phoebe. 'Bye-bye, sweetheart. Daddy will see you soon.'

It was hard not to be moved by the choke in his voice, and her returning, 'Bye, Daddy.'

He turned to me, and we gave each other a final hug.

'Good luck with your leisure empire,' I said.

'You'll call me?'

'And I'll bring Phoebe over on Saturday.'

'See you then.' He walked back to the front door, uncertain whether to go in. I got into the car and waved. As I drove down the gravel road, I was conscious of his figure in my mirror, hand raised, dwindling into the distance, until I turned the corner. At the junction, I hesitated for a moment. And then I thought that empires rise and empires fall; wars are fought, and then they end. We can choose to ignore the lessons of the past or let it move us in new directions. It's up to us. I switched the indicator light on, waited for a car to pass, and turned left onto the road into Whetstone. I accelerated at the final bend.

I did not look back.

LEST WE FORGET

2014

The clouds burst just as I reach Arthur's Stone. I run for cover, grateful for its protection as rain drums on the rocks above, pummelling the ground in front of me. Then, just as quickly as it started, it stops, and a thin crack appears in the cloud, glowing yellow. It is cold, but the light brightens the day, illuminating the stones as I search for the names I know are etched there.

It takes a while to find them. Twenty-three years have passed since Mum was here and many lovers have come this way since. *Jane loves Sam, Marlon for Adeola, Alan & Andy forever* – all variations on the same hopeful theme. Of course, I know from my own life that love doesn't always last, but then my parents never came here. They never made their mark, as their predecessors did. At last, after about 20 minutes, I find *EF & JF* in the corner, still looking remarkably fresh. *J loves R* is close by. Both serve as testament to the kind of love my parents never found.

Though I don't remember the time when Mum and Dad were together, I used to yearn for them to be reunited. I envied friends who were able to share Christmases, birthdays, holidays in the presence of both parents. But as I grew older, and realised how different they were, I began to understand why that was never going to be possible. Now I am here, their separation makes perfect sense. While Rachel and Joseph managed to find happiness, Leah and Jacob locked themselves into hopeless misery that lasted 40 years. Elsie and Jack may have loved each other, but after her death Jack consigned himself to the loveless union with Veronica that blighted his life. My parents were wise to walk away from that.

I take pictures of the carvings with my iPad to send to Mum, thinking she'd like to see them again. The setting sun emerges from under the dark storm clouds, colouring the horizon orange-black, signalling that it's time to go. I march back to the house, face and hands tingling with the cold, enjoying the fresh air, the sounds of sheep baaing, the kestrels flying overhead. This is a beautiful spot, but as I enter the grounds of Echo Hall and see the blank windows and grey stone, I am glad I didn't have to grow up inside its hard walls. That I grew up free of the malign influences that lingered here so long.

I enter through the back door, taking photos of all the rooms – mementoes of my visit for me and my parents. As I wander down the driveway, the sun has turned a fiery red; it lights up the windows of the house red-gold. For a moment, the place seems alive, almost happy, but then a cloud moves over it and it reverts to its usual gloom. I think then that it is fitting the house has become a tourist attraction. It is not a home where people thrive. Let it stand as testimony to the work of the Flint family, while those of us who are left get on with our lives.

On the way down to the village, I pause at the war memorial. A hundred years have passed since the first men from this village went to war, and now there is a new name on the stone, carved only 10 years ago: Simon Evans, killed in the futile invasion of Iraq. Another victim of another useless war. I think of Mum, who'll be wearing her white poppy with pride tomorrow, and how she works every day for an end to the cycle of violence. I think of Dad, who'll be at his British Legion parade, honouring his battalion's war dead, remembering the fallen – who, he says, died for us. Each in their own way is committed to a cause they believe in. And I reflect that, unlike Mum, I can disagree with Dad yet love him too. That my work for a charity providing medical relief to warzones has given me a way to honour them both.

I arrive at the stop just as the bus pulls up. I clamber aboard, watching Whetstone slip away from me. Picking up my conference papers, I settle into my seat and begin to read. My phone beeps as the bus turns out of the village – a message from a colleague, asking me to check my email. I am soon drawn back into my world of field reports and fundraising targets, barely noticing the journey till we reach Sandstown. I glance up to catch sight of the road leading to the old Walters home, where Rachel and Leah's conflicts first began. It strikes me that if my family history has taught me anything, it is that even the closest of siblings or the most loving couple can become divided. The bus takes me into the centre, depositing me close to the cathedral. On my way to the King George Hotel, I pass the Shire Hall and the Quaker Meeting House, a journey that feels simultaneously new but achingly familiar. I reach the hotel and gaze up at the gleaming white walls; the old building has been restored to its former glory. As I enter, it occurs to me that, though Echo Hall is behind me, its legacy will remain with me always.

I will not forget.